All the Rage

All the Rage

PAUL MAGRS

This edition published in Great Britain in 2002 by
ALLISON & BUSBY Limited
Bon Marche Centre
241-251 Ferndale Road
Brixton, London SW9 8BJ
http://www.allisonandbusby.com

A catalogue record for this book is available from the British Library

ISBN 0 7490 0568 8

Printed and bound in Spain
by Liberdúplex, S. L.
Barcelona

PAUL MAGRS is based in Norwich where he is a lecturer in English literature and Creative Writing at UEA. He is the author of four highly acclaimed previous novels and one collection of short stories.

For more information on Paul Magrs, visit www.pheonix-court.org.uk.

Acknowledgements

Thanks to:

Joy Foster, Louise Foster, Mark Magrs, Charles Foster, Gladys Johnson, Michael Fox, Nicola Creegan, Lynne Heritage, Pete Courtie, Brigid Robinson, Jon Rolfe, Antonia Rolfe, Steve Jackson, Laura Wood, Alicia Stubbersfield, Siri Hansen, Bill Penson, Mark Walton, Sara Maitland, Meg Davis, Amanda Reynolds, Lucie Scott, Richard Klein, Reuben Lane, Kenneth MacGowan, Georgina Hammick, Maureen Duffy, Victor Sage, Lorna Sage, Sharon Sage, Rupert Hodson, Marina Mackay, Jayne Morgan, Andrew Motion, Jon Cook, Louise D'Arcens, Malcolm Bradbury, Steve Cole, Jac Rayner, James Friel, Andrew Biswell, Gary Russell, Kate Orman, Jon Blum, Neil Smith, Patrick Gale, Patricia Duncker, Russell T Davies, Stewart Sheargold, Stephen Hornby, Jo Moses, Graeme Vaughan, Sarah Churchwell, David Shelley, Bridget O'Connor, Peter Straughan, Tiffany Murray, Roz Kaveney, Val Striker, and Jeremy Hoad.

Other books by Paul Magrs

Marked For Life
Does It Show?
Playing Out
Could It Be Magic?
Modern Love

Chapter One

I've got a horror of people who organise get-togethers. I'm suspicious of the whole idea of them.

They never work out.

What I feel especially bad about is the idea of getting together people who work in the same shop and who can't really stand the sight of each other.

There was no one in that shop that I wanted to spend time with on a Saturday night.

Why would I?

Except Shanna. She was all right.

She was my mate. Still is, I suppose.

She was the only one who would come out the back of the shop and have a fag with me when our breaks were synchronised and she would bitch as much as I did about the kind of tat we had to sell in Natural World and she listened while I bitched about our grinning manager, Pete.

The shop was one of many connected inside the mall by breezeblocked corridors where deliveries were made and we were supposed to clear up all the cardboard boxes but no one ever did.

Goods smashed in transit were chucked there and Shanna and I stood at our window smoking, looking through to the multi-storey beyond.

We flicked our still-burning fags through the bars and then worried that they'd plop into a patch of oil or a cardboard box and blow the whole place sky high.

Which could happen.

Which would be a shame.

We sold: Perfumed candles, ethnic artefacts, dried flowers in bleached wooden frames. Tat.

One fag during a coffee break off the shop floor was never enough. Two would make you dizzy, and you'd feel peculiar when you went back into Natural World, where it smelled of white musk, cinammon, vanilla.

I didn't want this works night out one bit.

But now I'm glad it happened. It led me on to be part of the biggest get-together I could ever imagine.

Once you start getting people together it goes on and on and soon everyone's all in the same place.

Shouting at each other and making me nervous.

It becomes an addiction, I think, this impulse to bully people to face one another.

But it was an adventure, as well.

Pete the manager had been on one of those courses that taught you how to be especially nice to everyone.

You had to be positive about absolutely everything.

If anyone asked you how things were going, you leaned towards them, fixed them with a stare and grinned: 'Everything's grrrreat!'

Like Tony the Tiger would.

It was Pete who'd organised this meal tonight. A bonding exercise for the staff of Natural World.

I had tried to wriggle out of it - saying I wasn't ready to start going out again yet - but Shanna made me come.

'Pete says it's fantastic. Surreal. It's run by this completely mad Chinese woman called Franky and it's on the second level of a multi storey car park in town. They do Karaoke and Franky does a fan dance sometimes and Pete reckons it's excellent. He's been with his fiancée.'

Shanna had a 2:i in Sociology and still, to my amazement, she didn't quite see sense.

I thought she perhaps fancied our boss, Pete with his waxed hair and his River Island suits.

Maybe she'd fallen for that grin. Maybe she thought it was real and, when he leaned in to hold her glance, she thought it was just for her.

'Pete won't sing,' I said, that afternoon in the hairdressers, where Shanna was having more extensions put in. 'He'd never willingly make a tit of himself. Not in front of his staff.'

'He'll have to,' Shanna said, as the stylist twiddled and fiddled with yards of her dark hair. 'He says we all have to muck in and enjoy ourselves.' She winced. 'He says it's good for morale.'
We went to a trendy cafe bar first.

We figured we might as well stay out till it was time to go to the restaurant in the car-park and see the others.

All the middle-aged, pouchy women we worked with.

'It'll be a big night out for them,' Shanna said. 'I can't imagine they get out much. We're doing them a favour by going. We're the young ones to them, you know. We have to remind them how to have fun.'

'Hm.' We ordered what the menu described as posh egg and chips. It arrived in deep white dishes. And a bottle of Chardonnay, frosted. Shanna reckoned we ought to eat something before we went to the restaurant. Chinese never fills you up.

'I thought the Chardonnay years were over,' Shanna said. 'That was the end of the Nineties. Now's when real life starts. Proper jobs in shops and things.'

'Great,' I said. Shanna was examining her extensions, looped and roped at the nape of her neck, in the wide mirrors behind our table.

'This town is looking up,' she said. 'Nice cafes where you can sit like this, and shops like ours, where you can fill up your house with decorous tat.'

'Yeah,' I said.

'I could almost think about staying here. Buying a house. I could fill it on staff discount.'

I wasn't sure if she was taking the piss. I wasn't sure that she didn't really fancy Pete and his whole life.

I wanted to tell her she had a crush on Pete's whole life and that's why she wanted to go to this meal tonight. She wanted to see him out of hours.

To find out what he was really like.

I could have told her. I was pretty convinced Pete was a twat.

But then, I'd felt like that about most people recently.

Shanna touched my hand. 'It's the break up. That's why you're cynical about everything. I should have realised. But you have to try to see the best in things, Tim.'

I was relishing this turn in the conversation.

I twirled one of the skinny chips left in my bowl. 'Why should I?'

'Because people will get pissed off and stop bothering with you, that's why,' she said briskly. 'I'll still like you, but I'm just daft. I can see the good in you.'

'Cheers.'

'No, I want you to have a good time tonight.'

'Can't promise anything.'

'You're missing Simon.'

'Am I fuck.'

'Hm.' She dabbed at her lipstick with a napkin. She missed the yolk on her chin. 'I reckon you are. But come on ... have a laugh. You should be more like Pete. He looks like he knows how to have a good time.'

I went quiet for a while after that.

I felt disgusted and stung.

I was quiet until we got the taxi up to the multi-storey.

Some of the others were already there.

Sitting at the long table in the middle, the middle-aged, pouchy women who were glad to be out of a night.

Shanna and I took our places at the end of the table and were told by the pushy Sue, who fancied herself management material, that Pete had phoned ahead and already ordered us Special Banquet D.

There would be lots of choice for everyone.

'Wait till you get a look at the owner,' Sue said, leaning in close to me, making me flinch. 'There she is. Look. Thinks she owns the place, swanning about.'

Fiona, who was slightly younger, leaned over. 'Fancy putting a restaurant in a car-park. It puts me off. All the fumes.'

I smiled.

Shanna was looking through the other leatherette menu. 'It's a list of all the songs they do for karaoke.' She flipped the laminated pages. 'They must take it quite seriously. Will you sing?'

'Course,' I said. 'So long as you do it with me.'

Sue dug me hard in the ribs. 'Do it with me! Go on, do it with me!'

At that point Pete appeared, gleaming and jogging.

The ladies noticed him at once and it was all they could do to refrain from clapping.

He apologised for being so late.

'How are you doing, Pete?' shouted Sue.

'Grrrreat!' he grinned.

'And will you being singing tonight? They want to get our requests in now, before the starters arrive.'

'Sing?' he said, and looked relieved when Anne, who was sitting on his other side, grabbed his attention. Something to do with childcare.

'He won't do it,' I told Shanna.

'He will if we will,' she said. 'I just think he's a whole lot more shy than he first appears.'

'And that's your considered analysis? That he's shy?'

Shanna coloured. She was already cross no one had commented on her extra extensions. 'Yes. What's yours?'

'That he's a twat.'

The second course (after the glutinous soup that no one would

touch) was the shreds of duck and the pancakes we lovingly
smeared with plum sauce and folded into fat cigars.

'This,' said Pete, down the length of the table, 'is almost as fine as
when I went to Hong Kong on that conference. That's why I suggested this place. It might not look like much, but the food is quite
marvellous.'

I scowled at Shanna.

'Peter!' came a shriek, and our hostess descended on us in a flurry
of yellow feathers and diamanté.

She put her hands on her hips and gave Peter a hard stare. 'You
never said your hellos to me, you naughty boy.'

The staff of Natural World giggled at this, and continued as
Peter took her large hand and kissed it.

'This is Franky, everyone. She's our hostess this evening.'

'And where is your lovely lady tonight, Peter?'

'This is a work's do, Franky. These are my people. Aren't they
grrreat?'

'I will be telling your lovely lady, Peter, when I see her, that you
bring all these nice and beautiful ladies out when you come here
alone.'

They laughed. I looked at Shanna. 'I feel left out. I'm no lady.'

'You're not.'

'And a young man!' Franky cried. 'You bring a handsome young
man to me!' She scooted around to my side of the table. 'Will you
all sing tonight?'

There was a ragged chorus of assent and some of the ladies hid
their faces.

'Oh, you will all sing!' Franky said. 'Everyone sings here!'

Pete spoke up. 'Will you do your fan dance for us, Franky? Like
you did last time?'

She glared at him. 'Fan dance? What is fan dance?'

'With the feathers,' he faltered. 'When you danced to the …
Chinese music and whatnot.'

'I need to be primed,' she said sniffily. 'If you want dance you must phone in advance.'

Then she was gone and everyone looked at Pete.

'She's obviously a star,' I called down the table to him. 'You can't just demand things off her.'

Pete went back to his duck pancakes, rolling too much of the shredded onion with the slivers of duck.

'Are they pictures of her, do you think?' Shanna was nodding at the framed studio portraits over the bar.

Against pastel backdrops and with her lustrous black hair back-combed and glistening with hairspray, Franky was posing in a variety of disco outfits.

'She looks about fifty years younger.'

I thought Shanna could be cruel sometimes.

On one of the pictures Franky was holding up a glaring white poodle with ribbons knotted in its hair. Her hands were round its throat like she was throttling it. It was as if she wanted to deflect attention from herself.

The main courses were set out on heated silver trays in the middle and competition became quite fierce.

I was letting all the ladies dig in first and I noticed, with satisfaction, that Pete's manners weren't as good. Pete was heaping things into his own little bowl.

All around me the ladies from Natural World were eating like gannets.

'Don't hold yourself back,' Shanna told me, reaching across. Then she touched my cheek. 'And smile!'

I really hate people doing that.

I decided that Franky must have taken to me, because whenever I waggled my empty glass half-heartedly, the proprietress would glare at a waitress and a new vodka orange would appear at my elbow.

I was set on becoming quite drunk as the rest of the party grew more animated, fuelled on water chestnuts and prawn dumplings and spicy ribs, and then Franky was hovering at my shoulder.

'Everything's okay for you, eh?'

'Wonderful,' I said, keen to let her know the night was a success.

Up the table Pete was outlining the new and exciting developments coming to the Natural World chain.

'You will like my daughter,' Franky said, in a lower tone. 'She is very beautiful and talented. And famous, too. My beautiful daughter has come back to her mother and tonight she will sing for us all.'

'Grrreat,' I said.

When the daughter came in from the kitchens and stood by the screens and mikes on the karaoke platform, I realised that I actually did recognise her from somewhere.

'They're starting,' said Shanna. 'Has everyone chosen their songs?'

Picked out in pink and blue spotlights, and in a red frock of some kind of crepey material, Franky's daughter was testing out the mike like a true professional.

Franky took up her place at the till and beamed.

'She's white,' said Shanna. 'Look, the daughter's white. How can a Chinese woman have a white daughter?'

'Good evening,' the daughter said. 'My name's Debbie.'

Belatedly Pete stopped addressing his staff and looked in her direction. He applauded loudly.

'Thank you. I hope you've all got your songs sorted out... because after my solo spot, I'll be getting you all up here. We're going to have a fantastic time.'

She had a rather squeaky voice. To my surprise, there was a round of cheers from the other tables. Looking around, the other, smaller parties were quite prepared to get up there.

They looked as if they could hardly wait.

Debbie launched into an energetic medley of rock and roll standards in a voice that was surprisingly confident.

I eased down in my chair, pleased I wouldn't have to be embarrassed yet.

'She's only got one dance move,' said Shanna. 'Thrusting her hip out and swinging one arm.'

Franky was grinning and watching over all the customers.

'That Franky can't be her natural mother,' Shanna added.

On the small stage, Debbie finished her solo spot with a tribute to Dusty Springfield. 'A blonde and a survivor,' she said, suddenly husky. 'Just like I am.'

Her mother shouted her approval and then again, more fiercely, at the end of 'You Don't Have To Say You Love Me'.

Two rough lads from the table in the corner were getting up to do Elvis. They were in old jeans and their hair was an identical matte black: one, the older one, wore his shorter.

They took up the stage with a louche casualness and Debbie was relegated to operating the machine as they growled out 'Jailhouse Rock'. They wouldn't need any help.

'They're rather good,' said Shanna.

'Brothers,' I said. 'They must be.'

I thought there was something almost sexy about them. Greasemonkeyish.

They stayed up for another Elvis, then a Roy Orbison, before Debbie reasserted control and got another party, a middle-aged one, onto the podium.

'She's Debbie Now,' I said, just as I framed the thought and the sought-after name clicked into place.

'Who?' Shanna had been talking with Fiona.

'From that band. Things Fall Apart, remember? She was one of the girls...'

Shanna shook her head. 'Can't be. She went into being a presenter on the telly. We'd recognise her.'

'No,' I said, scrutinizing the stage. 'She's the other one. The one who stopped being famous. There were two girls and two boys, remember? It was Brenda Maloney who went on the telly after the band broke up.'

Shanna's hair extensions were looking ropier than ever, coming loose from their knot and the Frascati she'd drunk hadn't done her any good at all. 'Whatever you say. I'd never know her in a million years.'

'I would,' I said quietly. 'They were Simon's favourite tacky band. He had the shittest record collection of anyone I've ever seen. But, to his credit, he loved every record he had. Everything meant something to him, which is more than you can say for most people. It was shit but it was consistently shit. And Things Fall Apart was his all-time favourite. The cream of his shit, as it were.'

Shanna had stopped listening to me.

'Right,' she said, 'We're up.'

She was uncharacteristically forceful in getting the other women up on their feet to help her with 'Killing Me Softly With His Song'.

Pete coloured and wouldn't be budged.

I let myself be dragged along, and stood at the back, mouthing the words, all the while stealing glances at the blonde at the karaoke console in the red frock and overdone eyes.

Her poodle perm was exactly the same as it had been when she used to go on *Top of the Pops*.

Everything about her was still in the early-to-mid Eighties.

Crouched over the karaoke machine and its blinking lights and scrolling screens and dinner plate sized CDs, she looked like she was guest-starring in *Blake's Seven*.

I was sure it was her. I had to think of a way to ask her.

But not yet.

Not while I was enjoying myself.

I grew bolder and kept my cigarettes and vodka with me on the podium, even though there was a sign saying I wasn't allowed to.

I graduated through the press of pouchy, middle-aged Natural World women and they were pleased when I took up first place behind the mike to duet with Shanna on 'Islands in the Stream' and then 'Up Where We Belong'.

Pete sat alone at the Natural World table and didn't look at his staff.

He was talking with the waitress for longer than could possibly have been necessary.

The two Elvis brothers good-naturedly clapped along and smiled.

The other tables were watching and I imagined that they recognised the shop's sales staff.

Everyone had been to Natural World to buy their homelies. All their homes boasted fragranced, natural tat.

It was like being recognised and celebrated suddenly and, next thing I knew, as one or two of the more embarrassed of my workmates opted out and returned to sample their banana fritters, I found that I was shouting into the mike and exhorting people from other tables to join me up on the stage.

A little cross-fertilisation was called for, I thought.

I was wanting everyone mucking in and enjoying themselves as much as I was, suddenly, oddly, as the vodka cast its heady spell.

I was welcoming others up to join me and I was the star of the show now, egging everyone on to greater degrees of devil-may-carelessness.

I just want to make a fool of myself for Debbie Now, I thought.

I want to make an impression on an erstwhile celebrity.

I want her to be able to remember this night amongst of a lifetime of engagements: That was the night that very pretty boy got up on my stage and sang his heart out (I could tell he was hurting, really, deep inside) and he, poor, lovely thing, made the whole restaurant join him in singing song after song.

Under layers of ginger, chilli and lemongrass I could smell Debbie's perfume, leaking out with the sweat of her exertions.

Charlie.

She came to stand with me and dance and we sang 'Puppet on a String'.

Next thing, before I even knew it, and through the skilful intercession of Franky, I was seated back at my table with the others.

Watching as the lights dimmed and Franky issued onto the larger stage area, taking tiny steps and lapping yellow feathers, long as her arms, over and around her black sheath dress.

Pete sat up. 'I knew she'd do it for me,' he told the others, and sipped jasmine tea with a grimace. 'Look at the state of her.'

Not to be upstaged by her guests' performances, or her daughter's, Franky even did an encore.

Franky finished exhausted, utterly given, on the polished parquet with the feathers, damp and quivering, clutched to her bosom.

Pete applauded wildly and the others followed.

'I know I can tell you, and that I can trust you, Tim, but I have to say I would never have gone into it, gone into that world, if I'd known then what I found out after.'

Debbie reached for the sparkling pink wine and I got there first, making sure she got the lion's share.

Grateful, she sat back in the chair, still faintly damp and glowing in her stage costume, and went on.

'My life's been really very hard, you know. It wasn't always all champagne. It was so hard and people can be so horrible. Something about me, it must have been, brought out the worst in everyone around me...' She shuddered.

'That can't be true,' I said and she glared at me.

'Well, it was. You know, I never believed it when they said, when people said, that some others will use you, use up your talent and then dump you. I never believed it of them. I always looked for the best in people and that was my downfall...'

It was one o'clock in the morning and most of the ladies from Natural World had gone.

Pete was talking with Shanna and one of the Elvis brothers. Pete looked embarrassed and cross that I had managed to get Debbie, our entertainer, to join us at the table. He had smiled but hadn't said a word to her.

I knew Debs was delighted to be sitting there.

She had come over and hovered, once the karaoke machine was switched off and stowed away, and she had told us all what a good crowd we had been.

How we had made her night.

My heart had ached for her as the ladies from Natural World looked her critically up and down, nodded, and turned back to pulling on their coats and sorting out the bill.

I knew Debs was needing a place to sit. I dragged up a chair and asked her if she would join us and I called for a bottle of fizz.

In return Debs had launched into the tale of her career.

'I knew it was you,' I confided. 'As soon as you came out on that stage, I said to Shanna, my friend over there: that's Debs Now, from Things Fall Apart.'

'So I haven't changed that much?' Her voice squeaked higher in pleasure.

'Still exactly the same. You were ... my favourite member of my favourite ever band,' I said rashly.

'Really?'

I nodded, forcing down bubbly with a squeeze of guilt.

Simon wouldn't mind me stealing his fiercest, most embarrassing love, I was sure.

'I'm glad to hear that,' she said softly. 'You just go on, assuming everyone has forgotten you. It's like someone suddenly says 'Game

Over' and then you get dumped back in the real world and have to start again.'

I nodded.

'But, for whatever I say, they were still great years, you know. They were still my glory years.'

'You must have some fantastic memories.'

She looked wistful as she stared into space, and I followed her gaze to see Pete getting up, grinning, putting on his jacket. The waitress was waiting for him.

'I have all sorts of memories,' she said. 'Unlike the other three, I have perfect recall of everything that happened to us. I can remember things that would make your hair stand on end.'

'I'm sure you can.'

'I'm off,' Shanna broke abruptly into our conversation, pushing her face into mine and smacking me on the back of my head with her extensions as she bent for a kiss.

'Oh, right...'

Both of the Elvis brothers were waiting for her by the till.

'You're not going off with them...?'

'They live in the rough part of town,' Shanna said quickly, 'But I'm not going to let that put me off.'

'You're getting into some kind of sick Elvis incest thing,' I warned.

She shrugged. 'We'll see.'

Debbie looked at Shanna over her glass. 'You go, love,' she advised. 'If I've learned one thing, it's never to let an opportunity slip by.'

I wondered if Debbie's pronouncements from the brink of stardom would ever start to piss me off.

'But they could chop her up and kill her!'

'Or,' said Debbie smoothly, 'She might just have a very nice, sexy time with a couple of incestuous Elvis impersonators.'

'Jesus,' I said. 'You watch yourself, Shanna.'

She smirked at me and then was gone, with the Presley brothers following at her heels. I was mad jealous.

At closing up time Franky became sullen, as if all the life had gone out of her. She slumped against the till and watched the last of our party go out for their cabs. Even with her daughter she was distant and strained.

'It's been a real pleasure meeting you,' I told Debbie, taking the hint at last and standing up. I was swaying.

She jumped up. She looked terrified at the idea of losing her audience. 'Look at me. I haven't changed out of my work clothes, I've been so busy nattering on...'

'Debs,' her mother called. 'Your taxi is on its way.'

'This is when I get you to sign all my records,' I said. 'But I haven't got any with me.'

'You could buy a CD,' she said. 'I usually carry some around in my bag.' She went shuffling back to the stage. 'I'm sure I've got some...'

'That would be lovely,' I said.

'All new stuff, all new recordings, solo stuff...' She came back, hunting through a sports holdall. 'They must be back at the house. But usually I bring some ... just in case someone spots me...'

'You've got new songs?'

'Old ones. Standards and oldies. The kinds of things I sing here.'

Suddenly I knew exactly what her solo CD would be like. It would be her singing along to the karaoke, recorded straight off the mike.

'I just do what the punters go for now,' she said. 'No point in trying to be artistic. We tried that, once.'

'Debs,' her mother shouted again. 'There is a horn peeping out in the car-park. It will be for you.'

Debs nodded and looked at me.

'Good night, then,' I said.

She grabbed my arm. She was surprisingly strong. 'Come with me. I'm staying at my mother's house. She's moved out, in with the bloke who owns the car-park. The place is my own now, for as long as I want it.' She was gabbling.

'Go back with you?'

'You've got me talking now, Tim. I can't wind down after a performance, especially not one like tonight. I have to talk talk talk. And I can dig one of my CDs out and sign it for you. Will you?'

I left with her on my arm. She held her head up and braved the stares of her mother's waitresses.

We went through the double doors and found ourselves up on the second storey of the car-park, where the late night wind whistled through and you could see the shops' roofs. There was only one car; our taxi, waiting there. The last cab in town.

'No, I've got one after all,' she said, with her head in her bag. She pulled out a CD case and passed it over to me. Her face was blue and shining in the lights as we cruised through the rough part of town. It would blaze orange every few moments as we went under street lights.

The plastic CD case was cracked. 'It was in with my shoes.'

'It doesn't matter.'

'Ten quid. If you don't mind. I'll sign it.'

The cover was laser copied in smeary red and blue. Debbie in the same outfit, on a small stage.

'Hey,' I said, 'these aren't all covers of other people's songs. You sing 'Let's Be Famous' on this.'

'Oh, that thing.' She sagged back. 'Well, I have to have that one prepared, part of the repertoire, just in case someone clocks me. That's for when I have to become the real Debbie Now and remind them of our most famous song. I hate it.'

'I love it,' I said. 'It's fantastic. But you never sang it for me.'

She smiled. 'Maybe I will.'

I went hunting through my pockets for a tenner and I was thinking about tomorrow, when I'd look up Simon's new number for the first time.

I'd ring him out of the blue and he'd be alarmed, then grumpy, then regretful, then envious at the sound of my voice.

I'd say, Guess who I met last night?

Guess what I bought off her as we went to her mother's house in the deepest, darkest part of town in the middle of the night?

Guess who's living in my town, in the middle of an estate of 1950s pebble-dashed council houses?

Simon would be so jealous he'd spit.

'Thanks for this,' I said. 'You've really made my night.'

She shrugged.

Then she put her hand on my knee and squeezed, making a small squeaking noise of her own.

I was thrilled.

'I'm sorry it's so warm in here,' she said, leading me into the dark front room. 'She's had it double-glazed throughout and I can't work out the heating controls.'

The lights sprang on, revealing a living room that didn't look lived in. It looked too neat and dusted, with its dado rails, empty bookshelves and TV on a table. One or two cardboard boxes were waiting to be unpacked.

I almost turned to Debbie and told her how she could spruce the place up by going to Natural World. She could use my staff discount.

'The heating's been on all day,' she said. 'It's really stifling in here. Well.' She slapped her palms against her thighs. 'Sit down. Make yourself comfortable. What would you like to drink? Excuse the mess. I haven't been here long.'

Now she had me here it seemed that she didn't quite understand why she'd bothered.

'Your mother just gave you this place?'

'Can you still smell her smoke?' She sniffed deeply. 'Her cats as well. I'd open the windows but it chills right through really quickly. Sit down.'

The warmth was actually making me feel queasy. I sat. 'Can I have a gin and tonic?'

'No ice,' she said. 'The freezer's jammed up with it, so I've got no cubes.'

'Chip a bit off...'

'Have it warm, eh? And then I'll find some music. Do you want the gas fire on?' She started disappearing in the direction of the kitchen. 'I'd better change out of these ridiculous clothes...'

'It's warm enough,' I said, struggling with my jacket and she was gone.

The room was dully lit and the colours were mostly greyish green and blue. I'd have expected something more flamboyant, really, from Franky. It didn't look very Chinese, either, apart from the couple of scrolls above the gas fire with that scratchy kind of Chinese writing on. And the empty wooden birdcage, maybe that was a Chinese thing too.

Maybe Franky was living in a more colourful place now. Maybe she'd upped and taken all the colour with her, leaving her daughter in this place.

I sniffed the arm of the squashy settee. Everything was permeated thickly with cigarette smoke. It would never come out. It was as if I could still see the restless smoke drifting around in the room, as if that's what her mother turned into, like a spirit, keeping an eye on her famous daughter.

I found my own fags and lit one, just to freshen the smokey smell up.

Debbie called through. 'Do you want a baked potato? I can do one in the microwave in a flash...?'

'No thanks.'

She reappeared with our gin and tonics. She'd scraped some ice out of the clogged freezer and dumped it in the glasses. They looked like Slush Puppies. 'I shouldn't be drinking more,' she said. 'I'll really never sleep tonight, but I don't care. I'm celebrating.'

'What?'

'My first, proper, successful night since I got here. Since I came back from the south.'

I nodded.

Then she started hunting through the cardboard boxes. They were crammed with old vinyl LPs. She had quite a collection, well preserved, apart from a few frayed and bent corners. She slid some out from the boxes, glanced over their covers, smiled and shyly passed them over to me. I sat forward on the settee.

'I used to buy every record I could get my hands on,' she said. 'That's how I got into the business. When I was a kid, saving up every penny and rushing to Woollies for the next new thing out. Did you?'

I nodded, though it wasn't true.

She looked at one cover and frowned. 'Twelve inch singles. I never saw the point of them. They were rubbish. Not worth the money.'

Barbra Streisand, Bananarama, Samantha Fox. 'Where are yours?' I asked.

'Ah.' Then she pulled out four records, shoved in with the others. She held them out to me. 'You'll recognise these ones.'

I looked at the covers. Let's Be Famous, Breakthru, White Noise, The Greatest Hits of Things Fall Apart. She'd signed her own copies in thick black marker pen. They looked shabbier than Simon's copies.

'Can we hear one?'

She winced. 'I hardly ever listen to these things. They're out of date. They're not what a young man like you wants to hear...'

'They are, I told you. They're my favourite.'

'Well, okay. But not too loud. They've got kiddies next door.'

She moved to the record player, eager now, and I watched her bend to slip the Greatest Hits from its sleeve with agonizing care. She held the record properly, against her palms, with her red nails splayed out of harm's way.

The needle hissed and the familiar drumbeat of 'Let's Be Famous' started, tinny and muted. She shuddered and turned to me with a grin.

'It's a rotten song.'

'I think it's great.'

'I don't play my own records all the time, you know,' she said. 'I'm not like some weirdo, listening to myself all the time.'

'No...'

'Mostly I listen to what's new in the charts. I like to keep up.'

I shrugged. 'I don't bother.'

She came to sit down with me, perching carefully. 'You're a funny lad.'

My ears started to burn. I could feel them glow red. Then I could feel her staring at them. I took a long sniff of her hairspray and squashed out my cigarette. She touched my ear gently with one of her nails.

'What kind of lad in this day and age still listens to songs by a clapped out old has-been pop star, eh, Tim?' She pushed closer along the settee cushion and I felt her breath on my face. Her hand came down to my wrist. She stroked my hand. 'Hm?'

A gay one, I wanted to say. A great big flaming handbag of a lad. But I was too choked up to say anything.

I glanced out of the corner of my eye and she was staring at me through her flaking eye makeup. She blinked. The next track started. A ballad in which Debbie took lead vocals. She hummed along with herself, lightly.

'I've not had a man in ages,' she whispered. 'I mean, I've not had a man back to mine, up this close. You'd think they'd be clamouring after me, wouldn't you? But I'm selective. I've not really had a man since Clive.'

My stomach flipped. The mention of Clive, her ex-husband, ex-band member, made the whole thing more real. This was really her. It was really Debbie Now pressing her breasts up against my arm.

I coughed. 'Isn't it a bit of a come-down for you, doing karaoke?'

The question came out more rudely than I'd wanted it to. She sat back as if I'd slapped her and lowered her eyes.

'I'm sorry,' I said.

'No, it's all right.' She picked up her glass.

'I didn't mean come-down,' I said quickly. 'I mean, it's just a change of direction, isn't it? It's just...'

'It's just some lousy job, one step up from a waitress, that's what it is.' She looked at me and seemed so hurt I wished I'd never recognised her in the first place. 'And, the truth is, if it wasn't my mum's place, I'd never even have that job at all. The other karaoke places won't have me.'

'Course they would.'

'They reckon I'm a prima donna.'

'You've every right to be.'

'One of them even accused me of impersonating myself!'

'That's ridiculous.'

'They want someone younger at the front.'

'You're young.'

She looked at me.

'You're still young,' I said.

She came closer again, until the poodle perm blocked out the whole room around us. 'Kiss me,' she said, so I licked my lips experimentally and shoved forward to kiss her.

She pulled away after a bit and said, 'It's the same job, anyway, in the end.'

'What is?'

'Doing the karaoke. It's the same job I always did. Cheering up the punters with songs they know. Making them feel part of it all.'

'I suppose it is.'

'It's more difficult, actually. Technical. You have to work your own machine.'

I pressed forward to kiss her again. Her skin felt soft and powdery. It was interesting, kissing a woman. Her hands went round my back.

'Another reason why I'm celebrating,' she said, popping her head on my shoulder.

'Hm?' I just felt still. I felt calm. I didn't feel like I was copping off. We were just having a bit of a hug. That was okay.

'There's some good news on the horizon.'

'Good.'

'Do you want to hear it? Do you want to know what my good news is?'

'Yeah. Course.'

She pulled back. 'Even the fan club bulletin doesn't know this yet. I'm waiting till it's definite. Do you get the bulletin?'

Luckily, I didn't have to answer, because she was hopping over to the mantlepiece and fetching a letter from behind the clock. She'd unzipped the back of her dress at some point, and shed one of her shoes.

She flopped down like she had no bones inside her and gave me the thick sheet of paper.

'It's a letter of agreement,' she said. 'Addressed to me, as ex band member and lyricist for Things Fall Apart, the legendary Eighties supergroup.' She grinned. 'That's how they put it in the letter, anyway.'

All the aggressive type was shifting into a blur. 'What does it mean?'

'Someone's wants to sing one of the songs and release it as a

single. It's going to be a big hit again. It looks like our moment
might be coming round again!'

She was really beaming.

I looked back at the letter. I fixed on a name. 'Shelley Sommers!'

'That's right,' Debbie said.

'But she's fantastic!' I couldn't stop myself sounding excited. 'I'd
heard she was starting on a singing career...'

'They all do. They get killed off in a soap and go straight to number one. And now Shelley's going to, with 'Let's Be Famous'. She
reckons it's her favourite song from when she was a kid. We're going
to be covered! I'm going to be covered!'

'Have you met her? Have you met Shelley Sommers?'

Shit, shit, shit. I sounded far too enthusiastic about the younger
woman. Debs wouldn't be pleased.

She took back the letter and folded it carefully. 'Not yet. I have to
go to London to meet her. Talk over her version of the song. She
wants my help.'

'That's amazing,' I said. 'Shelley Sommers!'

'Good news, eh?'

'Wonderful. Did you see the episode where she karked it?'

'I don't watch it,' she said. 'I don't watch telly.'

'It was brilliant.'

'Well,' said Debbie. 'There we go.' She put the letter on the arm
of the sofa.

I looked at her. She was staring at her one shoeless foot. There
was a ladder in her tights, starting at the big toe.

'Shall we go upstairs then?' I asked.

Simon told me once that I get myself into situations that I can't get
myself out of. He reckoned it was me being soft and pliable and not
making a stand. I told him it was just me being nice, not wanting to
disappoint people.

He'd said he couldn't live around someone like that. I was like one of them fake flower things you buy on the market. Clap or make a noise and it starts to dance around, waggling its head.

He said it was a quiet way of manipulating people. Make them think you're doing exactly what they want. Keep quiet about it as they tell you their whole life. Let them make themselves vulnerable to you.

He said that's what I did to him.

I told him he was a self-justifying twat. However soft I was with people it didn't excuse him for half the things he did. Sleeping with half the fellas down the club, for instance. Getting a job in Wales, where I couldn't and wouldn't follow him. It was never going to work.

In the end, he thought I was passive aggressive and I thought he was a cunt.

On the staircase Debbie held my hand and led me into the dark.

'How old are you?'

'Twenty-seven.'

I could hear her mind ticking over the sum. 'You were about three when we had our first single out! You were three when we did Eurovision!'

'I can remember it clear as anything.'

'Can you hell,' she laughed.

Her mother's room was at the end of the hall. This was where all the colour was. There were tissue paper kites, painted with faces, hanging from the ceiling. The headboard of the vast bed was collaged with pre-Raphaelite paintings razored from library books. The lamps were shaded with scarves and there were tassles and beads on everything.

Debbie lit some beeswax candles and got the incense burners going.

She stood by the bed and let her dress drop to the floor.

Her breasts were heavy and white, with those huge nipples that look purple and sore. I've always liked nipples of that colour and size. I didn't quite look any further down. I moved closer so I wouldn't have to.

'Well?' she said. 'Do I still look young to you?'

She looked even younger. I told her she was in wonderful shape, and she was. I hugged her again, through my smoke-filled clothes and I was amazed at how smooth she was.

'What about the others?' I asked.

She blinked in the soft light. 'What others? I'm here by myself...'

'I mean in the band. Clive and Brenda and Tony...'

'Oh, them.' I felt a shiver go across her skin. 'Look, can we get into bed, Tim? I feel a bit daft stood here in the nuddy. Especially if you're just going to talk about rock family trees.'

I nodded and she peeled back the continental quilt. When she turned her back it was white and her bum was all round and soft and dimpled. I felt a rush of compassion.

Plumping the pillows, she seemed to suddenly become self-conscious of her bare bum in the air, and hurriedly got into the bed. She looked up at me.

'Are you coming in?'

It was so warm in there. I couldn't believe how warm it was. My head was throbbing. I decided it was excitement. I wanted to be cooler. I wanted nothing more than to take off all my clothes.

Debbie watched me.

She watched me drop my clothes on the carpet and leave them where they lay. It was a bad habit I'd picked up from Simon. He was so careless it got so it wasn't worth even trying to make an effort.

Debs looked me over as I stripped. I turned slightly as I rolled down my jeans. I tried to make it seem I was fiddling with the buttons, but I was plumping my dick up, just like she had with her pillows.

'Come here,' she said, holding the covers open. 'I'll tell you what happened to the others afterwards.'

Afterwards. She'd tell me all about it afterwards.

She was bargaining me off for now with promises of stories she'd tell me afterwards. For now I'd have to do what she told me.

She took me to bed like a giant kitten and rolled me around under viscose sheets, my claws snagging on the fabric and static.

She pulled me down to her. She was urgent and dextrous, suddenly far less sleepy and drunk and underconfident.

I do her an injustice to suggest she was pulling me down, toying around with me, slipping me inside herself, against my will.

I was there. I was right in there. I was right inside her happily, snug as a gun in a hidden pocket. I couldn't believe how warm it was inside her. My first time inside another person's body.

Even through the clinging film of the condom she filched from the stencilled bedside cabinet I could feel her warmth.

I fucked to the rhythm of questions that crowded into my head so insistently. The questions all came in Simon's voice, surprising me with their urgency and the idea I'd kept his voice, his exact tone, recorded so carefully in my head.

Why did you break up with Clive?

When did you stop making music together?

How can you bear to write words that he won't put music to?

What became of Tony?

Was he brain-damaged forever?

Is he all right now, and happy?

Were the newspaper stories true?

We all know about Brenda, of course. We know her off the telly. Brenda's stayed famous and she's a household face.

But what is she really like?

What was she like when she was starting out, just part of the band?

Is she the bitch that everyone suggests she is?

Afterwards, afterwards, Debbie promised she'd tell me after this bout. After we'd both come and were exhausted with each other, lying a little distance apart in her mother's bed.

She'd tell me the stories then.

'Typical me, typical me, typical me...' she sang softly, and laughed her smoker's laugh. She waved the match dead and sank back on the pillow.

I was lying sideways and gazing at her uptilted face.

I'd had my brains fucked out. It hadn't happened before. I'd come inside her eventually and had been quite shocked by the whole thing.

I still didn't know what I thought about any of it.

Debbie seemed quite relaxed, as if it had all been fine, but not that great. I was acting the same, smoking with her, trying not to get ash on the polyfibres of the sheet.

'What's typical you?' I asked.

She looked me dead in the eye. 'Sleeping with a gay man again. It's a habit I got into at an early age. Can't shake it.'

She bent her knees under the quilt and balanced the ashtray on them.

I swallowed.

'Come on, Tim. What other kind of fella your age wets his pants over a career like mine? Only a gay boy.'

'Right,' I said, and felt more naked than ever.

'Besides,' she said. 'You don't screw like a straight bloke.'

Screw. It was such a straight word. I hadn't heard it applied to anything I did. I was in deep water here.

'Wasn't it all right?' I said.

'It was fine,' she smiled. 'Lovely. Nostalgic, actually.'

'But you could tell!'

'You made me come and all, but the ringing in my ears wasn't just that. It was the gaydar going off with klaxons and bells.'

'Shit.'

'Why did you do it, Tim? Why come to bed if you never fancied me?'

'I did, Debs. I swear...'

She gave me a long look. 'I'll believe you. I know it's complicated.' She touched my cheek.

'It wasn't just because ...' I sighed. ''Cause you're famous.'

'I'm not famous anymore. This...' She gestured around the room with the glowing end of her ciggy. 'None of this would get you kudos. No points to be scored with this kind of set-up.'

'Yes, there would be!' I said. 'If I went round telling people, they'd be dead impressed.'

'Would they?'

'Course they would. People remember.'

'So you still feel like a ...' She looked almost shy again. 'A star-fucker?'

'Completely. And I've never done it like that before. It was fantastic.'

'You got too excited.' She laughed. 'It was nice. Sweet to see.'

'So are you going to tell me stories, then?' I rolled over and snuggled in. Her whole skin was irradiated and glowing.

'Stories?'

'The story of your life.' I breathed in the smell of both of us. I was relaxed suddenly. The room seemed like the centre of the world.

'This,' she said, 'this is the story of my life. Sitting up in bed with a nice gay man and both of us naked and dawn coming up.'

'Tell me,' I urged, but I could feel sleep coming on. I still wanted to listen to her voice.

'I wouldn't know where to start,' she said. 'There's so much. And anyway, I'm not thinking about the past now. Not really.'

'You're looking to the future,' I murmured, my eyes starting to close.

'That's right.' She drew up the quilt and somehow I could feel her looking at me.

'You're waiting on your comeback,' I said.

I heard a sharp whistle as she drew in a breath. She paused.

I opened my eyes and looked at her, silhouetted against the tassled lamps. I was starting to get hard again.

'There can't be a real comeback,' she said softly. 'We couldn't do it. Not without Roy's help. Not without him. It was when Roy went that everything started to go wrong.'

It was a real effort to speak. 'Who was Roy?'

'Our guru. Our advisor. Our fifth member, in a way. The fattest, loudest, filthiest mouthed tranny who ever came out of Blackpool.'

Debbie lightly brushed my eyes with her fingertips until they were closed.

'He was our manager and our mother hen. Roy kept us all straight.'

Chapter Two

'It's your first time abroad,' her mother wept. 'And you aren't taking me.'

Debs was going on the hovercraft. She wasn't keen at all. She had three big bags and her stomach was churning round and round. She knew the others were already aboard and if Franky caused a scene in the departures lounge they would laugh at her.

She was the youngest and they all knew she had never been abroad. She was supposed to be acting tougher than this. She gulped down her tears and looked at her mother.

Franky's face was squinched up with emotion. 'I should be with you. What can I do? Watch it on the television when you win? That isn't enough. A mother should be with her daughter at these times.'

'We might not win, Mum.' Debs looked around nervously as the other passengers queued to go through the doors, onto the hovercraft.

'What kind of attitude is that to go in with?'

'I want to be realistic about this. It makes me nervous, otherwise.' She shouldered the heaviest of her bags.

'They should have someone to take your luggage,' said Franky. 'You are a star now. They should treat you like one.'

'I'm not a star.'

'People are buying your record! I am telling everyone! Everyone knows who you are. You take all of our hopes with you and you have to win.'

Debs felt her insides curdling. 'I wish I had never got into this now.'

'This Roy person will look after you properly,' her mother said. 'You are very precious.'

'Mum, I've got to go.' The last stragglers were heading towards the doorway, looking sheepish. She always makes me late, Debs thought. Everything important I've ever done and my mother keeps me talking and makes me late.

'You are so young. Going to Europe. Letting everyone in the world see you sing your song. How can you be so brave? A little thing like you...' But Franky looked proud.

'I'll be with the others,' Debs said. 'It isn't just me by myself. Thank God...' she added.

'The others...' Franky shook her head. 'I do not like the look of these others this Roy has given you. But they are there to make you look good. And at least you will have Tony. I have phoned him and his mother already. Tony will look after you.'

'Oh Mum, you didn't...'

'I did. That is a good boy there. He has always been in love with you. I am grateful he is in this group of yours. He will see you right.'

Debs shook her head. Her mother had never seen things the right way round. Debs had known Tony nearly all her life. She was *his* guardian, not the other way round. When he used to come to the restaurant and gobble up bowls of Franky's house specialities, it was because his mother had chucked him out and Debs was looking after him. Ever since he'd been thirteen his mother had been throwing him out of the house regularly. Debs had had to step in. She loved Tony, but there was no depending on him. And she knew that he was more terrified of this trip and this competition than she was.

At least I can sing, Debs thought. At least I know that much. When they put me on the stage and all the lights come on me and all of Europe is scrutinizing me; at least I know I can sing. Poor Tony doesn't. He just opens and closes his mouth. He's only there for the moral support. How must he feel now?

She had to go to him. She had to find him, somewhere on the

hovercraft. No doubt he'd have found the bar by now and he'd be needing to talk to her.

'Mum,' Debs rallied. 'I have to go. Otherwise they'll go without me.' She squared her shoulders.

'Without you!' Frankie exclaimed. 'They could do no such thing!' But she grasped her daughter in a quick, untidy hug, let her handbag drop to the floor and watched, sobbing, as Debs turned on her heel and hurried through the glass doors, down the tunnel beyond, and onto the hovercraft.

Franky thought it a very unnatural mode of transport. Through the smutty windows of the departures lounge she watched the craft's skirts belly out and the whole curious vehicle rise into the air with everyone aboard. Like something out of the space age and out of a nightmare. Unnatural at any rate, and she had consigned her only daughter to its protection.

She had sent her daughter off to sing in Europe and she had sent her alone. Franky watched the rubber skirt of the hovercraft tremble, as if in anticipation. It wasn't natural at all. It didn't bode well.

People were bedding down on their sun loungers with their hand luggage by their sides as Debs trawled the decks looking for Tony. Luckily, their manager had shelled out for two cabins for the band to rest in. He hadn't been so stingy as to suggest they stretch out on loungers on the deck as most of the other passengers had.

The clouds over the channel were massing and everything was cast in a yellow, funky gloom. Debs was sure there'd be a storm. And they would all drown.

Ten minutes into the channel and she was trying not to think about their position. She wouldn't look down at the sea. She didn't want to think about the ruffling, inflated bottom bit of the hovercraft. The noise was terrific as she hobbled in her clunky shoes on the damp, drizzly deck, weaving between the loungers and that was enough.

She wanted to be inside, pretending that she was on dry ground.

It was all right for the others. They'd all of them travelled before. Clive had apparently played in German clubs, when he had a band of his own. He was used to all this. Brenda had been a hair stylist on cruise ships. Even Tony had been on an exchange with a French pen-friend. She remembered that clearly enough. Her mother wouldn't let her do the exchange and she'd been livid with Tony for still going. He'd missed her, though, trudging round historical churches with his surly Jean-Claude, sending her postcards, saying how rotten it all was.

Now they were nineteen and they were travelling abroad under their own steam. Debs should feel buoyed up and excited. Tonight they'd be on the telly. They would know whether they had won or not. Either way they would be famous.

All she could feel was dread. There was an undertow of reluctance, dragging her back with every step across the deck. She glanced at the loungers on the way and some of the passengers had the *Mirror* or the *Sun* open, ruffling in the breeze, and she wondered if they would be reading about her. She knew she was in both papers. The tabloids were right behind the band, wishing them success this weekend in Europe.

No one peered at her over their papers. No one called out good luck. Her hair was ruined in the wind. Her bags, she was sure, would have let in the salty drizzle and everything would be spoiled.

Brenda was at the bar, hogging Tony. She had a glass of wine and he was gazing into a watery pint, trying not to look at her.

Brenda was unperturbed. She was rabbiting on, Debs thought, and making Tony listen to her every thought. She had already picked Tony out as the member of the band she could best bully. And Tony was just taking it.

Debs stood away from the bar for a second and watched them on their high stools.

Brenda's hair was like a helmet, Debs thought. You'd never think she was a stylist. It was a kind of soft, thick helmet of purple brown. She must have some kind of rinse in it. Brenda's hair looked glossy and healthy even in the murky grey light of the channel. Debs caught her own reflection and she looked mousey and her perm was hanging in tatters.

Brenda was perched on the very edge of her stool, with her powerful legs crossed and waggling one foot thoughtfully in the air with her shoe hanging off. Picture of nonchalance.

'The fucking French won't give us any points at all,' she was telling Tony in her slightly throaty voice. 'They never do. It's, like, political. Nor will the Germans, for the obvious reasons. It doesn't matter what our song's like or what we're like, we can't expect anything from the bastard French or Germans. What we have to do is aim at things like Switzerland and Israel. That's where we can make up the points.'

As Debs came up to the bar Tony was turning to look at Brenda. He blinked. 'You've got this all worked out. All the strategies and stuff?'

'You have to,' said Brenda. 'It's no game, you know. It's just like the war, but we do it in a more peaceful way. But there's still casualties and stuff. Oh. Look, it's Debbie.' Brenda sniffed and looked Debs up and down. 'You'll want that hair setting again, soon as we're on dry ground. It'll go all crinkly if you don't watch out. Thank God you made it. Roy was doing his nut about you.'

Debs' stomach gave a lurch. 'He wasn't, was he?'

'We were all supposed to come aboard together. The press were there.'

'It was my mum...' Debs found herself bleating. When she talked to Brenda her voice always came out in a bleat.

Brenda did her smirk and hoisted her legs, crossing them the other way. 'We did the pictures without you. Ready to set sail. I don't think they'll notice we were one down.'

Debs coloured.

Tony was patting her elbow, twisting round and trying to get her to sit. 'They all noticed, lovey. They were all horribly disappointed you weren't there. And Roy was stotting mad.'

'Great.' She tried to catch the barman's eye to ask for a bitter lemon.

'What I was saying, anyhow,' said Brenda. 'Those stage outfits are no good. It's just bland, generic disco gear, isn't it? We should have something a bit foreign on, to appeal to like, Israel or Norway. Then they'll like us. We could clean up on the international cabaret circuit. Now, that's big business. On the ships I saw them all come through, minting it...'

Tony cut in. 'Roy knows what's best. We've got to be big at home. In Britain. That's what we've got to do. Who cares if everyone in Finland loves us? Who cares about them? We want our mums and everyone to know we're famous at home. That's what we want.'

Brenda tutted. 'I'd prefer it if no one at home knew about this. Those crappy outfits ... that bloody song...'

Tony jumped in. 'It's a fantastic song!'

'It's crap.'

Tony hissed at her through his teeth. 'It's perfect for the Eurovision.'

Brenda darted a glance sideways at Debs, who was holding her newly-arrived bitter lemon in both hands. 'Oh, yeah. Sorry, Debs. Forgot it was your song. It's good for what it does. It's all right. I don't mind it. That okay, Tony?' She sagged back, as if she'd made herself apologetic enough.

'It's my favourite song,' Tony said, putting his arm around Debs' shoulders.

Brenda laughed and shook her head. 'You two. Honestly. You always look after each other, don't you? I don't know why Roy didn't just have the two of you. You don't need me and Clive at all.'

'Foursomes are in,' Debs said. 'That's what he reckons. That's what everyone wants to see. Two boys and two girls. We can't lose like that. They catch on because everyone wants to know who's going out with who.'

Tony was nodding.

Brenda looked them up and down. 'You two look as if you've been at it since you were at school together. You're never out of each other's pockets.'

Debs laughed and shook her head. She felt freezing drops of water plop from her hair onto her bare shoulders. 'My mum always thought we were a couple, too.'

Tony looked uncomfortable. 'It doesn't always work out like that.'

Brenda leaned forward and swished her hair out of her eyes. 'Now we're in the band, it can work out any way we want it to, sunshine.'

The channel seemed a lot wider than it was meant to be. After her second bitter lemon Tony took one look at Debs and said she ought to have a lie down.

'Roy got a cabin for us two to share,' Brenda said, with surprising concern. She passed her the key. 'Go and use it. I'm too worked up to want to rest. There'll be plenty of time to rest after tonight.'

Debs nodded and gave in. Tony offered to help her find the right deck and hoisted her bags.

'I want to know where Clive's gone,' Brenda said. 'He's a sexy fella, isn't he? When they pair us all up for publicity purposes I'm gonna have him. You don't mind, do you, Debs? If I take Clive? I reckon we look right together.'

Debs nodded and couldn't say anything more.

She felt Tony's arm go round her back as he guided her out of the bar.

'I hate her,' he muttered as they braved the sea spray outside and made for the stairs. 'She's a fat bitch and I don't know why we have to have her.'

'Foursomes,' said Debs. 'Roy reckons it's the right way to go.'

'And that Clive,' Tony went on. He was raving, Debs thought. He was off. 'That Clive is just an animal. Thinks he's a proper musician. Thinks he's wasting his time with the likes of us. We're just bubble gum. He's a musician. Fucking animal.'

Debs leaned on him as they ducked into the staircase and wobbled their way down in the gloom. 'I wish it was just us two as well, Tony.'

'They're older than us,' he complained. 'They look older. And they keep going on about everything they've done. What we haven't done. I feel like some daft kid.'

Debs heard the real hurt in his voice and saw how much he wished it was like it was last year and the year before. When the two of them had gone on *New Faces* together as a brother-and-sister act and cleaned up. They'd won through three rounds with three sappy ballads they both quite liked and that was how they came to Roy's attention. He placed them firmly under his management and they had willingly gone. They listened to all of his advice, agog, knowing that he was the maestro and couldn't put a dainty foot wrong.

Now Debs was having her first stab of doubt. She couldn't see the sense at all in trying to get on with Brenda and Clive. They were older and harder. The kind of people she and Tony clubbed together to protect each other from. The kind of people that made their self-protection necessary.

'Brenda only has a go at you because she's jealous,' Tony told her, trying to find the right cabin door for her. The ceiling was low and the whole corridor was swaying slightly. 'Because you're so petite. It drives her crazy. She looks like a right lummox next to you.'

Debs shrugged. 'Have you heard her range, though, Tony? She can sing anything. She's incredible.'

He tutted. 'Singing. That's got nothing to do with it. She'll run to fat by the time she's thirty and her legs are manky. She's not got what you've got, lovey. Here's your cabin.'

He propped her against the wall as he dealt with the lock.

The door swung open on the small, spotless, spartan room and they both gasped.

There was a steward facing away from them, yanking up his white trousers and checking his hair in the small mirror. He whirled around at the instant the door came open and turned a furious red. Behind him, on an uncomfortable looking banquette, sat Roy, tugging his hair into a rough pony-tail.

He was a monster of a man. He had a head the width and shape of a rugby ball and tiny eyes that needed all the making up they could get. When he spoke, opening those gross and fleshly lips, they could see all of his teeth. He had more square yellow teeth than he could ever use. To Debs he looked like a proper bruiser; the kind of man who could have been a wrestler if he'd wanted. Instead he chose to wear jewellery and kaftans, stilletoes and mini skirts. These outward appurtenances, though, were the only concessions he made to a femininity he believed was intransigently his.

'What the fucking hell are you doing?' he growled, grabbing up his auburn wig with one massive paw and giving it a ruthless shake.

The steward - a thin boy with a crooked nose - stood between them and their manager, trembling.

'Go on you, fuck off,' Roy grunted. 'That's your lot. Thanks for fixing that reading light. What are you waiting for? A frigging tip?'

The steward bolted past Tony and Debs and they watched as Roy watched him go, tugging his disordered chignon into place. He was wearing a voluminous sea-green kaftan and the largest silver slingbacks Debs had ever seen.

'What the bollocking hell happened to knocking?' Roy yelled at them, once he had his hair right. 'I could have been doing anything in here!'

'Brenda said this was mine and hers... the cabin, I mean ...' Debs stammered.

'Hm,' Roy sniffed. 'That bloody Brenda. I knew she'd be more frigging trouble than she's worth. She sings all right but she's got a big arse and a nasty mind.'

Tony crossed his arms and smirked. 'Sorry if we were interrupting anything.'

Roy narrowed his eyes. They were plastered in silver and green eyeshadow. His eyebrows were painted into incredulous arches halfway up his noble brow. 'Take that look off your face, Tony Bradley. Don't you start. If I want to make some fucking use of the ammenities, that's my business. You lot are so squeaky fucking clean. Don't you ever presume to judge me, all right?'

Tony shrugged.

Roy growled. 'You've got my poor heart going twenty to the dozen. I could have bitten that poor bastard's bollocks off. Never mind. No harm done. What's wrong with your face? You can't get sea-sick on a bloody hovercraft, girl. We're not even on the frigging water! Oh, come on. Lie down. Get a nap. We'll leave you in peace. I'm not having you go on that stage looking like that. You lie down there and get yourself pulled together.'

Roy heaved himself up, manoeuvred Debs onto the bunk with surprising care and tucked Tony under his wing. 'We'll let you know when we get there. You rest.'

Debs curled under the stiff polyester sheet and murmured her thanks.

Roy slammed the cabin door shut. He looked at Tony.

'Fucking genius, that girl,' said Roy. 'Fucking lyrical genius. We have to take care of her.'

Tony smiled.

Roy led the way back upstairs, his voice echoing down the passage. 'And you, too, Tony. You're a valuable asset. You're vital for all of this.'

'Me?' asked Tony, pleased. 'I thought I was just along for the ride.'

Roy looked him up and down. As he made his expert appraisal his wattles shook. 'You've got that kind of soft-boy look that some teenage girls like. The ones who don't cream their knickers over Clive will want you instead. You're the non-threatening type.'

Tony nodded.

'Mind, that fucking perm is a disaster. You look like a frigging queer.'

'I'll let it grow out.'

'That Brenda do it for you?'

'She did.'

'Well, you're not to let her. She's a star now. We can afford professional bloody stylists.' As they went up the stairs Roy was wheezing in exasperation. 'You bloody lot don't get the picture yet, do you? You all think we're just dicking about. But that's not how I see it. This is frigging serious. I've put myself behind you and I've told you I'm gonna make you famous. I don't piss-arse about.'

'No, Roy.'

Roy grunted. Tony was keeping up with him, jogging along at his elbow. 'So you bastards have to tow the line. No bitching, no slagging and no fucking each other, all right?'

'I reckon you should tell the others as well,' Tony said. 'Not just me.'

'Oh, I'll tell them all right. I just want to tell you, before we get there...' At this, he seized Tony's elbow. 'You watch yourself. I know what you're about. You're not so innocent. You pretend like you're the little boy, but I know your sort. When we get into that hotel and in the middle of that great big, sleazy city, you watch yourself. Don't you go mad. You know what I mean. You're a professional. Do the show tonight and make sure you give a hundred and ninety-nine fucking per cent. Then, afterwards you can let your bloody perm down, all right?' Roy winked in his face, with a throaty chuckle. 'You know what I mean.'

Then he led them both into the bar, giving Tony's arse a squeeze that made his eyes water.

The other passengers in the bar looked at Roy with alarm.

He headed for the high stools, where Brenda had been joined by Clive, who was in his black biker's leathers and looked like he hadn't slept for a week. Roy set his face in a determined grimace and strode across the sticky lino, brazening out the stares of his fellow travellers.

Don't you frigging stare at me, he thought. Stare at my stars. Keep your attention on them. I'm the fucking star maker and I'll tell you where to look.

Debs woke as they docked and she could feel the hovercraft settle on the shingle, letting gusts of hot air out of its voluminous skirts.

She was groggy and reluctant to get up and check her face wasn't green.

Brenda's bags were strewn along with her own, all over the floor. Outside, someone was banging on the doors, calling out in officious tones that it was time to disembark. She'd have to carry all of their stuff above decks.

She fetched out some travel-wipes her mother had given her at the last minute and scrubbed at her face. At least she hadn't thrown up.

I can't sing a note, though. I can't see how I'm going to go through with this.

It was the middle of the afternoon. There was only a few hours before they'd have to go on. There could be no backing down. All of Europe was looking at them.

Debs picked up all of the bags, one by one, thought about making the bunk up neatly, decided not to, and bundled herself out of the cabin.

The steward with the bent nose was knocking on the door opposite. He glanced at Debs and blushed again. She had a quick flashback to his arse-crack disappearing as he yanked up his trousers. He smiled at her bashfully.

'I know who you are,' he said. 'I'm coming to the show tonight. I love your record. That's what I was talking to Mr Kitchener about. He was saying he'd get me into the after-show party.'

He was stammering and blushing and Debs was delighted.

'You like the song?'

'Best of luck tonight,' he said. 'You're bound to win. You wrote the song, didn't you?'

'Just the words.'

'You're multi-talented. Let me take your bags.'

Gladly, Debs handed the whole lot over. 'Thanks...'

'David. The rest of the band are waiting with Roy ... Mr Kitchener. I'll take you to them. There's quite a reception waiting, you know.'

Debs hurried to keep up with him. 'Reception?'

'They'll treat you like royalty. And you deserve it. All our hopes go with you. You're doing this for the United Kingdom. And ...' He gave her his grin again. 'Even if you don't win, we'll still love you at home, for trying. You'll still be stars.'

'Here she is,' Clive said resignedly. 'At last.'

He was slouched against the wall in passport control, where Roy was haggling with a group of men in uniforms.

David the steward dumped the bags down with the others. He caught Roy's eye. 'She's safe and sound.'

'About fucking time,' Roy snapped. He looked Debs up and down. 'Have you been sick?'

'No.'

Clive laughed. 'She looks like she needs a bit of duty free.'

David stood to attention and saluted them all briskly. 'Good luck, everyone. I'm a great fan.'

Clive sneered and Brenda smirked at him.

'Yeah, yeah,' growled Roy, turning away. 'Fuck off now. We've got a public to face.'

Debs and Tony were last in the queue with their passports. His took a little longer because he looked so different with his hair permed.

'Why did I let Brenda do it?' he moaned. 'Roy says it's a disaster.'

'But we always have the same hairstyle,' Debs said. 'Me and you the same. That's our gimmick.'

He shook his head and she watched his hair bounce. 'Not now that there's four of us. First chance I get I'm gunna get this all shaved off.'

'Tony, you can't...'

They had been following the others down a glass corridor, not really paying attention. Now they looked and automatic doors were opening onto a tarmac expanse where a long white car was waiting for them.

'Look at them all!'

Sharing the tarmac with a thousand screaming gulls was a crowd of anxious, industrious pressmen. As Debs held her breath and let Tony grasp her hand, the flashbulbs were going off. The white car's doors flew open and Roy bundled them all inside.

'Did you see them all?' Clive crowed. 'I can't believe how many of them there were! Bloody foreigners - haven't got a clue.'

Roy shook his head at him. 'We're big business. You'll see. You shouldn't underestimate yourselves.'

The car was taking them through an industrial wasteland, which Debs could just make out through the smoked glass. Towers and pipes and belching fumes. Soon they were on a six lane motorway, humming along on the wrong side.

The band were able to spread themselves out on the cream upholstery and get their breath. Roy surveyed them all, twisting round from the passenger seat.

'Straight to the studios,' he told their chauffeur. 'Soundcheck first. We're late as it is.'

'Can't we go to the hotel first?' Brenda gasped. 'We haven't had a sit down yet, or...'

'Straight to the frigging studios,' Roy shouted. 'You'll do what I tell you. We haven't got time to go fart-arsing and prancing around in hotels. You're on a bloody treadmill now, you lot. And no bastard gets off till I tell them to.'

Crushed velvet trouser suits for the sound-check in red, blue, white and yellow. The four of them were instructed to change and warm up their voices and wait in their dressing room while Roy went off to harass the producers and check that their conductor had arrived safely.

They stood in the vast reception hall and watched him lumber off with his kaftan billowing and Debs felt bereft without his protection.

Everyone around them seemed to be speaking English, but it was a weird, accentless English that sounded to her rather sinister.

A very tall woman with Farrah Fawcett hair appeared and fawned over them for a while. She was the first in a long procession of helpers who told them what to do, where to be, how to behave.

'Whenever you see a camera or a photographer you must smile and say how much you are enjoying yourself here. You are an ambassador for your country. You must say that the Eurovision is a great chance for the nations to come together in perfect harmony.'

She was clip-clopping down a brightly-lit corridor, leading them away from the milling crowds in reception.

Clive was hanging on her every word. He turned to Tony. 'Are all the women here like her, do you think?'

Brenda scowled. 'She's a frosty bitch.'

'We do not have space to allot you separate dressing rooms,' their helper turned to say. She stopped them before a door labelled 'UK'. 'So this will be communal. Though this studio is a new complex built especially for Eurovision purposes, space is still at a premium. Nevertheless we will hope you are comfortable. Now change for your sound-check if you please.'

Grumbling, Brenda led the way into the cramped space.

'I don't think it's on,' Tony said, 'putting us all in one room.' He looked around and saw that it was actually quite a pleasant room. There was a view of a sluggish brown river and a quite impressive cathedral with a broken spire.

'It looks like a lovely city,' Debs said, unzipping bags. 'I wonder if we'll get a chance to explore.' She was determined to start enjoying the trip a bit more.

Clive had thrown himself into the single comfortable chair and hooked one leg over the arm. 'Come on then, get changed. Let's see you get your gear off, girls.'

Brenda was pulling a card off a neat bouquet of tulips. ''To UK from All at Eurovision. With love and luck for your performance this evening.'' She shook her head and started to unbutton her blouse. 'Where are those rehearsal outfits?'

Tony was checking out the shower stall. 'I still think it's wrong we have to share. I mean, we're in a band, but we don't have to live in each other's pockets, do we?'

They looked at him.

'Don't worry,' Brenda said. 'No one's gunna look at you when you've got nothing on.' She chuckled and started to unhook her bra, reaching around awkwardly. Debs started at her heavy breasts. 'While we're on this topic,' Brenda went on. 'Can we just agree on something? We're a band, right? And while we're in it, we do everything to make it a success, right? No bullshit ego stuff. Everyone mucking in. And no stupid sexual tensions and jealousies, all right? I can't be arsed with all that. I want this to be a success.'

The others were nodding slowly. 'Yeah,' Tony said. 'We're going to have to get on with each other for a while. If this all takes off, we could spend quite a while together.'

'Exactly,' said Brenda.

'I don't mind,' Debs said. 'I get on with anyone. I'm easy.'

'Clive?' Brenda asked. 'You're not going to mess it up, are you?'

He looked amazed. He spread his hands. 'I'm here, aren't I? Yeah, I'm here to do the best job I can, given what we've got. I'll give it a shot.'

'So no fucking about?' Brenda asked. 'No going all snotty and sneery about the material we work with? No suggestive remarks to me or Debs? No touching us up or playing us off against each other?'

Clive stood up and slouched over to them. 'No. We're family, right? If we're doing this, we're family. It won't be me bollocking around.'

Brenda made the four of them put their hands in the middle then, so they could all grab hold. She pulled out a bottle of whisky so they could toast each other and loosen up as they got changed.

Tony went to shower first and Debs watched Clive as he stripped down, out of his motorbike boy's outfit and realised she'd never seen anyone so beautiful in all her life.

Damn, she thought. I'm already out of order. She watched him scratch himself as he complained that the leather always brought him out in a rash.

On their way through the corridors to the studio they caught a glimpse or two of the opposition. A gaggle of extremely tall, haughty-looking Greek women swished by in feathers and Debs recognised the French singer. He was wearing a shirt with ruffles down the front and poking out of his sleeves. He grinned at them as he squeezed past and fingered his black moustache.

'Your conductor,' he whispered to the four of them. 'He is a cunt. He cut my sound-check short. You tell him what he is.'

'Will do, mate,' Clive said, and clapped the short man heavily on the back. Then he stepped out onto the stage and the others followed.

The auditorium was huge.

They stood in the centre of a stage built entirely out of blue glass.

Pyramids had been erected all around them and they were strewn with baubles and fairy lights. Above, in the rafters, there were clangs and shrieks as the lighting men hoisted lamps into place. Out in the stalls there were busy shouts and cries and the orchestra sat twiddling and tuning itself.

The four of them huddled together, staring into the darkness and realised how huge the seating area was. Debs felt Tony nudging into her. She felt his hand slide damply into hers.

'UK?' boomed a huge voice from behind the bank of television cameras. 'You are UK?'

Brenda straightened out her posture and stepped out across the gleaming blue glass. 'We are the UK entrants,' she shouted back. 'We were told you were ready for our rehearsal.'

'Debs?' whispered Tony.

'Yeah?'

'They're going to make us do it now.' He nodded at the centre of the stage, where four evenly-spaced microphones were waiting for them on stands. 'We'll have to run over there, sing and dance and everything.'

She looked at him and saw that his face was white. She gripped his fingers. 'That's what we came for, lovey,' she said. 'We've done it before.'

'Not like this. Not like this.'

The musical director was engaging in an energetic debate with the UK's entrants' conductor.

Brenda started to lead the four of them over to their mikes. There was a determined set to her head and shoulders. Her walk across the stage was pure bravado, and the others followed with their heads bowed.

Debs kept hold of Tony's hand, hoping he was going to make it.

Already she knew that she was going to be all right. This, if anything, was the most terrifying moment. Just them and all this space and that blackness beyond. All that shouting from people they couldn't even see.

'UK?' boomed the voice of the musical director. 'Are you ready UK? For your song?'

Brenda gazed out into the lights, shielding her eyes. 'Course we're ready,' she muttered. She made sure they were standing in the right order. Boy-girl, boy-girl.

'This is UK entry,' the voice bellowed. 'Let's Be Famous.'

He was interrupted by a rasping, booming voice that cut through the dense, hot studio with a mike of its own.

'All right, guys. We're all ready for you. Now, give it your best fucking shot. I'm out here and this time we're not fanny-farting about, all right? It's a rehearsal but I want to see you work your frigging guts out, okay?'

All four of them looked up and grinned as Roy's voice crackled out of the speaker system at them. It was like the voice of Zeus; like a benediction. They knew they were going to be all right.

Roy paused before cueing the UK conductor who, as Roy well knew, was as uppity a cunt as the French entrant claimed.

'Maestro!'

The music started and, whether it was being thrown in the deep end like this, or whether it was the excitement or the pent-up emotion of the hovercraft ride to this alien city, something clicked into place; some spark of pop genius took light and the four of them sang their hearts out in a way they had never quite managed before.

'Debbie?'

There wasn't any sound from inside their dressing room. Clive paused with his fist against the door. He tried banging again. 'Debs?'

There. He heard a snuffling noise. She was in there.

'Are you okay, Debs?'

The door opened a crack. He saw a slice of her face. One glistening eye, her trembling mouth. 'There you are.'

'It's you, Clive,' she said, and let him in.

He came loping in awkwardly. They looked each other up and down.

Outside it was dark and the broken spire was lit up. Fireworks were going off over the television centre and from here they could see them rippling and screeching over the dark rooftops.

'It's a lovely city,' Debs said.

They looked each other up and down. They were both in their spangly silver jumpsuits and they were both crusted with dried sweat. Debs let out a sob, stopped herself and shivered. 'Where's Brenda and Tony?'

He sighed. 'In the green room.'

'Is Roy with them?'

'He was on his way,' said Tony thickly. 'We should go there too. It'll look bad if we're not all there when the cameras are on. We have to put up a front. All of us together.'

'I know.' She bit her lip. 'I don't want to let us down.'

She didn't move, though. She seemed to be trapped in the middle of the floor, amongst their disordered luggage.

'We were shit,' she said suddenly and burst into fresh tears.

Clive took two strides and gathered her up. He crushed her wet face to his chest. 'We weren't shit,' he said, fondling her sticky hair.

'We were, we were,' she moaned, and felt snot bubbling out onto his chest hair. She snorted. 'The sound-check ... we were brilliant in that. We'd never been so good. But then after that, waiting for it, counting down the hours and ... all the others ... all the tension ... we got back on and it was shit. I was awful. I was shrill. I forgot all my steps. I bumped into Tony. What are we going to do? Roy will murder us.'

'No he won't.' He cupped both hands over her ears as if he could keep her from hearing what the other contestants were saying up in the green room. Clive knew Debs was going to have to pull herself together quickly if she was going to face that lot.

'He will,' she moaned. 'He'll dump us. We made a show of him. We were shit.'

'No we weren't. Come on, Debbie, love. Come on.'

He lifted her face till it was level with his and, bending down, kissed her quickly on the nose.

She blinked.

Then she kissed him back, hard. They were locked like this for a moment or two.

She pulled back, with a gasp.

'We have to go to the others. Support them. My mam will kill me if I'm not on the telly at the end.'

She imagined her mother watching the votes come in, along with the rest of Europe. It would be on the telly in the restaurant and Franky would shush the whole place as the cameras flashed into the green room to catch the instant reactions of the winners and losers. Franky would be totting up the scores on her own pad, and checking what votes the UK would need to let them win.

Except now there was no way that they could win. Most of the votes had already come in. Debs could imagine her mother's disgust as the scores from France, Germany, Spain came rolling in and the UK got a consistent three, four, two, null points.

'What went wrong, Clive? Why were we so shit?'

Clive was still holding her shoulders. 'I dunno. But it wasn't our last chance, you know. We can still make good.'

Debs went to pat some cold water on her face. She could feel Clive behind her, watching, and she hurried up. You had to smile to the camera and not look upset, no matter what votes came in. You couldn't be a bad loser. She thought back to the sound of her own, over-excited, whiney voice and wanted to die. Then she thought of how Clive had kissed her and the taste of him, his thick tongue pushing between her chattering teeth.

She let him hurry her away, back to the green room, where the cameras, the other contestants, and the rest of their group were waiting.

'Them Greek bitches,' Brenda cursed through her clenched teeth. She glanced over at the table where the three women were basking in the attention of the cameras and grinning at each other. 'They're gonna get it. They're miles ahead. They think they're bloody brilliant.'

'They were quite good,' Tony said, reaching for his drink.

'Good? They were ... pornographic,' Brenda hissed. 'Anyone could get up and do what they did. Well, if that's what Europe likes then Europe can keep it. Common bloody lot. Showing off their knickers and flashing their boobs. And their song didn't even make sense. It was just shouting.'

Tony pulled a face. 'Let's be graceful about it. Look, the camera's coming this way.'

With a crew of t-shirted men clinging to it, the camera was scooting across the carpet in their direction. 'Come and look at the losers,' Brenda sighed, and downed her gin. She set her face in a rictus grin. 'Where are fucking Clive and Debbie?'

Tony shrugged and turned on his own smile as the camera fixed on them. He raised his glass to the viewers at home and gave a wry sort of smile, as if to signify that he knew and didn't mind that, with one more set of votes to be announced, there was no way the UK were going to win anything tonight.

He knew his blonde perm was fluffy and damp. He knew he looked wrecked and disappointed. But some real relief and pleasure snuck into his expression as the camera fixed on him and beamed his image around the world. Tony could feel it bouncing that grin of his from satellite to satellite and he thought of his mum and dad watching at home, in St Anne's. They'd be proud. They would see he was a good loser. They would think he looked tired and handsome and that he'd done a good job tonight, even with Debs staggering clumsily into him during the lead break.

They might even think he was doing something worthwhile. They might stop telling him to give it all up.

Then the camera was gone, over to the next table, where the French entrant sat alone, moist-eyed and drunk, struggling hard not to look devastated at scoring even less than the UK.

A massive hand clamped onto Tony's shoulder. A gravelly voice spoke into his ear: 'Where the bollocking hell are the other two?'

'Roy!' gasped Brenda, choking on her drink.

Roy heaved himself around the settee and sat down carefully. He was in an extremely tight cocktail dress and took some moments to arrange himself. To Tony he looked as if he'd already had a few drinks to fortify himself.

'Clive went after Debs,' Brenda said. 'She ran off crying.'

'She's sensitive,' Tony said.

'She was shit,' Roy said.

Brenda smiled indulgently. 'She's too young. We should never have had her on board.'

Roy's eyes flashed. 'You were *all* shit. You were all a frigging waste of my time. I'm the star maker! I'm the big fucking daddy and I don't waste my time with shitheads. You lot had better shape up.'

Tony looked terrified. 'I'm really sorry we were shit, Roy.'

'Well,' said Roy. 'It won't happen again.' He darted another glance at Brenda. 'You were the worst though. When Holland was giving their scores. The camera went on you and you were slagging off the fucking krauts for getting top marks! Everyone saw you! Saw you clear as day going on about the bastard krauts!'

Brenda went pale.

Roy's head whipped around, as if alerted by some sixth sense. Clive and Debs were stumbling up to take their places at their table.

'There you are,' Roy sneered. 'You fucking wasters. Sit yourselves down. You've missed getting your faces on the telly.'

Debs sat down heavily. 'I don't mind. I look like shit.'

Brenda laughed. 'You sang like shit.'

'Brenda...' Clive turned angrily.

'What?'

'Just shut the fuck up.'

There was a huge roar then, from the audience downstairs and from the other contestants at the tables all around them, as the overall winner was announced.

'We haven't been paying attention,' Roy remarked, in his mildest tone all day.

They all swivelled round to see the cause of the jubilation. The three Greek women were jumping up and down, clutching each other and shedding feathers.

'That's that, then,' said Roy.

They took up residence in the hotel bar for their debriefing. Debs slumped next to Tony, dead on her feet, too tired to even touch her drink. Determinedly Roy had ordered them champagne and commanded them to drink it down like medicine.

Brenda watched, narrow-eyed as the French contestant slouched into the bar and waved at them. 'He can fuck off, as well,' she muttered.

'Leave him, Brenda.'

'Is he taking the piss?'

'He scored worse than we did,' Clive said. 'How can he take the piss?'

The Frenchman was nodding and grinning from his place at the bar.

Roy looked round. 'I think he wants to join us and our commiserations.'

The Frenchman nodded again, raising his glass.

Roy raised his voice. 'Why don't you just fuck off back to your room? No one here wants you. Go on. Bugger off.'

Brenda cackled and the French contestant turned away. Roy gave her a mirthless glare.

'I want a word with you lot,' he said. 'Get that frigging bubbly down you and listen up.'

They all sat forward. Debs put her head in her hands.

Roy started to talk then. He told them exactly what they had done wrong. He told them how disappointed he was with them. How he couldn't believe they had let themselves get so complacent and lazy with a performance. He told them he was giving them a second chance. He still believed in them.

For a moment Debs thought about the Greek girls, the winners, and what they would be doing now. They would be hitting the town. They would be dancing. They would have the world's press around them. They might be sitting down to dinner with flashes going off. Everything would come easy for them now. They were stars. No doubt about it.

'You're not going to have an easy time,' Roy told them. 'Your really hard works starts now. All right, so you've fucked up the Eurovision. We can deal with it. It's low-brow shit at best. But you can go further. I believe in you bastards. You can still make something of yourselves.'

'But how?' Tony asked.

'Back in Britain,' Roy said. 'You had the whole country behind you. That whole bastard nation was clamouring for you tonight. We can make something of that. You were crap, but they won't have clocked that. All they'll have seen at home is the UK getting stabbed in the back by a bunch of fucking foreigners. Same as usual. Now you can go home and capitalise on all the sympathy. Now we cash in.'

'On xenophobia?' Clive asked.

'Too fucking right,' Roy snapped.

'Great,' said Brenda.

'But you've got to sort your act out,' Roy said.

'That's what I've been saying all along,' Brenda burst. 'We were too sweety-pie. That crap song. All of it. Tinsel outfits. We need soul. I've got a soul singer's voice. We need proper material, proper...'

'Fuck that,' said Roy. 'You've not got a shred of soul, Brenda Maloney so just you stop there. Look. I don't give a gnat's twat for soul. You're not black. You're not a frigging yank. You're a girl with a big arse and you're in a cheap pop outfit. You'll do exactly what I say, don't get above yourself and we'll all be quids in.'

Brenda sat back as if she'd been slapped. Her mouth hung open.

Roy rumbled with satisfaction and hastily lit a cigarette. 'Right. We'll have no more talk of soul or integrity or anything like it. I mean you as well, Clive. I know you reckon you're a proper musician but you can forget that, right? You can stop wearing all your leather and thinking you're rock and roll. Bugger that. I don't want any of you hankering after Art. Art's got nothing to do with it. You're pop. Just pop. Stick with that and you'll be fine.' Then he rounded on Tony. 'Mind. I don't want musical experts, but neither do I want some tone-deaf twat groaning away up there. You have to sort that voice of yours out, Tony. Otherwise you're out. That goes for all of you. You do exactly what I say, otherwise you're out on your ear.'

He let that settle in for a moment.

Brenda gasped. 'But what about Debbie? You've slagged off everyone else, and she was the shittest out of all of us tonight! What about her?'

Roy glared at Brenda and then Debs from under his fake eyelashes. 'Ah, Debs. In a way, Debs has got the hardest job of all. She's our lyricist. She's got real talent. But to nurture that talent, to bring it out in the way she needs it, Debs will have to undergo the hardest challenges and changes. She has to tell the world what life is like in a way that the world will agree with, in a way that the world will recognise. And to do that, Debs, you'll have to suffer. It won't be easy. You'll have to suffer and pour all of that terrible life into each and every one of your lyrics...'

Debs looked at him, trembling, and blinked the tears out of her eyes.

'Can you do that for me, Debbie?' Roy asked.

She nodded dumbly.

'Right,' he said, and clasped his hands to his mammoth knees. 'Are we all in agreement? Shall I call for some more champagne and shall we toast this little resolution of ours?'

The four of them looked at him in awe. They nodded.

'Right we are then,' he said. 'Right we are. Then let's put this whole frigging night behind us. Let's get bollocks drunk and start all over again in the morning.'

He waved them all off from the foyer and watched as his group staggered up the stairs to their rooms.

He held Tony back, though Tony looked the most tired and drunk of all of them. He put an arm round the boy's shoulders.

'That's what you all needed,' Roy said, smirking as the others disappeared up the staircase. 'Get kayleighed and get it all out of your systems. I'm proud of you now, in a way.'

Tony was confused. He was pressed against his manager's bulk and it smelled of rank sweat and some kind of flowery scent.

'Yeah, proud. I've seen you all deal with disappointment and defeat. Best lesson you could learn.' Roy's voice was almost gentle. 'I'm gonna hit the town, I reckon. It's not even two yet. You coming?'

Tony looked guarded. 'Coming where? I'm shagged out.'

'Oh, come on, Tony. No you're not. There's somewhere right by here I was told about. Come on. You know you've been gagging to get out and about. It's not even two! Come on!' Roy was chuckling and patting Tony's arm.

'I think I'm tired.'

'No you're not.' Roy wheeled him bodily round and through the double doors of the hotel. Out on the steps it was freezing and there were still one or two fireworks sizzling through the night sky.

'Fucking Greeks,' Roy muttered. 'I wonder how they're feeling now.' He started lumbering along then, weaving them through a succession of almost empty streets. Tony hurried to keep up as the streets became narrower and more obscure. Soon he was lost but Roy seemed to know where he was going.

'We'll be successful,' Roy said, taking hold of him again. 'You'll feel how those Greek birds feel tonight.'

Then they were standing at the entrance to a club and Roy was speaking through a grille.

Tony stammered that he had no money and Roy waved his objections away.

'I'll pay up for you, Tony,' he said. 'Your manager's gonna pay for you. You'll see, son. Soon, every door will open for you and you won't have to pay a frigging bean. They'll fall over themselves to let you in for nowt.'

Inside it was warm and close and Roy was handing oddly-coloured foreign notes through a box office window.

'Is it a disco?' Tony asked as Roy turned and passed him a white, folded towel and a key attatched to a rubber band.

'No more music,' Roy laughed. 'No more frigging music tonight, please. Aren't your ears ringing enough tonight?'

He led the way down a carpeted corridor filled with lockers. There was a gurgling sound of water, distant splashing. There was even some faint disco music, playing softly through speakers hidden behind potted plants, but Tony didn't mention it. He shook his head so he could think straight and concentrated on following Roy, who marched ahead in his black cocktail frock with his bum swaying determinedly.

A thickset man with a pronounced chest came round the corner, flicking a towel around his neck. He nodded hello to them and

Tony was surprised to see he was soaking wet and quite nonchalant about the foot-long erection that preceded him.

'My kind of club,' Roy said, smacking his lips and turning the corner.

Tony watched him find his locker and start to fiddle his dangly earrings off. 'Would you unzip me at the back, Tony, love?'

Tony moved forward hesitantly, stealing a glance at the other men by their lockers. He felt them looking back at him. 'What kind of club is this?' he asked.

Roy winked at him and started to wriggle out of his cloying frock. 'You know. Come on. Get your gear off. Get that towel on.'

Tony sat on a bench and struggled with his shoes. He watched in shock as Roy stripped himself down and paraded his bulk for all the men to see. He was gargantuan and proud of it. The men there had perfect bodies, as far as Tony could tell, and still they stared at the massive Roy. He seemed to command their attention.

Tony found his locker and bundled his clothes inside. He fastened his towel and let Roy lead him through to the next room. 'Is it a sex club?' Tony hissed.

Roy laughed. He led the way past a pool and a bar and into an even darker area where Tony could hear the hissing of showers and the slamming of wooden doors.

'It's a kind of club for gentlemen to relax in,' Roy said. 'In any way they wish.'

He led the way to a steamed-up glass door. It was a murky, solid blue gloom inside. He yanked it open and clouds of steam gusted out. A sharp smell of pine needles.

A tall, thin white boy was on his way out. He paused and grinned.

Tony recognised the crooked nose.

'Mr Kitchener!' cried David the steward. He glanced down at the extra-large towel Roy had struggled to tie round his mid-riff. Then the steward looked Tony up and down.

'We're coming in,' Roy said gruffly. 'This is Tony. He's in my band.'

David smiled, caught on the steamy threshold. 'We met briefly, I think.'

Roy was trying to get past. 'Are you coming out or going in?'

David hesitated. 'Great show tonight, Mr Kitchener. I'm so sorry you didn't win.'

Roy snorted. 'Well.'

'You deserved to win.'

Tony smiled.

'Really. You were great. Specially you, Tony.'

'Look,' snapped Roy. 'I'm getting fucking cold hanging about out here while you two rabbit on. Tony's after a bit of cock, same as I am tonight. Why don't we all just get inside, eh? Why don't we get inside and close the frigging door behind us?'

It was hard to tell if there was anyone else inside. It was dark and fogged and Tony slipped at first on the hot tiled floor. He felt Roy lurch ahead and sit down heavily on a plastic seat that squeaked. He felt David the steward brush past him. He felt his way to the side of the small room and sat on a wet plastic bench and his head started to spin in the wet heat.

He felt David sit down carefully beside him.

And suddenly he was calm. He could breathe in the hot, pine-scented air. His whole body bristled and blushed with relief. He was out of the limelight. He was hidden away in a private club in a dark alleyway, hidden away in a city somewhere in Europe.

He heard Roy, across the room, groan and sag back, relaxing all of his bulk.

Here no one can see me, Tony thought. I'm not performing for anyone.

The steward's hand was reaching across his leg and pulling at his already sodden towel. Pulling it open and Tony felt his cock, already hard, already aching with not being touched, spring out into the hot air. The steward took hold of him and Tony felt his face push up against his neck. He let himself be kissed gently, insistently, before he touched the boy back.

'Come on, you boys,' Roy's voice rose out of the thick steam. 'Make an old fella happy. Let's see you fucking around, hey? Let's see the two of you boys play.'

Tony laughed. He swung around to take the sticky head of the steward's cock in his mouth and realised he was doing it as if Roy had given him permission to.

I'm eager to please, he thought. I jump to it every time.

And I will. That's okay. I'll be eager to please.

Chapter Three

You've tried to update yourself, I thought.

She was standing on the platform in a shaggy blue coat that came down to her knees and her tights were a kind of mauve. Debs looked immaculate and nervous as I hurried across to her. She was bouncing up and down and reaching for her bag because the train was already there and I was late.

It looked like it was going to be packed, all the way down to London. We'd be lucky to get a seat together. I had a glance through the window of the smoking carriage as I went by and there seemed to be those reserved tickets coming out of the top of every single seat.

Of course, we hadn't reserved seats. This had all been planned on the phone last night. Up until half an hour ago I hadn't been sure if I was coming along today at all. But here I was, dashing and gasping and clutching Debs in a hug.

She hugged back rather hard because she was so agitated.

'You came,' she laughed. 'You actually came.'

'I couldn't miss this.'

She grabbed my hand and dragged me to the train.

I'd phoned work to say I wasn't well. It was Shanna I'd talked to and she didn't believe a word of it. I'd sounded far too excited.

'You can't skive,' she hissed. In the background I could hear all the noises I associated with first-thing-in-the-morning at Natural World and my stomach twinged with dread and relief. I could hear the twinkly Natural World music and the crashing of the till as Shanna checked out the float. 'You can't! I haven't told you about Saturday night yet...'

'There's just something I have to do today,' I told her. 'It's important. You'll fob Pete off, won't you?' Shanna was used to making excuses for me. The last time had been over the Simon fiasco. Somehow Pete seemed to be able to swallow any amount of bullshit from Shanna.

'Getting me to do your dirty work again,' she growled.

'How are your extensions?'

'Fine. Still in.'

'How were the Elvis brothers?' I thought maybe showing some interest in her life might mollify her.

'That's what I wanted to tell you about! Now I have to wait! How long will you be?'

'I don't know. I have to go to London, with a friend. It's urgent.'

'Who, Tim? What friend?'

'I can't explain. I'll phone you.'

'Yeah, right.'

'I've got gossip too, Shanna. Stuff you wouldn't believe.'

Her voice went hard. 'Gossip's no good if you don't share it, Tim! You've got to make time for your mates!'

'That's what I *am* doing,' I said, and that was the end of the conversation.

I suppose part of the eagerness to go with Debs to London was just to skive off work. It was blissful to jump into that carriage and for the two of us to find a miraculously free table, plonk ourselves down as the train started shunting off.

Then we caught each other's eye. We laughed, as if we were both doing something naughty. As if we were running away.

Debs started unlacing her trainers and worried that her feet would swell up in transit.

The noise of the rails filled up my ears. I watched the town slide by either side of us. I breathed in the foggy scent of carpets, cigarettes and coffee.

I was looking at the shops and thinking; I could be stuck inside one of those all day, selling tat, if I hadn't met Debs on Saturday night.

'She phoned last night,' Debs said at last. 'Out of the blue. She phoned and said she wanted to meet me. Could I pop into town and have lunch and we could discuss her approach to the song?' She laughed. 'As if popping into London for lunch is what you do every day!'

'Mind,' I said, 'the trains are faster now. It's not as much hassle.'

'Of course I said I'd come. I had to try hard not to sound too worked up. She said she'd dying to meet me. I'm her idol. Imagine!'

'Well,' I said, 'you were doing all that stuff when she was still in nappies. She's only just starting out as a singer.'

'I wonder if they'll ask me to come to the recording.' Debs' eyes were lit up as she leaned across the plastic table. Her furry sleeves were soaking up a coffee spill. 'This is how it all starts again. I'm in demand, Tim. I'm not just the washed up has-been you saw on Saturday night. They still know who I am.' She lowered her eyes. 'I wanted you to be there. To be with me when it all started to happen again. Just so you know.'

'I already know,' I said.

She sat back again, seemed about to say something else, and then stopped herself.

She smiled slightly and looked out of the window.

Fields out there now, down gravel embankments, with horses standing around and crows wheeling kamikaze out of the clouds.

I was glad she hadn't gone on with her thought.

I was waiting for her to launch into some conversation about Saturday night and I really didn't want it.

I'd arrived home on Sunday lunch time and in my first rush of enthusiasm I'd tried to phone Simon to tell him what I'd been doing. He wasn't in. No answerphone. I sat in my flat, which was strewn with the same mess I'd left there before going out on Saturday morning, and thought over the triumph I'd wanted to boast about.

By Sunday night it didn't seem much of a triumph.

I didn't know what Debs was expecting of me. On Sunday morning she'd made a pot of thick black coffee and a heap of bacon sandwiches and packed me merrily on my way. At any moment I expected her to start quizzing me or making it all difficult. Asking me what I thought I was doing, going home with an older woman.

I was expecting her to go funny at any time.

Yet she didn't. Then she phoned, all breathless, that night, practically begging me to come with her to London. Moral support was all she was asking for. That was okay.

'We're pals, aren't we?' she was asking me now.

I held my breath. Nodded.

'Good,' she said. 'That's all I need. Just a pal.'

That seemed all right then.

King's Cross made her nervous. She said it was the high ceilings and everyone looking purposeful, striding over the waxy floors.

We had to sit in the pub for a bit while she sipped at a pint of fizzy lager.

'How can I go and meet this girl?' she asked me earnestly. 'I've been out of the loop too long. I was never any good meeting other celebrities. I always put my foot in it.'

'Debs, she's all of nineteen. You're her icon. She said so.'

She blushed. 'Well, not icon exactly.'

'You must have met everyone in your time,' I said. 'You'll know what to say when you meet her.'

On the table between us was a scrap of paper with the address of the restaurant where we were to meet Shelley Sommers. It was somewhere French on St Martin's Lane.

'The point is,' Debs sighed, 'she's famous now, right this minute. That gives her the advantage. Now's all that matters. She's on the cover of TV mags when I go to the corner shop for milk. She looks fantastic on the front of *TV Quick* even when I haven't got any make-up on.'

I was getting quite excited at the thought of meeting her. 'And she's fresh from a glamorous death on the telly.'

'If I was starting out now, I'd aim at a soap,' said Debs. 'I did it the hard way. *New Faces*, holiday camps, working men's pubs, gay clubs. It's not like that now.'

'Never mind,' I said. 'She can learn a lot from you.'

She brightened at this and suggested we braved the tube. 'London always scared me,' she said.

I never let on that it did me too.

She said, as we walked down to the steps, 'Roy used to say that they were all nowts down here. But you had to show you were as good as them and hold your head up. I used to come down with the others for things like *Top of the Pops*. I had my heart in my mouth the whole time.'

And back then, she had the protection of the others, I thought. It must be bonding, being in a group, with a pushy manager to steer you through the world.

Now Debs had to face it all on her own.

We stood strap-hanging on the tube, through a series of short stops, and she was gazing at strangers' faces as if they were familiar to her, as if she was searching out some point of contact.

The agent was waiting for us at the open front of the restaurant, peering up and down the busy street. She was in a tailored suit and her hair had been cut in a strange, assymetric style. She was clutching a whole sheaf of papers and, as we came bustling up, thinking we were late, she was squinting.

'Jenna, Shelley's agent,' she said, taking hold of Debs' hand. 'You should have taken a cab.'

'It's a waste of money,' Debs said. 'This is my friend, Tim.'

The agent looked me up and down. 'Shelley says to just go in and order. She's coming from a photo shoot and she's got some interviews this afternoon, so she can't give you long.'

'Right,' said Debs, and followed Jenna into the cavernous, tinkling restaurant.

It took my eyes a few moments to adjust to the lighting and, when they did, I saw a room reaching back for what seemed miles. There were hundreds of tiny tables and people were crammed together, all in suits, heads bent over their lunches and bottles of wine. They all had their elbows tucked in, for fear of knocking against anyone.

Debs was saying, 'It's exciting, being back in the big city. Brings it all back.'

'Hm,' said Jenna, and nodded at a bigger, secluded table to one side. 'I bet you're glad,' she said.

Debs slid along the leather seat and patted the space beside her for me to sit down.

Jenna flapped a huge menu at us and started leafing through her papers. She popped on a pair of glasses and gave Debs an appraising look. 'It took a while to find out who your agent was. But we sorted out the music rights and everything. The offer's generous.'

'Oh, very,' Debs agreed.

'The song will be quite a success,' Jenna said. 'We've booked her on all the big shows for the weeks we expect it to be number one. We've got the magazine covers that week. It's all going ahead.'

'You already expect it to go to number one?' gasped Debs. 'It must be good.' She blinked. 'So she's recorded it already?'

'Here she comes,' said the agent.

I'd already noticed the kerfuffle at the entrance.

The Maitre d' was leading a very small woman into the place, weaving through the tables as he guided her from the harsh light of the street. Diners were looking up, nodding and nudging each other.

'Oh,' said Debs. 'Look.'

Shelley Sommers was in the same shaggy blue coat that Debs had bought herself. In hers, she looked like a doll. Her complexion was smooth as an egg and she had a blond variation of her agent's assymetric haircut. A pair of candy pink Lolita sunglasses were perched on the top of her head.

She slipped into a chair at our table with her eyes cast down.

Debs plucked at the blue fluff of her own sleeve.

'This is Shelley,' said Jenna.

'Hello, Shelley,' Debs said.

'Hello,' said Shelley, looking up for a second.

I was gawping at her unashamedly. She had a rag of a dress on under that coat, I thought. It was made of some kind of filmy stuff. I didn't think she looked that great, all in all. Her voice was posher, too, than it had been on the telly. Even in that one word.

Jenna said to Debs, her voice suddenly warmer, 'Shelley wanted to meet you. She wanted to tell you what an influence your song had been on her. How she regards covering it and taking it to the top of the hit parade, a kind of homage.'

'Thank you,' Debs beamed.

Shelley dared another quick glance. 'What's a homage?'

'A tribute,' said the agent smoothly.

Shelley nodded. 'It's a good song.'

Debs' smile was looking strained. 'Thanks.'

We hung there for a bit, in awkward silence.

'I mean,' said Shelley, 'if we put some decent bass on, make it dancey enough, take some of the words out and have me shaking my booby-doos about on the video, it'll be a better song. It'll be all right.'

Her agent sent her a savage glance. 'Shall we order some wine?'

We had a little salad of spinach leaves and cherry tomatoes, which we slopped some balsamic vinegar on. Then we plumped for chips and fatty steaks that looked curiously like mocassins. I could hardly cut into mine, even with the jagged knife they gave me, and I could see Debs gamely struggling with her own as we inched through the meal.

Shelley sat with her salad and glass of wine, having refused the steak. She fiddled with a spinach leaf, shredding it slowly. She opened up slightly, to our relief.

I sat with my mouth open much of the time.

'It was your coat that shocked me,' she confided in Debs. 'The same coat.'

'Yes,' said Debs. 'Funny coincidence, that.' She gave an involuntary grunt as she dealt with her steak.

The agent was busy on her mobile with her head turned away, and Shelley seemed to break out suddenly.

'Thought it was bad karma for a second,' she said recklessly. 'The same coat. Thought you were taking the mick. Putting a bad hex on me. Do you believe in the goddess, then?'

'The what?' Debs looked confused.

'The goddess has brought me everything I have,' Shelley said solemnly. 'I truly believe it. All of my stardom is down to Shiva. That's how I came off the drugs and stuff. They told me all about her in the clinic I went to. The goddess is very strong in me and that's how I had the strength to put myself back together and return to the show and have my fantastic bowing-out episode.'

'Right,' said Debs.

'When they were writing me out, they said, we can leave the door open, Shelley, if you ever want to come back. But I said, no thanks. Give me a great ending, boys. Kill me off. That's what the goddess wants of me.'

'Really?' said Debs.

'That's why?' I couldn't help bursting out. 'You got yourself killed off because you'd gone religious?'

Shelley looked at me as if she hadn't noticed me yet. 'Of course. You have to die in order that you may live again.'

'You never said that in the interviews.'

She flinched. 'You read my interviews?'

'Every one.' I blushed.

Debs said, 'Tim's a big fan of yours.' She gave a nervous chuckle. 'Sometimes I think he's a bigger fan of yours than he is mine.'

'Oh,' said Shelley and looked from me to Debs. 'Do you have fans?'

I jumped in. 'Debs has got hordes of fans! She's a recording legend.'

'Oh, hush,' said Debs.

Shelley's eyes widened. 'Are you famous as well?' she asked me.

'No,' I said.

'You're better out of it,' Shelley said wearily. 'I've been famous for three years now and it's rotten. So many temptations.'

'There are,' Debs said, and I could feel her preparing to launch into some matronly good advice.

'But the goddess will guide me through,' Shelley smiled.

'The fucking goddess,' I heard myself mutter.

They looked at me.

Jenna the agent had finished her phone call.

'What did you say?' asked Shelley, incredulously.

'Well,' I said, 'it's a crock of shit, isn't it?'

Her lips did that quivering thing, just like they had on her death bed scene. The one I'd watched, only weeks ago, along with twenty-two million others. But I was bold.

'They've got you off the coke and stuff, but they've got you believing in some right old bollocks,' I told her. 'They're exploiting you, Shelley. They're making you look a tit. What's wrong with you? You look stoned right now. You haven't said one word of sense since you walked in here.'

Disappointment was fueling this, I thought, as my voice went shrill.

'Tim!' squawked Debs. She clutched my hand.

Jenna's face had gone stoney. 'Your friend is drunk,' she told Debs.

Tears were running down Shelley's face. I went in for the kill.

'I'm not having you sit there, talking rubbish to Debs. She's come all this way down the country and you two have built her hopes up! You made her think you were dying to meet her and you've not said anything worthwhile to her! You look as if you hardly know who she is!' I was gripping the edge of the table, having flung my knife and fork down. 'You've not asked her a thing about her career, have you? Either of you. It's like you don't care!'

'Tim,' said Debs. 'Don't. You're upsetting yourself.'

'It's not fair,' I snapped. 'They don't give a bugger about you.'

'All they want is the song,' Debs said quietly.

'And your blessing,' said Shelley Sommers. 'That's important to me. To have your blessing, woman to woman.'

Quietly, Debs gave it and Shelley and her agent made their preparations to leave. Jenna gathered her papers into her bag and clicked her fingers for the bill.

Debs reached across and touched Shelley's hand. 'You look after yourself.'

Shelley's eyes flashed. 'I can do that.'

'You need a good manager behind you.'

'I've got one,' Shelley said sullenly, and allowed herself to be dragged away from our table. The agent left without a backward glance at us.

Debs and I looked at the ruins of the table.

'It didn't go very well,' said Debs. 'I'm worried about her.'

I couldn't believe it. Shelley's character on the telly had been the young character with an old head on her shoulders, kindly, full of homespun wisdom. She'd knocked about a bit, been a bit of a tart, but she could be relied upon in the end. Which was why the nation had of course taken her to its heart and why we were all gutted when she was bumped off with that untimely brain tumour.

'That girl's a moron,' I said. 'It hurts me to say it. She was nothing like what I expected.'

Debs flicked disconsolately at her steak. 'She was probably just as disappointed with me. I was meant to be her childhood heroine. Yet she took one look at me - I could see her do it, when she arrived - and she wished that she hadn't bothered. I was nothing to her.'

'Then that's her loss. What does she know?'

Debs sagged even further into the leather seat and her shaggy coat. 'You shouldn't have gone yelling at them, Tim. That's not your job.'

'I wanted to stick up for you!'

'That was Roy's job. Or Clive's. What right have you got, to go shouting at people on my account?'

I bridled at this. 'I'm your friend.'

'And how long are you going to be around, Tim? Hm?'

I didn't have an answer.

She went on. 'Face it. You only came down here today because you thought it would be glamorous. You thought I could show you a world of glitz and fame.' She screwed up her napkin. 'Well, I can't. Now we both know. The world isn't welcoming me back with open arms at all. Not any more. The world doesn't give a bugger. I was stupid to even think it would.' She laughed bitterly. Then she took out another scrap of paper from her bag. 'Look. I even made a list of suggestions for which songs should be on the compilation greatest hits CD they would bring out after Shelley's single came out.'

I watched as she ripped up the piece of paper. 'Some use that was,' she said. 'I thought they'd want to know my ideas for what to do with my whole back catalogue. But they wouldn't have given a monkey's, even if I had got the courage up to show them. I should have guessed.'

'You shouldn't have ripped up that list,' I said.

'Why not?'

'Because it'll still happen, Debs. Someone will want to know.'

'It's a different world now, Tim. I got my hopes up, stupidly. You know what Roy would have said?'

'What?'

'He'd have called me a stupid fucking cow. He warned me, back at the start. If you get into this game, then you've got a shelf life. I'll give you your glory years, he said, but don't go trying to eke them out. Stick to your own time and don't push it too far.'

'He was using you, just like Jenna's using Shelley.'

'Maybe,' she sighed. 'Maybe he was. But I'd resigned myself to that years ago. It's all about consenting to be used, and I understood that. And I knew there'd be a time when I'd be left behind. But ... just look at me, when there's even a hint; the slightest chance, that my number's come up again. All the hope comes crashing down on me. I start thinking I can make it again. Hope is the cruellest thing in the world. But you have to act on that hope, don't you? Don't you, Tim?'

She was asking me as if I really might know the answer.

We stopped in Borders on Oxford Street so that Debs could show me the *Guinness Book of Hit Singles*.

We had stayed in the restaurant until the red wine was finished and, it was with blue mouths and teeth and in a dizzier, sillier mood that we left the place, linking our arms.

We strode off through the crowd and London smelled of diesel fumes and frying food.

We both felt optimistic again. We'd pieced together the jigsaw of Debs' backlist and we'd talked about all of the songs. Luckily, I had known them all and I could talk about each of them nostalgically.

We were still doing this, going up Oxford Street and into the bookshop.

I was explaining how 'Don't Worry Sweetheart (It'll Work Out Fine)' was in the top ten during my first few weeks at secondary school. I would eat porridge in our green kitchen, my stomach full of dread, and my mam would cajole me into feeling positive about the big school. We always had the Breakfast Show on the radio and it was Debs' voice that came on that winter, telling me not to work myself up with worry.

In Borders she fetched down the *Guinness Book of Hit Singles* and found the page with all her entries. There was a sizable list of the hits Things Fall Apart had had in the late seventies and early eighties. Bigger than I'd remembered. And there was her writing credit, on each and every one.

We were slightly tipsy that afternoon, swaying on the spot, gazing down at her credits.

'What people like Shelley Sommers don't understand,' whispered Debs, 'is that there's a responsibility involved in making records that millions of people will listen to. They listen to you for advice, for care, for consolation. And those records will last forever. They're written down here, in books like this. They turn up years afterwards on the radio and stuff. People buy them at car boot sales. Or there's a sudden revival. These things become a part of everyone's lives. None of it vanishes forever.'

I nodded.

'I was trying to think,' she went on, 'what it would be like if I was Shelley's age, and in her position. Well, for me, it would have been like ... meeting Karen Carpenter. I would have been in awe.'

'Karen Carpenter,' I said. 'Bless her heart.'

Debs slammed shut the *Guinness Book of Hit Singles*. 'Yes! Bless her heart! And Shelley Sommers has the nerve to speak to me about godesses!'

I laughed and Debs joined in.

We decided to get pissed in Soho. It seemed the best idea.

We ran down the escalator, cramming past the earnest shoppers.

'I'm not going home,' she said abruptly.

We were in a bar and I had all the gay papers out. I was scanning the contact ads and Debs was supposed to be helping me find a swanky metropolitan boyfriend.

She'd smoked her way through half a pack of black Sobranies

and, as I glanced up, I realised she was having an epiphany. I listened dutifully.

'I'm not going back home yet,' she said. An idea was taking shape behind her eyes. I could see it. 'I'm not going back to the north east and my mother like this. It's ridiculous.'

'It is,' I said. 'We're just starting to have fun.' Looking at the contact ads, a whole new world was swimming up invitingly. I couldn't believe there was all these men here, up for fun with no strings attatched.

'I'm not defeated,' Debs said. 'We've started something, now.'

I closed the papers. 'What are we going to do?'

She blinked. 'You're with me?'

'Too right.'

She misted over slightly. 'It meant a lot, actually. You shouting at them two in the restaurant. Being on my side.'

'They were bitches,' I said.

'Sssh,' she put out her cigarette. 'They were just misguided. They don't know what being a star is all about. They don't understand pop at all.'

'That's right. So what are we going to do?'

Debs grinned. 'If they won't do it for us, then we have to do it ourselves. Come on, Tim. You and me have got work to do.'

Chapter Four

She would always get to the recording studio in full make up.

Panda eyes and pale lipstick; hair teased up and bleached. Debs would dress every inch the star.

'Thinks she's Dusty Springfield,' Brenda told the others.

Seven o'clock in the morning and in would come Debs, making her demands, set on getting it just right. The other three fell by the wayside.

'What are we, light of my life?' Clive asked her, sitting with his coffee. 'What am I, eh? Chopped liver?'

She fondled his greasy hair but her mind was elsewhere, he could see. Her mind was on the song.

During these times, Clive would let her be.

'I have a vision', she said. 'Or rather, a sound in my head. I know just what this should be like.'

To the astonishment of the other three, Roy would draw back. He would let Debs get on with it. He watched her stand at her pages of music and smoke her first, solitary morning fag, reading over her notes.

'There's magic in her,' Roy told Brenda, Clive and Tony. 'There's magic all through the bones of her.'

'Arseholes,' Brenda muttered, and wished she'd done herself up smarter for the session.

Debs wouldn't actually sing a note until the backing track was ready and laid down and that, of course, involved the usual session musicians and the others, with Brenda filling in some backing vocals with her redoubtable and perky mezzo-soprano.

When that track was ready it was quiet please and Debs would pop on the clunky headphones and perch on her stool, confronting the mike and she would make further notes on her scribbled-over score.

She sucked abstractedly at a cigarette and they could all see, through the glass wall, that she was running it all meticulously through her head.

'You have to give it to her,' Clive whispered. 'She's a perfectionist. I've not given this song as much thought as she has. And I wrote the bleeding thing.'

'Pshaw,' said Brenda.

Tony glowed with pride, seeing Debs in her element.

When Debs was ready to sing lead, she would ask for the track to be played as loudly as possible. 'More track, more track', she would demand of the sweaty, oily, smokey fellas behind the glass partition. 'Louder and louder; crank it up. I can still hear myself. I don't want to be able to hear myself sing.'

They marvelled that she could still keep perfect pitch in amongst that welter of cranked-up sound. They watched, mouths open, as she flung out her arms and belted her way through the whole number. She would act as if she was on stage.

'You don't need to do that,' Brenda grumbled as they stood together, doing their harmonies. 'It's embarrassing.'

'Didn't you ever sing into a hairbrush, Brenda?' Debs laughed. 'Watching yourself in the bathroom mirror?'

'As a kid,' Brenda said. 'Not now. It's not like that now.'

Debs shook her heavily coiffed head. 'Yes it is.'

Debs would take home a rough cut, a tape of the day's work and she would phone Roy and the producer in the early hours. She supposed she was demanding, but sweetened it with utter self-deprecation.

'Oh, I was awful today. I was terrible. Everything I sang was wrong. I'm listening to it now. Could I have another go? Can we do it again? Hm? Please?'

She wanted to rerecord a phrase, a line, a verse. Just a little touch-up. Just a little more. When the rest of the band was satisfied, Debs always wanted to do a little more.

She would return the next day, and the next, and maybe, at last, it would be near perfect as dammit. She still wouldn't believe it and Roy had to talk to her and tell her they had run out of time.

There would always be another chance, he told her. They had to get on. There were other things to do besides records. Photo shoots, television, personal appearances.

But Debs would rather stay here, in the bare blank comfort of the studio, straining towards perfection. She imagined a perfect record. A perfect three minute single. Silvery perfection: always out of her grasp.

'She brainwashes herself,' Clive said to Tony, as they sat drinking late one night in a bar Clive knew. He had been spending a lot of his time with Debs, Tony knew. 'Did she always do that?'

'Even as a kid,' said Tony. 'She worked so hard when we did this shit as kids. At Butlins, Pontins, *New Faces*. You've never seen anything like it. I thought it was all just a laugh. It was never like that for Debs.'

'I think she's incredible,' Clive said, and knocked back his drink.

'I know you do,' said Tony.

Clive waved away his concern. 'I'll look after her. Don't you worry.'

But Tony didn't look convinced.

At home, Debs ran the rough cuts of songs backwards and forwards at full tilt until she knew the song inside out. She knew it better than the rest of the band in the first place, anyway, because she had written the lyrics and she had hummed and lalala'ed along with Clive as he fretted over his twelve string guitar.

There was a lot of fretting over Clive's twelve string round Debs' place during those days and nights. Writing the band's material had drawn them ever closer together. They would emerge from these writing times bonded and flushed in the face. Everyone remarked on their compatability and how long they sweated over their creations.

There was a long time between the writing and the actual recording, and by the time they were using up studio hours with the company paying, the song had become a difficult, complicated beast that Debs took it upon herself to tame.

She had to be inside of it.

Once a prototype was committed to acetate, she wanted to pore over every split second. She wanted to see what could be done with it.

Visitors to her small flat would at first feel that they were getting a scoop, a freebie, a startling, exclusive glimpse into the future of pop when they went round and found her singing along with this booming noise.

They discovered her dwarfed by the sound of her own voice: a mellow, velvety concoction; golden brown. Then husky, sharp, agitated, bluesey. Then silver, silver, silvery Debbie Now. A voice for all seasons. A miraculous voice, too good for pop.

'This is the next single,' she would bellow over some sketchily disastrous lead break from Clive's guitar. 'This is the one that'll sell millions for us.'

Her guests would nod, smile, act surprised and listen politely to the chaotic jumble of take one as Debs clattered around in her tiny kitchen, still humming, wielding kettle, frying pan, tea pot.

The guests would wait, slowly being deafened, listening to Debs as she toyed endlessly with novel inflections.

I could sing it this way. I could do that. I could change the whole feeling of the song by sounding bereft, disappointed, mortified, ecstatic, hopeful or glib.

I could go through ten mood-shifts in three minutes flat.

It's infinite, she would tell the friends who came to visit: I can do anything with this material.

You've no idea the world of sound that Clive has opened up for me.

Three minutes is endlessly elastic.

It's important, too, because songs stay with you. And not just you. The way they get recorded sticks just like that through all time.

She had to struggle, making everything she laid down, each note she committed to posterity, definitive.

She had to get it right.

There was never much stuff in Debbie's flat. She owned barely a stick of furniture. Too much clutter and she wouldn't be able to think. Too much to impede her and there'd be no more lyrics of searing honesty, truth and bravery.

She needed clarity and space in order to sit with her small leather book with its tiny lock and key (the one she'd kept since she was seven; sellotaping more and more pages inside till the spine was cracking and bursting apart).

She needed the open space in this flat to rehearse and revise herself.

Here she unleashed her voice in white rooms. She practised it like a fierce, unwieldy, private vice.

Tony stayed with her often. Flopped in a bean bag, mouth agape, hardly daring to breathe.

'You should sing like that in the studio,' he said.

Debs tried, but somehow the presence of the others and Roy and the sweaty, oily, smokey engineers put her off her stroke.

It was never the same as at home.

At home she could safely decant the white-hot brilliance that was still fresh from late night sessions with Clive. At home she could savour that heady aroma of composition and sex.

Her flat in Salford was the world to her. She'd been here a year. Alone apart from visits. Everything she needed was in walking distance, even Tony, and especially Clive. Everything she'd ever wanted.

How would it be, she worried, when she was married to Clive? Where would they live? Where would she be able to sing? How would she be able to be alone?

But there would always be the space she needed.

She managed to make Clive promise her this.

'Anything, anything,' he said. 'Sure.'

And anyway, she would be with him. Clive would be there to provoke that voice from deep inside her. He would give her new material and she would be wedded to that genius of his; one that knew how to draw out the genius inside her. That was worth any amount of compromise in Debs' book. She would have to learn to give up singing for herself. Maybe that's what being in love meant.

Hurriedly she stowed her stage outfit in a bag and ran out the back door of the club.

Her mother was waiting, ready in the cab, in the prearranged spot in the alleyway.

'Where's Tony?' Debs asked.

Her mother shrugged and looked up and down at Debs' track-suit. 'He took a taxi to the hotel half an hour ago. What were you doing?'

Debs looked back at the emergency exit, which had closed softly behind her. 'Signing.'

Her immaculate mother looked blank.

'Signing photographs for fans, with Clive and Brenda. They always make us sign.' She bundled herself into the back of the cab and Franky followed. 'We needed Tony there. There were girls waiting for him. What was the matter with him?'

'Headache,' Franky said.

As the driver took them off through the dark city centre, she decided not to tell her daughter that Tony had been crying when he'd left. That he'd been shouted at by their manager.

That the manager, the altogether shocking Roy, had fetched him a terrible clout around the earhole.

'It's a shitty night-time disco world,' Roy had told them all. 'That's the world you're going into for a while. It's all necessary and it mightn't look like hard work, but believe you me: it's a bastard. You just have to do one or two songs, ten minutes at the most, and you have to grab every fucker's attention.'

'Will we be singing for real?' Brenda asked.

'For real?' he laughed. A great chuckle that seemed to come from deep inside him.

'It's necessary, guys,' Clive rallied them. 'Just one more shitty thing to do on the way up.'

Drive to a disco in the centre of some town. Get smuggled through the back. Stand on a flashing glass floor and make the punters look at you. Distract them from their own dramas, their own sense of being stars under the heaving, ghastly lights and mouth at them the words of your song. Lodge it in their spacey addled brains. Imprint yourself upon your dancing punters. Take your bows. Sign some photographs.

'We could be just about anyone,' Tony complained, after their first few personal appearances. 'They go wild. They'd go wild at anyone walking on through the dry ice.'

'But it's you, you dickhead,' Roy snapped. 'It's you they're going mad for.'

'It isn't just anyone,' said Brenda. 'It's *us*.'

Franky glared at the muted lights of Middlesbrough swishing past. When she turned to her daughter her pupils were a flat, terrifying green.

'Not even singing,' Franky said. 'Miming along to your own words.'

Debs had rehearsed her response to this. She knew her mother would take this tack. 'Mam ... the song has to be exactly as it is on the record. We have to present it in the best possible, professional way. It has to be exactly the same, so all the people in the disco can go out and buy it tomorrow, and know what they're getting.'

'And you are not capable of singing it the same? You cannot do a good job?'

'You saw it in there. Smoke, dry ice, all the noise. We'd be fighting to be heard in all that.'

Franky nodded. 'It's not what I was expecting, Debbie.'

'We have to be perfect. We have to do it Roy's way. He knows what he's doing.'

Horrible discos, Franky thought. Friday nights in different cities, with people who looked like shop girls and bank clerks, jogging around. Sweating. Not even knowing how to dance. Not even paying real attention when the singing group came on to entertain them.

Franky had sat at a table alone, with a ridiculous green cocktail their Roy had bought for her. She had sat up at a height, watching over the rail, as her daughter and her band came rushing out to mime. Franky had heard the heckling, the catcalls, the laughter during the songs. She had seen her daughter dancing badly, knocking into Tony, trying to regain her place: pretending to sing her heart out.

Franky had assumed Debs would be the centre of attention. Not this; in this curious chemical-smelling cave of a place where no one cared if the group came on at all. Where people were having a good time regardless. This was Debs' success and what she was proud of. It was this evening's display she'd been so keen for her mother to see. To come all this way on the bus tonight, the night before the wedding.

It wasn't what Franky had been led to expect. Her cocktail tasted bitter, like liquorice. She threw away the paper umbrella when it broke apart in her fingers at the end of the last song.

The songs were insipid. Her daughter had laboured long over the words, Franky knew. In here, you could hardly hear them above the fuzz of the sound system, the thud of the feet, the pumped-up bass.

Debs had kept a little book with her since she was a kid. Everything she'd written in it and kept under lock and key, she fed into her songs. Franky had sneaked a look once or twice over the years. Just look what they'd done to her songs.

The last one tonight had had a plaintive refrain:

Remember when -
Remember when -
Remember when -
Remember when -

It roused the shop girls and bank boys a little; a few even joining in with the chant.

Franky remembered when Debs had decided to make herself the star of the show. When she was eight, at that holiday camp, and Franky had taken her and her friend from school, that very same Tony, and they had scooped up all the prizes, singing so sweetly together on the small, scabby stage.

Warming everybody's hearts. Singing along to a piano; sweet, old-fashioned songs. Making mums and dads around the tropical ballroom wipe away a tear and look at their own children and wish they had such talent.

Darling blonde-haired magical children, uncannily gifted. Shining faces under the primitive lights.

Franky hadn't stayed up through the nights, sewing their stage costumes together. By all rights, she should have. But she'd got her friend to do it; a childless woman in the next chalet whom she'd met at the beginning of that week in Llandudno, 1965.

Franky still had the trophy. For several years it had gone

back and forth between Tony's parents and her; dual residences on mantelpieces either side of their street. It was an ugly, wooden thing with Debs' and Tony's names stamped into the brass plate.

Tony's parents had lost interest, though, and the shield had come to stay with Franky, along with the other cups, framed photos, news clippings and rosettes. Tony's parents hadn't even been interested in the *New Faces* trophy for second place. That was how far he'd fallen out of favour.

He hadn't really spoken to his mam and dad in years. Poor boy, all alone in the world. No one to come out tonight, like Franky had, to see this little show of theirs.

She shouldn't be so hard on Debbie. Her daughter was slumped, a little defeated now, as the cab pulled up at the hotel. She looked nothing like a star in that tracksuit; her hair matted down and her lipstick smudged.

Tonight should have made her feel every inch the star. They're not doing justice to her, Franky thought, these people in this world that has sucked her in.

This hotel, too, she thought, grimacing at the plaid carpet and the dowdy rubber plants, is the place where businessmen come to get laid and they wolf their full English breakfasts and all the corridors smell of their socks and shoes.

My daughter has been placed in a twilight world of rancid, dancing men, late nights and not even being allowed to sing properly. I should make it up to her. I should have told her tonight she was wonderful. It was all a fantastic success.

She watched Debs wearily take the chunky key from the girl behind the desk. They had to share a room; Franky, her daughter, and Tony. Just as they had, all those years ago at the holiday camp.

I should tell her I am proud, Franky thought, stiffly following the girl into the lift. But I can't.

If she'd had a room of her own tonight, Debs would have wanted to listen to the songs again.

She couldn't help it. She had to hear them again and again. She got a rush of blood to her temples as the introductions came on, and another rush to the nethers as the choruses crashed in and she heard her voice twining around the others'.

If one of her songs came on the radio she stopped in her tracks and wanted to cry. It was still unbelievable to her.

Trying on shoes, zipping herself up in communal changing rooms, hearing the start of one of their songs, and a slow flush would come over her. She would feel exposed, as if the music was leaking out of her; blaring out through her skin; her whole body vibrating with it.

If it wasn't for me, she thought, this music would never exist in the world. There would be fewer songs in the world for people to hum.

And Clive, too - if it wasn't for him, as well.

They were, of course, a partnership.

She could still see Roy, clapping his fat hands with glee when she told him she and Clive were getting married. It was Roy who insisted they should do it when the single came out - the very day - guaranteeing extra publicity for both happy events. Brought together by their music; united harmoniously. Twin pop geniuses pledged to one another.

Debs had helped Roy pick out his outfit for the registry service: a surprisingly matronly number with a hat and a slight veil.

It didn't even strike her that no one was helping her decide on hers. Roy held her hand and patted her and she knew he was proud. He even gave Clive a bluff manly slap on the shoulder. She'd never seen Roy do anything like that before.

Clive could say anything and she just took it. It didn't matter what he said or did, Debs found that she could just deal with it because she loved him.

She knew she loved him because, no matter how rough or boorish he acted, he still made it clear she was the most important thing in the world to him. She had tamed a lout. The thought thrilled her.

He might have gone for the altogether more flashy Brenda. When Roy first pulled the band together, for Eurovision, it had seemed that might be the way of it.

The first time Debs let Clive into her flat, the night she knew they were going to sleep together, she said something to that effect. Brenda, surely, was the obvious choice for him.

'Dime a dozen, that sort,' he said, unlacing his boots. He'd brought along his twelve string, for when they were struck with inspiration through the night.

Debs drank her tea avidly, watching him. 'Really? You couldn't care less about her?'

He smiled. 'I look at Brenda and I think - Been there, done that.'

'Really?' asked Debs again.

All that night her voice stayed rather high, as if someone had turned her treble up.

That night, in her mostly empty flat, they wrote a song they thought they could maybe use, and they also recorded an improvised piece that lasted nearly an hour. It featured Clive's guitar, Debs' wordless ululations and then the various sounds of their bodies slapping together on the sheepskin rug in front of the gas fire.

He's freeing me up creatively, Debs thought. We're recording every scrap of ourselves and our art.

I could be Yoko to his John. Linda to his Paul.

When they were finished they took out the tape and looked at it, neatly spooled and shiny: a record of their first night.

They lay in bed the next day and imagined that the world's press had come to interview them. They were at the Amsterdam Hilton and under white sheets with nightcaps on. Everyone watching was agog at the spectacle they made. But, of course, they never cared. They were in love and this was art they were making. Every single thing they did was art.

Now she was in love, Debs knew this.

She flinched but forgave him when he said to her, as had so many kids at school: 'Your mam's Chinese! But you're not, are you? How's your mam Chinese and you're not?'

After she had introduced them in the Middlesbrough club foyer that Friday night and Roy had led her mother away to her reserved table, the band retired to their dressing room. Clive had wasted no time tackling this difficult subject. In her mirror, Debs saw Brenda sneer as she buckled her belt about her satin hipsters. Debs glanced at Tony, who looked shocked at Clive's frankness.

'How come your mother's Chinese then, Debbie?'

Clive wasn't meaning to be nasty. She was sure of it.

Awkwardly she replied: 'Yes, she's Chinese. And I suppose, deep down, somewhere, I must be Chinese, too.'

'Oh,' said Clive and that was the end of the conversation. The band went on dressing and then they were ploughing through the dark and the noise and the fake mist, ready to do their show.

He mustn't mind, thought Debbie. He doesn't mind at all.

Back at school she had howled and blubbered and wailed her protest. She had locked herself in the horrible and fishy fourth form bogs.

'She's not Chinese! My mam's not Chinese! Fuck off! Fuck off!'

Girls her own age crowded outside, chanting and calling for her to come out and take it like a good sport. They waited, bent double with hilarity, until Debs came out and they could follow her all the way back to her house. Chanting, Ching Chong Chinaman: Debbie Now's a yellow chinky; a slitty-eyed chong.

Debbie's face was purple with rage, pent up, turning black, as she pelted home past playing fields, hawthorn hedges, and the row of shops. Finally she was home with hordes of crowing schoolgirls at her back.

Each night she came home like this and each night her mother would ask why. Whenever Franky came out to the front door to see what horrors had pursued her daughter home, the girls squealed and scattered. They fled shrieking back up the Avenue.

You eat cats. You eat dogs. Your mother feeds you monkey brains.

Debbie ground her teeth together, lying face down on the leatherette settee.

'You must tell me,' Franky said at last, hardening her voice. 'How these girls make your life so miserable. How they are spoiling your life.'

Debbie howled and sobbed into a crotcheted cushion. 'They're saying that you're Chinese!' she cried, muffled.

'What?'

Debbie raised her face and everything was blurred and red. She looked at her mother's concerned face and hated her.

'They were saying you were Chinese.'

'But I am!'

Debs looked at her. Then she burst into tears.

She felt her mother's fingers going through her hair.

'It's nothing to cry about, Debbie. I'm Chinese and maybe that is unusual here. Perhaps. But I am proud and you should be, too. You may not look much like me, more like your father. But deep inside, you are Chinese as well.'

Debs screamed. 'I'm not! I'm not Chinese!'

'Hush now, Debbie Now. You are. You are. You're Chinese, too.'

Debs paled and sobbed and couldn't believe her ears. She hauled herself up, pushed past her mother, staggered through the hallway and threw up on the carpet in the downstairs loo.

Her head pounded and she sat herself on the toilet seat, looking at her sick. Why can't we have normal food?

She thought about going over the road to Tony's house. There they ate baked beans, fish fingers, beef burgers, chips, jam roly poly, Yorkshire puddings, garden peas and tinned peach slices. She thought about Tony's parents - him with his beer gut, her with her frizzy hair and tarty skirts.

'But at least they're not Chinese,' she moaned.

Playing out on the street with Tony, she'd always felt betrayed by the spicy sweet smells that came wafting out of Franky's kitchen. Sweet and sour. You eat dogs. Your mam cooks cats. You held my grandad prisoner-of-war.

When Tony came for tea she watched him look mystified and pleased at the delicate little bowls, the won-tons and the thick, unidentifiable soups.

'We never have rice round our house,' he'd told Franky.

She patted his shoulder and turned back to the wok, which was spitting impatiently. We're unusual, Debbie had thought at the time, tapping out a tune with her chopsticks. We stand out around here and just then she had been proud of her mother and her cooking and how they'd seemed to Tony's eyes.

Unusual.

In the downstairs toilet she started sobbing again.

'We are Chinese!' she cried out.

That night her mother lay beside her on her bed and soothed her brow.

'Never feel ashamed because of the things they shout. They know no better. They should only be ghosts to you, Debbie Now, and they may never touch you.'

'Ghosts?'

'See how pale they are?'

'I'm pale as well. I'm the same as them.'

'Hush now, Debbie Now. Not the same.' Debbie felt her mother stretch out and look at the ceiling. 'When my mother first came here, she lived with her aunt, who was already here. In Manchester, where people were, on the whole, kind, though wary. She learned you must treat them all politely if you want to get by. And if they mock you and if they shout at you, you must remember they are ghosts. Pale things that cannot harm you.'

Debs took a shuddering breath. 'Am I all Chinese? All the way through?'

Franky nodded gravely. 'And you ought to be proud.'

'Oh, God.' Debs blinked and stared up at the aertex. 'Everything's different.'

'No,' said Franky. 'You are still the same girl as you woke up this morning.'

'Chinese,' said Debs. 'Was my dad Chinese?'

'Your father's part of the family was Irish,' said Franky. 'Not Chinese and no good at all. Tinkers and gypsies. No good. They do not count.'

'So I'm not completely Chinese?'

'These things do not matter, Debbie.' Her mother straightened up and took out matches for the nite lights.

She left her daughter staring at the pale flames, lying down on silky sheets, hair stuck to her face.

I thought she had adopted me. I thought she had found me in a phone box. But it's true. What they shout at me: it's all true.

When she told Tony this, walking to school the next morning, he shrugged. He was chewing on crispy strips of chilli beef Franky gave him when he came knocking. Terrible thing to have for breakfast. 'So what if it's true?' he grinned.

Look at how lovely and pale his skin is. White, so white he's almost blue. His yellowish hair, all tufted from sleep, unwashed. Debs realised his uniform was unwashed too and unironed. Yet Tony didn't tell her much about the troubles they had round his house.

'This is the worst thing that's ever happened to me,' she said.

'At least they're not lies,' he said.

'What do you mean?'

'The things they shout about you in school and all the way home. At least you know they're all true.'

Debs hung her head. 'Yeah.'

'That's just like me. You hear the things they shout about me.'

She blushed. Bum boy. Queer boy. Pansy arse-fucker. She nodded.

He winked. 'They're all true as well.'

She gasped.

'So we ought to be glad, oughtn't we? That everyone knows. That they care so much they feel they have to shout it in the streets.'

The school gates were looming up. Kids were hanging about, watching, perking up in interest and Debs and Tony wandered up.

He addressed them all.

'She's a chinky dog-eater and I'm a queer who touches up boys. And we're both gunna be famous for it. Anyone got a problem with that?'

The kids at the gates smirked and snorted at Tony's bravado.

He led Debs triumphantly past.

That wasn't the only thing, though, that they shouted after Tony. They also said he smelled, came from a dirty house and that his mother was a whore. He didn't mention any of those things and Debs thought she'd better not, either.

Chinese!

Up on the seventh floor of the hotel Debs gave a timid knock, wondering if Tony had fallen asleep already.

They shuffled in to find the room half-lit and Tony sitting on his divan in his pyjama bottoms, cramming his face with wedding cake.

'Oh, God,' he moaned as they stood staring down at him.

Between them, on the rumpled hotel duvet, the cake lay in a state of ruin. He'd clawed great chunks out and scattered crumbs, dried fruit, clods of icing all through the sheets.

He wasn't even using a knife to cut proper slices, let alone a paper plate. He looked at them with his mouth bulging, frozen with guilt.

'Tony?' asked Debs.

He spoke through his mouthful, trying to swallow. 'It was supposed to be a surprise.'

Franky picked up the fallen bride-and-groom ornament.

'You're eating my wedding cake?'

He struggled up, still swallowing. 'I made it for you. It was my present.'

'And you ate it?'

'I kept it hidden in my bag. All the way here ... it took me weeks to make...'

Franky sat down and picked up a crumbled piece. She tasted it delicately. 'Very good.'

'Why are you eating it?' Debs asked, her voice quite steady.

He looked down helplessly. 'I don't know. I just came back and ... I started.'

'It's destroyed,' said Debs.

'Nah,' said Franky. 'Come and sit with us, Debbie. Eat your cake now. Plenty left. It is very good.'

Debs strode past and stormed into the ensuite. She locked the door with a very loud, satisfying crack.

Franky watched Tony sag backwards and lie on his back, crumbs caught in his sparse chest hair. 'What have I done?' he said.

Franky brushed her hands free of crumbs. 'The question is, *why* have you done it, Tony?'

'I don't know.' He didn't look at her.

'You take all the time to make a beautiful cake for my daughter's day and then you spoil it on the night before.' She narrowed her eyes. 'You are upset. You have just realised what is happening.'

He glanced at her and rolled onto his elbow. 'What's happening?'

Debs' mother rolled her eyes. 'My daughter is marrying this man, Clive. You are losing your best friend to him.'

'Oh, him,' Tony scowled. 'Well, I knew about that a long time ago.'

'It does not upset you? You think he is a good man?'

'I wouldn't know about that. I think so.'

'So.' She nodded slowly, looking at the remains of the cake. The ensuite toilet flushed noisily, efficiently. Debs didn't reappear.

'I hope you will find yourself a good man, too, Tony.'

He blinked at her.

'Hm,' she said. 'It was never any surprise to me. The way you are made.'

He smiled weakly. 'I carried the cake in my holdall. I thought I'd been careful enough. When I got back tonight, I thought I'd have another look, to check it and because I suppose I was proud of it. And when I looked, great chunks of icing had dropped off.'

'And so you thought you might as well eat it?'

'I don't know what came over me.'

Franky sighed. She looked at their wedding day outfits, all three of them, hanging ready in the wardrobe alcove. 'You always ate, back when you were a small boy. You ate when you were upset. I thought you must have hollow legs or a demon living inside you. You would come to our house and I would have little things ready for you. Nibbles. I knew you would devour them for comfort.'

'Was I always upset?' he asked. He realised just how long he'd known this woman.

'You were. I do not think you were very happy as a child.'

'I remember the things you made. The food you gave me. I thought you were just being nice.'

'A sad ghost inside you,' Franky said. 'Making you eat. You should be fat as your Roy by now. Why are you so unhappy now, Tony? Tell me.'

He shook his head slowly. 'If I could put it into words for you, Franky, I would.'

'Try. As a boy you told me many things. I had never met such a talkative child. I used to wish my Debbie was more like you. She would write things down in her book instead of talking to me.'

'Really?'

'I used to tell her. Learn to talk. Be like your friend.'

'I can't really say, Franky.' He hoisted himself up from the bed and reached for his striped pyjama top, suddenly shy, pulling it on, fastening it over his skinny chest. 'If I told you about my life now, how it really is ... I'm afraid you'd be rather shocked. You wouldn't think I was still the nice boy I was then.'

She looked at him shrewdly. 'I may be shocked. I may not. You can't tell. But if you cannot tell me now why you are a sad boy, that is up to you.'

'Thank you, Franky.'

'So have some more cake, Tony.'

'I feel a little bit sickly now.'

'I will have some more, I think,' she said. 'In honour of my daughter, who will marry tomorrow a man I hardly know.'

Tony smiled at her.

She said, 'Everybody's life gets more complicated, Tony. Everyone does things they cannot be proud of. Do not assume that when I hear about how you live this life of yours, that I will hate you. We all have lives that are private and make us sad.'

She nibbled at a hunk of cake. She was eating it like a bird. 'I think you are too sensitive for this world of dancing and hotels. But you must learn first, not to feel ashamed. Embarrassed, yes, when you mouth your words in an embarrassing discotheque and you have to smile at strangers. But never be ashamed, Tony. Surely, never be ashamed.'

Chapter Five

Debs gobbled a spicey lamb pasty on the platform as we tried to work out how the Circle and District Line worked.

Then she had a chicken sandwich, thick with mayonnaise, that made her mouth go all gooey. I was glad the day hadn't spoiled her appetite. She was eating quickly, as if that would get us where we wanted to be.

We were travelling north again, through the night, and we hoped to get into Blackpool on the last train, changing in cities I'd never been to. We were going up the north west, which wasn't where I belonged and Debs was making the journey into the night seem like a race against time. She'd jumped into action, still dragging me.

I was trying to remember that Auden poem, about the trains that run all night bringing the post, while the good people of England are safe in their beds. I hadn't read much since my degree. I'd put myself out of the habit; sickened by literature.

But that night we were the night post, hurtling north and I wished I could read the poem again. It hit me, once we were on the train, that Debs and I had put ourselves out of normal life, just by not going home again that night.

I still wasn't even sure where we were supposed to be going.

'Poor Tim,' Debs said, a few times. She wiped at the black patent leather of the window.

We had a table again. The train wasn't full.

'When we were touring we'd take a sleeper up and down the country. They had these funny little rooms with four bunks. Imagine that. All four members of Things Fall Apart laid out on these tiny shelves. It made it awkward when me and Clive were married.' She smiled. 'Though that was awkward all round, anyway.'

I said, 'I don't think they have beds on trains anymore.' What did I know? I rarely went on trains.

'I think they stopped all that. Things got faster. No need for sleepers.'

I thought it sounded a horrible idea. Passing out on tiny shelves, under thin sheets and waking up in just another British town. What a disappointment: I'd expect somewhere fabulous and exotic: Prague, Moscow, Hong Kong. Walking out on a platform half asleep and smelling spices and bodies and everyone looking different to how you'd expect.

'I make our lives as stars seem less glamorous with every story I tell, don't I?' Debs asked tiredly.

It was true. I kept waiting for her to reach the moment in the tale of her career when it suddenly turned fantastic. When everything became polished and easy. When there was no more worry or fuss. It had become important to me, to hear the whole thing; to stick with Debs until she reached that turning point in her fortunes and then I would know.

As she teased through the past she seemed just as surprised as I did, that it didn't all seem like one glamorous romp.

'You look punch-drunk,' she told me as tall and supercilious buildings fell away and we shot into tunnels again. Yellow light crackled through the carriage.

'Cheers.'

'I've bludgeoned you with my stories till you look half-dead. Even an obsessive fan would be knackered by now.'

I roused myself on the mucky plush of the double-seat. 'No, no,' I said, feeling bruised all over. 'I love you telling me this stuff.'

'I know. It's not fair, though. I'm taking up all your time. Now I'm dragging you off somewhere else.'

I leaned forward. 'What's in Blackpool?'

She didn't hear me. 'It does me some good, though, talking to you. You're a godsend to me, Tim.'

I shrugged. 'It's all right.'

'But I've spoiled the illusion a bit, haven't I?'

I knew enough by now to deny this flatly.

Debs perked up. 'Selfish me. Typical me. I hardly know a thing about you and your life, do I? I've never really asked a thing.'

'Not much has happened to me.'

'Really?' she grinned. 'Remember, I grew up with a gay man. Tony told me everything. I know how much you guys pack into your lives.'

'We're not all alike,' I said stiffly.

'Near enough. I bet you've got some stories to tell.'

I found myself becoming quite grumpy. I was quite short with her. 'What's in Blackpool then?'

But she still wouldn't tell me.

I wanted to sleep on the train, but there was just no way. It seemed like a twisty kind of route, with the carriages shifting tracks every now and then and jolting us about. It was as if the train driver didn't know the way exactly. This set off alarm bells for me. I started thinking about all the rail disasters in recent years.

'Did you read about that man who'd been in both big train crashes?'

'Hm?' Debs looked as if she'd been managing to rest. Her eyes had that smudgy, unfocussed look.

'He was in the Clapham Junction crash, and climbed out of the window to safety. Then, a year afterwards, he was in that Paddington crash too. Can you imagine? You'd feel ridiculous, the whole thing happening over again...'

She squinted at me.

I went on, 'He got out the window again, using the hammer they put in the little glass box. Now he carries his own hammer in his briefcase, even though it's illegal. Just in case. I think I would, too.'

'Why is it illegal?' Debs muttered.

'What?'

'Why is it illegal to carry a hammer in your briefcase?'

I blinked. 'Offensive weapon.'

'Oh.' She looked blank. Her head fell against the rest again. Her hair looked really mussed. I thought, there was something very naive about Debs, if she couldn't figure out that a hammer kept in a brief-case could be counted as an offensive weapon. As if the thought would never occur to her on her own. I suppose that's a good thing, that she could still be that naive. But I didn't understand how she could have survived in the nightmare world of showbiz being as innocent as she seemed to be.

But then, she hadn't really survived in that world, had she? She'd been pushed out.

She had closed her eyes and her mouth had fallen open and I felt ashamed for thinking along these lines.

Then I realised my responsibility. I was along for the ride because I still thought of Debs as a star. She wanted me with her because I was her witness.

I couldn't stop backing her up even for a moment. I imagined that if I stopped for a second, her whole confidence would vanish. There'd be nothing left on that double-seat apart from her blue furry coat.

When at last we arrived there was no one else in our carriage.

We stumbled up the aisle as the train shunted in. We were gasp-ing after clean, night air.

I felt a bit conspicuous, with our lack of luggage. I was wonder-ing what we would sleep in, what we would wear tomorrow, and how we would brush our teeth. I didn't allow myself to wonder exactly where we would do these things.

I was supposed to be in work tomorrow. The whole of the

Pennines were between me and work; ugly black crags and miles of rolling moors. There was no way of getting back in time.

We moved up, past tables and seats, strewn magazines, newspapers and foam coffee cups with scum already forming.

I saw the front page of the *Evening Standard* before Debs did, but she snatched it up off the seat as she went by.

She held out the picture before me.

'That cheeky, lying mare,' she said.

It was Shelley Sommers, grinning in disco gear, under a banner headline. Debs skimmed the tiny article.

'She's already recorded the song! It's coming out at the weekend...' Debs looked at me. 'That lunch ... her asking after my advice ... it was all a farce. It was all lies.'

She thrust the paper into my arms and made for the door. From the few sentences I managed to skim, I made out that Shelley was debuting the single on *Kiddies in Krisis* on Saturday. *Kiddies in Krisis* was an annual, star-studded telethon and she was bound to get a lot of publicity from it. I rolled the paper up and hurried onto the platform after Debs.

The only people there were an elderly couple in long coats, who were being greeted by a younger woman - their daughter, I thought. A little girl - the granddaughter - was in a silver padded jacket and she was rollerskating in circles around her elders and their luggage.

I caught up with Debs and saw that there was a new set to her face to go with the determined spring in her stride.

'Now I know we're doing the right thing,' she glowered.

'And what's that, Debs?'

She stopped and looked at me. 'We have to see Tony. He needs to know what's going on behind our backs.'

She got a cab to take us off into the empty streets of Blackpool. We shot out of town with barely a glimpse of the tower, into the spaced out houses of the suburbs.

'Why did Tony leave the band, anyway?'

'You're not up on your history, are you? I thought you were a proper fan.'

I tried to recover this slip. 'I thought there was some other story. Something that didn't get to the public.'

'Well, that's true enough. It was the accident, really. He couldn't concentrate. He didn't have the energy or the commitment. He couldn't give it a hundred per cent.'

'You didn't kick him out..?'

'No!' Debs looked ashamed for a second. 'Clive wanted to. He'd never really liked Tony. You have to remember, we were all thrown together by Roy. We were forced to get on, because we were the right combination. It didn't mean we'd automatically become best of pals.'

'Clive was jealous of you and Tony.'

'He knew that there was nothing in it. He knew for a fact Tony was as gay as a goose.'

I still found that exciting, hearing it from Debs. 'I'd always realised. Seeing you all on *Top of the Pops* and Saturday morning TV. I was just a kid ... I hardly knew what being gay meant. But I knew something Tony wasn't saying.'

Debs sighed. 'He was so sensitive and sweet...' She talked about him like he was dead.

'It wasn't just that. The way he looked and talked and laughed...' I said. 'It was the first time my youthful gaydar went off...'

I remember once being glued to the screen when the four of them came on. They looked gawky and pale in their stage outfits, sitting on beanbags, surrounded by kids and their TV studio hosts. They were clutching phones and answering questions, and then they were setting a competition and bringing out goodies - signed LPs and posters and mugs - for prizes. Tony was fumbling in a per-spex box for the winning entry to last week's competition and I'd hoped he'd pull out my card ('Answers on a postcard to...') I entered every week and never won. I wanted to hear Tony read my name on TV and I wanted the delicious irk of his mispronunciation of it.

I watched them doing their new song, miming to it live. They looked so happy. They were in their New Romantic phase and sported feathers in their hair, lacey collars and cuffs, robotlike make-up with sharp cheekbones, eyeliner, lipgloss and beauty spots. Tony was in tight-fitting silver jodhpurs. I remember his getting me hot and bothered.

'He never used to wear pants, did he? Under his stage outfits?'

I remembered his mischevious bulge; tongue-in-cheek.

'Never.'

I bought a magazine or two that interviewed him and I pored over them. I kidded myself he liked girls and forced myself to believe it when he said in interviews he hadn't met the right girl yet. He always said Debs was his best friend. In photo shoots it was always them two larking around together and the other two were aloof, grown-up.

Somehow it became linked in my head; that if Tony really did like girls, then I did too, and everything would be okay. Nothing to worry about. But I still stared into the photos, hoping for signs and intimations of something or other. I still found myself looking at boys in the showers at school. Around that time I became a fantastic swimmer, through practising so much. Evenings and weekends came to smell of chlorine to me and so did I: hanging around in changing rooms.

In many ways Tony was responsible for the whole thing. His was the first grown up body I'd wondered about, and dreamed about. I wanted to know what it was like. I wanted to see it and touch it and it made me wonder what my own grown up body would be like.

Debs was leaning forward to whisper to the cab driver. She had her address book out and I could see the address and phone number printed in her clear, careful hand. It was as neat as the list of songs she'd ripped up that afternoon. There was something touching about the neatness of Debs' handwriting, as if she wanted to impress someone. As if some teacher was going to come round and check on her legibility and give her a gold star.

Something so hopeful about her.

'I've had this written down for years,' she told me. 'And I haven't been to see him ever. I hope he's still there.'

The taxi cruised into a leafy cul-de-sac. It was a street that looked as if it had been the same for decades.

She paid the man. We got out with stiff legs.

'Did you and he fall out, then?' I'd be surprised if it was true.

'No, never.' She watched the taxi turn off and away. 'God, I hope we're in the right place. He might not even be here.'

Behind the hedges, the stuccoed house we'd arrived at was dark. Not even the carriage lamp on the porch was lit. But it was late.

'We didn't keep up with each other...'

She opened the gate and it screeched. I realised she was whispering. 'It was kind of because of his boyfriend at the time...'

Now I had very mixed feelings.

I wanted Tony to be single and about twenty-one again; gangly and young with lacquered, blonde-streaked hair. He should be jumping about on Saturday morning TV and, when the camera went in for his close up, his hair would be falling into his eyes.

I wanted to see him roll his eyes again, as if the whole thing was a big joke.

When I was a kid we kept ourselves pretty much to ourselves. Mam would talk about how, at one time, it used to be different and, on Bank Holidays and Easter Sunday, everyone in town would dress up in their new clothes and troop up and down the main street, showing off. They would visit grandparents and aunts for tea; everyone piling into cars with their immaculate children and letting old people tousle their kids' hair, making the kids kiss pouchy cheeks. The best china would be out on white linen.

By the time I came along, that had all changed and me and Mam lived in a different town, with no one nearby we could visit. They seemed like fairy tales to me, her stories of the big fair that came to the top of the town and how those neatly-dressed families would ride the wooden horses and the dodgem cars. She talked about the hot, heavy, smokey air; the chips and beer and electric lights. It sounded like something from before the war, but I suppose Mam was talking about the sixties.

So we never went round other people's houses. We stuck to our own company and I was the odd one out at school; not going round a friend's for tea, not doing sleepovers, not playing video games in some other boy's bedroom. Other houses took on an air of forbidden romance. They had their own smells and allure.

As a teenager I dreamed about the insides of other people's houses. It set me up for a life of visiting strangers at home. In some ways, this trip with Debs seemed like the fulfilment of a youth spent wondering and it took my breath away, to step so blithely through the porch, into Tony's house in Blackpool.

I didn't want to talk about my own life in this. My own life, that is, prior to the night I met Debs. I wanted to keep myself quiet, turned down low. As she led me through this, I wanted to let Debs' voice speak up and turn it into an account that was for her, not me.

Debs was nervous and still she went crashing into situations. She was only brave on the surface. You'd think she would need an awful lot of courage for the things she did; standing before the whole of Europe and singing words she'd written herself, alongside people she hardly knew, apart from Tony. But hers was a nervous courage, like someone going down on a cruise liner who suddenly, knowing they're about to die anyway, flings herself overboard.

She was easily embarrassed and I think Tony was the same. I'd gathered as much from what she'd already told me. When they were at school together and when they'd first performed as gleaming wunderkinder in the holiday camps of the north west, they had made each other brave. They would clutch hands, making each others' fingers water and smart.

They had walked into the big bad world of pop like the woodcutter's children in the old story; when he abandons them and, trustingly, they try to find their way out, leaving an uncertain trail. They only wend their way further into the wood.

Yet, when I met him, the night we showed up unexpectedly at the house in Blackpool, Tony was different to Debs, in that he seemed to have always believed in what they were doing. Debs gave off a good deal of self-doubt. Tony might never have believed in himself much, but he had always believed in her.

It was as if a person didn't really exist without at least one other person staunchly beside them, on their side; investing their faith in the hopeful, tawdry, dodgy things they do.

Though he told us we had to be quiet, Tony and Debs greeted each other with squeals and shouts in the dim hallway.

He couldn't get over the fact that she was actually there. He accepted my presence without question and barely paid any attention to me.

His eyes were bright and he turned bright red and he couldn't let go of Debs. She was flushed and excited and then he seemed to glance up the staircase and abruptly calmed down.

'He's asleep. We'd better ... get in the kitchen. He's not been sleeping well ... my partner, Kris...'

We followed him into the kitchen, which seemed to be equipped with nothing but Italian appliances, all of them lightly filmed with dust. Wide windows looked out on a dark garden.

Tony busied about, putting on lamps rather than the strip

lighting, which made it seem like a louche restaurant; a tiny, smart, continental one. Then he put on an Eartha Kitt tape.

> *If I love you then I need you*
> *If I need you then I want you around*

Tony had a perm not unlike Debs', partly grown out, ruffled, tired-looking. He looked apologetic.

'I'm sorry about shushing you out there. It's all to do with Kris and him not sleeping...'

Debs nodded and added, unnecessarily, to me: 'Kris is Tony's partner.'

I hate that phrase, which has, far as I can tell, only recently come in. I can never figure out what's meant by it. It was one of those words used to denote something that used to be fun, but isn't anymore.

Tony made us coffee and went bustling silently about. He didn't seem used to having company and kept looking at us, to check we were still there.

'Five years,' Debs said quietly, as we sat ourselves on stools at the breakfast bar. 'Five years since we've seen each other.'

It was certainly him. I'd have recognised Tony as easily as I did Debs - easier, probably. He'd put on some weight. His face was not unattractively chubbier. He was in a dressing gown of paisley silk, over cotton pyjama bottoms and fluffy rabbit slippers. You could just glimpse his hairless chest under the gown.

As the coffee brewed and he came to sit with us and handed out the white cups and saucers, a Dusty Springfield song gave way to one by Cilla Black.

'I've been going back to the roots of pop,' he said. 'The proper stuff. These women and everything I remember from being a kid. What got me started in the first place.' He looked at Debs. 'I've gone back into the past. I can't be doing with what they're recording now...'

Debs laughed and shook her head.

'You can hear what these women are singing about. Cilla, Dusty, Lulu. Nowadays, they make the words sound like nothing.'

He sounded like a right old fart, but I did feel for him.

I was dead on my feet and wondering when Debs would tell him we would need to sleep. She seemed to want to talk, though, and her hand was over his. Her hand looked chapped and red, as if she'd never moisturised enough. Tony had. His skin looked okay.

'What it is about a three minute song...' Debs said, 'Is that it's concentrated...'

'Exactly,' said Tony.

'Like, if you put together all the songs we ever recorded, they'd come to ... I don't know. Have you ever listened to them all together and seen how long it took?'

'I don't know,' I said, and felt like I'd failed a test. She pouted.

'Three hours and about thirty-five minutes,' said Tony. 'That's what it comes to.'

'Is that all?' she said.

He nodded. 'Including the gaps between and time to change the records over.'

'Well, there you go,' she said. 'Now, if you think, that three and a half hours is, in concentrated form, the very essence of the four members of the band and all of our lives. Imagine taking the meaning of your whole life and squashing it down to three and a half hours?'

I drank my coffee. I doubted I could even fill that much.

I remembered Liza Minelli singing a song and explaining exactly what proportion of your life was spent sleeping, washing, working, and then she decided that maybe all the best moments in your whole life added up to about a single minute. Silly bitch, I thought at the time - I bet she's had more fun than that in her time. Who's she think she's talking to?

How much fun had I had? And I found myself thinking of

ejaculating as the most fun I could have and then I was thinking, if you strung all those orgasms together, how much would they add up to? Could concentrated blasts of pleasure like that be the equivalent to a whole career in pop?

I needed to sleep. I really did.

That's when I had a dreamy interlude, face down on the scrubbed pine breakfast bar. I could still hear the excited, chalky pale, hoarsely-whispering voices of the two of them over my head. I thought they were selfish.

I was, meanwhile, in an Egyptian tomb of some sort, which appeared to be under Blackpool Tower. I was a tongueless priest (I could feel the useless stump of tongue stirring and stinging) and I had priestesses Lulu, Cilla and Eartha standing by in gauzy outfits. They were paying homage to Dusty in her sarcophagus, all of them intoning and harmonizing on 'I Just Don't Know What To Do With Myself'.

They were reading the lyrics from papyrus scrolls and popping the jars containing her precious organs into a little cupboard that already contained her gold and platinum records.

During a lull in the ceremony Cilla nipped over and warned me that I had no place, observing their sororal rites. I didn't have any songs to sing. I looked round at my cowled fellow priests and they turned out to be a perplexed Debs and Tony. Even they were saying, What was I doing there?

Then Shelley Sommers, in a shaggy blue coat, was stooped over Dusty's shrine and being invested with secrets.

I woke with a painfully full bladder in a dark living room, naked under a candlewick bedspread.

Debs was on the phone in the bright hallway when I shambled through. The sun was streaming through the glass of the front porch and she had her back to it as she listened intently to someone on the other end of the trimphone.

I realised that the walls were papered with signed, framed record sleeves.

Debs looked me up and down as she listened.

I had the thin green bedspread pulled around me and my face was stiff with sleep. I hadn't been able to find my clothes in the chintzy living room.

'It's very important,' she said, as the person on the other end let her get a word in. 'I need to get in touch with him this morning...'

She waved me through to the kitchen as she talked.

I've never been a morning person. I glowered, but did what she said. I didn't even care that I was naked in a stranger's house. I'd got over that one a long time ago.

In the kitchen Tony was wearing a powder blue fluffy shellsuit. The washing machine and dryer were going full pelt. Cilla Black was singing again as the washer flew off into a throbbing spin cycle. Tony was poking about in a packed leather holdall, stopped, looked up at me and grinned.

'Just giving your things a scrub,' he said, going over to the kettle. 'Debs said you both came away without any luggage, so I thought I'd...'

I hoisted myself awkwardly onto a chrome stool, which was cold. 'Yeah, cheers.'

I'd turned surly. What was I hoping to accomplish? Yet Tony responded to that with a small glow and set out breakfast things for me.

'You fell asleep right here. You must think we're awful - gossiping on all night.'

My head was still thick with dreams. Cilla seemed to be singing directly to me:

> 'Let me find you a place
> where the curs of this world can be buried away
> wipe that the smile off your face...'

or something.

'Who undressed me?'

He chuckled. No, he laughed. Chuckled is too smug. There was nothing smug about him. 'Don't worry - Debs did.' He gave me a funny look. 'She said she'd seen it all before.'

I looked down at my cup.

He apologised. 'I always say something wrong. It used to get me into trouble.'

That's right. On Saturday morning TV, on a panel judging and commenting jokily on other bands' videos, he'd come out with that line about Simon le Bon. Brenda, of all people, had said Simon le Bon had gone all porky. Tony had burst out with: 'I still wouldn't kick him out of bed for eating crisps.' And it was in the papers the next day. Reporters asking if he was gay - as if they'd never suspected.

'One slip of the tongue,' he was saying now, when I reminded him of the story, 'And it was laissez-faire.' He sat down opposite me. 'So I'm sorry if I embarrassed you. I should just walk around with a hob-nailed boot in my mouth. Debs explained that you and her aren't really ... together. That you're just friends, really.'

I nodded.

'Do you want an egg?' he asked hopefully.

I shook my head. He went to pop one on the boil anyway. 'I think it's nice,' he said, 'that people can sleep together and have a nice, sexy, safe time and still come through it as friends afterwards. That's how it should be.'

'Hm,' I said. Actually, I was thinking I'd prefer it if you never had to see that person ever again. That you could just get on with your own, boring, ordinary life afterwards. But, as I say, I'm not a morning kind of person and maybe in an hour or two I'd be excited again about visiting Tony (my early adolescent wank-fantasy, after all). Maybe.

'Who's Debs phoning?' I asked. 'She seemed all wound up and red in the face.'

He looked very serious. 'Clive.'

'Oh.' We both looked away. The mention of Clive put a distance between us, as if he was the real thing, somehow. Clive was someone with a connection to Debs that put the two of us in the shade.

'It's necessary, she said.' Tony did a kind of facial shrug. 'She's right. We have to be united on this.'

I realised they had talked further and more seriously into the night than I'd thought.

He nodded. 'We're getting the whole band together. That's what we've decided.'

He pushed the local paper under my nose. Shelley Sommers was on the cover of this one, too. In the photo she was coming out of a nightclub, looking a bit sweaty. And with her, arms around her tiny shoulders, was an older woman with a dark bob: *Brenda Maloney. Let's Be Famous Again!* the headline said.

'Debs is right,' Tony said. 'If this Shelley Sommers person can make a fortune out of our song, out of our band, then we ought to, as well. We have to put all of the differences of the past behind us, and be ready to reform.'

'Right...' I said. 'What's Brenda doing, knocking about with Shelley Sommers?'

In the photo Brenda's head was flung back and she was laughing like she was feral. She was apparently enjoying the company of her new protege. Brenda wore a far more spontaneous, unguarded look than she did on the telly, when she hosted her game show or occasionally supervised the drawing of the balls for the lottery.

'Shelley Sommers is going to be on the telly with Brenda this Saturday. On this *Kiddies in Krisis* telethon thing. She's debuting her travesty version of our song. Of Debs' song.' Tony's voice was curiously hard.

'It might not be a travesty.'

'Course it will,' he snapped. Then softened. 'All I know is,

Debs is being ripped off. She'll make next to no money out of it. Her agent's a twat and she hasn't had proper management for years. None of us have. Not since Roy went. So we have to club together and make our presence known, so we don't get taken for a ride.'

'You're going to cash in on their cashing in?'

'Exactly.' He listened for any signs of life from the hallway. 'If we can pull it off.'

'So you're packing?' I looked at the holdall. Soft Italian leather. Everything in the kitchen seemed to be Italian.

'Yes,' he said guardedly. 'That's the next problem. My partner, Kris.'

'He doesn't want you to go.'

Tony sighed. 'He doesn't want me to go anywhere, ever. He's very protective.'

'What'll he say?'

'God knows. He's a bit eccentric.'

I drank the last of my coffee from the bowl. I chewed on the gritty dregs for a moment. 'Can I get a shower?'

'Top landing,' he said. 'Third door on the right. Don't get the wrong one and wake Kris, for gawd's sake. He's murder in the morning.' Tony shuddered. He looked terribly nervous over this whole thing.

'You don't have to do this. You can just let these people - Shelley Sommers, or whoever - cash in. You don't have to become famous again. People remember you anyway...'

But I didn't say it.

What did I know anyway? I was in the wrong town. I felt sticky with sleep. And I wanted to wash my hair.

'When your things are dry, I'll leave them out on the landing.'

'Thanks.'

After my shower, I found he'd done just that.

Yesterday's outfit was clean and still warm, neatly folded and waiting. I couldn't believe Tony had been folding up my jeans and ironing (ironing!) my shirt and my Calvin Kleins. He'd bundled my socks into a little ball.

Chapter Six

That first night in the city, Brenda Maloney dreamed that the streets and canals of Venice were filled with apes. It was the wine and the rich food that had done it.

On arrival here they had descended on a small square and they had dined outside at dusk - the band, the video film crew and the people from that ridiculous TV show. A whole horde of them, chattering away, when what Brenda really wanted to do was explore the dark city alone.

It was interesting to Brenda, though, hearing what the TV crew talked about.

Of all the things they had seen and talked about yesterday, it had to be the monkeys that stuck in her mind. (Over dinner Tony had been perplexed over the question of whether monkeys had hair or fur. And what did dogs have? Cats? Horses? It was the kind of question Tony lent a lot of thought to.)

To Brenda, it was as if sleep came washing into her head when she could no longer hold it back and it carried off all but one or two thoughts, which created a tideline around the inside of her skull. A scummy residue, and it was this that she had to put up with all night.

In the case of her first night in Venice, it was the spectacle of apes lurching and shambling over humpbacked bridges and trailing their arms over smooth stone banisters. Chattering and nipping at each other (Brenda's dreams were always full of conflict, for some reason), the apes were wearing Edwardian period costume, playing out some Simian drama for her benefit. Apes standing on gondalas, braced on hairy legs above the warm green water. Apes in stripey jumpers, wielding their massive oars with expert care.

In the morning - a fine, steamy morning that caught her breath as she stepped out of their hotel - she couldn't let go of her dream.

I have an extremely vivid imagination, she told herself; a very visual imagination. The director of the video they had come here to shoot had told her exactly this yesterday. To pass time on the plane she had described some of her more convoluted nightmares to him. She had been waiting to hear him say, 'You should be in pictures,' or some such nonsense, but he didn't.

She knew this morning that she wanted to tell him this monkey dream because, really, some of the images from it should be incorporated into their video, which was supposed to be a magical, fantastic affair, after all.

Brenda set off round the backstreets, with only a sketchy knowledge of where she was. She was determined to get another string to her bow, and felt that this camera crew held the key. She thought she should maybe be behind the camera, behind the scenes.

Or better still; in front of the camera, presenting.

With skills like those, she would be prepared when the bottom finally fell out of her current career (as it surely would.)

She knew the production team would all be in a certain off-licence that served breakfast, quite close to the hotel. They'd been talking about it last night, before everyone trooped off, exhausted, to their rooms. She was still smarting from being given a pokey room at the back of the hotel, while the others all seemed to have ones with arched windows facing out on the Grand Canal. They wouldn't appreciate the view. She knew they wouldn't.

Sure enough, the directions were right and there was the off-licence, across a canal from a small boat yard.

At the tall bar inside she found the soundman and the director with chunky looking sandwiches and small glasses of pale pink wine.

'For breakfast?' she winced.

'It's 5p a glass,' said the director. 'It's locally made and very fortifying.'

She leaned against the bar and abstractedly rubbed Ambre Solaire into the tops of her arms as she waited for the owner to come over. He was busy fiddling with the bottles that lined every yard of the walls, all the way up to the ceiling.

Funny place to have breakfast. She was feeling bilious. She let the director, Mitch, order for her in his halting Italian and then she launched into a description of her monkey dream and how images from it might come in useful for the video.

'You said you were interested in my dreams,' she finished.

'Yes,' he said.

In the morning light, she thought, he actually looked a bit of a grubby man, stuffed in an old cardy with wisps of white hair coming through the neck of his polo shirt. One of those blokes where you can't tell where stubble finishes and chest hair begins. Never mind.

'Where would we get monkeys from?' he asked.

Brenda hesitated.

'See?' he said. 'You have to think of practicalities like that if you want to get on in this business. If you want to see your dreams on that screen.'

The soundman was nodding and sipping his pink wine, rather genteely.

'Anyway,' said Mitch. 'I can't see what monkeys have to do with this song of yours.'

'It's not my song,' said Brenda tightly. 'It's Debbie's.'

'The band's song,' he said. 'What's it called? 'When I am an Angel'? What's that got to do with monkeys?'

Brenda's drink arrived and she slurped at it self-consciously. Her stomach growled in protest.

'You can't get carried away in this business,' said the director. 'We have a very tight brief for this. Get you lot onto gondalas and bridges in a variety of get-ups - Tony doing his solo spot as an angel - the rest of you as Harlequin, Colombine and what-have-you. Get you all dicking about, a spot of night filming, a few fireworks and mist ...'

The soundman put in, 'All of that's complicated enough, without bringing your dressed-up monkeys into it.'

'And then,' said Mitch, 'we still have to include them two brats and their mother from that TV show. Dress them up as a heavenly choir and sail them around on a canal. No, we've got enough to be thinking about, without you going all artistic as well, Brenda, love.'

She swallowed hard, furious. This was her video, wasn't it? She was one quarter of the band it was meant to promote. Why shouldn't she put in her own ideas? She was the one on the line here, doing the performing.

'I just thought I'd tell you my idea,' she mumbled.

Mitch shrugged. 'Well, thanks.'

She glanced over his shoulder then, as Derek Strand came into the bar. He wore shades and a shellsuit with leg warmers; a hotel towel around his neck. He grinned and spread his hands.

'I knew you'd all be in here.' He glanced Brenda up and down. 'And a lovely lady, too. This is a bonus.'

Brenda smiled. 'Morning, Mr Strand.'

He wanted whisky and, still looking at her, ordered, and nipped the end off a cigar. 'You want to be in telly, don't you, Brenda?'

She gasped. 'How could you tell?'

'All the questions you were asking me on the train yesterday. I can tell ambition like that a mile off.' He wrinkled his burst-veined nose. 'I can smell it on you, Ms Maloney.'

She rubbed at her bare arms again and suppressed a shudder. 'Well, good,' she said. 'I can't see this band malarkey lasting much longer. I think I'm a natural for the box. Doing anything. I'm sure I could.' She beamed at him. 'You're the expert, though, Mr Strand. You should know.'

He jabbed his cigar at her, making her blink. 'You're right,' he growled. 'Ten years this show of mine's been going. I know Light Entertainment inside out. I know what telly's about.'

'And have I got it?'

'You might have.'

She shrank back a little.

Who was he to tell her anything? He thought he was fantastic. One poxy little show and he thought he was god. It was a crappy programme anyway, with a clumsy title - *Derek'll Sort It All Out* - on which he made children's dreams come true.

Here they all were in Venice, because some brats had written in, saying they wanted to be in a video with Things Fall Apart. Two whingey sodding twins who had recently lost their daddy in a tragic accident, and their pasty-faced mother, tagging around with them for a week. And it was all because of Derek Strand and his crappy TV show and because the nasty old letch wanted a free week in Venice.

She could see it was a corrupt world that she was eager to be in on.

'What would I have to do to switch careers?'

'Ah, well,' he said, warming his glass and lifting up his shades to reveal pinkish, sensitive eyes. 'You're a step ahead already. The public know your face. You, Brenda Maloney, might just get an easier ride than most.'

She brightened. 'Really?'

'You might,' he chuckled, 'get a very easy ride indeed.'

Tony popped next door to see what Debs' room was like. He found her sitting at a wickerwork table, staring at the canal and pulling petals off a rose, the ruins of breakfast set out before her.

'Hey,' he said. 'You've got Michaelangelo's David on the wall behind your bed.' He looked at the mural. 'I should be in this room.'

Debs shrugged.

'Where's Clive?'

'Showering.'

'Isn't it fantastic?' He hurried over, kissed her good morning, and eagerly sat down to get the view from her window. 'They've really done us proud this time. After years of grotty clubs and motorway services and shopping centres and TV studios, we've actually come somewhere nice to work.'

'Hm,' said Debs.

'Sitting here,' he grinned, rolling up his white sleeves, 'I actually feel, for once, like a successful pop star. Sitting in a palace with the water rubbing up against the window.' He shook out his hair, still damp from the shower.

A vaporetto crammed with passengers went sailing by and he whistled at them, waving both arms.

Debs watched as a couple of older women on board flung out their arms to him enthusiastically.

'They responded *con brio*,' he said.

He's just showing off, she thought. Sitting there with his shirt unbuttoned, waving like royalty out of the hotel window.

'I've been doing that all morning,' he said. 'It's really like being famous.'

'You could cause an accident,' Debs said. 'It's just the same as waving at buses and taxis on the High Street. Imagine sitting here and watching one of those big old water bus things smashing into a bridge just because you distracted the driver by waving. You'd feel terrible.'

But Tony was off again, waving at the next one. 'I'd just pull the curtains and pretend it wasn't me,' he said. 'They'd never trace it back to your particular window. There are hundreds of windows along these palace fronts.'

It was true, thought Debs. Arriving yesterday, they'd all looked like crumbling slabs of cake to her, pushed up together. The windows were dark, inscrutable slits.

'Thank god there aren't excitable tourists waving out of every one of them,' she said.

'We're special,' he said. 'Friendlier. Stars.' He turned back to look at her. He was more handsome here, she thought. In this light, with his stubble lit up golden. Italy was doing him some good. His skin seemed to shine.

She knew that she, on the other hand, looked washed out. Only ten minutes ago she'd been throwing up. Clive had done his nut, having to shower in a bathroom that still smelled of her vomit.

'I've got to thank you, Debs,' Tony said, 'for all of this. You've made this trip for me.'

'How?'

'You wrote the song for me. You're letting me have my moment.'

'You deserve it. Anyway, you won that fan club poll for the most popular member. You should have a star moment.'

'You know what I mean,' he said. 'I'd never be anyone without you, Debs.'

She was embarrassed but pleased. She looked back at the canal and saw a bus almost empty. There was only one couple aboard and they were inside, under glass, facing front. He had his arm protectively around his wife and there was no chance of their waving back to Tony.

'Why aren't they sat out on the nice bit at the back?' asked Tony. 'It's empty up there on top - the best seats. Why are they under the glass? It must be roasting hot in there...'

He really can't understand, thought Debs. That's me. I'd be like them. Picking the most sensible place to sit; inside, covered from the elements. Not too conspicuous. Certainly not throwing out my arms to the hotel windows and waving. That would be me: not getting the full experience.

Tony reached across the console table and the wreckage of her breakfast to take her hand. 'I'm glad I met you, Debbie Now. You've made all the difference to my life.'

Her eyes filled up immediately. 'It's no good, Tone. I have to tell you...'

'What?'

The bathroom door flew open and Clive came out in billows of steam; glistening, lobster pink, stark naked. He tutted at Tony. 'I thought you'd be in here. Checking out whether we had a better view.'

Tony looked at Debs and her eyes were dry suddenly. She'd managed to blink back her tears.

'You might well have the better view,' Tony told him, turning back to Clive and taking the opportunity to look him over.

'It's gunna be a long day,' Clive said. 'And we have to look after fucking kids and pretend we're enjoying it. Two film crews and fucking kids following us about, as we dress up as frigging angels and stuff and mime along to a bloody song about you, Tony.' Clive rubbed his balls thoughtfully. 'A fucking long day.'

Tony smiled. 'Sounds good to me.'

'Yeah, well. The kids are evil and so's Derek Strand.' Clive towelled his hair. 'The mother's okay, though. Looks a bit like Lady Di.'

The day's shooting went on and Tony and the others grew hot and self-conscious in their fancy dress, attracting stares from passersby. The two kids from *Derek'll Sort it All Out* became bored. Derek was having nothing to do with them until the moments he had to appear on film with them, pointing out landmarks and patting them on the head.

'He's such an objectionable man,' Tony said, adjusting his strap-on wings as they sat having a break with ice creams.

'He's all right,' Brenda said.

Debs was quiet. One look at the huge, multi-coloured cornets the others were cramming into their mouths had set off her stomach again.

'It's hopeless,' said Tony. 'We're trying to shoot two things at once at the height of summer in Venice. It's bound to be a shambles.'

'It's a very professional crew,' said Brenda. 'They'll do it. We just have to stand where they want us and do what they tell us and it'll work out fine.'

Clive laughed. 'Which one are you nobbing, Brenda? You know a lot about how telly crews work, suddenly.'

It was true, Brenda had been observing and commenting on the technicians' work all day.

She glowered at him.

They were sitting on a sun-warmed wall in their costumes, watching as Derek put a fatherly arm around the shoulders of the twin girls and was filmed pointing out the Rialto bridge to them. Their mother stood behind the crew, awkward and concerned.

'They want us in next,' said Debs. 'We've got to come walking round the corner and meet them, as if it's all a big surprise and we've made their dreams come true.'

'Bollocks,' said Clive. He looked at her. 'You know, you look terrible, Debs. You look green.'

'The colour of the canals,' put in Brenda.

'I'm all right.'

Some kind of fracas had broken out amongst the crew. Derek Strand was storming away from the kids. Left alone at the water's edge in their yellow-knitted jackets, the two kids looked like abandoned chicks. Their mother dashed over to them.

'Apparently,' said Brenda, 'those are two very badly behaved kids. Derek says they're driving him mad. They swear like troupers and keep doing it on tape. He points out some spectacular view - like on the plane yesterday when they were filming - and these two little brats take one look and go, 'Bugger me! Look at that!' She shuddered. 'Badly brought up, if you ask me. I'd tan their hides.'

'If you ask me,' Debs shot back, 'It's a good job you haven't got kids, Brenda Maloney. You'd be a rotten mother. You're just out for yourself. You're a selfish cow.' With that, Debs slid off the wall and hurried away in her Pierot costume.

'Debs?' Clive shouted.

'What's wrong with her?' Brenda said. 'What brought that on?'

'I'll go after her,' said Tony, jumping up.

'Leave her be,' Clive said. 'She's been funny ever since we got here.'

Brenda looked smug. 'Roy will sort her out. He'll sort this whole thing out and get us through.'

'Oh,' said Tony, 'I'd forgotten. He arrives this afternoon, doesn't he?'

Brenda nodded. 'And he'll sort out Debs' attitude problem and everything else.'

She turned to see Clive walking over to the film crew, taking loping strides, full of confidence, even in his doublet and hose. Then he was chatting away with the mother of twins under the silver umbrellas and the microphone boom. The mother flicked her blonde hair away from her face and, in a few moments, they were laughing.

'Roy will sort it all out,' Brenda said, 'when he turns up this afternoon.'

Tony gave her a worried smile. 'He always does, doesn't he?'

Debs came back in time for the afternoon's shoot: a gondala ride with the kids and a mollified (and drunk) Derek Strand down a more obscure green canal that smelled of damp wool.

They had three black gondalas yoked together and two guitarists and a singer performing arias for them. Debs held her stomach in and tried to smile as they sailed back and forth under the same dark, dripping bridge and were filmed from above.

Tony kept patting her and rubbing her back, but it didn't do any good. She glanced across to where Clive sat, beside the kids' mother on the next gondala and she could see from there that he was rubbing his leg against hers the whole time.

Brenda was, meanwhile, giving it all she had, plumping up her cleavage for the cameramen above and grinning beatifically, making sure she had screen presence. Derek Strand sat chewing on a cigar with the two kids who were supposed to be having the time of their lives.

'It's wank, this,' Debs heard one of the little girls say.

The other one looked as sickly as Debs felt. She looked up as they came by for yet another shot and the gondoliers started singing again and then she saw Roy's face glaring down at them. She jumped in surprise. He was in his auburn wig and what looked like a Marks and Spencers summer maternity frock. He looked appalled at the spectacle below.

Debs nudged Tony. Tony looked up. 'Christ,' he said.

Roy didn't look very pleased at all.

This isn't how it was all supposed to be, thought Debs. This song was a quiet ballad, an album track; a little showcase for Tony and his voice, which had improved no end this last year. But the record company had taken it and decided that because it was about angels, it should be their Christmas single and have oodles of cash pumped into it. Debs hated the over-produced monstrosity it had become; a full orchestra, shimmering sound effects, angelic choruses and little girls intoning a haunting rhyme about heaven in its closing moments.

'A sure-fire frigging number one,' Roy had said. 'You'll see. This'll be your great fucking Christmas Number One. If you get that - if any band gets that - then you're immortal. Look at Slade. You'll be in the charts every fucking Christmas and it'll be played in shopping centres and on the radio every year from here till frigging doomsday.'

But they had taken Tony's tremulous ballad about mortality and self-doubt and made it into a kind of glittering Busby Berkley affair. Debs was already dreading the night filming, tomorrow night, with the fireworks and all the boys dressed up as angels, with Tony, rapturous, at their head. The storyboards looked nauseating.

What Roy had neglected to mention - and what Debs suspected - was that, if you have a hugely-indulgent song like this under your belt, your days are numbered.

This was the kind of success that some bands went out on.

There was a disturbance on the gondala in front, where the kids and Derek and Brenda were sitting. One of the kids was saying something into the mike; something that had wiped the smile off Brenda's face. She was shouting it now and Brenda was rising up off the satin cushions.

'You're not my favourite, anyway,' the kid was bawling. 'Tony's my favourite. You're just a fat cow.'

Brenda slapped the kid hard about the face.

'Right!' Roy screamed from up on the bridge, even before the director could call, 'Cut!'

'That's it!'

They were dragged to the side of the canal and the gondoliers and guitarists looked mystified. Roy supervised the disembarking and simmered with rage in his summery frock.

Stepping up out of the gondala, Debs felt her vision begin to swim and she called out Clive's name once, before falling into a dead faint on the wet stone.

'Brenda's being a fucking bitch,' Roy said. 'She wants out.' He was crumbling dry bread onto his side plate. 'Well, none of you spoiled bastards are irreplaceable. She'll find that out.'

Roy was raising his voice and others in the tiny trattoria were staring. He was conspicuous enough in his summer dress.

Tony looked down and smoothed the gingham table cloth.

A quiet dinner out for the two of them. It felt ominous to Tony.

'She wants to go into telly, doesn't she?' Roy growled. 'And now she's sucking that creep Derek Strand's cock.' His eyes flashed at Tony. 'The only cock any of you lot need to suck is mine. You all know that.' He shook his massive head. 'This hook-up with Strand's show was a mistake.'

Bravely, Tony said, 'Debs thinks this whole video's a mistake...'

'Does she?' grunted Roy. 'She'll see. She'll fucking see. She'll thank me one day.' He seemed to relent. 'When she's fifty-odd and haggard she'll have this bit of film of you lot at your most beautiful in Venice. Yeah, dressed up like frigging ponces and singing a pretentious bloody song ... but you'll be luminous. You'll see.'

Tony smiled.

They were in a trattoria on the left bank that Roy knew of old. It was homely, ersatz, down at heel; waitressed by a gaggle of what Roy called amiable ex-whores; wizened, motherly types in stained aprons. Their particular waitress had rather large hands, and spindly arms and legs. She looked almost simian, with thin, dyed black hair. She never batted an eyelash at the sight of the huge, bewigged Roy. She simply clasped him like an old friend and winked at Tony and pinched his cheek. She brought him a rose and quoted Shakespeare in Italian to him. Tony blushed and felt honoured.

The waitress mixed up their orders and every dish of every course that she tottered over with was wrong. She set her head at an angle, put her hands on her hips and sighed. 'Oh ... taglietelle, lasagne ... it is all the same.' Then she took a cigarette off Tony, pinching his cheek again. Roy was shovelling up his nondescript pasta with relish.

Tony glanced sideways into a mirror that had a disturbingly cheerful clown painted on it.

Luminous? Beautiful?

'You're all at your prime,' Roy said, looking up and catching him. 'You're all great.'

'Thanks, Roy.'

'You're past that awkward, gawky stage like when you started out. You've grown into yourselves. You've got confidence now. You especially, Tony. I've seen this happen before to girls and boys like you lot.' He put down his fork and dabbed his lips with a paper napkin. 'It's all downhill from here on in.'

Tony's heart sank slightly.

'Oh, you've a couple of years left in you.'

'What if Brenda wants out?'

'We get another fat-arsed tart in. No one'll notice.'

'Oh.' Tony was surprised. He couldn't imagine the rest of them welcoming someone entirely new. The four of them had been together from the start. It would be too weird. They didn't get on like the best of pals - but they were used to each other, at least.

'No, the one I'm really frigging worried about,' said Roy, with a soft belch, 'is that Debbie.'

'Debs?' Tony looked down. Debs had gone back to her hotel room for the afternoon and the twin crews had worked on shots she wouldn't be needed for. It was meant to be exhaustion she had - what with the heat and all - and an afternoon's rest would do her good. Tony knew there was more to it, though no one was saying anything. Roy voicing his doubts now, over their little dinner for two, made Tony's suspicions come flooding back.

'She's up the fucking duff,' Roy said. 'Silly moo.'

'She's told you..?' She hadn't said a word to Tony - her oldest pal - but now it was out in the open, it made perfect sense.

'Course she hasn't,' Roy snapped. 'Even that dopey bloody Clive hasn't got a clue yet. Mind, he's too caught up in trying to shag the arse off those kiddies' mother tonight.'

'What?'

'With Debs safely put away for the afternoon, he's been running around with that one, while the twins were off filming.'

'Clive wouldn't...'

'You're fucking dopey, as well, Tony. Clive's been shagging all sorts of tarts, wherever we've been. He always has.'

Tony's eyes widened. 'Does Debs know?'

'Course she does. That's why she's so worried about being up the stick. She thinks he'll fuck off, soon as she tells him, and she's probably right. Fucking toe rag. Oh, I can see the fear in her eyes.' Roy winced. 'I've got an instinct for these things.'

Tony had an impulse to get up and leave. 'I have to see her.'

Roy clamped a fat hand on his wrist. 'Don't be fucking daft. She doesn't need you. She just needs a sleep. It's another long day tomorrow.'

Tony sat back, taking it all in. He said at last, 'If Brenda runs off to be on the telly, and Debs is pregnant and Clive leaves her ... that's the end of it all, isn't it?'

Roy swirled his pinot grigio round and stared down into it, watching the grainy sediment. 'Could be. Could well be, Tony, love.'

'And this - this *fiasco* we're filming - could be our swansong.'

Roy shrugged. 'Not a bad thing to go out on. A Christmas single at Number One. Fannying about on gondalas dressed as angels. I'd say that was a pretty good swansong.'

'We've only had four years ...' said Tony. 'We're only just getting successful ... after everything.'

'That's how it goes, sometimes,' said Roy. 'Anyway,' he smacked his magenta lips and clicked his fingers for the bill. 'We know fuck all for sure just yet. Wait and see, pie.'

He settled back and Tony allowed himself a rebellious thought: You're grotesque.

'You've exploited us. You've run us right into the ground.'

Roy's lip lifted into a snarl.

'You've always known this,' he told Tony. 'That one of these days your time will run out. One of these days I'll have to let you drop. I made you stars and then, suddenly, it will have to stop. You knew that.'

'We've hardly done anything yet...'

Roy sighed. 'You'll see in the end. You've had a lot out of me. A whole load of good stuff. This video you're filming now - it'll make you a star in your own right. Use it, Tony. Use us all and all the opportunities before you. Think of yourself, you silly bugger.'

Roy scrunched a handful of foreign notes into their waitress's spidery hands. She scuttled off.

'I thought we were still having fun,' said Tony sadly. 'All of us together.'

'You might be. I might be.' Roy shrugged. 'The others aren't. They've grown up. Marriage trouble, babies, ideas for further careers. That's the fuck-awful world they live in, Tony. A grown-up world you'll never be part of. No wonder you can still enjoy yourself.'

Tony looked down.

Roy touched his hands again. 'My friends here - these nice ladies - always fix me up while I'm here.'

Tony looked up, into a blurry view of Roy. 'What?'

Roy widened his eyes and smirked. 'Boys,' he mouthed. 'Good, old-fashioned Venetian boys, with webbed-feet and salt water in their delectable veins. They always sort me out. And they'll be waiting for us, just outside the hotel. Two clean-limbed Italian boys with few scruples and whangers like babies' arms.'

Tony shook his head. 'I just want to rest.'

Roy grabbed his upper arm. 'Two of them, Tony.' He helped him up. 'We're going back and we're going back to my little appartment. I've a nice big bed and cherubs all over the wall. A great frigging mural of God making man behind the headboard. The perfect setting. We're taking some of this nice pinot grigio and I'm going to sit in my chair by the window overlooking the canal, and you and these two nice local boys are going to keep me diverted all night.'

'I can't do this anymore, Roy...'

Roy laughed and marched him out of the restaurant, waving airily at the waitresses. 'Yes you fucking can, sunshine. It's part of your job - keeping me entertained.'

The alley outside was dark by now; filled with the unnatural, overlapping sounds of the canals.

'I want to stop playing your games, Roy. They scare me. I want my own life. I want to find someone for myself...'

Roy shook his head. 'You love it. You love me being there. You love the boys I fetch for you. You'll love these two tonight.'

'I won't.'

Roy turned savagely and Tony ducked, expecting a slap.

Instead, Roy touched his cheek gently. 'I've missed you this last week. Even just this week, while I've been in London, away from you, I've missed you, Tony. I haven't seen you strip for me. I haven't seen you hard. I've missed that smile you do, and the way you shudder, when you come...'

Roy chuckled and shook his head. 'Can't you see, Tony? It's you who's the one with all the power. You've got power over me.'

He laid his bare, heavy arm over Tony's shoulders and led him back, at a leisurely pace, to their hotel on the Grand Canal.

Chapter Seven

'He will see us, after all,' Debs said. 'Apparently, he's managed to find a window.' Her face was thunderous.

Tony was whipping up some lunch; tomatoes, mozarella, olive bread. He'd nipped to the deli round the corner, leaving me alone in the house with Debs fulminating through her phone call and his still-unglimpsed partner hanging around upstairs.

'A *window*?' Tony cried. 'For his ex-wife?'

'It was his personal assistant I talked to,' she said. 'He was in a meeting.'

'A meeting!' said Tony, slicing bread roughly.

'What is it he's doing now?' I asked.

'Managing,' she said and perched herself on a stool, scowling.

I didn't think I should ask what exactly it was he was managing.

She went on. 'He's in some village in Yorkshire. Near Halifax. We're to go there and see him at nine tomorrow morning. He can spare us half an hour.'

Tony shook his head. 'I'll open a bottle of wine. Anyone ready for a drink?'

'Yes,' she said. 'Half an hour!'

'Well,' said Tony. 'He'll give us longer when he hears what all of this is about.'

I said, 'I thought Clive was still making records. He is, isn't he?'

I was trying to move the conversation on, but I could see from the looks on their faces that I'd said the wrong thing.

'Occasionally,' Debs said.

'If you can call them that,' Tony added. 'They're not what I'd call pop.'

'I've never heard them,' Debs said.

'Oh, I have,' said Tony. 'I even bought the last one.' He went to a rack of shiny CDs on the window sill. 'It was the soundtrack to that TV series about eskimos and what-have-you. All the original instruments made out of reindeer hide and bones and that. Shall I put it on?'

Debs grimaced. 'No.'

Tony glanced at me. 'It's a far cry from what he was doing with us.'

'And he's managing people as well?' I asked.

Debs looked at me crossly. 'Yes, he's very successful. He's still in good work.'

There was a crippling silence.

Tony shrugged and went on shredding basil leaves. 'I'm not working. I get enough from residuals for my few wants and so does old Kris upstairs.'

'Kris gets residuals too?' I asked.

Tony nodded proudly. 'More than I do. He was in a band, too.'

Furiously I set to thinking who Kris might be. And thinking, what an odd world to live in; where everyone in your ken used to be well-known and isn't now.

'And I,' said a steely-voiced Debbie Now, 'have to eke out my miserable life getting complete tossers up to sing karaoke.'

Tony gasped. 'Karaoke! Oh, Debs - you aren't...'

'Um,' she said. 'But it was only to help my mam out and to keep my hand in. In the restaurant, you know.'

'Oh,' said Tony.

'She's very good,' I said. 'She got me and all my work-mates up, singing...'

'I'll bet she's good at it,' Tony smiled proudly. 'She's used to letting others share her limelight. She was always generous like that. But don't the punters recognise you, Debs? When you get up there?'

For a second it seemed she was about to lie. You could see her, deciding not to. 'No one did,' she sighed. 'Except my new friend here.'

I beamed at this.

'Tuck in, everyone,' Tony said and fetched out chunky tumblers for the wine.

'No one ever recognises me, either,' he said, once we were all sitting round. 'It's incredible. But I've thought it over. When we were famous, it was, like, in the early Eighties, wasn't it? We all wore thick make-up and, like, pantomime clothes.'

'Space outfits,' Debs shuddered.

'Angel costumes,' he laughed. 'And then we had that leather S+M type gear for *Top of the Pops* that time.' He whistled between his small, square teeth. 'Dunno how we got away with it. Anyway, what I think is, because we were always dressing up and that and we had all that big hair, then it was like we were in disguise. We look too plain now. We look too natural.'

Debs pulled a face. 'Maybe you're right.'

Tony was obviously in the grip of an idea he'd thought long and hard about. 'No, it's true. We fell out of fashion when all that artificiality went down the pan; when all the dressing up stopped. In the late Eighties and early Nineties ... well, it was all about the Natural Look, wasn't it?' He crammed tomato and mozarella into his mouth. 'No more hair gel and spray. No more man-made fibres.'

'But we could have been natural!' Debs protested. 'We could have gone like that ... if we'd known...'

'Too late,' he said. 'Remember the last show we did? Remember how out of it we felt?'

'We'd been on a treadmill,' she said. 'No wonder we lost track of the world.' She shook her head savagely. 'But the music was always natural,' she said. 'It had real soul, didn't it? Even under the sparkly production and the gloss...' She winced. 'Underneath that, the words were ... naked and real. Weren't they?'

'Yes,' I said, scared she would start to cry. 'Of course they were.'

'That's not how they came across, lovey,' Tony said. 'Not to the punters out there.'

Debs stared, horrified, into the deep pale green of her wine. 'Shite,' she said.

Tony gave a self-deprecating giggle. 'There's this show on Radio Two on a Sunday night. We listen to a lot of radio round here, me and Kris. Anyway, they do this thing - One Hit Wonders - and what they do is, phone up someone who was a One Hit Wonder; someone that people would be interested to hear about. Where they ended up ... what they're doing now...'

Debs was looking at him narrowly.

'Well, one week, they read out a letter and it was someone asking where the members of Things Fall Apart had gone to. What had become of them.'

Debs' eyebrows shot up. 'We weren't One Hit Wonders!'

He nodded and laughed.

'We had *nine* top ten chart hits!' she said, her voice going up. 'We recorded three studio LPs!'

Tony rolled his eyes. 'You don't have to tell me.'

'What were they talking about on Radio 2, then?' she demanded. 'One Hit Wonders! I hope someone put them right.'

Tony banged down his glass, still laughing. 'No! They didn't! They just started this whole conversation, in the studio, the daft DJ and the girl who answered the phones. They were coming out with all sorts of rubbish.' He was creased up with laughter. 'They said I'd died of AIDS or I'd been beaten up and killed in funny circumstances. They knew about Brenda, of course, because she'd become even more famous on the telly and all...'

'What did they say about me?' Debs asked, steel in her voice.

Tony flinched. 'Nothing.'

'Nothing at all?'

He gave a tiny shake of his head. 'So anyway, Kris was nagging on me. He was going, phone them, phone them up and tell them that you're not dead and that you were more than a one hit wonder...'

Debs banged the table. She was getting quite worked up over Tony's story. 'Good for Kris.'

'He was egging me on to greater folly,' said Tony. 'I phoned up and they wouldn't believe me at first, when I said who I was.'

'God,' she said.

'They believed me eventually and I got to talk to the DJ and I put him right about a few things. He said he was glad I wasn't dead.'

Debs stared at him.

'And you know what? I was really excited. I was standing in that hallway at the foot of our stairs, talking away into our trimphone like I was on MTV or something. Kris was in the living room, listening to me on the radio. I thought I was great. They even dug out the single of 'Let's Be Famous' and played it, there and then. It was like a proper interview.'

I was smiling, but Debs looked stricken.

'This DJ,' Tony said, 'he asked me if I was still singing. And I kind of laughed and said ... I said, 'Only in the bath these days.'' He shook his head.

'Why?' Debs gasped.

'Because that's the only time I do get to sing these days!' he burst. 'It's true! I only sing in the bloody bath. I can't even carry a tune anymore. My voice has all gone. And I told him that, this DJ, live on Radio 2. It was out of my mouth before I could even think.'

Debs was aghast. 'You told him you couldn't sing anymore?'

He looked down. 'This DJ said he was very sorry to hear that. He was sure it wasn't true. He asked me if that meant there was never any chance of Things Fall Apart getting together again, for a comeback tour - just like everyone else has done.'

Debs touched his hand. 'What did you say?'

'I said No. Never.'

We absorbed this for a second and then Tony seemed to come t his senses. He jerked upright. 'I haven't taken Kris his lunch upstairs.'

'Can't he come down?' I asked.

Tony gave a tight shake of his head. 'Not while he's dressing. It takes him till this time in the day to prepare himself.'

'Every day?'

'Every day,' said Tony stiffly. 'He's still an artist.' He went to the side, where Kris's tray was laid out ready, with a small vase of blue-bells from the garden brightening it up.

Debs looked at Tony steadily. 'Will you tell him, now, when you go up, that you're coming with us?'

Tony made for the door. 'I'm not sure.'

'You'll have to do it soon. If Clive wants to see us tomorrow...'

'Look,' Tony snapped. 'I'm not sure, Debs...'

She stood up. 'You mean you're not sure about us getting back together?'

'It's hard, all right? It's harder for me than it is for you.'

With that, he was gone, hurrying into the hall and up the stairs.

'How does he know?' Debs muttered, not even looking at me. 'How does he know it's harder for him?'

Debs and me took a ride into town, just to get out of Tony's hair. They obviously had a sticky conversation coming up round his house. Debs knew more about it than I did. She'd sat up much of the night, talking with Tony, and his relationship had come into that.

Tony seemed relieved that we could take care of ourselves and didn't need looking after. He'd changed into leather trousers and a vest and a studded cap when he came down with a back door key we could borrow.

'Kris likes me to wear this lot when I'm hoovering round,' he said.

'Right,' said Debs, taking the key off him.

We got the minibus at the end of his street, with a couple of old grans and some skiving school kids.

'I always took the bus,' Debs said brightly, as we sat ourselves at the back. 'Even when I could afford not to. Beause it's where you hear real life. Some of my best lines come from things I heard, riding round on the buses.'

'Really?'

'Really. You know the line that goes, '*Don't worry sweetheart / It'll work out fine / Don't worry sweetheart / All it takes is time...*'? I heard that on a bus, once. I wrote it down.'

I smiled. 'Do you still keep your little leather book with you? The one your mother gave you?'

'Not anymore.' She shook her head. 'It was full up.'

We got off at the end of the prom, where the fair was.

Blackpool was slack. It was a bright, chilled day, early in the season. We stood to watch empty carriages thunder through the Big Dipper, to prerecorded shrieks and squeals.

We wandered through the amusement arcades, accompanied by the tinkling and crashing of money, by cheap music played too loud.

'Maybe Tony's right about not being up to it anymore,' she said, walking close beside me. 'Maybe we have been left behind, after all.'

I didn't know what to say.

'Do you know what struck me?' she asked. 'When I looked at that list of all our singles in that book yesterday - all the titles ... I thought, well, they tell the whole story, don't they? As if we'd known ... as if I'd known, back then, what would happen to us. It's all in the titles. Remember When. The Good Old Times. Together Again. Leaving You (Behind Me). Lady Obscura. Those were some of our biggest hits. It's like we were made with a kind of...'

'Self-destruct mechanism,' I said.

She shivered and hunched into her blue furry coat as we walked back into the bright air of the prom. She tugged up her collar.

'What band was Kris in?'

We still hadn't seen the mysterious partner. He was upstairs, dressed and prepared for the day, but was busy at his computer, Tony had told us. He was dealing with his email correspondance, which was always heavy and involved.

'He maintains several websites,' Tony had explained.

'Sounds like a big spider!' Debs laughed and Tony gave her a funny look.

Now she was asking me, 'Do you remember the Dominators?'

I stopped walking. 'Kristopha Katastrophea?'

'That's the fella.' She smiled wistfully.

'But he was huge! They were massive!'

'That's right.'

'I thought they'd vanished in America ... on that big tour in the late Eighties...'

'They self-destructed,' she said, 'far more than we ever did. And Kris came slinking back home, hiding from the world. He's off the drugs and all that now, but, according to Tony, he's still dressing up every day. Still reinventing himself, even with no one to see it. Every day, Tony says, his creations become more and more outlandish.'

'With no one to see it? Only Tony?'

'Tony says Kris has moved beyond music ... even, beyond gender...' She shrugged. 'Whatever that means.'

'And they're together?'

Debs led the way across the road so we could lean on the rails and look at the sea, which was sludgy and manky-looking.

'They have been for years. I'm not sure it's good for Tony.'

'Not if Kris makes him dress up in leather-boy outfits all the time...'

Debs counted off on her fingers. 'And do all the housework, and cook all the meals, and run out for groceries and shop for all the bits and pieces Kris needs for his ridiculous costumes.'

'So Kris Katastrophea has turned himself into a living work of art...'

Debs chuckled. 'He might as well. His records were rubbish.'

'Actually, I loved them,' I said, before I could stop.

She turned to me.

'You're not really what you claim to be, are you, Tim?'

'What?' I was rumbled.

'My biggest fan. Things Fall Apart's biggest ever, most devoted fan.'

I flinched. 'Maybe not the biggest...' I leaned against the rail, paint flaking on the sleeves of my jacket. 'Really, Simon was. My ex. He was obsessed. That's how I know so much. By secondhand, really.'

'Secondhand,' she sighed and lit a cigarette. 'Thought so. Like every fucking thing.'

'Hey,' I said. 'Would you rather I'd never come along?'

'What,' she said, sounding frightened, 'are you going to go home?'

'No. There's nothing back home. I'd have lost my job anyway. I feel involved here.'

'I need your support, Tim. You mightn't be all excited, after all, at the prospect of meeting us all ... but you are a pal...'

'I am excited!' I said.

'Not as excited as a real, hardcore fan would be,' she said. 'That's how I knew you were fibbing to me. We always said we'd never come back. A real fan would be having kittens if they'd overheard what you have.'

'Sorry.'

'It's all right. So...' She tossed her ciggy onto the beach. 'Are you disappointed then?'

'What with?'

'That Tony's got a fella? A fella he's still in thrall to?'

I opened my mouth and she laughed.

'No, don't tell me. But I know you are. You were dying to meet our Tony. That's why you've kept along with me.'

'That wasn't it...'

'You thought you were in with a chance with the gorgeous Tone...'

'No I didn't...'

'You said you'd loved him as a kid - not the whole band. I believed that much, at least. And I've seen you looking at him in that kitchen, all morning. You were sat there like a little tom cat, preening yourself.'

Had I been? I hoped not. I didn't have the heart to tell her I didn't find Tony all that red hot in person. He came across a bit whingey and gone to seed. And that servant boy outfit had turned my stomach.

She linked arms with me and hustled me towards a chip shop. 'You might still be in with a chance,' she hissed conspiratorially. 'If we can manage to wrench him away from his domineering, queeny boyfriend. I'd rather see Tony with you than him...'

We ducked into the chip shop just as it started to rain.

'I'm still hungry,' she said. 'That was a tiny lunch he gave us. Let's have chips.'

At the counter there was a very tall black man in a striped pinny and cardboard hat. He was grinning broadly as Debs stepped up in her shaggy coat.

She blinked. 'What is it?' She fluffed at her damp hair.

The black man sighed. 'Debbie Now,' he said. 'Fancy you showing up here.'

Her eyes went wide. 'You recognise me?'

'Anywhere, hon. I'd recognise you anywhere.' He slapped the thick wad of newspaper for wrapping chips in. 'I can't believe this. Whatever you want, is on me!'

'We just want chips...'

'Just chips then - on the house!'

He made her sign a chip bag, which he said he would frame. He made her sign it to Timon, which I thought was a strange name, but I didn't say anything.

Outside, Debs was beaming and reeking of vinegar. We were both standing in the rain.

'That's it!' she said. 'That's decided me! They still recognise me, Tim. At least someone does. He did. We're going to do this, Tim! You've got to help me persuade Tony and the others.' She led me at a brisk march up the prom. 'We can still come back, I know we can!'

'He's taking it very badly.'

We hurried into the kitchen, sopping wet. On the way back we'd been caught in the worst of the downpour and we'd sat steaming on the bus all the way back to Tony's house. Now Tony was slumped at his breakfast bar, still in black leather, glaring at us as if Kris's mood was our fault.

Debs tried to hide her delight. 'You've told him you're coming with us?'

There was a great crash from upstairs. The ceiling above us shuddered. A voice bellowed, 'Fuck!'

Tony shook his head. 'His hard drive keeps buggering up.'

There was another crack and screech from upstairs. 'Fuck!' Then someone was stamping on the floorboards.

'Every time he shouts like that...' Tony touched his rib cage, 'I feel it here. I feel like he's inside of me ... raging and banging about...' His voice had gone quiet.

Debs was frowning. 'Does he often have tantrums?'

'Tantrums?' Another burst of noise upstairs. 'I'm not sure if I'd call them that ... but, yes. Most days.'

Debs set her face determinedly. 'He sounds bloody bonkers.'

'It's not like that,' Tony said wearily. 'He doesn't sleep well and his computer has some kind of glitch or ... it always seems to go wrong on him and shut down, wiping things off forever. And he gets furious and paranoid and scared. He thinks someone is doing it on purpose ... cutting down his only link with the world and all his fans out there. Someone is purposefully destroying that lifeline...'

Debs whistled. 'Jesus, Tone. You can't shut youself up in here with someone bonkers.'

He looked at the rain as it slid in torrents down the kitchen window. 'I already have, lovey.'

I spoke up. 'But you're coming with us. And you've already told him you're coming with us.'

Debs shot me a sly look. 'That's right,' she said.

A louder crash then, as some piece of hardware was slung against the wall. Tony cringed.

'We'll have to have the repair men in again. That'll be an adventure, if it's anything like last time. They were terrified of him.'

'Can't he just buy a new computer?'

'We're not rich, Debs,' Tony said.

'His band was bigger than we were. Course he's rich.'

Tony shook his head. 'The last of his money he injected into the most prominent vein he could find in his dick.' Tony glanced at me. 'Excuse my coarseness.'

I shrugged. I didn't know how I felt, hearing about Kris Katastrophea's veiny dick.

'He's going to have to come to his senses,' Debs said. 'I'll talk to him.'

How doleful Tony looked: as if it was all out of his hands now. He looked scared. 'He wants to talk to you anyway. At five o'clock. We're all to have sherry in the front parlour.'

'Well,' she said nervously. 'Good.'

'He won't let me go, Debs. Even for a week. Not without a fight.'

'That's ridiculous,' I said. 'He's not utterly dependent on you...'

'He is.' Tony stood up and stretched. His leather chaps creaked. 'I'd better hoover round in the parlour so it's ready.' Then he was gone, treading carefully into the hall.

Debs turned to me. 'Sherry? Tony doesn't even like sherry.'

Their front parlour looked quite different from when I'd slept in it.

A fire was blazing and there wasn't a scrap of dust to be seen. Tony had set out a drinks trolley, with dainty, gold-rimmed glasses ready.

'I'm quite nervous,' Debs said. Her eyes were imploring me. 'What are we doing, Tim? We're interfering,' she lowered her voice, 'in a marriage.'

'I suppose we are.'

'I'm not one of those who thinks it's any different because it's a man with another man. They've made that commitment and I'd call it a marriage. I'd stand up in court or in church and say so. It's just the same as me and Clive.' She bit her lip. 'Except they're still together. Clive chucked me out.'

'He chucked you out? I thought you left him.'

She shushed me. 'What have they got those pictures up for?'

The walls were covered in those framed portraits of Victorian children. Each with one glycerine tear running down their smutty cheeks.

'I think they're awful,' she said. 'Weren't they all cursed? Wasn't there a lot of housefires and they said it was all down to them pictures?' Debs was babbling now. To me, the pictures fitted in with the shire horses, the flying ducks, the pot dogs and everything else dusted to a shine in the parlour. Another strange affectation of Tony's - or more likely - Kris.

Tony appeared at the open door. 'He's coming down.'

He shuffled over to the record player in the corner of the room and gently nudged the needle into place.

Within a few crackly, booming chords I recognised the opening to 'Love Monster Autobahn Parade (The Orgiastic Mix)': a twelve inch I'd coveted, adored and lost a good long while ago. Even with the pounding bass and the sonorous vocals starting, I could still hear footsteps on the stairs.

Tony had his eyes cast down. I caught Debs' glance and smiled reassuringly. Her lips tightened and went pale.

As the song crashed into its chanting chorus, an incredibly tall shape filled the doorway. It lifted up its sinewy arms and blazed its eyes at us.

It was all I could do, not to applaud and suddenly I understood that this was Tony and Kris's tea time ritual and it went on whether visitors were there or not.

Tony moved round to the drinks trolley, his bare shoulders bowed resignedly as he started to pour the sherry. It looked thick, like molten sugar.

Kris was miming the words to his song. We stared at him. Debs' mouth had fallen open.

He was bright orange, all seven feet of him: from head to stilet-toed foot. He was skinnier than I had ever seen him: his ribs, shoulder blades and cheek bones sticking out like a roast after Sunday night sandwiches. Every visible inch of him had been painted a gorgeous, citrus orange. On top of that he wore scarlet fishnet stockings, a bolero jacket of livid green feathers, and a balaclava of golden chainmail. His pupils were scarlet; glaring at us from under his ridiculous lashes as he sang. His bangles - a dozen on each arm - rattled up and down his skinny arms as he flung himself about, dragging the twelve inch up to its diabolical conclusion.

When silence fell, I couldn't hold back any longer. I clapped till my palms were sore, and Debs did the same, less enthusiastically. Tony was applauding very gently. He switched the record player off.

Kris tore himself away from his spot on the threshold of the room, and flung himself down on the blue chaise longue.

He took the sherry glass Tony passed him and held it in his massive talons so that it glinted in the firelight. He drew his spindly, fishnetted legs up under him and rested languidly, looking at us beadily from inside his glittering balaclava.

'Please,' Tony told us throatily. 'Do sit down.' He shoved our glasses into our grasp.

I downed mine and nearly choked.

'Kris,' said Debs warmly, 'it's so lovely to see you again.' She blinked as his gimlet eyes raked over her. 'You still look ... extraordinary.'

Those eyes seemed to soften somewhat. 'Debbie Now,' he said and his voice was harsh, as if from disuse. 'I never thought we'd see you round here. Did we, Anthony? We'll never see her round here; that's what we thought.'

'Well,' said Debs and rested her tiny glass on her palm. 'Here I am.'

Kris's eyes swivelled to take me in. 'And this is your boyfriend. This child.'

'Not my boyfriend, Kris.'

Tony put in, 'He's her friend. He's a fan of Things Fall Apart, Kris.'

'Really?' said Kris.

'And a fan of yours, too,' Debs said eagerly. 'He was telling me this afternoon. He loved the Dominators and you almost more than he loved us.'

Kris's eyes narrowed. Even under the balaclava, you could see his nostrils flare with pleasure. 'Oh, really?'

I nodded. 'I'm Tim.'

Kris gave a rasping laugh. 'Do you take it up the arse, Tim? It looks to me like you take it right up the shitter.'

I felt myself blush. 'No,' I said, 'but I give fantastic head. Will that do?'

He cawed with laughter again. 'I should have known Debbie Now would still be schlepping up and down the country with a little gay boy. That's what she always did. Couldn't be without one, could you, dear? What was it? Did you love the smell of poppers? Or couldn't you hang onto a normal man?'

'Kris...' warned Tony.

'Oh, fuck off, Anthony,' Kris snapped. 'I can fight my own battles, thank you.'

'He meant,' said Debs, 'to protect me.'

'Protect you!'

She leaned forward and lashed out in a way that surprised me. 'You always were a poisonous fucker.'

Kris drew back away from her and seemed, for a second, almost panicked. 'Would you mind not leaning so close to me, dear? I'm afraid I can smell your cunt.'

Debs was on her feet. 'That's it. I'm not listening to this.' She rounded on Tony. 'I knew it was a mistake trying to talk to this frigging freak. He's worse than ever. He hated me then and he still hates me now, after all these years. Well, sod you. I'm going.'

'Debs,' Tony gasped. 'Wait...'

'He's not talking to me like that.' She was over by the door.

Kris was chuckling away, pleased with himself at the uproar he'd caused. I stood up awkwardly and put down my sherry glass.

'Oh,' said Kris. 'You're not going as well?'

I nodded.

'But you're such a fan of mine, aren't you, Tiny Tim? I thought you were an acolyte. I thought you'd want to see what has become of your icon; your favourite star in your own personal pantheon.'

Debs shouted out, 'Yes! Take a look at him, Tim! Look what's become of him!'

Kris was rivetting. He snarled and held a talon up in front of his visor. 'I have evolved. I have gone on in my own way and evolved beyond what any of you talentless fuckwits could ever have imagined. You all gave up the ghost. You all, in the end, clung to some tawdry modicum of normalcy. You only wanted to be famous - fleetingly, tragically, pathetically. Whereas *I* ... I wanted to go on. And I have done so, with the help of faithful Anthony here. Whom, I might point out, is only alive and sane these days because I took him in, under my wing, and loved him...'

'Loved him!' Debs bellowed. 'You call making him dress up and scurry round like your personal slave, loving him?'

Kris blinked. 'Of course I do. Tell me this, Debbie Now. Who else wanted him, hm? After the accident? After his breakdown? Who else would take him in?'

'I...' stammered Debs. She looked at Tony, but he kept his eyes on the swirling pattern in the carpet.

'You wouldn't, you selfish cow. You were married to that neanderthal prick, Clive. You couldn't have given a flaming fuck about the lovely Tony. No ... it was me who took pity on him. Me who let him join me, live with me; help me with the daily craft and grind; the slow accretion of this heavenly carapace. This gradual, glorious, evolution of a self.'

'You're insane,' Debs whispered.

'I'm a whole new race,' grated Kris.

Debs looked at Tony again. 'He's insane.'

Kris settled back. 'I'm actually toying with the idea of giving up on human language altogether.'

'Jesus,' said Debs. 'I'm going.'

'Don't you see? Tony needs me. He's tied to me. All the way. Tony is with me all the way.'

'He doesn't need you,' Debs spat. 'He never has.'

Kris's feathers seemed to bristle in the firelight, as if they had a life of their own. 'Have you, Tony?' he asked, quieter now. 'Have you ever needed me?'

Tony wouldn't look at him. 'Yes,' he said dully. 'I have.'

Kris laughed. 'I put you back together again, didn't I, Tony?' His laughter became shrill. 'See? I know exactly how to put a person together. The Tony you see here, Debbie Now, isn't the one you knew. He's no longer your private, personal fag. He's *mine*. I *made* him into what you see here.'

'And you can destroy him, I suppose?' Debs suddenly cracked out laughing. 'Jesus Christ, I've never heard such crap. What is this? What are we doing? Listening to the rantings of some bloke who looks like a great big bloody parrot.'

Kris stiffened and clutched his arm rest. It was true. He looked like a parrot.

'Just let him go, Kris,' Debs said. 'Give over, eh?'

'You were the one who did him the most damage, Debbie Now,' Kris said, his voice dangerously low. 'You used him and confused him and put him in danger.'

Debs was white. 'He was in an accident ... that wasn't anyone's fault but...'

'I'm not talking about that. I'm talking about how you made him follow you and your pathetic dream. You used him and dragged him into a world he couldn't cope with. You talk about slavery - but it was you who made him get up there and sing when he can hardly sing a note. You made him go on telly when he's so insecure he can hardly string a sentence together!'

'But that's not true!' Debs shouted. 'Of course he can!'

'And it was you,' Kris said, 'who gave him to that evil fuck, Roy Kitchener. You gave him to that old fake to fuck and to toy with. Roy Kitchener used Anthony as a dildo for years.'

'No,' said Debs.

'Don't pretend you didn't know.'

'Tony?' Debs asked.

'The worst thing,' said Kris, 'was that you made that boy fall in love with you. You kept him beside you, when you knew he was queer and you made him feel it was okay to fall in love with you; that he'd be safe there forever. You let him believe that his real world, his own world, was a scary place, full of exploitation. You made him think he would be safe with you. But then you ran off into the arms of precious fucking Clive. You cast Tony off, and he falls at the feet of anyone who will have him. Anyone who will use him. Because that's what he'd grown accustomed to. *That's* what destroyed his nerves, Debbie Now. *That's* what happened.'

Debs had sunk back into her chair.

I didn't know where to put myself. The room started to tilt and I hoped it was the sherry.

'Tony,' said Debs, 'it wasn't like that, was it?'

He looked up, very slowly, at her. He nodded quickly.

'Oh fuck,' she said. 'Oh fuck.' She looked round wildly at me. 'I've got to get out. I've got to get away.'

I moved forward to help her up, as if she'd aged terribly all of a sudden.

'Hang on,' shouted Kris. 'I thought this young lout was going to suck my cock for me?'

We froze. Kris thought at first it was because of what he'd said. But then he saw the expression on Tony's face.

'You monster,' Tony said thickly.

Something shifted in Kris's hooded eyes.

'You're a monster,' Tony said again.

Then he moved swiftly to the door.

'I'm going with them, Kris. I'm going with them tonight.'

Chapter Eight

Debs never got to like their Kilburn flat. She couldn't understand why, in London, people seemed to pay a fortune to live somewhere they thought of as posh and, when you went round, it was dog rough. With things like the Co-op and all night takeaways and nasty pubs only yards from their front door.

'It's the Metropolis,' Clive told her. 'That's what it's like.'

They moved into the place that Christmas, when it seemed certain that Roy was right after all and the Angel song, with its Venice-shot video, was headed for the top ten.

'We're gunna be loaded,' Clive said. 'This is where it starts.'

He threw himself into decorating their four large rooms, as if determinedly working out his frustrations on the accreted layers of ancient wallpaper.

As he worked at plastering and papering and painting - turning his skilled hands to everything - Debs sat in her new kitchen, at a spanking new stripped pine table and drank coffee, staring at a frozen garden. She watched cats chase birds and snow come down.

Every day Roy or Tony or Brenda would phone. There were TV appearances to do and Debs was huge. Her costumes would have to be let out. Roy decided he could use her as a unique selling point, because her baby was due at Christmas and people would like that.

Debs didn't know how she could face all this. Singing that song. She tried to back out of doing the TV shows, claiming stress and exhaustion. The band shared the duties round and went on separately. Brenda stepped into the breach, getting her mug on the telly as much as possible. Luckily they could just show the video - that ludicrous extravaganza. It seemed a million years since they had made it.

At home, Clive worked till late in the night, shirt off, getting covered in paint and paste. There was, Debs noticed, a kind of ethnic look to the rooms as he completed them.

She couldn't stir much interest in the flat. She dreamed of heading back to the north, and into the care of her mother. Franky, of course, phoned every day, offering to leave her restaurant and to come and look after her daughter. But Debs held her off. Clive would never put up with that.

The single came out at the start of December and it shot straight into the top ten.

Debs sat at her table, watching the neighbours' cats through the freshly-painted french windows and thought: I could walk out of here, round the corner, and onto Kilburn High Street and everyone would recognise me. That huge pregnant woman ambling through the Christmas shoppers ... why, she's a star! She sings about angels on the telly almost every night. She floats past the screen in a gondala, wearing a mask.

They would all know her. The thought made her very tired.

Clive wanted to throw a Christmas party, once the decorating was finished. He wanted to show the whole place off.

'Better not,' she said, thinking of the elderly couple next door.

'We'll invite them,' he said.

Next door lived an incredibly old couple who Clive had befriended shortly after moving in. They were delighted to have famous next door neighbours and, when he wasn't working on the flat, Clive often disappeared round there. The old man had travelled the world, by all accounts, and he had a huge collection of records. Clive had been sucked in and would disappear to listen to bizarre music from the Amazon, the Andes and chants by Aborigines.

Alone, Debs would hear the alien music vibrating through the clean, damp walls.

'It's authentic music,' Clive told her. 'Proper soulful stuff that means something. Played on real instruments.'

The old man next door had a collection of exotic devices, made from gourds and stretched guts from dead animals. In the time he took out from decorating, Clive was learning to play them all, under the old man's careful tutelage.

'This could move me in a totally different direction,' Clive said, 'musically-speaking.'

He brought back odd-looking objects and blew into them while strumming them, sitting on the bare boards of the half-done living room.

'It's called World Music,' he said, in the middle of one night when Debs came through in her dressing gown, sleepless and dismayed at his honks and grunts.

'How am I supposed to make up words to go with that?' she asked.

'You'll do it,' he said, wiping saliva from the mouthpiece of something that looked like a dried-out stomach. His eyes were bright. 'We can do anything. We're going to be the Christmas number one with that commercial piece of shit. Now we can do anything. We're famous. The public will follow us anywhere...'

Debs wasn't so sure.

She went back to bed, thinking it over, leaving Clive to make obscure notes to himself on sheafs of paper. Once she was lying down again - awkwardly, oppressed by the weight of her bump - the honking and grunting started up again.

'Whatever happened to pop?' she thought, and watched the snow drift down, picked out against her muslin curtains by the security lights.

That Sunday, the weekend before Christmas, they went to number one.

Clive had the radio on as he worked at painting the ceiling in the living room and his hair was spotted with beige. Debs was lying down with a cold flannel over her face. She felt like she would never be able to move again. The baby was due in a week and she couldn't give a shit about the charts. Clive wouldn't feel her tummy when it kicked - even though it only kicked feebly. He said it gave him the creeps.

The old woman next door - Monica - kept a herb garden in her conservatory. This past month she had knocked every morning on Debs' french windows and brought her a milky drink, flecked with green, all blended up. She said the drink would do Debs and the young'un a lot of good. Dutifully Debs gulped it down, but the special drinks from Monica had done nothing to ease her pains, which she felt weren't natural. Her doctor told her there was nothing to worry about. Every pregnancy was different and she was to ignore whatever her friends said.

Yet none of the people she talked to knew anything about pregnancy anyway. Tony, Clive, Roy and Brenda. What experience did they have? When she asked her mother what childbirth was like, even Franky was evasive. 'Listen to your doctor. I'm sure it's okay. Are you sure you don't want me to come down?'

But she didn't want Franky there. She'd only get on Clive's nerves. Debs couldn't put up with any kind of atmosphere. She felt bad for her mam, thinking like that.

A suitcase was packed ready for the hospital, waiting at the foot of the bed.

That Sunday night, at exactly seven o'clock, there was a great cry and a crash as Clive jumped off his stepladders. He was yelling out in excitement and Debs could feel the bare boards tremble in the other room.

Then the sound went up; full blast on the hi-fi.

They were number one.

In a phoney transatlantic accent the DJ announced:

'Their first number one - this year's Christmas number one: 'When I am an Angel' - by Things Fall Apart.'

And then the twinkling, shimmering, opening bars of their record.

It had never sounded so glossy, so perfect, so proper before.

Debs felt curiously detatched from everything. She was a receptacle; a collection of numbed limbs and stretched-out organs.

Clive came tearing through. The bedroom door banged open. He looked ecstatic.

Everyone came round their flat in Kilburn that night. Tony was first, with a boy he had started seeing and a bottle of pink champagne.

Their single was playing on a continuous loop and Clive was in an ebullient mood, clapping Tony on the back, and even welcoming his new boyfriend (who looked a bit cowed by it all.) Debs had never seen Clive like this.

'You're like a little boy,' she laughed, putting out bowls of crudites and crisps.

'It's all I've ever wanted. A Christmas number one.' He looked at her. 'You could be more excited, too.'

She brushed her hair and set to welcoming her impromptu, delighted guests; feeling as if she'd failed some other test in Clive's eyes. She kept thinking how he'd called the record a commercial piece of shit.

'Debs...' Tony took her quietly aside. The flat was quite full by now, with some people she didn't even recognise. It was hard going down the narrow passageway with the bump. He looked at her steadily. 'You look terrible. White and thin and washed out.'

'I'm due in a week,' she reminded him. 'How am I supposed to look?'

'Radiant,' he said softly. 'And you don't.'

'It's exhausting,' she said. 'I didn't think it was going to be like this.'

Then Roy was arriving in a brand new and colossal Savile Row suit, bang on the heels of Brenda, who looked at the newly done-up flat with a sniffy expression. She was living in Shepherd's Bush, now.

Roy gathered them up like his chicks and beamed at them, rather startling with his pink bald head and single glittering earring.

'Didn't I tell you?' he cried. 'I told you all, didn't I? You listened to all my pep talks and now you've done it. You're immortal now; every one of you.'

'We can't go wrong!' Clive grinned, uncorking a bottle he'd been saving. 'We can do anything now!'

Roy blinked his false eyelashes, cast a careful glance round at his entourage and said, 'Not quite, sunshine. Now you'll need my guidance more than ever.' He lowered his rumbling voice a full octave and added, 'Now you've got the follow-up to work on. You can't get that fucker wrong.'

'We have to consolidate our success,' Tony put in, and Roy gave him a strange look.

'Quite.'

'That's all sorted out,' Clive said. 'It's already written.'

Roy raised a delicate eyebrow. 'Is it now?'

'He's been writing all week,' said Debs. 'It's almost done.'

'No one told me,' Roy said.

'It's a kind of change in direction,' said Clive. 'A radical shift for us.'

Roy frowned. 'I don't like the sound of this.'

Debs touched his massive arm. 'You'll love it, Roy.'

Roy was holding Clive's glance. 'Don't go all independent on me. And don't you dare get Art. Remember what I said about Art.'

'Art is death,' said Tony, nodding.

By midnight Debs' head was reeling. The looped song had brainwashed them all and a curious, sluggish atmosphere had stolen over the assembled group.

Couples were slow-dancing in the underwater gloom of the living room, their feet scraping on the bare boards.

It was snowing again outside and, staring out of the bay windows, it struck Debs for the first time that Christmas really was coming.

She sat on a tassled pouffe by the towering tree that Clive had bought, wedged in a bucket and neglected to trim.

She'd had a few jabbing pains tonight, but managed not to show it. It was important to her to be a perfect hostess in the new flat. Everything was changing and she had to look like she could deal with it all; flat, baby, success, new year.

Brenda flopped down beside her. She looked the picture of health and Debs felt a twinge of envy at Brenda in her batwing sweater, leather skirt and cowboy boots.

Brenda nodded at the old couple from next door, who were cheek to cheek and swaying in the middle of the floor.

'Who are those old fogies?'

Debs told her, and how the neighbours had become good friends of theirs; Clive especially.

'You've become a middle-aged suburban couple,' Brenda said.

Debs thought she was being sarcastic.

'No,' said Brenda. 'I mean it. I'm glad you and him have settled down. He's calmed down a lot, has Clive. He's a nicer person. You've been good for him.'

Debs was surprised. Brenda sounded almost friendly.

'We've all mellowed,' Brenda said. 'All of us. Even Tony's a little less skittish and scared. More happy inside his skin.' She dangled her empty glass. 'We've all grown up.'

The pains were returning now.

Debs could feel a film of cold sweat settling on her face like a mask. Her hair was damp suddenly, and she was rooted to her low seat by the force of the pains.

She would never be able to get up by herself. She would have to break in and stop Brenda talking and just at the moment when Brenda was sounding almost human.

She would have to ask Brenda for help. Ask her to hoist her up on her shaking legs.

Brenda looked at her, and caught her grimacing.

'I think I'm ready to move on, Debs. I'm glad we've had this success. It means we can go out on a high point. But I think it's time to leave.'

Debs' voice was strained, as she tried to make it sound normal. 'You're going to leave?'

'I've been offered a job presenting. Breakfast TV. It's my chance. I can't do that as well as the band. I have to prioritize.'

'When?'

'Soon. I need out, Debs. I need to be out.'

There was a terrible, rending pain then, that blotted out Brenda, the dancing guests, the music and the muggy air about her.

It was the worst surge yet and, as she screamed out and waves of blackness came pulsing in, Debs knew that it wasn't right. It wasn't the right kind of pain to feel.

Chapter Nine

Naturally it was me relegated to the back seat of Tony's clapped-out Morris Minor.

He threw open the garage door as if he'd never been near his car in years and we all climbed in quietly, hardly banging the doors, like we were scared his boyfriend was going to come dashing out of the house, squawking curses and flinging himself in the path of our getaway.

I still couldn't believe the performance I'd witnessed.

Revving the ancient engine, turning it over grimly, Tony was shaking. Debs sat patiently beside him on the ox blood leather and put her hand on his arm. 'Hey,' she said, as if reminding him who we were.

'I've never seen him like that,' he whispered. 'Ever. Even at his worst.'

Debs bit her lip. I could see she was dying to say something. You're best shot of him. Or maybe she was going to apologise for causing all the upheaval; and for calling his boyfriend a parrot. But she stayed quiet.

'I've really done it,' Tony said, louder now, as we swang off the drive, into the empty cul-de-sac. 'I've left him.'

Debs cast a glance back at the house, as if she couldn't quite believe it, either.

'Tim,' said Tony, as we hit the main road. The car was juddering along and he didn't look that confident driving. 'If you feel about in the pocket behind my seat, there should be a map.'

I was to be navigator for our journey into deepest, darkest Yorkshire and our confrontation with Debs' ex-husband.

'I've got no spatial or visual imagination,' Debs said. 'Clive himself told me that.'

As it happens, I'm bollocks at reading maps as well.

Once we got on the motorway Debs went rooting through the glove compartment and found a Best of the Eighties tape. The atmosphere in the Morris Minor was lightened somewhat by Kim Wilde, Duran Duran and Bananarama.

'Hey, are we not on this?' she asked, turning over the tape cover.

'We were hard to get the rights to,' Tony laughed. 'We were fairly exclusive and classy, you know.'

The two of them even started singing along after a while. I closed my eyes and listened to them doing Nena's 'Ninety-Nine Red Balloons'. It was as if their two voices, so long-used to singing together, were being reintroduced. They took a few moments to recognise each other. Then, they both grew more confident and embraced each other, twining and matching perfectly.

I settled back and watched the lorries on the motorway.

'It's a road trip,' Debs said. 'We're in a road movie, aren't we?' She looked back at me. 'Okay back there, Tim? Or do you feel like our hostage?'

'I'm fine.' Although I did feel like a hostage. A happy one. One keen to see what came next. Happy to have all responsibility lifted off me, though I knew I'd have to phone Shanna soon and find out what was happening at work.

If I claimed that I had, in fact, been taken away against my will, then no one could get at me. My rent money was due at the weekend. My whole life at home was falling apart.

I could say that they'd held me at gun point as they went off on their road trip. I was the sex slave of has-been Eighties pop stars.

But I looked at the backs of Tony and Debs' heads and realised no one would ever believe they'd do anyone harm. They were too tender-hearted.

For now at least, though, while we were in transit, I was exonerated from doing anything about my real life. I was glad none of us had a mobile phone. As it was, I would just have to wait till we came across a call box.

Sitting alone on the back seat reminded me of a few runs-out in the country we'd had, when I was ten or so and Mam had hooked up with a new boyfriend, a country and western enthusiast called Rick. He'd taken us to a country and western weekend in Northumberland. We weren't used to bombing around the place in a car. We'd quite got to like it, though the thing with Rick didn't take off in the end. He'd wanted someone without kids.

Tony and Debs started to talk about where we should stay tonight. What our plan of action should be with Clive, the next morning.

I sifted through the accumulated junk on the back seat (MacDonalds wrappers, coke cans, jumpers, a tartan rug) and was surprised to find a hardcore gay porn magazine.

I had a flick through as we made our way cross-country.

'I can't go into it now, Shanna, but I'm nowhere near home. It's kind of a long story.'

'Are you still in London?'

'Not quite. I'm somewhere between Lancashire and Yorkshire. Some motorway. I don't know what it's called.'

I heard her sigh on the other end of the line. A pause.

At least she wasn't shouting. I was glad I'd waited to phone her at home. It was remarkable; Shanna was a different person at home. At work in Natural World she was hyper with tension; lashing out and having to apologise to people later.

'Are you coming back or not?'

'I'm caught up in something.'

'It's some fella, isn't it, Tim?' She laughed. 'You've met some lodgy bloke and he's dragging you all over the countryside.'

'Yeah,' I said. 'He's the bloke of my dreams. Of course he is.'

There was some kind of kerfuffle at the other end, in Shanna's flat. Male voices. 'Just put it over there,' she said.

'Who've you got round?' Shanna wasn't keen on having people in her place. Even I - her best mate - had been allowed to visit only a handful of times.

'Oh...' she said. 'Ian and Mick.'

'Who?'

'You know. The Elvis twins.'

'Oh, yeah?'

'They're shifting furniture around for me. I might as well make use of them.'

'Right.'

'Okay. So tell me who this bloke is who's ruining your life.'

I only had fourteen pence left on the phone meter. 'It's not a bloke. It's Debs - the woman from the karaoke on Saturday night.'

'Her? What are you doing with her?'

'She needs my help.'

'I hope you're not biffing her, sonny.'

"Biffing'?'

'I'd have something to say if you suddenly started getting it together with older women.' There was a slightly pained gap in the conversation.

'Well,' I said. 'I'm not. She's a pal and we're going to visit her ex-husband.'

'Cosy,' Shanna laughed. 'I hope this Debs person knows she's screwing up your career.'

'Career?'

'At Natural World.'

'Oh, that.'

'Pete's stotting mad. Furious. I've been covering for you, but he's starting to think you don't take your retail career seriously.'

'Cheers, Shanna ... look, my money's gunna go...'

'He means it, Tim. If you don't get back by the end of the week, he'll sack you. You haven't rung in properly or anything...'

'Listen - that's the pips going ... I'd better ...'

'We've had to change all the frontal gondolas and window displays without you and ... You'd better phone again, Tim...'

The line went dead. I was left looking at the receiver and I felt suddenly exposed, standing in the middle of some service station on a motorway whose name I didn't even know.

I felt inept, and show-off, too; shouting in a corner, all alone, all about my life.

But no one was taking any notice. I was between the Ladies and the sweetshop, across the tiled floor from Burger King, where Tony had taken Debs. No one had been listening to my conversation.

What was Shanna doing with those two rough Elvis fellas round her flat? All sorts had been going on since I'd been gone. She wouldn't have let them in if I'd still been there. They would trick her and rape her and kill her and it would all be my fault.

I'd have lost my job, Shanna would be dead and that's how it would all happen.

Outside, it was dark. I was hungry. Another ridiculous, action-packed day. Time to talk plans with the others in Burger King. Time to shake off my child-on-the-back-seat-taking-no-responsibility role. Time for a big fat burger and grease and extra salty chips.

We had an early night in one of those funny travel lodge places. I'd never been inside one, but Debs seemed to know the routine and it was she who led us across the dark car park to the silvery foyer.

She wanted a good night's sleep after all the excitement of recent days and to be ready for tomorrow, seeing Clive again.

Tony and I just went along with her. He gave me a kind of look, as if to say, don't argue. I wasn't going to. Debs had offered to pay for our stay, just as she had for petrol and our train tickets the previous day. I didn't think she could be rich; not if she needed her mam to put her up and give her that house to live in. But it was like she was trying to spend all the money she did still have, as if that would make some more arrive. She'd already told me how, when they were famous, Roy would give them pocket money to live off and that was how they'd got by. Maybe she had never clicked out of that mindset.

Thinking about it, that's how I behaved as well. Everything I earned was pocket money. Never saving for the future. Trying not to think about it.

The travel lodge was a bit fuctional and bleak. In the tiny foyer you had to phone up some central service and ask for the rooms you wanted. Then you gave your credit card to a girl behind a glass partition. She was sitting there with a display of essentials people might have forgotten; toothbrushes, tampons, bottled beers.

It looked like a place designed for people who were running away.

Tony and I stood around as Debs dealt with it all. Tony had slipped back into some kind of shellshock, now he wasn't doing something immediate, like driving or eating. He stood there in his jacket with the sleeves pushed up to the elbows and his jeans gone all baggy at the knees. It was like he was waiting for someone to tell him what to do next.

Businesslike, Debs held up two keys and said, 'I'm putting you two boys in together, tonight. I just got a single for me. I need to get my head together.'

I opened my mouth to protest.

'Okay,' said Tony quietly. 'We understand.'

I looked at my watch. It was the last present Mam had bought me, for starting university. It was lasting well. Twenty-five past eight. Early night.

'We should set off about half seven tomorrow morning,' Debs said. 'I don't know what I'm going to do for clean clothes.' She pushed her hair out of her eyes.

'We can tell Clive you've gone all grungey,' Tony said.

'What?'

He shook his head. 'We'll think of something.'

She led us down a corridor. We were on the ground floor. Plastic potted plants and a strange cheesey smell. And no sign of anyone else.

Debs gave a tight smile and vanished behind her own stripped pine door after struggling with the key.

'Here's ours,' Tony said.

He put the telly on and found we had satellite and he sat on the end of one of the beds, waiting for the tiny kettle to warm up. Those travel kettles and two-cup teapots always make me sad. I watched Tony fill it and click it and the smell of burning dust that came off the kettle made me sad, too.

At home, even if I was making tea just for me (usually the case) I'd make gallons, and waste them, rather than just making a sad single person's amount. Even though he didn't live alone, Tony seemed used to brewing small quantities.

He was glued to the local news.

He was going to make a move on me, I was sure. It was obvious in the way he was keeping his eyes on the telly and not on me. I'd have to find a way to let him down nicely.

The soft furnishings in the spartan room were all from the mid-Eighties, just like Debs and Tony. They should feel at home. Horrific jarring patchwork patterns in lilac and lime green. Like migraine.

The beds were very close together, with light switches in the headboards. I'd have to lie there all night, inches from Tony. I didn't know if I could handle it.

I was standing looking at him and it wasn't like I fancied him. He looked a bit care-worn and as if he could burst into tears any moment. He wasn't really registering my presence. But I knew that all that night, I'd be lying awake, thinking of the boy he'd been, back when I'd been frustrated and well under-age. I knew I'd be awake, pent up and needing to touch him, just so I could tell myself that I had.

Wasn't there a terrible tension in the air between us right now? Or was he just caught up in the weather reports, being enunciated slowly by a woman who looked like a frog? Was that a frisson of desire and erotic nostalgia palpable in the sterile air of the room or was it all, in fact, in my head?

I grabbed a clean fluffy towel off the rail and hurried into the ensuite for a shower. It seemed the easiest thing to do.

In that tiled and sealed compartment I looked at myself in the mirror and ignored the bags under my eyes and thought: He'd be lucky to get anywhere near this. Then I felt ashamed and thought about how he'd left his fella just that afternoon. He'd had a tricky time.

I stood under the fierce shower and wanked myself off quickly, as though it had nothing to do with me. If there were games being played here and frissons being bred, then they wouldn't be mine. Coming first, neatly, efficiently, would let me act natural and blithe with him.

But I came out in a towel with hair dripping down my face and he was lying on his bed in boxer shorts, staring at the ceiling. His body, it has to be said, was delectable even with its few extra pounds. The sight of him had me back where I started from.

The telly was turned down. I sat on the other bed and looked at him, at the blondish hair of his armpits and his small, pink nipples.

He opened his mouth and it turned out he wanted to talk.

'I'm amazed about Debs,' he said. 'I wouldn't want to see Clive, if I was her.'

'You didn't like him in the first place,' I said.

His eyebrows went up. Lying down, his face looked more like it had done when he was younger. He didn't look so thickset on his back. 'Didn't I?' He frowned. 'It's hard to say. It was all just a given. We were family.'

'And I've got all my sisters with me,' I quoted.

'Hm?' Tony blinked. 'He treated her like shit, you know.'

I remembered something. 'I always thought she'd got rid of him and chucked him out. I thought that was how it had happened. Debs said something about it being the other way around.'

In fact, I was remembering the video of their last ever single, when it was still the original four of them. 'Blues of the World', it was called. In that mini-narrative, Debs had been the wronged woman who threw out her boorish, philandering man and sang her song, tramping round a snowy park, pausing under trees and beside a river bank, wearing a long herringbone coat with her hands plunged into her pockets. Tony and Brenda had sang the chorus; exhorting her to be brave and to learn to live her life alone.

Who could blame me for thinking all of that was real?

'He dumped her,' Tony said. 'Quite unceremoniously. Out of the blue he told her it wasn't working anymore. He wanted to move in new directions and explore new avenues. He didn't want to write songs with her anymore.'

'That's when he started doing his instrumental stuff with eskimos?'

'And he diddled Debs out of her rights, too. There was something wrong with the contracts and he got most of the money. It turns out that the music counts for more than the words.'

'Not to me,' I said.

'You should tell Debs that.' He rolled over and propped his hand on his palm, looking at me. 'I reckon Clive will be making a packet out of this Shelley Sommers business, anyway. I don't think, when Debs sees him tomorrow, he'll be all that helpful.'

'He's been rotten to her the whole way through,' I said, 'from what I've heard. It's just as well they didn't have kids.'

Tony's face fell. 'Jesus. Whatever you say, don't say that to Debs. Or Clive.'

'Why?'

'She was pregnant up until the day we went to number one. That Christmas. A little girl. Gemma.'

'Oh.'

'Debs took bad at a party they had round theirs. She knew the baby was dead inside her. They rushed her into hospital. We all went, even Brenda. But Debs knew the baby was dead. The doctors knew straight away, too. But they wouldn't operate till after New Year. No staff.'

'God.'

'That whole week, when we were number one and it was Christmas, she was waiting. I stayed with her. She said to me, I've got to walk around with this dead thing inside of me. It lasted a hundred years for her. She said, I know the blood's not moving around. I know she's not kicking or breathing. Why are they leaving me like this?'

'That's horrible.' I felt sick. 'What was Clive doing?'

'To be fair, he was supportive. He was devastated as well. He loved her that much. But you could see at the same time, he was still excited about how many records we were selling. He was furious we couldn't go on *Top of the Pops*. And he was writing the follow-up single, this thing that was all, like, South American bongos and pipes. Debs couldn't write any words for it, of course, so he just had us chanting, like, tribal chants in the background, me and Brenda. And that was his big change in direction.'

'I remember that song,' I said. 'That was a big hit, too.'

Tony nodded and rolled over to grab his Lambert and Butler off the bedside cabinet. 'It was meant to be a tribute to little Gemma. Roy hated it. He said we were doing it all wrong and we'd come a cropper. It was the first time we'd really disobeyed him and stuck to our guns and he was livid. Debs might have listened to him in time, if she'd been in a fit state. But she wasn't and we let Clive bully us, instead of Roy.'

'Poor Debs,' I said. 'And she's not found anyone since Clive?'

'Oh, it dragged on with Clive a little bit after that. A couple of years or so. Almost as long as the band did. But he was more open about all the other women and what he was up to. It broke Debs' heart. And there was never any more talk of kiddies, either.'

Tony fell quiet. I wondered whether Debs would ever have told me what he just had and whether she would be angry that I knew all this now. With me she liked to put on this resilient act; like an old trouper, well-versed in the ways of the world. Nothing shocked her. I was shocked now, hearing how she'd had to go about with a dead baby inside her.

'At least she's had you,' I told Tony.

He glanced at me, smoking and blowing it at the ceiling. 'Not as much as she should have. I remember telling her, again and again, that no man would ever be with her as much as I was. But that was a lie. We haven't seen each other in five years.'

'Maybe that's her fault as well.'

'I don't know. I've been so locked into my world, and Kris, that I wouldn't know anymore if it's my fault or not.'

'You were there for her back then.'

'Maybe.' He sighed and stretched out. I heard joints cracking, like he hadn't been able to stretch out in ages. 'I had my own stuff going on. I couldn't give her all the support she needed.'

'Right,' I said, not knowing whether I was meant to ask what his 'own stuff' had been.

'I got into some strange stuff with Roy. Because of Roy. Debs never really knew about that and I never told her.'

'I'm not sure I like the sound of Roy,' I said.

Tony chuckled. 'He could make you feel fantastic. It's funny - a big, fat, ugly, queen like that ... but one word from Roy and I could feel like the most beautiful boy on the planet. I could do anything.'

'He made you do stuff,' I said.

Tony laughed again. 'Yeah, he did. All sorts of stuff. And I wasn't to tell anyone. He'd bring these blokes in, wherever we were, he always found a supply of boys. Roy's big thing, that always got him off, was watching me doing stuff with them. It went on for years.'

'You didn't have to...'

'I did. I'd have been dropped, just like that, if I hadn't.'

'You don't know that, Tony.'

'Roy told me straight.' He squashed out his cigarette. 'You see, I wasn't very good, Tim. You've got to appreciate that. I was crap. Couldn't really sing, couldn't play anything. I was only there because I was Debs' mate and I kept her sweet. And Roy liked to watch me with other men.' He was quiet again. 'It got dangerous,' he said. 'He put me right in danger and he did it for kicks. And I just went for it. I was kind of addicted to it - just like I was to sleeping pills, Lambert and Butler and cheap white wine.'

It didn't sound much of a rock'n'roll lifestyle to me. A surplus of boys, fags, wine and pills. Tony looked shattered as he told me all this, though; as if he'd not really gone over it in years.

'Did Kris know all this about you?' I asked.

'Course he did. Kris got me through it all. We met and he was coming off all sorts of stuff and leaving the business and we sort of hooked up and helped each other through it all.'

Tony sat up, pulled his holdall towards him and rooted around inside. 'That's all gone now, too, isn't it?' he said. 'It's like I'm out of that life now - the one I thought would last forever. And I'm back in my old life, as if nothing has changed. No, more than that. I'm helping Debs to start it all up again, as if I want my old life back, suddenly.'

'Don't you?'

'I didn't think so.' He was going though crumpled clean clothes. He yanked out a half full bottle of Moscovskaya vodka. 'But I came along quick enough, didn't I?'

I smiled.

'Hey,' he said. 'I've brought a bunch of clothes. You can wear something of mine tomorrow.'

'Cheers,' I said. I watched him sit up stiffly and fetch our emptied tea cups. He came back and passed me mine and I realised, with a blush, I'd watched his prick slide and nudge inside his shorts. 'What stopped the arrangement with Roy?' I asked. 'What made him leave you alone, in the end?'

Tony's laugh was drowned in glugs of vodka. 'Didn't you know?' He shook his head. 'You're not as big a fan as Debs thinks you are, are you, Tim? You'd better not let her find that out. She thinks you're our number one obsessive.'

I blushed further and sipped raw vodka. The fumes made my eyes mist over.

'Roy vanished,' said Tony. 'That year, after Debs lost the baby. We thought he was dead. At first, it seemed he was. But he survived and then he vanished, leaving us all alone, to fail on our own, vainglorious terms. No one's seen hide nor hair of Roy Kitchener, of Mr Starmaker himself, ever since.'

Tony drained his cup quickly and poured us two more shots. 'Have you not heard the tale?'

I sat back. 'Not yet, I haven't.'

Tony sat down heavily. 'You'll hear it sometime, I expect.' With that he seemed to have shrugged me off and he disappeared inside himself for a while.

I asked, 'Shall I turn the telly off?'

He smiled and nodded.

I walked over, switched it off and thought; here's the awkward part. We seem to be bedding down. Even if there's no frisson, I'm still in a damp towel. I'd left all my things in the bathroom.

I went back for my pants, put them on, and returned to the room to see Tony standing and facing away from me, sliding down his boxer shorts with a whisper of silk. Then he slipped quickly into his bed.

He'd waited till I'd left the room.

I got into my bed and we looked across the space at each other.

'Tim,' he said softly.

'Yeah?'

'Listen ... I'm not wanting to sound like I'm ...' He rolled his eyes. 'I don't know what I'm trying to say.'

'Go on,' I urged him, stretching out under the thin duvet, pushing into the cool places.

'I'm just not interested, you know?'

'Oh. Right.'

'Is that okay?'

'Yes,' I said, quietly. 'Course it is.'

'Okay,' he said. 'I'll turn the light out.'

Chapter Ten

It was just what he'd always wanted.

This is what Tony had always aimed at being. He'd thought about Diana Ross in a sheath dress with the Supremes behind her, all of them wriggling tightly on the spot. They were hemmed in by fans in the studio. The camera would have to fight to keep them in the picture.

On all those Sixties music shows you could feel the excitement, blistering off the TV screen. It was like licking the screen and your spit making it turn colourful. Tony did this once, as he watched Dusty come down the stairs on *Ready, Steady, Go*. She was nervous and regal; her voice booming out of the speaker. Tony licked the screen just once; to feel closer to her, to feel inside the studio. Her voice was making all of his insides vibrate.

This is what he had always wanted to be. The singer on a TV show, making someone at home feel just like that. He wanted to be on that podium with lucky teenagers dancing mindlessly about him; all of them unable to believe their luck.

Trying to touch you. Getting as close as they possibly could. All of them stewing under the lights.

And, having got here, having reached this studio, what was he trying to do but push them away? He stood on the stage for *Top of the Pops*, ready to go for a take. And it struck him: the fans couldn't dance. They were dressed horribly. They looked unwashed. They weren't really there for Things Fall Apart. They couldn't care less. When the song was announced and it was time to mime, the fans let out an almighty whoop, but only because the floor manager had told them to. It all rang hollow in Tony's burning ears. He knew they whooped for everyone.

Jaded and worn out; that's what the four of them were. They

now took appearances like this in their stride. It took hardly any energy to muster the smiles or the correct synchronised moves. All of them knew where the camera would be for their own special close-up. They all knew the song inside out. Even this new, difficult song, 'El Nino'.

Maybe, he thought, what he was missing was that special status conferred on him last Christmas, when he was the soloist. Maybe Roy was right and what he really wanted was to be performing alone all the time, perched on his glass stool. On the New Year show - the very day that Debs had been in hospital - he had gone on in his angel wings and a leather jacket, a twist of tinsel round his head, and he'd sung his tribute to her, ringed by fans. He'd impersonated the whole band all on his lonesome. Was that how he wanted to be all the time?

Had he grown up?

Roy said he'd lost his boyish *joie de vivre*. Something had snapped and gone in him this year and Roy wasn't happy. Roy wasn't happy with any of them. Sure, this new, experimental, ethnic song had gone to number three, but he still didn't like it. Roy didn't like Clive's dicking about with exotic instruments and authentic sounds one little bit. He thought it was a blind alley and in no way true to the spirit of the band as Roy conceived it.

The rest of them, Tony knew, were going through the motions and so Clive was getting all his own way. Tony couldn't help thinking that, maybe if they'd listened to Roy, and done things his way, they would have a second number one now.

But at least they were on *Top of the Pops* again. They were still a success. This was Debs' first appearance since her illness. It was late July, and no one would be watching anyway. They'd be out on lawns, on day trips. And meanwhile, here they were, in outfits made of chamois leather with tassles and boots. A kind of S+M look, but in beige.

Debs had her figure back. She looked unnaturally fit and well, as if nothing at all had happened to her. She would brush off anyone's concern for her. This being her first appearance back, people were rightly concerned, but she would shrug them off with a laugh. She'd never felt so great, she said, and she was towing the line over Clive's song, too. She thought it was a work of mature genius. Even though she had had almost nothing to do with the song, she was right behind it.

Now they were making music for adults. That's why the teenagers around them, on this show, seemed so inappropriate. Music for grown-ups, Clive had told them, didn't have to be for fun. People had grown up with pop and it would continue to be a big part of their lives. This was the big market for them now, he said; something more mature, sometimes more challenging. Sometimes easier on the ear - music for dinner parties and gatherings and driving down the motorway. They should leave their teeny bopper audience behind.

'What a load of bollocks,' Roy had sighed. 'That's a man getting into his thirties talking. There's a man thinking he's a real musician talking. And the world he is in is crap. It's ephemeral crap. And it won't put up with highminded bullshit from the likes of him.'

'You know what, Tony?' Roy asked him, that July. 'Your mattress absorbs a bathful of water from your body each year. There's more water in it than there is in you. That's why you're so frigging sourfaced these days. Your mattress has absorbed all your personality. And what you send out into the world is just a miserable husk. You've left the best part of yourself back in your bed, Tony boy...'

And Tony thought: I've left it in your bed, too, Roy. Sweat, piss, tears, blood and spunk in your bed and beds all over the country and Europe-wide. There's me in all them places. No wonder I'm dried up already. No wonder I'm a husk.

He'd read somewhere that booze dehydrates you as well, just like mattresses do. So there was that going on as well.

He might as well turn into sand.

Past his prime. His prime had been in Venice, last year. This summer, he wanted to go back to Italy. It was better than here. Suited him. He was a different person there. The world didn't embarrass him.

Embarrass him like Brenda Maloney did.

Brenda, he thought; you big fat bag. She'd have sweat patches coming through the suede of her stage costume because she was shaking herself for all she was worth. She was going hell for leather next to Debs, who seemed so serene and calm as she did the chanting. Brenda was giving it all she had; a dervish in a tassled mini skirt, pouting at the camera with all the bravado of a woman who knows what her next career move is. Soon, Brenda could let go of all this tacky sexy shit; she would have no need of it.

She was being groomed for breakfast telly and afternoon telly and she needed to be the lady next door, in suits and jumpers in plain colours, doing cookery, gardening, healthcare and sensitive interview slots. This was her last big fling as a temptress, this song, and she went at it mockingly, with nothing to lose.

Telly all through the daytime was to be the next big thing, Brenda had announced to them all. And she was going to clean up. She was just the sort of presenter than unemployed people or housewives would want to see in the middle of the day. She'd be full of good tips on how to run your life. She would advise on the tiny things that made up your life.

Tonight her hair was teased up huge. She was starting to look like someone who could fill up a whole TV screen easily and with aplomb. When Brenda talked about the future of TV, Tony believed every word. He could imagine it belonging to the likes of her. It was funny, how her brashness softened when she was on camera and she came across as vivacious and sparky, and never edgy or vicious. It was as if by reducing her to millions of transmittable particles, TV tamed the bitch Tony knew, at heart, she truly was.

When they appeared on talk shows as a group, it was Brenda who coached them on how to behave and how to represent themselves. It was she who did most of the talking. She knew just when to touch the chat show host's knee or call out to the audience and get them on her side. She had that knack of mass rapport. The band would watch the recordings of these shows afterwards and marvel at how wooden and unsure they all looked, apart from Brenda. And, against their better instincts, they would warm to her and think of her as the stand-out member of the band. She was the one with the common touch; the one your eye naturally went to.

'Let her have that attention,' Debs had said. 'If she wants to be that kind of celebrity so badly, then that's what she should do.'

They would lose her though, and none of them would miss her. They weren't sure yet if it would damage them in the public eye, to be one member down. But Roy said you could turn a thing like that to your advantage. He tapped his nose and nodded and didn't elaborate just yet. Then he was off, enthusing about his other projects on the go. Other bands, younger bands, new songs, different looks. Roy had his fingers in more pies than ever.

That's how they'd been able to get their own way with this experimental song. Roy was spending less time on them. His mandarin's painted eyes were looking elsewhere.

The ethnic song was called 'El Nino' which, as Clive explained, was a scientific term to do with meteorology. It was the warmth in the atmosphere as it pushed and shoved its way around the world, tossing monsoons, tornadoes, ice storms and floods into cities unprepared for such things. Natural disasters were taking over the world because of this boistrous, restless, broiling atmosphere. Probably it had all to do with pollution and people using hairspray.

The world was getting smaller as it was getting hotter and Clive's new song was a pointed reminder of that. He was timely. They all thought so, and he was venemous over Live Aid and the fact that, although Bob Geldof cracked on that all the major pop stars of the past and present were taking part, Things Fall Apart hadn't even been asked.

'Abba haven't been asked, either,' Debs said.

'They're not together anymore,' Clive said.

'Nor have Bucks Fizz,' she pointed out.

'Them?' he laughed. 'That's some fucking consolation. We should be up there, at Wembley. We're proper. Especially now.'

This was last Saturday, as the two of them sat with pizza and lager in the Kilburn flat, watching Bowie at Live Aid. 'Just across town,' Clive said. 'We should be over there, in that fucking stadium, doing our bit.'

Secretly, Debs was glad. She couldn't imagine standing at the head of a full stadium like that, being expected to dance about and wave her arms. She imagined your voice would come back at you like a tidal wave, lifted and swelled out by the many voices of the crowd. It would be terrifying.

Yet Clive was right. They ought to be thinking about their profile and their standing. It was ridiculous that this event should be going on while they were number three in the British charts with an innovative single and still no one had asked them to appear. It was a right poke in the eye.

Bowie - lizard-sharp in powder blue - sang 'Heroes' and Clive was pulling on his leather jacket and lacing his Doc Martens.

'I'm going out for a bit.'

Off to relieve his tension, she thought, down one of the Irish pubs he'd taken to. The ones on Kilburn High Street that she would never dare go into.

'It does make me feel guilty,' Debs said. 'Those pictures of starving people and us sitting here eating pizza. It makes our lives look so excessive.'

'You're just falling for all the rubbish they spout on there,' he said. 'All that lot on the telly, they're just getting a good advert, by doing their old bloody songs.'

'They're doing some good. We aren't!'

'Is that our fault?'

'No ... but...'

'You watch. Whatever they do on there, it won't make any difference. They might get loads of money sent in, but that's not what they need. Not only that. They'll throw money at it because it eases their conscience.'

Debs said, 'It's consciousness-raising. That's what it is.'

'What?'

'I ... don't know. I've never used that phrase in my life before.' She looked perturbed.

'Well, where did it come from?'

'I don't know.'

'Consciousness-raising,' he mimicked, and laughed. 'What a load of crap.'

'I wonder where I picked it up from.'

He was heading out the door. 'God knows. You watch too much telly, you know. I remember a time when you used to sing round the house, training your voice. I remember when you used to write songs, Debbie Now.'

She sat waiting for the door to slam. It's true, she thought, that's what I used to do.

'Anyway,' she called after him. 'What do you know about it? You've never been to Africa. You don't know anything.'

'Exactly,' he said. 'And I wouldn't bloody well want to go to Africa. And I don't know anything about it.' He pointed steadily at the TV. 'But neither does anyone on there. I'm a musician, for god's sake. I'm a fucking pop star. What do I know?'

Nowadays, everything had reversed, it seemed to Brenda, and it was Roy who needed the looking after.

After the recording that night, Brenda took the initiative and went to find him in the BBC staff bar. He was in a flowing off-white muslin shirt that came down to his ankles and his head was shaven bald. He'd let the drag slip quite a lot of late.

She found him standing with a bunch of cronies at the bar, boring them and slurping at neat egg nog.

'Brenda Maloney,' he bellowed. 'How was the show? Are you still Top of the soapy-tit-wanking Pops?'

She lowered her head. She knew some of these TV people by now. She looked at Roy and decided he was something of a liability these days.

She tried to drag him from the bar, two hands around his meaty forearm.

'You're coming home with us. The car's out the back.'

Suddenly his face was right in hers. He smelled of lemons. 'I don't know why you've even stuck with them this long, Brenda Maloney,' he slurred. 'You never gave a flying fuck about them.'

They were wedged in the doorway and others wanted to be in. 'What?'

'You never had any respect for what they were doing. Poor kids. You thought they were wankers.'

'Come on, Roy.'

He struggled to keep up with her, down the grey corridor. He raised his voice and it was choked up. 'You're going to leapfrog over all over them. You're going to be on the telly.'

She swung around. 'Yes, I am, you fat fuck. But that's up to me, isn't it?'

'Is it?' he leered.

Brenda took a deep breath. 'At one time we let you run our lives, Roy. You told us where to live, what to wear and sing and eat and who we could see. You said it was the only way. But we're older now.'

'And you don't need me.'

'Actually, no.' She looked him up and down. 'You perverted bastard.'

Roy reeled for a second on the spot in his sandals. They were in a corridor of framed photos from old TV shows. He couldn't keep them still and in a line. 'I knew you were bad news from the start, Brenda.'

'Oh, did you?' She started stomping away. 'I'm going to fetch the others.'

He roared: 'Rot in hell, you fat fucking bitch.'

Then he went stumbling in the opposite direction.

Debs was glad to be out of her suede bikini and back in a tracksuit. She hurried out of her dressing room, into the lime green of the underground corridor and the thought came to her very clearly: That's the last time we'll ever be on *Top of the Pops*. That's it for us.

She looked over to Tony's dressing room and saw a very young girl waiting outside. She had bangles on and her hair was up, crimped and stained pink. 'Are you waiting for someone?' Debs asked.

The girl wouldn't look her in the eye. 'We were in the audience,' she said. 'You were great.'

'Thanks,' said Debs. 'Look, if you're waiting for Tony...'

'I'm waiting for Rob. My boyfriend.'

'Oh.'

'Tony's signing his plaster cast for him. He broke his leg in three places playing football. But he still wanted to be in the audience on *Top of the Pops*.'

'That's great,' Debs said. Now that she thought, she could remember this girl dancing around next to a dark-haired boy with his leg in plaster. 'Didn't you want anything signed?'

The girl shook her head. 'Didn't have nothing. Tony told me to wait out here. He's very good-looking, isn't he? Up close.'

'Yes,' said Debs, and banged on the dressing room door. 'Tony?'

She opened it and peered in.

At first she thought they were having a little rest. It was absurd, but that was the first thought she had. The boy was stretched face down on the dressing table, with his plastered leg stuck out awkwardly. He already had a few names and messages scrawled on it. What she could see of his thighs were covered in dark hair. Tony was resting on top of him, still wearing much of his beige bondage gear. The leather kilt and shorts were off and, as Debs suddenly got the whole picture, Tony jumped up suddenly. He darted a look at her and his cock jabbed out of the boy's arse, as if it had been hiding there.

'Debs!' he shouted.

She tried to slam the door shut, but the girl was standing behind her and she'd seen. Debs had banged her elbow.

The boy struggled to lift himself up, alone, as Tony groaned and slammed off into his shower room.

Debs was caught between them all. She turned to see the pink-tinted girl scurry off, crying, down the corridor.

Tony's voice came loudly through the shower room door. 'They shouldn't have been allowed in here anyway!'

She was left to help the poor, mortified boy with the plastered leg get himself off the dressing table. She found it almost touching, the way he tried to cover his ebbing erection. 'You didn't see nothing, did you?' he stammered. 'You didn't see nothing, did you?'

'Nothing,' Debs said, capably helping him into his single-legged jeans. I could have been a nurse, she thought.

Once she'd packed him off, worried at how badly he was trembling, she sat down in Tony's dressing room and listened to him splashing in the shower.

'How long have you been doing that?' she asked, when he came out in a towel.

He gave her a mutinous look.

'How long have you been shagging our fans?'

He turned away and dried himself off quickly. He was over-generous with the talc, dousing himself in savage gusts.

'It's not fair, Tony,' she said. 'It's awful.' She watched him dress. 'That poor girl, stuck out there waiting. She had no idea.'

He turned on her. 'Course she did. She knew the score. She just about shoved him in to get laid. They were both into it.'

'I can't believe it's you, saying these things. Doing ... that.'

'I have to do it some time, Debs.' He fumbled with his shirt buttons. 'Jesus. Can you stop being all sweetness and light, for just one second? This is the world we're living in, Debs. There was nothing wrong with what you just saw. We were all getting something out of it. They both got their brush with fame in the raw and I badly needed a fuck.'

His face was dark. She knew that underneath he was embarassed really. She couldn't shake off that image of him cramming himself up inside that poor boy.

'Did you use protection?' she asked and knew, as soon as she asked, that he hadn't.

'I'm okay,' he muttered, slinging his gear in a bag.

'For fuck's sake, Tony...'

'I'm okay, all right?'

She kept quiet.

'There's got to be perks for doing this shit,' he said at last. 'And anyway - Brenda does it.'

'I don't care about Brenda.'

'She shags everything that comes her way.'

'I said...'

'And so does Clive!' he said. 'If you want to have a yell at anyone, Debbie Now, it should be at him, shouldn't it?'

She caught her breath. 'Clive?'

Then Clive was in the doorway, hair wet, reeking of shower gel and Old Spice.

'There's trouble,' he told them. 'Roy's gone beserk. He's running amok, Brenda says.'

With her new and expert knowledge of the interior of TV centre, Brenda led them breathlessly through a series of dark, empty corridors.

'Everyone's gone home,' Clive said.

'It's like being on Scooby frigging Doo,' said Tony.

'What's Roy doing all the way back here?' Debs asked. 'He'll get lost. We'll get the security men after us and...'

'He was pissed,' Brenda said, clip-clopping down the shiny lino. 'He was out of it on Advocaat.'

'What was the matter with him?'

Brenda sighed. 'I just told him a few home truths. About how we don't really need him anymore.'

'Oh, Brenda,' said Debs. 'You didn't.'

Brenda gave her a sickly look Debs couldn't decipher.

As they carried on in the gloom, Debs couldn't help thinking about how fat Roy was. After she'd lost the baby Debs had immersed herself in medical books and now she was haunted by images of how large and inflamed Roy's heart must be, underneath all those layers of abused flesh.

She imagined his heart wouldn't be able to withstand much upset. She pictured it as swollen to the size of a melon. At any given moment it might burst. She tried to chase the image of that angered, exploding heart out of her mind and pick up her pace.

Now she was seeing Tony's inflamed cock instead; interrupted, furious and red.

What's happening to us all? she thought.

Brenda stopped and pointed to an emergency exit in a wall of glass. Someone had left it ajar and the cool of the night was fresh on their faces.

'What's out there?' Clive asked.

Debs frowned. She could smell honeysuckle and, underneath, the loamy smell of turned earth.

'That's where he went,' Brenda said.

She led the way out into the dark and cold and the ground was suddenly springy under their feet.

They were in a lush garden, walled around and protected. Dimly, they could make out stirring leaves all around them; as they moved into the lightest patch, snagged all the way by rustling branches.

'It's that garden,' Tony said, in a voice that sounded more like his own again. 'From that kids' TV show.'

As their eyes grew accustomed to the milky weak moonlight over Shepherd's Bush, and the curds of violet cloud nudged obligingly out of the way, they all saw at once that the kids TV garden had been completely trashed.

With tremendous force and persistance, someone had set about ripping up every carefully-tended shrub and bush.

Flower heads and bulbs and clods of earth were strewn on the lawn. Even the turf had been torn up in places. The pewter memorial statue of the kids' show's very first pet dog had been shoved off its plinth. The wooden bench named for a sponsored blind quadropeligic had been tossed over backwards.

And the bronze sheet of the goldfish pond, pride of place in the middle of the dark garden, had been irrevocably polluted. Vomit floated in a yellowish scum on its surface.

The four members of the band were staring, however, past the scum, and at the still, lumpen shape of their manager, lying face first in the water.

Chapter Eleven

'In the end,' said Tony, as he got us back onto the motorway, glancing anxiously at lorries from the sliproad and giving me the willies, 'it was all a bit like Who Shot JR.'

'What do you mean?' I was wishing he was a better driver.

In the passenger seat, Debs was still quiet. She hadn't spoken much at all this morning.

'Like on *Dallas*, when JR was shot? About twenty years ago?' At last, he got us into the right lane. I sighed with relief.

'I'm not that young,' I said. 'I remember JR getting shot. Kristen did it. Sue Ellen's sister.'

'Right,' Tony said. 'But he survived, right? With no ill effects. Well, we all thought, when we saw him lying drowned in that fish pond, Roy had karked it, too, and gone off to that great fat tranny nightclub in the sky.' He wrenched the Morris's steering wheel rather sharply. 'But he was okay. We dragged him out between us.'

I could see Debs' shoulder tremble. She was in a denim shirt of Tony's. He'd taken her some clothes to her room this morning. She'd been grateful, but I could see her thinking: She was hardly going to look very glam for this reunion. Maybe she didn't want to.

'We tried to pump the water out of his lungs and massage his heart,' said Tony. 'I even had a stab at the kiss of life, but none of us had a clue. We hadn't done first aid or anything. Brenda was sucking pond water out of him, and she could never stand him. Anyway, when the ambulancemen finally turned up, they said it was good we hadn't gone too far, trying to resuscitate him, because we might have done more harm than good. Jumping on him and whatnot. They whipped him into casualty and he was in for three weeks.'

'And he lived?'

Tony nodded. 'And he wouldn't see any of us. He absolutely refused to. He set a message, eventually, resigning as our manager and said we could make our own way in future. He'd had enough.'

I let this sink in for a moment. 'He wouldn't see any of you?'

'None of us have clapped eyes on him since then. But there were rumours. Most said he'd wanted to leave the business for ages. That all his financial affairs were in a mess. That he'd lost his golden touch - and even he saw that it was time to get out.'

Debs grunted. 'The financial stuff was certainly right. We were properly messed up with money.'

Tony laughed. 'Some said he'd retired to an island on the west coast of Scotland, where he was living as a full woman. A big fat spinster who raised rare breeds of birds. He sent us one note. Said that he'd felt the cold hand of death clutch hold of his heart. And he'd taken it as a sign he had to get away from his current lifestyle. We were all deadly to him. He wished us the best for the rest of our lives. And that,' smiled Tony, 'was that.'

I got mixed up with the snarled multicolours of the road map and I could feel Debs and Tony tense up each time I misdirected us over the moors. We were high above sea level and it seemed like the whole horizon had hoisted itself up and we were coasting some vast ochre scrubland plateau at the top of the world.

The road unspooled along sloping hillsides and all we saw for a while were disgruntled sheep in long yellow grass and various road-kills, scarlet in their raggy overcoats. The light was good and I was cheered, until Debs reminded me that it was somewhere round here, out on these wilds, that Brady and Hindley used to take their own day trips and photograph each other larking in the tussocky grass. Great.

I fineigled a route into the relevant valley and the old car crept down through dank, ancient villages, past limestone houses and hawthorn thickets.

When we got to the town Debs wanted to walk about and get some air before bearding Clive in his den.

All the houses were stone built and the people we saw were dressed for walking in the hills. It was one of those towns in the middle of nowhere that the well-to-do had taken over. We stood outside a flower shop and couldn't recognise anything on display. Nothing you'd normally see in Yorkshire. I wondered if Debs was thinking of taking him some flowers.

She hurried over the road to watch frothy water tumbling from underneath a road bridge and across flat green rocks.

'We always said we'd live in the country,' she told me. 'Miles from anywhere. It was our fantasy retirement environment, like Paul and Linda McCartney. I used to dream about them two. Buying a whole island and sitting on the beach with a fire going, singing about the Mull of Kintyre. I used to think, well, why can't we do that as well?'

Just then I could picture Debs as she should have been by now. She could be properly middle-aged, living in a farmhouse and wearing big jumpers, making soup in her farmhouse kitchen. Then she'd walk in the fields they owned, throwing sticks for the dogs and feeding the ducks. Maybe she would have a horse.

Tony said, 'I always thought I'd be where I am now. In a house like the one where my parents lived. I looked forward to it. After all those shared houses and hotels. I wanted a house with pebble dashing and a porch and neat hedges around.' He glanced over the wall into the jade water. 'The countryside's all right to visit. But it's not really for me.'

Clive's house was more impressive than any of us had expected. It was at the top of a hill overlooking the town, hidden from the cluster of renovated cottages that Tony inched the Morris Minor past. He was terrified of the incline and wasn't sure the car would make it to the top. Debs and I peered out at the numbers and the twee name plaques and at last we found Clive's place.

It was a cottage wedged into the old rock of the hillside, the kind that seemed deceptively small from the front, but backed into large, cool, subterranean rooms.

In a horror film, I thought, his would be the haunted cottage, high over the feudal town under lowering clouds. Clive would be the spectacularly rapacious Count waiting inside. As it was, he was just the richest semi-famous person in town.

The whitewashed front of the house was densely crowded with climbing plants, so that the windows were almost obscured. The house looked as if it was frowning at us.

When we got out of the car I noticed that Debs' mouth was set in a grim line. I didn't blame her. I would love to end up in a house this nice, though I wasn't sure about the thatched roof. There could be all sorts living in that.

Debs and Tony led the way up the garden path and I watched them knock into each other, as if accidentally, just the way they always had during dance routines. Now it seemed like something they did habitually, for luck.

Tony rapped on the old wood of the door and I hung back, conscious again of my lack of role in this.

When the door opened it let out the most wonderful breakfast smells; fried sausage and bacon, coffee and eggs. For a moment I thought of the fairy tale and the ogre who must live inside, preparing treats to fatten his visitors up.

Clive himself had come to the door, in a heavy cable-knit cardigan and reading glasses. He now wore his hair cropped short and he had a sharp, pointed beard, streaked with silver. He looked like someone retired from the Secret Service; someone ready to jump up, whenever the call to arms came again.

There was a bristling energy to him, thrown into relief by the travel lodge weariness of his visitors that morning. Clive looked to me like a man who was used to sleeping soundly in his bed at night.

I could tell that, at the sight of him, Debs was rigid, like an antelope realising the lion's just clocked her.

'Thanks for seeing us, Clive,' she said limply, at last, shielding her eyes from the Yorkshire sunlight, winching an overlong denim cuff into her fist.

Clive grinned and his eyes twinkled green. I felt an instant rush of attraction; sold on him completely. I would have to stiffen my resolve and not fall for his straight man's charm. He had, after all, fucked up Debs' life.

She was hugging him, awkwardly at first, then, without warning, giving in completely and burying her face in his cardigan. Clive looked over her shoulder to Tony.

'I knew I'd be hearing from you,' he grinned. 'We were about due for a get-together.' Clive held out a large, scarred musician's hand and pulled Tony roughly into their hug. Tony went eagerly and I stood watching the three of them.

When they finished and looked up, all damp-eyed, Clive was introduced to me and he nodded briefly.

'So you're only giving us half an hour?' I asked.

Clive frowned. 'Who said that?'

'Your assistant,' said Debs. 'She said you were busy today.'

He shrugged. 'I make the decisions, not her. Come in, come in, anyway...' He led us into a hall brightened yellow and blue by the stained glass at the top of the front door and decorated throughout with hunting prints.

'That assistant of mine, Jo, she's only about twelve and she's really terrifying. She keeps telling me what to do...'

He took us through to a living room with a cool stone floor and expensive rugs and lamps. There was a whole collection of his prized arcane instruments from around the world, all of them perched incongruously on shelves and chairs and on top of the dusty black

piano. Cassette tapes and CDs were strewn everywhere, out of their
cases and all over the floor. I kept an eye out for where I was treading.

'I'm sorry it's such a fucking tip,' he said, rubbing the shaved
back of his neck. 'I was up all night, working on something...'

'Still writing your music?' Debs smiled.

'Oh, yes,' he said and, in one swift movement, scooped a spotless
white cat off the piano stool, where it had been studiously cleaning
its paws and ignoring us. 'I was working with this little beast.'
Clutching the startled pet to his broad chest, he hurried to the
stereo and started to play us an excerpt from his current work.

Debs' and Tony's eyes widened in alarm as the distorted and
reorganised screeches and yowls of this very same cat came full blast
through the speakers.

It was ghastly.

Clive set the cat down and it shot off to safety. He clicked off the
tape triumphantly.

'It's almost human, isn't it? That sound? If you play her backwards, slightly slowed down, she very nearly sings actual words...'

Debs' mouth was hanging open.

I thought Clive must have too much money or time on his
hands, if he was following the cat around the house with a microphone.

'You aren't impressed, are you?' he laughed.

Luckily, this broke the tension and suddenly we could all laugh.

'The singing cat!' said Debs. 'You almost had me believing you
then...'

Clive shrugged and rubbed his neck again, ruefully, and watched
Debs fling herself down on his antique sofa. She was making herself
right at home and I almost felt sorry for Clive. I think he had been
quite proud of his cat tape.

'We have to talk business,' Debs said, and patted the space next
to her. Tony parked himself obediently.

'I thought we'd have some breakfast first...' Clive began and she shook her head.

'We have to move quickly on this, Clive. Someone's pulling a fast one.'

'Shelley Sommers?' he chuckled. 'I don't think she's bright enough for that.'

'Her management is,' Debs said.

'Who is her manager?' Tony asked.

'I don't know,' Clive said. 'The contract I got for the song rights was all a bit garbled...'

A horrible thought struck me. 'It isn't you, is it?'

Debs gasped and all eyes were on Clive.

His eyes narrowed at me. 'As it happens, no. Though I'd love to get my hands on her.' He sighed and sat down, hitching his corduroys over his knees. 'The acts I manage are a lot less prestigious. Pub and club singers, mostly. Though I do have a new act on my books I've been meaning to get in touch with you about...' He dug around in a heap of CDs on the shelf beside his head.

He found the one he wanted, smiled almost nervously, and gave it to Debs.

Her face hardened. She passed the CD to Tony.

'What's this?' Tony said, not understanding at all. 'Things Fall Apart Again?'

'A tribute band,' Clive said smoothly. 'They're all the rage now, these days. Tribute bands do good business in the clubs, on the nostalgia circuit. Two girls, two boys. What more can you ask for? All dressed up in the kind of gear we used to wear.'

Debs and Tony held the new disc between them and stared at the picture on the cover.

'They look nothing like us,' Debs said at last.

'They don't have to,' said Clive. 'It's not our actual faces that people remember, is it? It's just the music, the feel of it all. That's all they need.'

'This is all our hits on here,' said Tony quietly. 'They've covered all our greatest hits.' He looked close to tears. 'And the one who's meant to be me is ugly.'

'Barry?' Clive smiled. 'Ugly? Do you think so?'

'Yes,' said Tony.

Suddenly Debs was on her feet. 'You're doing it as well!' she yelled. 'You're just the same as Shelley bloody Sommers! Fleecing us for a quick buck!'

'Calm down, Debbie,' Clive said and there was an edge to his voice that I didn't like at all.

'It's true!' she burst. 'We came here in all good faith, to talk about protecting our shared interests, to discuss the legacy of our music - and you're doing this! Organising some tacky, horrible so-called tribute band to exploit us even further!'

'They'll only do clubs and student union nights,' he said levelly. 'You should be flattered, Debbie. At least people want them. At least they remember.'

'But they should be seeing us!' she cried. 'It should be us up there, doing those shows. Not some younger lookalikes.'

'No,' said Clive. 'I don't want to perform anymore. I'm happy doing what I'm doing.'

'With your eskimos and frigging cats,' said Tony bitterly.

'Some of us have got to go on performing,' Debs said. 'Some of us have no choice. Some of us didn't come away with all the publishing rights in our pockets.' Debs seemed to run out of steam then, and she sat back down in her place.

'Is that what this is about?' Clive said. 'Is it about money, Debbie?' He sighed. 'And I thought you'd come all of this way just to see me. Because maybe you still thought something of me.'

She looked uncomfortable. 'Yes, it did have something to do with money. It was ... I don't know ... it was everything. Seeing you ... of course it was seeing you again.'

'It's a shock, though,' said Tony. 'Seeing how rich you are, Clive.'

'Rich?' He looked around. 'Most of what I've got has come from what I've done since Things Fall Apart ... fell apart. Incidental music from TV documentaries. You should know that.'

'Yes,' said Tony. 'I bought one of those records.'

'Well, there you are, then.'

There was a pause.

'I'll make us some coffee,' Clive said.

Debs stopped him a moment. 'This tribute band,' she said. 'Are they any good?'

'I've only seen them rehearse,' he said. 'They're brand new, as it happens. Four lovely kids. Really nervous about their first show, just like we were. It's this Friday night, for Durham's student union. Some kind of ball thing in a marquee. I'm supposed to go through and see them do their thing.'

He got up to make the coffee.

'Doesn't it make you feel strange?' Debs asked. 'Watching them, being us?'

Clive frowned and shook his head. 'Maybe for a second it did. But no, not really. It was all a long time ago, wasn't it? It hardly seems like the same people anymore.' He smiled gently, that charm of his coming to the fore again. 'I'll make some bacon sandwiches too, eh?'

Once he was out of the room, Debs turned to the two of us and whispered harshly. 'He's timed it like this on purpose. He's got this band starting out just as Shelley Sommers releases her single. It's all planned. He's going to cash in, as well.' She threw the tribute CD down on the stone fireplace. Tony and I both winced as it cracked clean across.

'He's just another one ripping us off!' Tony hissed.

'He knew!' Debs said. 'I was right! Soon as Shelley's single comes out, there'll be a huge amount of interest and nostalgia. I said so - and Clive knows it, too. Only he's doing something about it...'

'So what do we do?' I asked. I thought Clive's plans had probably ruined everything. He had made it clear he wasn't interested in the band coming back for real. I knew that's what Debs wanted more than anything.

'We'll have to work on him,' she said thoughtfully. 'I don't know. Emotional blackmail, or something.'

We all sat back on our tapestried seats and fell quiet. Tony noticed the *Radio Times* on the coffee table, which had that red monkey thing on the cover, the mascot for the children's telethon. 'Is that this week's?' he said. 'Chuck it over.'

He riffled through to Saturday, grunted, and showed us yet another picture of Shelley Sommers with Brenda, both of them grinning fit to burst.

'Brenda's put on a stack of weight,' Debs observed. 'And she's had her chin done.'

'Huh,' Tony said. 'Listen to this. 'The main attraction of the evening will be at nine pm, when, live from the Metro shopping centre in Gateshead, soap starlet Shelley Sommers performs her new smash hit single, 'Let's Be Famous' for the first time. Introducing her will be one-time pop diva and TV sensation, Brenda Maloney.''

'So? We know all that,' Debs said irritably. 'Why don't you rub it in a bit more, Tony?'

He shook his head. 'But we never knew exactly where or what time this performance was going to take place.' He stroked the page thoughtfully. 'Nine pm on Saturday in the middle of Gateshead. Now we know exactly where it is.'

'So?'

'Well, I've just thought of a way we can get round Clive,' he said. 'I've got an idea that just might interest him...'

We were taken outside to admire Clive's hilltop garden, which was rather wild and spacious. He sat us at a mildewed bench in his gazebo and came out with a tray of coffee things looking quite pleased with himself.

Debs sat slumped and I noticed she had panda rings around her eyes. I hadn't slept much either. I'd listened to Tony snoring through the night and cursed him for that, but also his presumption in telling me he 'wasn't interested' in me. As if I was the one angling for his attention and giving him the gladeye all the time. He'd made me feel like a groupie, like a ridiculous, horny fanboy and, this late in the morning, sitting under the stirring green shadows of Clive's garden, I was still resenting him furiously. Especially when he came to sit right beside me on the bench and nudged his thigh into mine, accidentally, a couple of times.

We sat there for a couple of hours, slowly unwinding. Clive turned out to be a pretty good host, dissolving the tension they'd drummed up during their conversation about money and diverting us with chat on a variety of topics. He even asked me about my life, which was a novelty these days.

From the open door of the study behind us, came some curious ambient music that I assumed was his own. It seemed a funny thing, to listen to your own music. But what did I know?

After a while we relaxed and even Debs sat with her face tilted up, to catch the sunlight. Clive announced that it was almost lunchtime and he should probably open some wine for us. 'I hope you're staying for lunch.'

'We should be going,' Debs said. 'I thought you had a full day on, today.'

He stood there in his outsize cardy, holding the tray of dirty cups. 'How often does my ex-wife come to call? I don't need to work today.'

He went in, passing the white cat on its way out.

We watched the musical cat stride nonchalantly onto the lawn.

'I wonder if it really does sing words,' Tony said.

Debs tutted.

Tony's knee nudged mine. I pulled away.

'So what about you two boys, hm?' Debs smiled, pulling up her shirt sleeves.

'What about us?' I asked.

'You know,' she said, rolling her eyes. 'Last night. Locked in a motel room together.' She reached over and took hold of our hands. 'I don't want the gory details, but I do want you to thank me for being a fantastic matchmaker.'

I couldn't believe her. I half expected Tony to get all upset at her insensitivity and storm out. I had half a mind to do so myself.

Instead, he coughed and said, 'Well. You know how it is...' And he let his voice dwindle away.

I looked at him sharply.

Debs squawked. 'I knew it! I knew it from the start! I knew the two of you would just adore each other...'

Tony shrugged. 'Early days, yet. Early days.' Then he turned to look at me.

'I have to piss,' I said coldly, and took myself off into the house.

Behind me, I heard them start to whisper, heads close together over the table.

I found Clive in the living room, pulling bottles off an iron rack. He looked me up and down as if he'd never seen me before in his life.

'Could I use the loo?' I asked.

'Did you shag her?' he asked, picking up a heavy corkscrew and getting to work. He looked at me when I didn't reply. 'Come on. You can tell me. I'm not even married to her any more.'

'I...'

He whistled between his teeth and held the dusty bottle between his knees. I watched him yank the cork free and jumped at the gunshot. 'She's an attractive older woman. She's still a looker. And, from what I remember, Debbie was always a goer. So have you shagged her? Have you shagged my ex-wife?'

I really needed to go to the loo. That strong coffee of his had gone right through me.

'You're not a very articulate young man, are you?' he smiled.

Now that really hurt.

'Yes,' I said. 'We slept together on Saturday night. After...'

He stepped lightly across the stone flags of the living room and punched me in the mouth. I fell down. Bang on the coccyx.

'Jesus,' I said quietly, holding my face.

The corduroy trunks of his legs swayed before me.

'Stand up.'

'I fucking can't.'

'I had to do that. She isn't mine anymore. Hasn't been for a long time. But it was a gut reaction. I couldn't help it.'

'Is that meant to be an apology?' I couldn't make my consonants very clear. I tried to stand up and slipped on the rug.

'I knew it,' he said. 'I knew it by the way you came walking in here so cockily. Little squirt like you, walking in my house like that. I could see it all over your fucking face. You were thinking; I've shagged his missus. And he doesn't know.'

'I wasn't looking like that!'

'Yes you were.'

He thrust his massive paw into my face. I flinched, expecting another smack. He grasped my hand and hoisted me up to my feet.

'No hard feelings,' he said. 'I could just smell her on you and it got too much for me. That's all it was.'

'Right.' I could feel my eye puffing up in front of him. I willed it not to.

'You'll understand one day. When you're my age and you see some young bloke strutting about like that. I just had to get it out of my system.' He clapped me hard on the back. 'You can have her. No, really. I don't mind. I'm happy if you can make her happy.'

'But I...'

'We'll say no more about it. Now we've sorted it out like men.'

I was seeing double by now, and all I could do was nod.

'You want the loo, right? Back out in the hallway. At the end. I'll go out and talk to my guests. I'm going to persuade them to stay till supper. Why don't you go and piss and put some water on that eye, and then bring out this nice Chardonnay and four glasses, hm? And we'll forget this ever happened.'

'Okay,' I said, 'All right, Clive.'

As he left for the garden again, a new spring in his step, I reflected that he'd always been my least favourite member of the band anyway.

I turned to find the loo. I was bursting. Before I went, I picked up one of the rather smudgy glasses, the one I would give to Clive and took it with me so I could aim some piss in it. Topped up with the rubbish Chardonnay he'd so expertly opened, he'd never notice.

We got drunk that afternoon. We watched the singing cat gambol on the yellowy grass and the shadows stretch tall and then slant away as the occasional breeze swept in and italicized the lawn.

We were sheltered and dozey with our wine, smoking and chatting; the atmosphere piquant with plans and revenges, as I watched Clive sip appreciatively at my own piss spritzer and Tony prepared to hoodwink him into going along with our plan.

And meanwhile Debs grew happily drunk, thinking Tony and I were suddenly an item and, I imagined, she was thinking herself lady of this Yorkshire manor. She was wondering, not unhappily, what it might be like, to be married to Clive still.

'Do you have a lady friend at the moment?' she asked him, out of the blue. Lady friend rather than girlfriend, I noticed, out of deference to both their senses of their own maturity.

'I do, yes,' he smiled. 'Cassandra's in publishing. She works in London through the week. She edits children's books.'

'Oh,' Debs nodded and stared into her glass. 'Cassandra's a nice name.'

'She's got two little girls, both away at school.'

I saw Debs look up at him. 'How old?'

'Six and nine,' he said. 'Ariel and Rosalind. They're gorgeous. They're just like my own.'

Debs nodded and smiled and, for a horrible moment, it seemed like she wouldn't be able to stop herself nodding.

No one had noticed my swelling eye. Either Clive had warned them and explained it away, or no one was looking at me very hard. We were picking at fat black olives from a hand-thrown bowl, glazed blue. The others seemed content to while away the rest of the day like this, taking in the sprightly Yorkshire air.

It was as if Clive had put some kind of spell on them, to deter them from their quest.

They talked about their past adventures; about Roy and the clubs they had played together. Clive asked politely about Debs' mother and Debs said, 'You know Franky. She'll never change. She's got some new man who gives her everything.' They talked about when they went on the Eurovision and it turned out Clive had a videotape of that whole competition. They could watch it later, if they liked, after supper.

Suddenly it seemed that we had agreed to stay.

Then they talked about the videos they had made, back when videos for singles were brand new things and they were at the forefront of the art form. 'I watch these so-called art house movies,' Clive said, 'and all the effects, all the things they do, just come straight from what we did then.'

'The best one we ever did,' said Tony haltingly, his teeth blue with the red wine we'd moved onto, 'was the one in Venice.'

Debs laughed. 'Just because you were the star in that one.'

'It was good,' said Clive, with a sigh. 'It was fucking good. It still holds up if you watch it now. It's quite spooky and surreal. And we all look fucking gorgeous.'

'Roy was right,' said Tony. 'We were all at our best, that summer. It was all downhill after that. We looked fucking marvellous.'

They all looked at me then, as if they were expecting me to be in my prime, since I was the youngest in our midst. But I was already a good few years older than they'd been in Venice.

'The one I like,' Clive said, 'is 'Blues of the World'. The one about Debs throwing me out and starting off on her own life. That's a beautiful video. It still makes me cry.'

Debs looked moved by this. 'Really?'

He nodded. 'Cassandra won't let me watch it. I cry every time. I get to thinking about everything I've messed up.'

I saw her heart go out to him. I wanted to piss in his glass again for that. He was winding her around his finger.

'Do you think,' Tony began. 'Do you think we should have stayed together?' He picked up the bottle and gave us all another slosh. 'Sometimes I think we gave in too easily. I'd got myself on the rails again. We could have pushed it further...'

'No,' said Debs. 'It got too messy. We would have killed each other.'

'I've thought about this,' said Tony. 'I think we would have been okay. We were a team, remember? We still looked out for each other. It was us against the rest of the world. I still think we could have made it.'

Clive looked thoughtful. 'I won't complain about my life since Things Fall Apart ... I can't really, things have been great. But Tony's right. I do think about what we might have all done together.' He looked sharply at Debs. 'Do you still write lyrics?'

She blushed and looked down. 'I've just started again.'

This was news to me.

'These past few days,' she said, 'going over it all again in my head ... it's really inspired me to write some more words.'

'Really?' asked Tony. 'That's great!' I could feel the pressure of his leg against mine again.

Clive said quietly, 'You know, Debbie. I'd really love to hear what you've written. That is, I mean, if you're ready to go public with it. I always loved your writing. You know that.'

She looked delighted and flushed. 'It's very rough.'

Tony was wringing his hands together under the table. 'You're writing songs again! I can't believe it!'

She looked wistful. 'There's no music for them. They're just words so far.'

Clive snorted. 'Music's easy. Any fool can string some chords together and make them sound good. That stuff, it's just in our bones, in the very marrow. We just have to let it out. It's in everyone. That's why even the cat can sing.'

Tony gave him a funny look. 'Go on, Debs. Get your notebook. Read us some new words.'

Then, quite distinctly, I felt Tony's hand reach, under the cover of the mildewed table, and touch my leg. His fingers rested there, warmly, for a moment, and then were gone. I swallowed.

'Read them to us, Debs,' I said, rather woodenly. 'Please.'

She laughed, mock-protested and, at last, felt around in her handbag for her notebook. She cleared her throat and tossed her hair out of her eyes.

It was late in the afternoon by now and the light was mellow, having shed that particular sharpness hours ago, back when I'd stopped wondering what time it was and what time were we going to leave.

Tony's hand reached out for my leg again and this time, his fingertips stayed there, lightly on the fabric of the jeans I'd borrowed from him. As Debs found her page and started to read aloud, slowly, quite clearly, he put more pressure on his hand and his palm cupped me. He rubbed my leg very slowly as we listened, so slowly that it hardly seemed to be happening at all. But by the end of Debs' reading, his whole hand was had found its way to my inner thigh, and his thumb and index finger had made their first thoughtful contact with my tense, alert crotch.

'This really is quite rough still,' Debs said. 'But here goes.'

'Time, there's been so much of you between us
Time apart can tear apart your soul
But now my soul is full of forgiveness
And I think it's time that we gave it a go
Again
Why don't we give it a go
Again
And make it just like it used to be
When
We were together
When
We used to have fun back
Then
We can do it all
again
There's nothing to stop us!'

She looked at us and closed the book. 'That's kind of the first verse and chorus. The rest will be similar. But I haven't got to them yet.'

'That's great!' Tony grinned and, under the cover of his words, nudged his strong thumb into my balls.

'And,' said Clive warmly, 'it's really about us, isn't it?'

Debs hugged herself and slipped her notebook away. 'I suppose it is. Underneath everything.' She looked at us all. 'It's just how I feel.'

'I've got some wonderful oxtail and tongue in the freezer,' said Clive. 'I make the most fantastic stew. Why don't I get it going and we can open some more booze? I feel like celebrating.'

'Yeah,' said Tony lazily, as Clive got up unsteadily and Debs basked in their appreciation. Tony flicked again at the head of my cock through those jeans of his I was wearing and kept on doing it, while I sat there and watched the sun swing round the other side of the hill.

Chapter Twelve

'I do the After Nine slot. That's the time in the morning when the kids have been packed off to school. Husbands are long gone. The kitchen is a mess of crumbs and plates and half drunk coffee ... and what does Mum do? She has a sit down in front of the telly. She needs someone on the telly just after nine o'clock. Someone like a best friend, sitting on a sofa and talking about things women will be interested in. Health issues. We have a sexy doctor who comes on twice a week to read out letters and allay fears. An Agony Aunt does the same on a Monday morning. Dieting. Exercise. Consumer news. We do showbiz chat.

'Maybe Mum even has a portable telly in the kitchen now. People are, after all, more affluent than before. Where once she had a transistor radio in the kitchen and she listened to the pop charts as she started the breakfast washing up and made out her shopping list and loaded the washing machine, maybe now she watches me on the After Nine slot. It's not enough anymore, to listen to some disc jockey blethering on about pop music. She doesn't need pop stars in her life. She's a working mum and she wants to know about things directly pertinent to her life.

'That's where I come in,' said Brenda Maloney, still wearing her fuschia suit with the boxy shoulders and her hair frozen solid with lacquer at eleven o'clock in the morning. 'I'm her best friend and I'm popping round.'

Tony had taken to watching her in the mornings and he hadn't realised how much Brenda knew about ordinary life. When did she get the time to discover how normal people functioned?

She laughed at him for asking. 'They write it all down for

me, Tone. Everything I say I read it straight off a screen. Can't you tell?'

He'd really thought she was making it all up.

Clive, who'd half-heartedly slotted himself into the role as their new manager, badgered Brenda in the early days of her new job.

'You could have us on there and you could interview us. That would be good publicity. You could pull some strings for us.'

At eleven o'clock in the morning Brenda was shattered. She was delirious from lack of sleep and an excess of chat. At the moment she was more concerned about what she'd look like on the video they were shooting this afternoon. A fucking swamp donkey, she thought; that's how I'll look. She glared at Clive with hooded, magenta lids.

'Conflict of interests, Clive,' she said. 'It would look terribly nepotistic.'

He snorted. 'You don't care if this song never sees the light of day, do you?'

She opened her mouth to protest and decided she wouldn't bother.

It's all chat, she thought. Everything's chat. I can't engage with anything at any serious level. This gave a her a warm, protected feeling.

They were sitting in a cafe by the frozen riverbank where the action of the video was to take place. Debs had found them the location and the cafe, so they could sit with greasy cups of tea over checquered cloth and warm themselves through before the shooting.

Brenda could sense the presence of the lorry-drivers, recently left, who had sat in this same place through the night.

Debs didn't want any more tea. She had gone out, walking up and down the crackling gravel of the towpath, getting herself into character.

'What character?' Brenda asked. 'It's your character! You're only meant to be playing yourself!'

Debs was terse. 'I have to get it right.' Her hair was longer, tousled and gentle. She was in a warm, long coat. Debs was looking brave and fine-boned that morning. She was dignified, thought Tony. They could see her perfecting her stride and they watched her through the cafe windows.

Beside Debs, Brenda looked brash and too heavily made-up. Soon she'd have to have it all scraped off and replaced with something more subtle. They'd be under the pearly open air this afternoon; not studio lights. For this video, Brenda had to blend into the background, alongside Tony, and let Debs take centre stage.

Thank Christ this will be my last one, Brenda thought. She hadn't told the others this yet. She was waiting for the right moment to explain that it was embarassing for her, to be the sensible-woman-next-door on early morning TV, only to undercut it by appearing in videos for songs about love affairs and being wronged. Her TV work was being put in a bad light by the songs, she felt. The songs were all about losers.

The make-up girl, the stylist and the video crew, all hired at great expense, were waiting on the cold tour bus, which was new and had been bought, at great expense, by Clive. He thought the bus would be a morale boost to them all. It was only small, and they didn't really fill it, but the idea was to make them feel more of a going concern. It was even big enough to sleep in, so it would save on hotel bills. Clive had spraypainted, with stencils, the words 'Things Fall Apart!' across both its silvery flanks. And Clive did all the driving.

Brenda thought it was a wasteful gesture, but didn't say anything. It wasn't like they arrived in towns on that bus to hordes of excited, screaming fans. This tour he'd set up, working without Roy's contacts and methods, seemed a pretty shabby affair to her, on the whole. Clive didn't have the right touch. Anything he did for the band was just to appease Debs. Brenda could see that. He felt bad about her and she'd been far gone in depression for months. Which was why she was writing miserable songs.

What's the point of me cheering up housewives on the telly, only to sings songs that tell them love is hopeless? That they should chuck their cheating husbands out?

And I'm not, thought Brenda Maloney savagely, spending the rest of my life going up and down the country in a bus. Specially not one with 'Things Fall Apart!' written on its side. Even the band's name was embarassing to her now.

On the table, amongst their tea things and Clive's half-eaten bacon and eggs was the cover art for their *Greatest Hits*, which the nice woman at K-Tel had sent on for their approval. It was a new photo of them and, looking closely, you could see how they'd aged. Tony had put on a few pounds. Clive had gone the other way; gone mad in the gym, pushing himself to some ridiculous idea of perfectability and his muscles looked jagged and unreal. With the two boys either side of the girls, the band looked lopsided now.

They had gone back to talking about the record, which was due out at the same time as the miserable single. We haven't even done a new LP, Brenda thought. Just one new song on an album of old ones. If I was a customer, I'd definitely feel ripped off. I'd see this as a last gasp.

The boys were still wrangling over the running order of songs (radical because non-chronological) and the non-inclusion of Clive's personal favourite, 'El Nino'; that chanting song. Brenda could see they were getting quite worked up about it.

'For God's sake,' she burst. 'It's not even...'

They looked at her.

'Well,' she said. 'It's not like we're the Who or the Stones, is it? I mean, it's no big deal what they've put on or haven't. It's only a shitty K-Tel compilation. It'll sell next to nothing and everyone, even the few fans we've got left, will see it as a rip-off...'

Tony gasped. 'There's nothing wrong with doing a Greatest Hits LP. Even Kate Bush has done one...'

Clive brightened at the mention of Kate Bush. To him, she was the acme of musical integrity.

'The whole thing's cheap,' Brenda said hotly. 'All of it's cheap.' She flicked the cover art desultorily and stood up. 'We're living cheap lives.' She looked around and shouldered her handbag. 'We're wasting precious time. I'm going out to the bus to get my slap on.'

Once she was gone, Clive muttered: 'What she needs is a bloody good slap.'

'If Debs was here and listening,' said Tony, 'she would use that line. "We're wasting precious time." She'd have her notebook out on that table and she would write it down. Soon she'd have a whole song written around it. It would express how we all feel.'

'Yeah, she would,' said Clive. Though he knew that Debs hadn't written anything for months. He shuffled the cover art back into its portfolio and led Tony out onto the tow-path by the river.

At that moment it started to snow. They were the fat, feathery kind of flakes that wouldn't melt, even after they'd landed on you.

They stuck in Debs' hair and on the collar and shoulders of her heavy coat as she pretended to sing for the camera, later that afternoon.

'Honestly, Tony,' Debs said. 'I think I'm going bonkers.'

They were driving back into London on the tour bus. It was late and the snow hadn't let up all day. They were eating their way through a packet of Jammy Dodgers, their favourites.

It had been a perfect day for shooting and Clive was confident that the footage they'd got down was ideal. Chilled through, they had finished the day with the hired back-up crew in a country pub, where Clive, playing the gracious host, bought round after round of drinks.

Tony was slumped against Debs on the back seat of the bus. 'You're not going bonkers, pet.'

'I just can't stir myself out of this mood.' She shook her head as if to clear it and peered round the headrests to have a look at

Clive as he drove them down the motorway. 'He's so cheerful and optimistic,' she complained. 'And I can't share in any of it. I don't know where it's coming from, this mood of his.'

Tony pulled a face, stopping himself from saying that she ought to enjoy it while it lasted. It was only a matter of weeks since he'd had Debs going on at him about the black funk Clive had sunk into. How he'd smashed up all the exotic instruments he owned. She had told Tony about Clive's frustration and temper and she'd looked frightened, whispering as if Clive could hear her, wherever she was. Now she was mithering because Clive had come out of that and was on the up again. He couldn't do right, far as Debs was concerned.

'Maybe you've been cooped up together too much,' Tony said. He gazed out of the bus windows, at the dark high rises and the warrens of streets below the flyover. He didn't look at Debs, who would, he knew, be staring at him as if to say: What would you know about it? And it was true, Tony had never had to live inside someone else's pockets. He didn't know anything about the constant friction of rubbing along with someone when everything wasn't exactly hunky dory. He had no right right, really, to comment on Debs' relationship and he could feel the resentment coming off her in waves. All she wanted him to do was sound a bit sympathetic.

'There's something I don't know,' she said, crunching into the jam at the centre of her biscuit, spilling crumbs. 'Something that's changed his mood. Something he's keeping secret from me.'

Tony gave a hollow laugh. 'All men have secrets, Debs.'

'Do they?'

'Hm.' Now here was something he did know about. Now she'd have to listen to him. 'You can't expect to know everything. They all ... we all ... keep certain things locked away and you'll never know about them.'

'Things you're ashamed of,' she said huffily.

'Not necessarily,' he murmured.

'God, Tony,' she said, trying to lighten the tone. 'You know what? You're sounding almost philosophical.'

'Maybe.' He shrugged and it was as if Debs' reflective mood had starting seeping into him. 'I just know it's true. Whether it's shame or not, all the fellas I've ever known have things they're never likely to tell anyone about. I mean, like, no one.'

He could feel her inching away from him, sitting back on the seat. 'That's so weird. Fellas are so weird. Women aren't like that at all.'

'Oh, no?'

'Much more open.'

'Like you and Brenda are with each other?'

'That's different,' Debs said. 'We've never been friends.'

'It's not just friends you tell secrets to.'

Debs felt even more confused by now. She'd been depending on Tony to be fairly straightforward and just listen to her woes and maybe commiserate with her over what a bastard Clive was. But Tony was dwelling over things, too, these days and sounding quite unlike himself.

No wonder, Debs thought, we can't make bright, happy songs anymore. It's like we've all broken through something, some realisation, separately and together, and realised that life isn't like that. We can't make happy songs in any kind of good faith, because then we would know that's it's just a lie. If I went on *Top of the Pops* tomorrow, she thought, I'd be lip-synching in bad faith. If I had to sing to camera I'd be in tears. No amount of professionalism would save me. I'd be in bits. Well, that's no way to carry on.

'We should all have a rest,' she told Tony. 'After this single's out. We should take a break from each other.'

'After Brenda's left, you mean?' Tony whispered, watching the back of Brenda's head, further down the gangway. 'Roy wouldn't have approved of a rest. He would have said, when that fat tart's gone, that's when we need to be working hardest. Keeping ourselves in the public eye. Not letting them think we're defeated. We're one down but there's no holding us back.' He turned and looked Debs straight in the eye. 'That's what Roy would have said. That kind of thing.'

'Maybe we have been defeated, after all,' Debs said.

'Rubbish.'

'Look at that list of tour dates Clive's been pushing under our noses lately. All those tatty clubs and second rate joints. Could you really face doing all them, Tony? Doesn't the thought of them make you feel sick?'

He lowered his gaze and she went on.

'Well, I'll be honest, if no one else will. He's booking us into crappy venues. It's all a step down from what we're used to. Everything we've built up is slipping away and all that confidence and bravado of his is just covering it up. We're on the way out, Tony.'

He licked his lips. 'What are you saying? That we should pack it all in?'

She rubbed her face with both hands. 'I don't even know. I feel disloyal even thinking it. I feel like I'm tied to Clive whatever mood he's in and I can't escape from whatever he's planning for us. I can't even say when I disagree...' She looked at Tony almost pleadingly. 'But you aren't tied. You could put up a fight. You could say that we all need a break...'

Tony looked uncomfortable.

'I can see us all ten years from now,' she said bitterly. 'doing summer season in some shitty end-of-the-pier show. Trotting out in the same old routine. I'm exhausted, Tony ... I'm exhausted now ...'

Tony nodded, but didn't say anything. He thought of Debs that afternoon, looking careworn as she trudged about in the snow for the cameras. It hadn't been acting.

What did she want him to do? Step in and effectively break up the band? Get him to cancel their engagements so they could all blame him? If they stopped working suddenly the public would forget them - that's what Roy had always warned. They couldn't suddenly let themselves get tired. Best keep moving. If they stopped they'd be finished.

'It's not about the band, this,' he said abruptly.

'What?'

'It's about you and Clive.' He'd gone hard and cold. To Debs he sounded almost shirty. 'You're dragging me into your marriage problems. This isn't about the band at all. Sort it out with Clive. Talk to him.'

Tony stood up and started to move away. Debs watched him, her mouth hanging open.

Chapter Thirteen

After we'd finished watching the Eurovision the tape ran blank and scratchy and the others sat looking at the dark screen.

I was wedged at the end of the settee, between Tony and the musical cat. The three of them had barely taken their eyes off the telly the whole time.

'It was so close,' Debs said at last. 'I'd forgotten how close we'd come.'

'Brenda was right about the voting,' Clive said. 'About the bastard French and the fucking Krauts. A few more points from them and we might have got it.'

When it had come to the close-up of Brenda in the green room, mouthing her curses for all of Europe to see, everyone had laughed, almost fondly.

'We were good, weren't we?' said Tony. 'We were really good.'

'Would it have made much difference if we had won?' Debs asked. 'Would we have been more successful?'

Clive shook his head. 'We wouldn't have had the success we had. That's what I think. Our consolation prize was a string of chart singles. The British public love good losers. That's what we were.'

Debs nodded gloomily, her face lit up by the telly.

At least Tony hadn't rubbed his leg against mine anymore. I wanted us to get a chance to be alone. I wanted to know what he was up to, handling me like that. But there hadn't been the chance.

He sat forward.

'We've got a proposition, Clive,' he said, and Debs looked startled.

Clive got up to switch off the telly, breaking the spell of our stillness. 'Go on,' he said.

'I've thought it through,' Tony said excitedly, 'and it could well work...'

Maybe, I thought, that's what all the rubbing of my leg had been about. Maybe that's what Tony did, unconsciously, when he was thinking things through.

'This lookalike band of yours...'

'Things Fall Apart Again.'

'Yes, them. You say they're doing a gig tomorrow night?'

'In Durham.'

'Well, then we go and see them. Give them a surprise. We all go together and then we go up to Gateshead. Ready for Friday night and the telethon. We get in the crowd. We get your lot on the telly while Shelley Sommers is on. We upstage her.'

Everyone was staring at Tony.

'Go on,' said Clive.

'We make everyone think it's us reincarnated. We show the public what they ought to be seeing instead of some soap star. We put the band on instead.'

Clive sat down. 'We sabotage a charity telethon? That's what you're saying?'

'It'll be fantastic!' Tony said. 'Everyone will love it. And it will be a wonderful publicity coup for your band.' He turned swiftly to Debs. 'That's what we want, isn't it? To remind people. To make them want to bring us back and buy the records again? We could do it. We just have to get up there at the right time. It's all live in a shopping centre! We can do anything!'

'Jesus, Tony,' Clive shook his head. 'You're talking like a fucking terrorist.'

'But it would be wonderful,' he said. 'Imagine. Brenda introduces Shelley doing our song. Then Things Fall Apart turn up - or what *looks* like Things Fall Apart. Everyone will think it's been planned!'

Debs had been holding her breath. 'I think it's a great idea.'

'I think you're both fucking mad,' Clive said.

'It'll give Brenda something to think about,' Debs laughed. 'Don't you reckon? Wouldn't you love to mess up one of her immaculate TV specials? Can't you just see her face? And then she'd have to pretend it was all under control. She would have to look pleased...'

Clive laughed ruefully. 'We've all got scores to settle with Brenda Maloney...'

Debs gave him a narrow look. 'We certainly have.'

'And it would be good publicity for my band,' he said. 'They could always use telly exposure.' He laughed again. 'You two never give up, do you?'

'Us?' said Tony.

'You two. You've been the same since you were kids, singing at Butlins. Desparate to be up on the stage. Taking over. Showing off. You can't let go, can you?'

'No,' said Debs. 'Not now we can't. If we don't do this, I'll never forgive myself. I don't care if they arrest us and chuck us in prison. But we have to do this.'

I'd become quite caught up in the idea myself. 'It would be hilarious,' I said. 'Clive, you have to...'

He glared at me, and seemed to consider for a moment. Then: 'I've got something to show you all.'

And he led us through the house, to the interior door of the garage.

He paused on the threshold.

'I'll do it,' he said. 'I don't know how you've managed to convince me, but you have. I've got my life all steady and sorted out these days. I feel like an old fella in retirement. I could just let it all go on and not bother. But...'

'But?' said Debs.

'But it would be good, wouldn't it? To knock that smile off Brenda Maloney's face?'

Debs and Tony grinned.

'And I've got the transport,' said Clive mysteriously, leading us into the dark garage. He clicked on the light.

'You kept it!' cried Debs in a shrill voice.

There were three cars in the cavernous, reeking space. But furthest from us, taking up more room than the three sports cars put together, was the dusty, stencilled, silver bulk of the tour bus.

'It's all ours,' said Clive mildly. 'It's what we'll arrive in.'

Tony was jubilant. 'You knew we'd do this some day! You still wanted to!' He hurried over to the bus.

'I don't know why I kept it,' said Clive. 'Maybe sentiment. Maybe not.'

Debs touched his arm.

'So,' he said, 'that's how we go north tomorrow. We'll pick the kids up in Durham after their show. And we hit the road again.'

Chapter Fourteen

'She's not even part of the band anymore,' Debs said. 'Why should we bother? Who cares?'

The kitchen was dark and there was crockery piled high on the surfaces. She'd let the whole place slip.

Tony took off his cycling helmet and sat down at the kitchen table.

'That's a bit rough, Debs,' he said.

'It's how I feel. What right has she got to ring us up at all hours? She didn't want anything else to do with us.'

He sighed and fished around in his jacket for his cigarettes. Debs hadn't offered him so much as a cup of tea since he'd arrived, breathless from cycling full tilt from Peckham.

She was sitting in her blue fluffy dressing gown, looking very caught up in herself. It was almost one in the morning.

She'd been lucky to catch him at home in his flat. He'd just got in, the phone was ringing and Debs was demanding that he come back across town immediately.

And it was all because of Brenda.

'She's scared,' he said.

'It's her own fault.'

'She didn't ask for mad people hanging around her front door.'

'That's what happens when you go on the telly,' Debs said. 'You put yourself in the firing line. She should just grow up and deal with it.'

He shrugged helplessly.

'If it was one of us having trouble,' Debs said. 'there's no way she'd come running round at all hours to help us out.'

'That's not quite fair,' he said. 'When you were in hospital she came and saw you. Remember? She was there with the rest of us.'

'Yeah,' she admitted. 'But I don't see why she has to phone us up and ask for Clive all the time. Getting him to race around in the dead of night. Just because she's seen some funny people hanging about.'

This had all started a month ago.

After the initial showing off and flouncing about, Brenda had settled into her life as a TV personality and ex-band member. Their last single together, the one with the snowy video and Debs in a long coat, had failed to make the top ten and, following that, Brenda had seen no reason not to make her split public and final.

They'd all got a few good headlines out of it, and sales of the Greatest Hits package improved slightly. Which was all well and good. Since then, the remaining members had been considering how to go on.

At night Debs claimed to hear the ghostly voice of Roy telling her to hold auditions for another girl. A less bolshy one. One with a smaller arse. One who would do what she was told.

Clive was quite into the idea of a new girl.

They had expected Brenda to slip out of their lives. She would just be a face that they saw on the telly occasionally or on the front of women's magazines.

It would be a relief not to have to deal with her, Debs had thought. Not to have her turning up her nose every time she got on the tour bus or when she read through lyrics Debs had sweated blood and tears over.

But Brenda was still in their lives.

A month ago, she had phoned, breathlessly distraught, and neither Debs nor Clive could get any sense out of her at first. They had held the receiver between them and talked her out of her panic.

Apparently, hard-looking women were hanging about on her street.

Brenda knew that they were waiting for her.

'*Lesbians,*' she hissed into the phone. 'I've got the lesbians after me.'

She said there had been a lot of funny fan mail sent to the TV studio. Brenda could never bin her fan mail out of hand. She had to pore over every scrap sent in the post and lots of it, she said, was innocuous enough. It had increased tenfold since she had started on daytime TV and most of it simply requested a signed photo by return of post.

'And then the lesbians started,' she whispered. 'They love me, they say. And they send it direct to my house. Fuck knows how they got hold of my address. Someone at the studio is in on this. But why do I attract lesbians? What is it about me? I hate lesbians! I always have! They turn my stomach...'

'Hang on,' Clive said. 'What's so disturbing about it? They're just fans, like everyone else. You should be flattered.'

At the other end of the line, Brenda took a shuddering breath. 'You wouldn't believe it. The things they say in their letters. One or two of them, they tell me what they want to do to me. What they want me to do to them. It's sickening, Clive. Really sick. I think it's some kind of organisation. And ... they've started sending me polaroids with their letters, too.'

'Fucking hell,' he said.

'What's she saying?' Debs asked.

'Do you think I should get in touch with the police?'

Clive wasn't sure. That first time, he suggested that he drive around and take a look at the evidence himself.

'She's over-reacting,' Debs told him, as he left. 'She's just showing off.'

'It sounds to me like she's terrified,' he said. 'You wouldn't like it.'

Debs shrugged.

Clive had stayed round all that night.

He came back at dawn, stubbly and rough-looking. He told Debs he'd been sleepless in Shepherd's Bush with Brenda out of her mind.

He too had seen leather-jacketed women hovering outside Brenda's house, just out of range of the street lights.

'All night,' he said, 'like phantoms. They'd give me the willies, too, if I were Brenda. And they stuff they send to her is really filthy.'

It became a pattern after that.

On irregular nights, the phone would go and Brenda would be sobbing at the other end, squinting through curtains at her dark street and asking for Clive.

Debs simply passed the phone to him, every time, with hardly a word and Clive put his jacket on and went.

'If it's that bad, it's a police matter,' Debs said. 'She's taking a lend of you, Clive.'

He fiddled with his car keys. 'Brenda doesn't want the coppers because that'll mean publicity. If this gets out into the papers, everyone's going to think she's a lesbian as well. Dykey fans, dykey TV personality. She doesn't want that. Of course she doesn't want that.'

Debs shook her head. 'She wants to get a bloody grip on herself.'

But Clive was gone, purring into the night in his new car.

Night after night he went round to Brenda's in Shepherd's Bush.

After a month of this, Debs decided she had had enough.

'I've tried phoning her,' she told Tony. 'But she's not even picking up the phone. I was letting it ring and ring and thinking, what's she up to? Why doesn't Clive pick it up? And then I realised. She's been getting pestering phone calls as well. She's ignoring them.'

'She could be,' said Tony. 'I would.'

'I almost called a cab and went round there myself,' said Debs. 'To see what's going on.'

'This is ridiculous,' he said. 'We're hearing more about Brenda's life than we ever did before.'

'She thinks she's so bloody famous,' Debs said. 'She thinks she's got every right to disrupt all our lives.'

Tony looked at her squarely. 'You want me to bike round there, don't you?'

She brightened slightly. 'If you would.'

'Well, all this will certainly keep me in trim.'

Actually, she thought, Tony didn't look all that fit, really. He was squashed into his cycling gear and he'd obviously had a fair bit to drink tonight. He looked flushed and red. But that was nothing new these days.

'I just keep thinking...' she said, 'that whoever it is intimidating Brenda ... well, they might well be complete loonies. They could have guns or anything. Clive's putting himself in danger by being there. I've tried to tell him, but he thinks he can cope with anything. It's a slur on his manhood apparently, to say he might be hurt by lesbians.'

'Well,' said Tony, getting up and lifting his cycling helmet again. 'It's not a slur on mine. Tell you what. I'll whiz round there, see what's going on and ring you back from Brenda's. Deal?'

She nodded. 'Deal. And, thank you, Tony. You're a real star.'

It was raining as he made his way through the emptying streets.

He hadn't reckoned on how far he'd have to bike around tonight but, as he got back into his rhythm, he quite relished the edge of drama and urgency that Debs had forced on him.

As far as he was concerned, Brenda had every right to be scared. He was even a little - sneakily - pleased she was so scared.

It was her homophobia that had obviously blown the whole thing out of proportion.

Tony's real concern was how all of this was getting to Debs.

She could do without Brenda on the phone every night, calling her husband away; demanding his immediate attention.

Crossing the dark streets in the slashing rain, his face streaming and freezing over, Tony found himself struck by a terrible thought.

He increased his pace.

He hoped he could remember where Brenda lived.

In streets that looked suburban and gentle.

The kind with chintzy bistros on the corner and very little litter at all.

There couldn't be anyone knocking about, intending harm. Not on a night like this. No assassins lurkng in doorways, no phantoms flitting with knives. No one ready to pounce and break in. They'd get soaked.

As he slowed and counted the house numbers to Brenda's place, he saw one lone figure at the end of the street.

He stopped and peered through the silvery rain.

It was a woman. And she was joined by another.

They both seemed to register his presence and they conferred briefly. He watched them part on the street corner.

One of them hurried to her parked motorbike.

Tony stood there, propping his own bike, as she roared off.

And the street was empty again.

He dashed up the front path to Brenda's and rang the bell.

He rang it three times, each time more insistently; convinced that someone was walking up the path behind him with a bread knife in her hand.

He tried to calm himself down.

Brenda was right, he kept thinking. They really are cruising her street. I'd be watching my back, too, if I had that.

He opened the letterbox and yelled into Brenda's hallway: 'It's me! Tony! It's all right...'

It was dark inside, he saw, as he stepped back to look at her windows.

He imagined her switching everything off; pretending she was out and cowering in some corner. A prisoner in her own expensive boudoir.

He repressed a slight shiver of glee.

'Brenda!' he shouted again. 'It's Tony! Let me in! Clive!'

Only the bedroom gave off a dull, peachy glow.

They were hiding up there.

He jumped as a large silhouette appeared abruptly behind the frosted glass. Brenda was struggling with a whole barrage of new locks and, at last, she opened the door a crack.

'Tony!' she gasped, looking pink.

'I believe you,' he said quickly. 'I've seen them out there. One's on a motorbike. They look hard as nails. Let me in...'

He eased past her and took a look round at her house.

She hadn't had him round in ages.

She followed him into the living room, where everything was Art Deco and spotless and the walls seemed to be covered in highly-polished copper. She went round clicking on shaded lamps and the walls glowed with some kind of inner intensity.

'You've had this done up nice,' he said limply.

'You saw them?' she asked, folding her arms across her dressing gown. She looks dishevelled, he thought.

'Two of them at the end of the street. They saw me and they nicked off again. Debs told me what was going on. That you're under siege and that Clive...'

There was a thudding of footsteps on the thick pile of the stair carpet and Clive appeared, in an open-necked shirt and his jeans.

'Tony,' he said.

'I saw them out there,' Tony said. 'I thought Debs was exaggerating, but...'

Clive hurried to the curtains and eased them back. Brenda peered from under his armpit, hugging herself.

'Fuck,' said Clive. 'I thought they'd gone for the night.'

'One had a motorbike,' Tony said, watching them stare into the rainy street. He looked down at their bare feet. It took him a second to register their two pairs of bare feet, white and blushing at the toes on the plain, dove-grey carpet.

Why were Clive's feet bare? He could understand Brenda making him take off his shoes before coming in. But why didn't he have any socks on?

'They're really going to get me,' Brenda was saying, in a whining tone. 'And I don't even know why. Why do I appeal to lesbians? What is it they want from me?' At this, she turned on Tony. 'You should know. Tell me. You understand all that stuff.'

'I'm sure I don't!' he said. 'Why should I understand?'

Brenda scowled at him.

'Are you still getting the letters?'

'Threatening ones now,' she said. 'Because I never reply to them. They've got hostile and even sicker.'

'There are some sick people out there,' Tony said. 'Clive, how come your feet are bare?'

Clive dropped the curtain and turned around. 'What?' He looked incredulous, as if Tony had said something completely off the wall.

'You haven't got anything on your feet.'

They all looked down.

'Jesus,' said Brenda.

'I...' Clive said.

'It just looks odd,' said Tony. 'That's all.'

'Fucking hell, Clive,' Brenda cursed, and stomped off to the drinks cabinet. She hissed through her teeth at him as she unscrewed the Bushmills.

'Well, I didn't know it was him turning up, did I?' Clive burst out at her. 'It could have been anyone knocking at the door. I just came running down, didn't I? I didn't have time to put anything on my feet...'

Tony was staring at him levelly.

Clive paled. 'It's because I'm pretending I'm Brenda's fella. If them dykes see me coming in and out, they'll realise that Brenda's not like them and maybe they'll leave her alone. Isn't that right, Brenda? That's what we're doing...'

She tipped the glass up to her mouth and said, 'Jesus,' again.

'You're pretending to be her fella?' Tony said. 'Really?'

'Don't tell Debs,' Clive pleaded. 'She's been down enough recently. She'd be furious if she knew. But it's only to protect Brenda...'

'It's a pretty thorough pretense,' said Tony, 'if it involves leaving your shoes and socks off. So what, you're meant to look as if you've dressed in a hurry? I'd say that was a pretty thorough thing to do.'

Clive didn't have an answer for that.

'Just tell him the truth,' Brenda said. 'Go on. Bite the fucking bullet, Clive.'

He shook his head. 'I don't want to hurt Debs. Anything we say to Tony will get straight back to her.'

'What are you two up to?' Tony asked.

'Go on, Clive,' Brenda said. 'You might as well.'

'Oh, you can't be,' Tony moaned. 'You can't do this to Debs, Clive. It'll ruin her.'

'It just happened,' said Clive. 'The first time I came round ... it was, I don't know. Just something we had to do.'

'God, that sounds lame,' Tony said. 'You just *had* to shag her? I don't believe any of it.'

Brenda snorted and handed Tony a drink.

'She isn't in the band now,' Clive said, aggressively.

'What difference does that make?'

'We always said we wouldn't get into those games,' said Clive. 'We wouldn't endanger the band.'

'So what you mean is, soon as she leaves, jump on her bones?' Tony laughed and glugged down the whisky. It burned him pleasantly and made him cough. 'Can you imagine what this will do to Debs? She's already worse than I've ever seen her. There's hardly any fight left in her at all. She already knows about the other dodgy women you knock about with...'

'Oh, thanks a fucking lot,' Brenda snapped.

'She knows?' Clive gasped. 'How does she know?'

Tony scowled. 'Cause I told her. I didn't mean to, but I did. She needed to know, though, Clive. You've treated her like shit.'

They looked at each other for a moment.

Brenda perched herself on the arm of a silk-covered settee. 'All this melodrama. Just like one of Debbie's piss-awful lyrics.'

'What?' Tony found himself bellowing. 'You ungrateful fucking bitch! How dare you say that about Debs? She's worth twenty of you.'

Brenda sneered. 'Maybe to you, she is. Not to anyone else. She's a mopey, self-indulgent woman who's never grown up. She's stuck in some kind of twisted sexless incest thing with you.'

'Me?'

'Yes, you, Tony. It's you that's spoiled Debbie's life, not Clive. It's you she loves and cause she can't have you she treats everyone else like second best. She's never really had time for Clive. Not in any real way...'

'I'm not listening to this.' Tony thumped his glass down. 'I'm not listening to all your self-justifications. I think you're both evil bastards and I don't want anything else to do with you.'

Clive shoved himself in Tony's way as he tried to leave the room. 'And that's it? That's the end of the band?'

'I suppose it is,' said Tony. 'I reckon between the two of you, you've fucked it up good and proper.'

'I'd call it a joint effort,' Brenda said. 'Now we have to work out who's going to tell Debs.'

'I will,' said Tony. 'I'll tell her the whole lot.'

There was a great clattering and banging at the front door just then.

Brenda jumped to her feet, rigid. 'What the fuck...?'

'Please!' someone was screaming from the pathway. 'Open the door! Please! I know you're in ... we need help ... there's ...'

Clive pushed past Tony, who stood there stunned.

'Don't! Clive!' Brenda shrieked. 'It'll be them!'

'Please!' came the woman's voice again. 'There's been an accident...!'

'It's not them,' Clive said. 'She sounds...'

He hurried into the hall, followed by Tony and Brenda.

In the glass door panel they saw the shape of a woman with a wild, white face and what was evidently blood glistening on her temples.

Clive stepped up and threw open the door.

The woman collapsed into his arms.

'What is it?' he asked, and the strength seemed to have gone out of her.

'An accident...' she gasped. 'Out on the main road. No one else will let us use their phone...'

'What kind of accident?' asked Tony, staring at the woman's leather gear. 'Motorbike?'

She nodded and wouldn't look at him. 'My friend...' she sobbed. 'I was thrown clear, but she went right into the phone box. Didn't you hear it? I think she's dead...'

Clive rallied into action and dragged the girl into the living room, where she lay slumped, bleeding on the silk cushions.

'Brenda, phone for an ambulance. And the police. Tony, come with me...'

Clive bent down to peer into the girl's eyes (they could all see now, that she was quite young), shook her out of her daze, and made her give him directions.

'Tony,' he insisted. 'Come on.'

With the white telephone receiver cradled against her chin, Brenda turned to see them go. She stabbed nine-nine-nine and looked from the girl, who was fading into unconsciousness on the armchair, to the front door of her house, which was yawning wide open, and letting in the rain.

Clive led the way at a run.

Tony panted and gasped after him and wanted to tell him that he didn't think this was how it seemed.

There was more to this.

He had already seen the motorbike and that girl.

Clive swung himself round the corner of the street, under the rolled awning of the restaurant on the corner and, there, at the end, they could both see the phone box and a motorbike lying crushed up against it, one wheel still spinning.

There was a figure crumpled on the floor.

Tony watched Clive dart up to the scene.

God, he loves it, Tony thought. He's probably already thinking of the headlines. Clive the hero.

Tony followed at a slower, winded pace and suddenly realised: there was no glass. The phone box was undamaged.

The bike hadn't crashed into it at all. It couldn't have. Someone had just laid it carefully down to make it look as if there'd been an accident.

'Clive..!' Tony called and pelted towards him.

Clive was bending over the injured woman. It was hard to make her out in the dark and the wet and the copious blood.

Gingerly, he reached out to touch her, to see if she was conscious still. She gave a tiny groan.

'It's okay,' Clive said, in his most reassuring tone. 'We're getting an ambulance. You're going to be...'

Tony almost barrelled into him. 'Clive! It's not real! None of it's real!'

Clive's head whipped around, furious at him. 'What the fuck are you talking about now?'

Tony stared in horror as the injured woman's eyes sprang open and, almost as swiftly, her hand flew upwards, clutching a half brick. She smashed it down on Clive's head and he dropped, heavily, on top of her.

'Christ,' said Tony.

The woman scrambled up and pushed Clive away from her, kicking him for good measure.

She swore and brushed her blood-matted hair out of her face.

There was nothing wrong with her. Nothing at all.

She looked at Tony.

Very slowly, Tony started backing away through the rain.

'You're the lesbians,' he said.

She snarled at him, still brandishing the brick.

Having made her calls, Brenda hurried across the room to secure the front door again.

Before she could get there, the apparently concussed girl flung herself onto Brenda's back, making her spin about the room, screaming. The girl had her hands around her throat.

'Shut it! Shut it! Shut it!' the girl yelled.

Brenda was past hearing her. She span around as if she could somehow shake the girl off.

'I hate your fucking voice!' screamed the girl. 'You've got to shut up! You've got to stop!'

Brenda panicked as the girl's cold, wet hands gripped harder on her throat and she felt something inside crack and start to give. She gurgled at her.

'You'll only hurt yourself,' the girl warned. 'I'm only doing this to warn you. You with your fucking recipes and your keep fit. You with your bright orange face and your breakfast TV...'

Brenda lurched across the carpet, feeling the heels of her attacker's heavy boots jab into her ribs. With the part of her mind that was still the slightest bit rational, she struggled to keep her balance and control her trajectory.

For a second the girl thought she was giving up, and relaxed her own grip.

In that moment, Brenda flung herself and her assailant backwards across the room until they connected, hard, with the burnished metal wall.

The girl grunted once and all her limbs went limp.

She slid off Brenda's back in one smooth motion.

Brenda squawked and sprang free. She whirled around, with her dressing gown hanging open, to see the girl, collapsed on the floor.

Her eyes were flickering and she was still muttering incoherently.

Brenda backed away slowly.

She glanced about wildly, looking for a weapon.

A heavy glass object came to hand. She looked at it dumbly.

A paperweight. The only award she'd ever won. For coming fourth in the Eurovision Song Contest.

The girl, still locked in her position on the floor, was struggling to focus; to drag herself back up.

Brenda thought about clonking her on the head with the award.

She couldn't. She couldn't do it.

She ran into the hallway instead, where the door was still gaping open on the dark.

The first thing she registered was heavy footsteps, pounding down the street towards her.

She yelped out once more in terror and held up the glass award.

'Clive?' she called. 'Clive?'

She edged her way outside, with the rain lashing down and the wind billowing her gown around her.

'Clive!'

Two figures came hurtling around the corner. Two dark, indistinct shapes, breaking their run, gasping and grappling with each other.

'Brenda!' she heard Tony shout.

They fell headlong onto the path, one of their hands lashing out to grab Brenda.

She raised the award in both hands and brought it, with all her might, crashing down on Tony's head.

She could see it was his, immediately, because he flopped backwards, as if shot, and hit his head again, on the paving stones.

He made an awful crack and he was out cold.

The other lesbian was quite still, lying partly on top of Tony.

She looked from him, up to Brenda, who was shaking.

'You've killed him! You've cracked his bloody skull open!'

Then she lifted herself off him and backed away down the garden path.

'You're a maniac!' she shouted at Brenda Maloney.

Then she turned on her heel and fled.

Brenda fell to her knees and slapped at Tony's face.

He didn't even stir.

'Tony? Where's Clive? Tony?'

She said it again and again until she heard sirens coming up her street.

Tony hadn't come to, but the girl in the living room had.

But all she did was come to stand in the doorway of Brenda's house as the ambulance and the police car pulled up and, hazily, she tried to make sense of it all.

When Tony came out of hospital they knew he wouldn't be able to look after himself for a while. Debs and Clive took him in like he was their child.

For a while he kept forgetting things, the simplest things. He had raging headaches, fits of temper and the strangest dreams.

Once he cried out in the night, from where he was sleeping on the sofa in their living room. Debs came running and he was rambling, half-awake.

'I've had this idea ... I've seen it all, like, in a vision. What we should do is a concept album ... a whole story ... a science fiction spectacular that will get made into a film that will be the biggest-grossing movie of all time ...'

Eventually Clive ambled through into the half light of the living room. He slouched in the doorway in his boxer shorts. Debs was soothing their guest's brow with a damp flannel while he mumbled on about alien beings.

'Leave him, Debs and come back to bed.'

But she wouldn't.

The next morning, the idea still had Tony in its grip. A concept album. With a gatefold sleeve. They would all be characters in this long, unfolding story. Over breakfast Tony started to badger Clive. He wanted to learn to play guitar properly, so he could write songs for himself.

'It's about time I started earning my keep in this band. I'm full of good ideas, honestly. That bang on the head might have been a blessing in disguise, you know. It's freed me up, like, artistically. Somehow I feel more able to express myself...'

'Forget it,' Clive said, without even looking at him. 'I can't teach you to play. I've never taught anyone.'

Tony kept on at him. 'But you can. You make it look so easy. You'll be a natural teacher and I pick up things dead easy.'

'Like herpes, yeah,' Clive laughed.

Debs shot him a look. Already he'd made a few *sotto voce* comments about Tony using their bathroom while he was staying with them; and about the kinds of things he might be carrying. Debs had been appalled to hear Clive saying these things and was desperate for Tony not to hear them.

Tony went to pick up Clive's shining beloved twelve string guitar, where it sat on the arm chair in the corner of the kitchen. 'Go on, Clive. Who knows, I might...'

Clive took the guitar off him. 'You've got absolutely zero coordination, Tony. You're too old to start learning now.'

Tony had gone red. 'I'm not! I...'

'I started learning the guitar when I was eight,' said Clive steadfastly. 'You're no musician. You're backing vocals and that's about it. Sorry.'

Tony skulked off and Debs felt her heart go out to him. She hissed at Clive, 'What did you have to go and do that for?'

He scowled at her.

'That's the first time he's showed any interest in anything since his accident - and you have to go and crush him like that...'

'He's like a kid,' Clive said. 'Moping about all the time. When's he going to move out? That's what I want to know.'

All three of them had been on standby while Tony was getting over his head injury. They had been waiting to see what he was like when fully recovered.

'You're just pissed off because you can't write any new songs,' Debs taunted Clive. 'Now you won't even let Tony write any...'

'We don't need new songs,' Clive said, through gritted teeth. 'We just need to get on that bus again and on the road and do a few dates. We've wasted enough time and money. Don't you see? We just need to sing the old songs. Nobody's expecting us to come up with new material. Our time for that has gone already. All we have to do is rake in the bit of cash we can from the old stuff, that's all.'

She was shocked. 'I thought you were supposed to be some kind of artist.'

He looked at her: sitting by the French windows in her chenille batwing sweater, twisting a piece of knitting in her hands and going on about art.

'It's got nothing to do with art,' he said.

Debs raised her eyebrows and looked back at her knitting. 'That's not how you went on about it before. You went on like you were Bob Dylan or someone...'

He glowered at her.

'And now poor Tony gets a couple of ideas and you bite his head off. You won't even help him...'

'Debs... the world doesn't really need Tony's concept LP about aliens...'

She bit through a strand of wool with her teeth and knotted it. She inspected her handiwork. 'I don't see why not. All sorts of things are getting into the charts these days. You don't know what it'll be like until you've tried it.'

'Christ.'

He headed for the door.

'Where are you off to now?'

'We're not recording any of that puff's alien songs and that's that,' he snapped.

'You've missed the point, as usual. He probably won't even write any songs. He probably can't. The point is, Clive, if you had the tiniest bit of sensitivity about you, you'd see this ... Tony just needs something to do ... to get himself back together ... to get his confidence back...'

Clive couldn't see how a bang on the head could have robbed someone of their confidence. He refused to see. He thought Tony was being weak. It had been three months since that awful night with the lesbians round Brenda's.

'I've given him enough support. We've let him live round here. We've babied him. I think we've done enough...'

'He's part of our family,' Debs said primly.

'He might be part of yours. But he's not mine.'

'He's part of the band...'

Clive snorted. 'He might be, if he'd get off his fat arse and came and did some shows with us. But until he does - there's no such thing as the band. The band might as well be finished.'

Debs watched with her knitting on her lap, as Clive yanked on his jacket.

'I'm off out.'

She wondered who he was knocking about with. They hadn't slept together in months. Since before the night of Tony's accident, in fact. There had been one occasion of intimacy; that night in the hospital after she'd made sure Tony was okay, after Brenda had gone, making a statement to the police and the papers and blanking Debs in the hospital corridor. Debs had sat with Clive, at his bedside all night. He slept fitfully, waiting to have his skull X-rayed in the morning. She knew he'd be all right though. It was Tony with the hairline fracture.

Clive had made her pull the plastic curtain around his bed in the middle of the night; pull back his sheets; hitch down her jeans and sit on his cock. Playing doctors and nurses. It had been the final, humiliating event in a ridiculous day. It was the last time they'd come close to any kind of sex. Debs had ridden up and down on him - surprised at how hard and keen he was - and dreading the curtain being whisked back by some night nurse or fellow patient. Imagine finding two pop stars *in flagrante* on the ward. Maybe they should have gone with BUPA.

Since then, he'd been nowhere near her and she knew he was getting it somewhere else. He had no interest in her.

After he was gone that morning, she went into the dark living room, to find that Tony had rolled up his futon and duvet neatly and had stowed them away behind the heavy leather sofa. He didn't want to impinge on them too much. He was the perfect guest, really.

In the slatted morning light from the half-open blinds, he was sitting in a wicker chair, with one of Clive's less treasured guitars; an old one, flat on his lap, plucking aimlessly at the strings.

'It's about time I left you and him to get on with your own lives,' he told her.

'You don't have to ... I want to make sure you're okay...'

'I'm okay,' he insisted. 'It was only a crack on the skull...'

She knew it was more, though. It was as if something had leaked out of him. He hadn't gone out at night since. He wouldn't. It was an odd reversal: she had been used to going on at him about wandering the streets and the Heath at all hours and his casual pick-ups and so on, and now she was the one telling him he should get out more.

'I should go back to my flat,' he said, 'though I dread to think what state it's in. I'll have squatters, probably...'

'Let's go there,' she said. 'I'll help you clean it up. We'll...'

'I was thinking of going further away,' he said. 'Maybe Italy. A little holiday.'

'By yourself?' she squawked.

'I don't always need my hand holding.'

'You've hardly been over the doorstep in months, Tony! Don'
you think this is biting off more than you can chew?'

'You know me,' he said, 'in at the deep end every time.'

He was grinning and strumming at the guitar strings and she wa
thinking: but that isn't true. Given a choice, Tony would rarely op
for the deep end. He'd do a little plodging in the shallows first. Bu
maybe that was just how she saw him. Maybe there was a braver sid
to him that she knew nothing about; the secret Tony who used to
sally forth in the night, meeting up with strange men in the dark fo
the hell of it - while she watched telly, knitting on the sofa, countin
herself lucky if Clive stayed in on a night.

'Italy,' she said.

'It'll bring me back to life,' he said. 'I can feel it. I can feel m
blood, eager for all that vitamin D, or whatever it is in the sun
light...'

She ruffled his hair, which felt soft. It was short now. He'd had i
shaved for a while, after the accident and it had grown back softe
and darker.

He bit his lip. 'If I go I want to go quite soon, while the plan i
fresh in my head. It'll mean I can't do any gigs or anything...'

'Obviously,' she laughed.

'I don't know what I'm saying ... I mean, I don't know how lon
I'll be away for ... whether that means I'm leaving the band or not..

'Tony - your place will always be open for you. We wouldn't le
anyone else in.'

'You wouldn't chuck me out?'

'Course not.'

She watched him toy with the taut strings. His strumming wer
on for a while, then he stilled the noise with the flat of his palm
'Why can't I be talented?' he said at last. 'Why isn't there something
I always assumed there was. I went along with you all, just assumin

I was as good as all of you. Good at something. I thought - because
I was with the three of you - and you were all marvellous at what
you did - I thought, I must be talented too.'

'But you are...' Debs said.

He laughed. 'What at, Debs?'

She stammered.

'You don't have to answer.' He took both her hands in his. 'It was
bad of me to put you on the spot. But I'm going to find out what I
can do, Debs. Even if it takes a couple of years. I'm going to go off
into the sun and hang around a bit, all by myself and I'm going to
find out what it is I've got inside of me. There's something there.
I'm sure there is. Something worth having.'

Chapter Fifteen

'You touched me,' I told him at last.

'Hm?' Tony was looking out of tinted windows at Yorkshire scudding past. I was in the seat in front of him and it was like we had the whole tour bus to ourselves. It smelled slightly musty and unused on board, but Tony had made himself right at home.

'I said, you touched me. Yesterday. Last night. Sitting outside in Clive's garden.'

He looked perplexed. 'No, I didn't.'

Down the gangway, Debs was in the seat beside the driver's cab. You could see her, almost bouncing up and down with supressed excitement. Clive, too, seemed buoyed up, with both meaty hands clamped on the steering wheel, his foot firmly on the accelerator. As I talked to Tony our driver was experimenting with the sound system and each of the speakers in the ceiling of the bus gave a discreet cough and a crackle. Then their Greatest Hits came on and Tony grinned sheepishly.

'You had your hand on my leg the whole time,' I said.

He frowned. 'I really don't remember. I don't think so.'

I wanted to punch the headrest between us. 'But that's ridiculous. I know what I felt.'

He shook his head and looked out of the window. The blue tint did odd things to the colours out there. The hills and fields and the sky itself came up brighter, somehow. I watched passengers in the cars alongside us stare at the tour bus and read the spray-painted legend down the side. Maybe they were thinking that the band had got together again. Maybe they were keen to get a glimpse inside.

Clive turned the volume on the sound system up and I had to laugh.

'You're a liar, Tony.'

'I don't remember,' he said dully, looking away again. 'Honestly, Tim. That's what I'm like.'

'Oh, yeah?' He was really getting on my nerves. All this blowing hot and cold.

'I have these memory things. Lapses. Whole spots of time vanish. Sometimes I don't even know what I'm doing while I'm doing it.'

'Right.' I wasn't buying any of it. He was coming on like someone doo-lally in a novel by Virginia Woolf. As I say, an English degree can really bugger up your later life.

He looked me in the eye and I realised he was serious. 'It was the bang on the head that did it. Hairline fracture on my skull. You can feel it through my skin, still. It's like things seep out of it, all the time, and I don't even know what my body's doing...'

'This is the accident that Debs was on about...'

'Yeah. I got smacked on the head. Defending Brenda from ... from what we would nowadays call stalkers. I suppose.'

'And you're still affected by that?'

'For three months I could hardly remember my name. That's why I had all that time out.'

'When I am an Angel' started up and we could hear Debs singing along, up at the front. After a second, Clive's voice joined hers.

'Oh,' I said. 'Well, I'm sorry.'

'I might have been touching you. I don't know. I'm sorry if I did. But it wasn't really me.'

'I thought it meant...'

He looked blank. 'What?'

'What you'd said the night before. About not being interested. I thought this meant that you'd changed your mind.'

He looked even blanker. 'I said I wasn't interested?'

'Yes. In the Travel Lodge. Before you went to sleep.'

'I said I wasn't interested in you?'

'Yes.'

'Oh. Right. You mean, like, sexually?'

'I reckon that's what you meant.'

'I actually said that?'

'As good as.'

'Jesus,' he said, whistling through his teeth. 'I don't remember any of that. This moving around from place to place is really getting to me. I was less erratic at home.'

'So where does that leave everything, then?'

'I don't know!' he grinned. 'But if I said I wasn't interested in you, like, sexually, then I must have meant it. That must be how I feel.'

'Right.'

'Though,' he went on, 'if my hands were all over you, instinctively, hidden from everyone else's view ... well, that might be even more true than what I actually said in words. Because that's like ... a gut reaction, isn't it?'

'Yeah,' I said, and felt suddenly exhausted.

'So, I don't really know, Tim,' he finished brightly. 'Are you interested in me, then? Is that what this is about? Are you into me?'

He looked almost hopeful.

'Nah,' I said, and turned back in my seat.

We stopped just once, at a motorway services that afternoon. Clive was antsy because we'd set off so late in the day. The clear Yorkshire air had got to us all, made us sleep in late, each in our separate rooms in his cottage. He let us out at the Services and gave us only fifteen minutes before we had to be back on the bus.

I took a deep breath and phoned Shanna at work.

'Oh, it's you,' she said.

'I'm back in the region,' I told her.

'Well,' she said. 'Good. Pete's sacked you, you know.'

'That's a bit quick!'

'I warned you.'

'Has he replaced me?'

'Uh-huh.' I could tell she was serving someone at the till while she was talking to me. I suddenly felt nostalgic for Natural World. I felt jealous of Shanna's ease as she wrapped whatever piece of precious tat her customer wanted and popped it into a recyclable bag. But then you always get a bit funny and nostalgic over something just as you lose it.

'And wait till you hear who he's drafted in.'

I went cold. Pete was such a twat I'd believe him capable of anything. 'Who?'

'It's all worked out okay, really,' Shanna said, and I heard her swiping someone's credit card through the little machine. There was that dreadful moment of suspense, of credit-rating-checking before the receipt came chundering out.

'Tell me,' I said, 'Who's he replaced me with?'

'Simon,' she said.

My bloody ex-boyfriend.

'He's in Wales!'

'Natural World didn't quite work out in Aberystwyth,' she said smoothly, like some corporate mannequin. Something had happened to Shanna while I'd been away. 'And, as Pete pointed out, Simon is management material and too good to waste on a shop that's going under. Your vacancy came up here and Pete drafted Simon back to fill your shoes. Pete wants to groom him.'

'Groom him!'

'Like he was grooming you, though you never appreciated it.'

'But I was coming back!' I said. 'He can't just sack me!'

'He can,' she said.

'And bringing Simon in is just like adding insult to injury.'

Shanna sighed heavily. 'It's interesting, really, to hear Simon's side of things.'

'Oh, is it?'

'You treated him pretty badly, Tim. And it all fits with your behaviour this week. Running off. Running about all over the place. Simon reckons it's your fear of commitment. How he gave you everything and you could never be that open with anyone.'

'What?'

'It all rings true.'

'And Simon's just a fucking all-giving, all-dancing saint...'

'He's a nice guy, Tim. And you really hurt him.'

'I can't believe this is you talking, Shanna.'

'It's nothing I didn't want to say before. You block people out, Tim.'

'Jesus,' I said.

'So where are you going now?' she asked, with a lighter tone, as if the counselling part of the conversation was over and she was content with how she'd trashed my whole personality.

'Gateshead,' I said, 'for the charity Telethon tomorrow night.' I was answering automatically and the squeal she gave as I said this surprised me.

'But we're going to be there!' she said. 'All of us from Natural World. We've been raising money and we're going to hand over a big cheque to Shelley Sommers on the telly!'

'You're going to be in the Metro Centre?'

'Yes,' she laughed, 'but because it's Natural World, we have to dress up as fucking pandas and tigers and all that. Actually,' she added, 'I'm dressed up as a panda right now and it's fucking boiling in the shop. But what the hell, eh? It's all for charity, isn't it?'

Debs was still on the phone to her mam when I left the booths. She wanted Franky to meet us in Gateshead. Franky, she said, wouldn't miss this for the world.

We were all going to be there.

And, I suppose, underneath the Simon shock, I was excited.

I couldn't imagine what it would be like, crashing a national event like that. We'd be sabotaging and maybe jeopardising something that was in a charitable cause. The poor homeless and abused kiddies. But maybe, the spectacle Debs and Tony were planning would make the whole thing even better.

I went to sit in the blustery car-park and smoke. I watched the sun smack off the silver sides of the tour bus.

I didn't want this to end. I wanted to be on that bus forever.

I wanted to be able to sing along with all the tapes, with Debs and Clive. I wanted Tony sitting behind me so I could crane round and bait him some more. No, that was unfair. I wanted to be able to keep talking to him.

He was hapless and useless and he couldn't even remember - he didn't even always perceive - what he'd been doing.

He'd be useless for me, surely, and I'd end up just looking after him. He couldn't even talk to me, not really. His eyes would slide away and he'd be thinking about something else. The further away he got from home the worse he got like that.

But then, when it was me who wasn't paying attention; when I was earwigging on what Clive and Debs were saying, I'd find Tony's eyes on me, with a surprising frankness.

I watched him come out of the Services with bags and bags of sweets and drinks cartons. I watched as he dropped a couple of things, swore, and tried to grab them up again. He looked up and saw me.

'I did remember,' he said, as he came over and stood with me. 'Really.'

'Remember what?'

'Holding your hand.' He looked down. 'Though I did forget for a bit.'

I nodded.

'It just seemed the thing to do,' he said. 'I wanted to. You were there and I could feel the warmth of you. Does that sound stupid?'

'No.'

'And you never shrugged me off. You never asked what I thought I was doing.'

'I didn't,' I agreed.

'So I thought it was okay.'

I found myself lighting a cigarette off the last one. 'I don't know where I am with you, Tony.'

Abruptly he started to walk away. His behaviour was getting more erratic by the minute. He turned on me again. 'It's just what everyone expects, isn't it? Put us two together and, of course, we're going to get off. They all expect it.' He looked firm. 'I'm not doing it. I always used to do it. I'd feel obliged. I felt like I'd be letting someone down if I didn't.'

I sighed. 'It's up to you if you want to ... get off with me, or not.'

'It's not been like that for me,' he said. 'I ran around dizzy. Being made to do it. People offering themselves. I felt obliged.' He was squinting in the sunlight. He hadn't shaved and his stubble was like white filaments. 'So I put my foot down. Debs shoved me on you ... like it was some kind of reward.'

'Reward?'

'For coming with her. For being supportive this week. And I'm the booby prize. Your reward is a shag with me.'

'That's not what I want...' I said.

'It's how she's thinking. But she means well.'

'We don't have to do anything.'

'We haven't,' he said.

'That's okay, then,' I said.

'But I really want to! After everything I've said - about putting my foot down and that - I've still been really into you since I first saw you, Tim. That night at ours. It seems like weeks ago already. You looked wonderful. Confident and shy at the same time. Nice, but there's an edge all the same, like you're not giving anything away, like you're not giving an inch. And I just wanted you from that first night.' He grinned, lopsided. 'I still do. Badly.'

'This is ridiculous,' I said. 'You're either daft, or this is the most conniving and roundabout seduction in the world.'

'Neither,' he said. 'I'm drawn to you. I want you.'

'Yeah?'

He nodded and beamed. Guileless.

'Then,' I said, watching Clive and Debs approach. 'We'll just have to see, won't we?'

Franky was going to go to Gateshead anyway. She and the girls from her restaurant were going to do an act on the stage that had been erected in the shopping mall. Franky had had her fan-dancing feathers dry-cleaned.

'She never mentioned it last week,' Debs said, as we hit the motorway again.

'She's very deep, your mother,' Clive said, wrestling with the wheel.

'She reckons they've only just decided to do it. To raise money for the kiddies. Apparently there's an amateur slot to entertain the crowd before Shelley Sommers comes on.'

'That's it, then,' said Tony. 'Franky can be our person on the inside. Maybe she can sneak us behind the scenes and we can crash it like that.'

Debs smiled. 'I'm a bit nervous thinking about it,' she said. 'It could all go horribly wrong. We could end up in prison.'

Clive gave a booming laugh. 'Nervous! How can we be nervous? How can you? You've done Butlins! The Eurovision! You've played the roughest dives north and south and across the continent! What difference does one shopping mall make, Debs?'

'It's a shopping mall *now*,' she said. 'Right now. And that makes a difference, Clive.'

Durham.

We used to come to Durham to shop when I was a kid and I thought I'd end up there or a town like it. Somewhere with narrow stone streets and tiny windows and low doorways. I could sit in the Cathedral grounds and look down over the leafy city and brood on ... I don't know ... deep ideas. And yet everywhere, up to and including the shop where I worked till recently had been breeze-blocked, prefabbed Sixties architecture. The schools I went to, the estates that we lived on, the university I ended up attending. All of these buildings were from the stuccoed Sixties.

What I was thinking about as the tour bus went trundling down into Durham and the castle and the cathedral appeared in our widescreen windscreen was that, maybe if I'd lived and studied somewhere like this, everything would have been different. I'd have specialized in mediaeval art or modernist poetry or theology or something.

We were driving into an ancient town and I was thinking about how I'd got myself caught up in trash. The rubbishy world of pop in all its forms had reached out and sucked me in. It had happened a long time ago.

'Look,' said Tony, 'they've opened some nice cafe bars here, too. The old place doesn't look quite so gloomy.'

It took hours to park the bus. We got out and walked to a bridge and I looked over the side, hundreds of feet down, into the stillest green water.

I heard Clive explaining to Debs that their descendents, Things Fall Apart Again, would never need a tour bus. All the backing music they needed could fit onto one gleaming disk, thanks to advances in modern musical technology. The four of them never even needed to see a musician in the flesh, not even in the studio.

'It's amazing,' Debs said. 'We thought we were futuristic, even back then, didn't we? When it was all synthesizers coming in and drum machines. With all of those we thought we were it.'

'We were state of the art at the time,' Clive said. 'Though the sound of our records, when you hear them now, is strange. Transparent almost. Clashing. That very jarring, too clean synthesizer sound.'

'I still like it,' said Debs. 'It's our sound. It's just a bit out of date. But in its own way, one day, it'll sound as distinctive as Phil Spector or Motown...'

Clive looked unsure. 'We'd better find out where the show is meant to be. Time's getting on.'

He put on a pair of Ray Bans firmly and led us across the river to the Student Union building. We stood waiting as he explained that he was the manager of that night's band.

'It turns out they've got four bands on,' he growled, writing out the address and directions for us. 'Our lot impersonating us, a Bananarama tribute, a Human League tribute, and a fake Kim Wilde.'

'God,' said Debs. 'They're keen on lookalikes, aren't they?'

'I wonder what they'd say,' said Tony, 'if they knew they had the actual real things here...'

No one answered him.

Briskly Tony and I were packed off to entertain ourselves and get something to eat in one of those cafe bars we'd seen out of the tour bus windows.

'Clive and I are going on ahead,' Debs said, looking worried. 'Just turn up before eight at the right place...'

We nodded and let them tell us exactly what to do.

We walked down the hill back into town.

'You've soon slipped back into taking orders,' I said.

'Well,' said Tony, 'I actually like it. Gives me less time to think for myself. I really liked being in a band.'

'I really hate being told what to do,' I said. 'It's only happened since I started work at that shop. I could never quite take orders seriously. They used to phone from head office and tell us how to display the shite merchandise, and they'd take it all so seriously I'd just want to laugh. Still, that's over.'

We'd reached the cafe. The door was all scrolling ironwork. Inside it was chrome, lillies and chaise longues. It was that sort of cafe bar.

'What do you mean, it's over?'

I told him about losing my job.

His face crumpled. 'Because you've been with us? Oh, that's awful, Tim.'

I sat down heavily on a low sofa that was harder than I'd expected and watched him settle opposite.

He was in shorts now, with a loose-necked shirt and sunglasses and he looked sharper than I'd expected him to. It was me, I suspected, who looked as if I'd been on the road for days on end.

'I feel like we've been responsible,' he said, slipping his glasses off, 'for ruining your career.'

'Nah,' I said. 'I would have left or been chucked out anyway.'

We talked for a bit about his abandoned boyfriend.

'It had to finish, too,' he said. 'Really. I'd already thought that. I'd started thinking, projecting ahead, ten years, twenty years, and imagining what we'd be like. Stuck in a rut. Him madder than ever. Me running around for him. Getting older.'

Suddenly he went pale. 'I've left my mobile switched off.' He fished around in his little bag and switched the cellphone on with a musical chime I recognised as the opening bars of 'Let's Be Famous.' Tony looked aghast. 'Fifty-two messages and all from Kris.'

'Jesus,' I said.

The waitress was hovering with her pad and she looked self-conscious in her bra top so I quickly ordered two pints of Kronenburg.

'Bitter shandy for me,' said Tony and she smiled and went.

'Are you going to listen to his messages?'

He weighed the phone in his palm. 'What's the point? They'll be full of venom. Him squawking away. They'll start furious, go into terrible threats and end up pleading. I can't deal with all that now. I don't even want to remind myself of what his voice sounds like.'

'You'll go back to him,' I said.

'What makes you say that?'

'You must love him still.'

Tony looked stymied by this. 'I don't know.'

'Where did you meet him, anyway? How do famous people meet each other?'

Our drinks arrived and Tony waited till we were settled with them before he carried on.

'We met a few times, at different do's, like the Rock and Pop Awards or *Top of the Pops*. Over the years, when we were in the charts at the same time. And he was different then, you know. Tall and gloomy and he was, like ... artistic. I thought he was fantastic then.'

I nodded, remembering.

'And,' said Tony, 'I'd sucked his knob a couple of times at different parties and stuff. Just whenever our paths had crossed. I knew he was really into me. But Roy had put the fear of God into me about getting hooked up with anyone permanantly. He didn't want me to have a boyfriend. Anyway,' he took a long, appreciative sip of his bitter shandy. 'Roy went, Brenda went and I had my accident and was packed off, when I was fit enough, back to Italy, which I loved. I think it was Debs and Clive, really, sending me away while they split up and they dissolved the band.

'They called it my Italian rest and recuperation, but it was really because they didn't think, in my vulnerable state, I would be able to cope with what was happening to the band.'

I couldn't imagine, either, what it must have been like, for Debs and Clive to explain to him that it was all finished. They had things they could go on and do. They could have other careers in music and performing. Tony wouldn't have stood a chance by himself.

'I was in Florence,' he said. 'I was doing the Merchant Ivory thing. All that white linen and panama hats. I was just swishing about, learning the language, loving Italy. Getting my addled head - literally - back together. And one day my hat blew off while I was staring up at the statue of David. Can you believe it? It rolled across Palazzo Vecchio, between tourists and pigeons and, because everyone's so lovely and friendly there, five people made a grab for it as I came running. It was quite an expensive hat.

'Anyway,' he smiled, and I realised that his eyes had brimmed with tears. 'The person who actually managed to catch up my hat was this very, very tall man in black. A man with very pale skin and green eyeshadow who held out my hat to me and grinned. It was Kris. He'd appeared there like magic.'

I imagined Kris stood there, like a huge black crow.

'He flew me with him to the States, where he was fronting his last tour with the Dominators and I was with him when he finished the whole thing in Philadelphia. When he told them all, before the last encore: 'This is the last show we'll ever do.' Honestly, I'm like a Jonah. I'm the kiss of death to whichever band I'm with.

'I remember standing in the underpass at Philly airport at the end of the Eighties with Kris and we were both having a fag. Taxis were going up and down and pulling up and these fellas were dashing up to us, saying where did we want to go. It was so hot and bright in Philadelphia and the two of us looked like white-faced zombies by this time. Well, you know what Kris looks like. He was in his Bela Lugosi phase just then. We were both finishing our ciggies and these blokes were saying, Hey, guys, where do you want to go, guys?

'And Kris and I took one look at each other and one of us, I forget who, said: 'We just want to go home. It's time to go home."

'And you moved back to Blackpool?'

He nodded. 'Do you know what we should do now, Tim?'

I fingered the menu. 'Eat?'

'Find a hotel. For a couple of hours. Until we have to meet the others.'

My mouth went dry and I had to swallow down the rest of my pint suddenly.

So now it was me, following him, and doing what he was deciding and going to a hotel by the river that was an old coach house converted.

I hung back in the foyer while he did all the transactions and suddenly he looked less hapless than he had done of late; signing the receipt and telling the blousey woman that we wouldn't be needing breakfast.

The hotel was quite swanky and Tony was treating it blithely like a cheap motel.

She showed us to the room, up winding steps, ambling ahead of us terribly slowly. As she led the way Tony reached back and squeezed my hand.

We watched her unlock the door and I was hard already. The end of my dick was wet.

When the door came open he bundled me past the proprietress and once we were both inside (more chintz; green and pink and lacquered furniture) he slammed the door in her astonished face.

Tony was on his knees in front of me, grasping my arse in both hands and pressing his face into my jeans, finding the zip with his tongue, teasing it down with his teeth.

All of this, very deftly done.

He eased my cock out with his mouth and the warmth and wet of his mouth covered me. It was shocking almost, the completeness of it. But also because of how familiar it seemed, to have him take me like that. My cock was already well-covered in come, just from anticipation and he groaned at this, kneading my thighs and rolling me around in his mouth.

Different people's mouths feel quite different, of course. His teeth nicked at me as we both got used to this. He sucked me and I felt I was filling him up, right down his throat.

He pulled back, at length, and carefully kissed the tip of my cock, which was bursting and red. And then we started, hurriedly, to undress.

He smelled milky. He lay back on the duvet and we rumpled the thick covers and I took in the smell of him, pressing my face to his neck. There was a distinct smell of milk, an almost sour smell.

I lay on him and we pressed our weight together, grinding our cocks together and we paused, as if we didn't know how to go on. He kissed me hard, pushing his tongue into my mouth and it was rough. Rougher than I'd expected, the way he carried on; pushing his strength onto me and rolling me over onto my back. He wanted to be on me, pushing down on my chest and kissing, then sucking hard, at my nipples. As if he could get something out of me that way.

It had all happened so fast I hadn't seen him fully naked yet. I reached down for his cock, which I could feel, nudging its busy way against my thigh, and he was rock hard and smaller than I'd thought. He had a snug cock, hand-sized, with a tight foreskin that hurt him slightly when I pumped him, too hard, in my enthusiasm.

'I want to come on you,' he said, breathing hard into my face. His breath was all bitter shandy. 'From when I first saw you, I wanted to come all over you. All over your belly and chest. I want to come in your face and in your hair.'

'Do it,' I said. 'It's been a while since anyone has.'

I had a momentary stab of guilt about Debs then, who'd climaxed so nicely. Who'd been so friendly. This wasn't like that. Tony was kissing me fiercely and throttling my cock, bending it back as far as it would go, rubbing it hard on his tight, heavy balls.

We came quickly that first time and both of us, so pent up, came so hard it shot up past both our faces into my hair, the pillows, the padded headboard.

'We came together!' he crowed. 'That's never happened before!'

Simon would always jump up at this point, to rub us both clean and dry with towels. Like that advert for paper towels where they show you how much chip fat they can absorb. Nasty allusion. But Tony was content to lie with me, hugging me hard, in both our mess.

We kissed a bit more and recovered ourselves and then, without even thinking much about it, did it again.

Time was getting on and we had to meet the others and attend to business. But in a very leisurely and absorbed fashion, a formerly famous Eighties pop star manoeuvred us both into a position we'd be happiest with, and fucked me very deeply. But it was just Tony. Tony who I'd known for a few days. And Tony who I'd assumed would be hopeless in bed.

He squeezed himself up inside me and grasped my chest like there was nowhere on earth he'd rather be.

Afterwards we showered together and my legs were shaking. We dried, dressed and left the hotel and took a taxi to the marquee at the college, just outside of town, where the graduation concert was taking place.

It was eight o'clock and the sky was a lambent blue above black trees. To me, at least, the night smelled of lager, excitement and the milky scent of Tony's spunk.

We could hear the music, the shouting and dancing as we got out of the cab.

We heard it all before we even went round the trees and into the field and saw the vast white tent full of students and lookalikes.

'You touched me,' I told him at last.

'Hm?' Tony was looking out of tinted windows at Yorkshire scudding past. I was in the seat in front of him and it was like we had the whole tour bus to ourselves. It smelled slightly musty and unused on board, but Tony had made himself right at home.

'I said, you touched me. Yesterday. Last night. Sitting outside in Clive's garden.'

He looked perplexed. 'No, I didn't.'

Down the gangway, Debs was in the seat beside the driver's cab. You could see her, almost bouncing up and down with supressed excitement. Clive, too, seemed buoyed up, with both meaty hands clamped on the steering wheel, his foot firmly on the accelerator. As I talked to Tony our driver was experimenting with the sound system and each of the speakers in the ceiling of the bus gave a discreet cough and a crackle. Then their Greatest Hits came on and Tony grinned sheepishly.

'You had your hand on my leg the whole time,' I said.

He frowned. 'I really don't remember. I don't think so.'

I wanted to punch the headrest between us. 'But that's ridiculous. I know what I felt.'

He shook his head and looked out of the window. The blue tint did odd things to the colours out there. The hills and fields and the sky itself came up brighter, somehow. I watched passengers in the cars alongside us stare at the tour bus and read the spray-painted legend down the side. Maybe they were thinking that the band had got together again. Maybe they were keen to get a glimpse inside.

Clive turned the volume on the sound system up and I had to laugh.

'You're a liar, Tony.'

'I don't remember,' he said dully, looking away again. 'Honestly, Tim. That's what I'm like.'

'Oh, yeah?' He was really getting on my nerves. All this blowing hot and cold.

'I have these memory things. Lapses. Whole spots of time vanish. Sometimes I don't even know what I'm doing while I'm doing it.'

'Right.' I wasn't buying any of it. He was coming on like someone doo-lally in a novel by Virginia Woolf. As I say, an English degree can really bugger up your later life.

He looked me in the eye and I realised he was serious. 'It was the bang on the head that did it. Hairline fracture on my skull. You can feel it through my skin, still. It's like things seep out of it, all the time, and I don't even know what my body's doing...'

'This is the accident that Debs was on about...'

'Yeah. I got smacked on the head. Defending Brenda from ... from what we would nowadays call stalkers. I suppose.'

'And you're still affected by that?'

'For three months I could hardly remember my name. That's why I had all that time out.'

'When I am an Angel' started up and we could hear Debs singing along, up at the front. After a second, Clive's voice joined hers.

'Oh,' I said. 'Well, I'm sorry.'

'I might have been touching you. I don't know. I'm sorry if I did. But it wasn't really me.'

'I thought it meant...'

He looked blank. 'What?'

'What you'd said the night before. About not being interested. I thought this meant that you'd changed your mind.'

He looked even blanker. 'I said I wasn't interested?'

'Yes. In the Travel Lodge. Before you went to sleep.'

'I said I wasn't interested in you?'

'Yes.'

'Oh. Right. You mean, like, sexually?'

'I reckon that's what you meant.'

'I actually said that?'

'As good as.'

'Jesus,' he said, whistling through his teeth. 'I don't remember any of that. This moving around from place to place is really getting to me. I was less erratic at home.'

'So where does that leave everything, then?'

'I don't know!' he grinned. 'But if I said I wasn't interested in you, like, sexually, then I must have meant it. That must be how I feel.'

'Right.'

'Though,' he went on, 'if my hands were all over you, instinctively, hidden from everyone else's view ... well, that might be even more true than what I actually said in words. Because that's like ... a gut reaction, isn't it?'

'Yeah,' I said, and felt suddenly exhausted.

'So, I don't really know, Tim,' he finished brightly. 'Are you interested in me, then? Is that what this is about? Are you into me?'

He looked almost hopeful.

'Nah,' I said, and turned back in my seat.

We stopped just once, at a motorway services that afternoon. Clive was antsy because we'd set off so late in the day. The clear Yorkshire air had got to us all, made us sleep in late, each in our separate rooms in his cottage. He let us out at the Services and gave us only fifteen minutes before we had to be back on the bus.

I took a deep breath and phoned Shanna at work.

'Oh, it's you,' she said.

'I'm back in the region,' I told her.

'Well,' she said. 'Good. Pete's sacked you, you know.'

'That's a bit quick!'

'I warned you.'

'Has he replaced me?'

'Uh-huh.' I could tell she was serving someone at the till while she was talking to me. I suddenly felt nostalgic for Natural World. I felt jealous of Shanna's ease as she wrapped whatever piece of precious tat her customer wanted and popped it into a recyclable bag. But then you always get a bit funny and nostalgic over something just as you lose it.

'And wait till you hear who he's drafted in.'

I went cold. Pete was such a twat I'd believe him capable of anything. 'Who?'

'It's all worked out okay, really,' Shanna said, and I heard her swiping someone's credit card through the little machine. There was that dreadful moment of suspense, of credit-rating-checking before the receipt came chundering out.

'Tell me,' I said, 'Who's he replaced me with?'

'Simon,' she said.

My bloody ex-boyfriend.

'He's in Wales!'

'Natural World didn't quite work out in Aberystwyth,' she said smoothly, like some corporate mannequin. Something had happened to Shanna while I'd been away. 'And, as Pete pointed out, Simon is management material and too good to waste on a shop that's going under. Your vacancy came up here and Pete drafted Simon back to fill your shoes. Pete wants to groom him.'

'Groom him!'

'Like he was grooming you, though you never appreciated it.'

'But I was coming back!' I said. 'He can't just sack me!'

'He can,' she said.

'And bringing Simon in is just like adding insult to injury.'

Shanna sighed heavily. 'It's interesting, really, to hear Simon's side of things.'

'Oh, is it?'

'You treated him pretty badly, Tim. And it all fits with your behaviour this week. Running off. Running about all over the place. Simon reckons it's your fear of commitment. How he gave you everything and you could never be that open with anyone.'

'What?'

'It all rings true.'

'And Simon's just a fucking all-giving, all-dancing saint...'

'He's a nice guy, Tim. And you really hurt him.'

'I can't believe this is you talking, Shanna.'

'It's nothing I didn't want to say before. You block people out, Tim.'

'Jesus,' I said.

'So where are you going now?' she asked, with a lighter tone, as if the counselling part of the conversation was over and she was content with how she'd trashed my whole personality.

'Gateshead,' I said, 'for the charity Telethon tomorrow night.' I was answering automatically and the squeal she gave as I said this surprised me.

'But we're going to be there!' she said. 'All of us from Natural World. We've been raising money and we're going to hand over a big cheque to Shelley Sommers on the telly!'

'You're going to be in the Metro Centre?'

'Yes,' she laughed, 'but because it's Natural World, we have to dress up as fucking pandas and tigers and all that. Actually,' she added, 'I'm dressed up as a panda right now and it's fucking boiling in the shop. But what the hell, eh? It's all for charity, isn't it?'

Debs was still on the phone to her mam when I left the booths. She wanted Franky to meet us in Gateshead. Franky, she said, wouldn't miss this for the world.

We were all going to be there.

And, I suppose, underneath the Simon shock, I was excited.

I couldn't imagine what it would be like, crashing a national event like that. We'd be sabotaging and maybe jeopardising something that was in a charitable cause. The poor homeless and abused kiddies. But maybe, the spectacle Debs and Tony were planning would make the whole thing even better.

I went to sit in the blustery car-park and smoke. I watched the sun smack off the silver sides of the tour bus.

I didn't want this to end. I wanted to be on that bus forever.

I wanted to be able to sing along with all the tapes, with Debs and Clive. I wanted Tony sitting behind me so I could crane round and bait him some more. No, that was unfair. I wanted to be able to keep talking to him.

He was hapless and useless and he couldn't even remember - he didn't even always perceive - what he'd been doing.

He'd be useless for me, surely, and I'd end up just looking after him. He couldn't even talk to me, not really. His eyes would slide away and he'd be thinking about something else. The further away he got from home the worse he got like that.

But then, when it was me who wasn't paying attention; when I was earwigging on what Clive and Debs were saying, I'd find Tony's eyes on me, with a surprising frankness.

I watched him come out of the Services with bags and bags of sweets and drinks cartons. I watched as he dropped a couple of things, swore, and tried to grab them up again. He looked up and saw me.

'I did remember,' he said, as he came over and stood with me. 'Really.'

'Remember what?'

'Holding your hand.' He looked down. 'Though I did forget for a bit.'

I nodded.

'It just seemed the thing to do,' he said. 'I wanted to. You were there and I could feel the warmth of you. Does that sound stupid?'

'No.'

'And you never shrugged me off. You never asked what I thought I was doing.'

'I didn't,' I agreed.

'So I thought it was okay.'

I found myself lighting a cigarette off the last one. 'I don't know where I am with you, Tony.'

Abruptly he started to walk away. His behaviour was getting more erratic by the minute. He turned on me again. 'It's just what everyone expects, isn't it? Put us two together and, of course, we're going to get off. They all expect it.' He looked firm. 'I'm not doing it. I always used to do it. I'd feel obliged. I felt like I'd be letting someone down if I didn't.'

I sighed. 'It's up to you if you want to ... get off with me, or not.'

'It's not been like that for me,' he said. 'I ran around dizzy. Being made to do it. People offering themselves. I felt obliged.' He was squinting in the sunlight. He hadn't shaved and his stubble was like white filaments. 'So I put my foot down. Debs shoved me on you ... like it was some kind of reward.'

'Reward?'

'For coming with her. For being supportive this week. And I'm the booby prize. Your reward is a shag with me.'

'That's not what I want...' I said.

'It's how she's thinking. But she means well.'

'We don't have to do anything.'

'We haven't,' he said.

'That's okay, then,' I said.

'But I really want to! After everything I've said - about putting my foot down and that - I've still been really into you since I first saw you, Tim. That night at ours. It seems like weeks ago already. You looked wonderful. Confident and shy at the same time. Nice, but there's an edge all the same, like you're not giving anything away, like you're not giving an inch. And I just wanted you from that first night.' He grinned, lopsided. 'I still do. Badly.'

'This is ridiculous,' I said. 'You're either daft, or this is the most conniving and roundabout seduction in the world.'

'Neither,' he said. 'I'm drawn to you. I want you.'

'Yeah?'

He nodded and beamed. Guileless.

'Then,' I said, watching Clive and Debs approach. 'We'll just have to see, won't we?'

Franky was going to go to Gateshead anyway. She and the girls from her restaurant were going to do an act on the stage that had been erected in the shopping mall. Franky had had her fan-dancing feathers dry-cleaned.

'She never mentioned it last week,' Debs said, as we hit the motorway again.

'She's very deep, your mother,' Clive said, wrestling with the wheel.

'She reckons they've only just decided to do it. To raise money for the kiddies. Apparently there's an amateur slot to entertain the crowd before Shelley Sommers comes on.'

'That's it, then,' said Tony. 'Franky can be our person on the inside. Maybe she can sneak us behind the scenes and we can crash it like that.'

Debs smiled. 'I'm a bit nervous thinking about it,' she said. 'It could all go horribly wrong. We could end up in prison.'

Clive gave a booming laugh. 'Nervous! How can we be nervous? How can you? You've done Butlins! The Eurovision! You've played the roughest dives north and south and across the continent! What difference does one shopping mall make, Debs?'

'It's a shopping mall *now*,' she said. 'Right now. And that makes a difference, Clive.'

Durham.

We used to come to Durham to shop when I was a kid and I thought I'd end up there or a town like it. Somewhere with narrow stone streets and tiny windows and low doorways. I could sit in the Cathedral grounds and look down over the leafy city and brood on ... I don't know ... deep ideas. And yet everywhere, up to and including the shop where I worked till recently had been breeze-blocked, prefabbed Sixties architecture. The schools I went to, the estates that we lived on, the university I ended up attending. All of these buildings were from the stuccoed Sixties.

What I was thinking about as the tour bus went trundling down into Durham and the castle and the cathedral appeared in our widescreen windscreen was that, maybe if I'd lived and studied somewhere like this, everything would have been different. I'd have specialized in mediaeval art or modernist poetry or theology or something.

We were driving into an ancient town and I was thinking about how I'd got myself caught up in trash. The rubbishy world of pop in all its forms had reached out and sucked me in. It had happened a long time ago.

'Look,' said Tony, 'they've opened some nice cafe bars here, too. The old place doesn't look quite so gloomy.'

It took hours to park the bus. We got out and walked to a bridge and I looked over the side, hundreds of feet down, into the stillest green water.

I heard Clive explaining to Debs that their descendents, Things Fall Apart Again, would never need a tour bus. All the backing music they needed could fit onto one gleaming disk, thanks to advances in modern musical technology. The four of them never even needed to see a musician in the flesh, not even in the studio.

'It's amazing,' Debs said. 'We thought we were futuristic, even back then, didn't we? When it was all synthesizers coming in and drum machines. With all of those we thought we were it.'

'We were state of the art at the time,' Clive said. 'Though the sound of our records, when you hear them now, is strange. Transparent almost. Clashing. That very jarring, too clean synthesizer sound.'

'I still like it,' said Debs. 'It's our sound. It's just a bit out of date. But in its own way, one day, it'll sound as distinctive as Phil Spector or Motown...'

Clive looked unsure. 'We'd better find out where the show is meant to be. Time's getting on.'

He put on a pair of Ray Bans firmly and led us across the river to the Student Union building. We stood waiting as he explained that he was the manager of that night's band.

'It turns out they've got four bands on,' he growled, writing out the address and directions for us. 'Our lot impersonating us, a Bananarama tribute, a Human League tribute, and a fake Kim Wilde.'

'God,' said Debs. 'They're keen on lookalikes, aren't they?'

'I wonder what they'd say,' said Tony, 'if they knew they had the actual real things here...'

No one answered him.

Briskly Tony and I were packed off to entertain ourselves and get something to eat in one of those cafe bars we'd seen out of the tour bus windows.

'Clive and I are going on ahead,' Debs said, looking worried. 'Just turn up before eight at the right place...'

We nodded and let them tell us exactly what to do.

We walked down the hill back into town.

'You've soon slipped back into taking orders,' I said.

'Well,' said Tony, 'I actually like it. Gives me less time to think for myself. I really liked being in a band.'

'I really hate being told what to do,' I said. 'It's only happened since I started work at that shop. I could never quite take orders seriously. They used to phone from head office and tell us how to display the shite merchandise, and they'd take it all so seriously I'd just want to laugh. Still, that's over.'

We'd reached the cafe. The door was all scrolling ironwork. Inside it was chrome, lillies and chaise longues. It was that sort of cafe bar.

'What do you mean, it's over?'

I told him about losing my job.

His face crumpled. 'Because you've been with us? Oh, that's awful, Tim.'

I sat down heavily on a low sofa that was harder than I'd expected and watched him settle opposite.

He was in shorts now, with a loose-necked shirt and sunglasses and he looked sharper than I'd expected him to. It was me, I suspected, who looked as if I'd been on the road for days on end.

'I feel like we've been responsible,' he said, slipping his glasses off, 'for ruining your career.'

'Nah,' I said. 'I would have left or been chucked out anyway.'

We talked for a bit about his abandoned boyfriend.

'It had to finish, too,' he said. 'Really. I'd already thought that. I'd started thinking, projecting ahead, ten years, twenty years, and imagining what we'd be like. Stuck in a rut. Him madder than ever. Me running around for him. Getting older.'

Suddenly he went pale. 'I've left my mobile switched off.' He fished around in his little bag and switched the cellphone on with a musical chime I recognised as the opening bars of 'Let's Be Famous.' Tony looked aghast. 'Fifty-two messages and all from Kris.'

'Jesus,' I said.

The waitress was hovering with her pad and she looked self-conscious in her bra top so I quickly ordered two pints of Kronenburg.

'Bitter shandy for me,' said Tony and she smiled and went.

'Are you going to listen to his messages?'

He weighed the phone in his palm. 'What's the point? They'll be full of venom. Him squawking away. They'll start furious, go into terrible threats and end up pleading. I can't deal with all that now. I don't even want to remind myself of what his voice sounds like.'

'You'll go back to him,' I said.

'What makes you say that?'

'You must love him still.'

Tony looked stymied by this. 'I don't know.'

'Where did you meet him, anyway? How do famous people meet each other?'

Our drinks arrived and Tony waited till we were settled with them before he carried on.

'We met a few times, at different do's, like the Rock and Pop Awards or *Top of the Pops*. Over the years, when we were in the charts at the same time. And he was different then, you know. Tall and gloomy and he was, like ... artistic. I thought he was fantastic then.'

I nodded, remembering.

'And,' said Tony, 'I'd sucked his knob a couple of times at different parties and stuff. Just whenever our paths had crossed. I knew he was really into me. But Roy had put the fear of God into me about getting hooked up with anyone permanantly. He didn't want me to have a boyfriend. Anyway,' he took a long, appreciative sip of his bitter shandy. 'Roy went, Brenda went and I had my accident and was packed off, when I was fit enough, back to Italy, which I loved. I think it was Debs and Clive, really, sending me away while they split up and they dissolved the band.

'They called it my Italian rest and recuperation, but it was really because they didn't think, in my vulnerable state, I would be able to cope with what was happening to the band.'

I couldn't imagine, either, what it must have been like, for Debs and Clive to explain to him that it was all finished. They had things they could go on and do. They could have other careers in music and performing. Tony wouldn't have stood a chance by himself.

'I was in Florence,' he said. 'I was doing the Merchant Ivory thing. All that white linen and panama hats. I was just swishing about, learning the language, loving Italy. Getting my addled head - literally - back together. And one day my hat blew off while I was staring up at the statue of David. Can you believe it? It rolled across Palazzo Vecchio, between tourists and pigeons and, because everyone's so lovely and friendly there, five people made a grab for it as I came running. It was quite an expensive hat.

'Anyway,' he smiled, and I realised that his eyes had brimmed with tears. 'The person who actually managed to catch up my hat was this very, very tall man in black. A man with very pale skin and green eyeshadow who held out my hat to me and grinned. It was Kris. He'd appeared there like magic.'

I imagined Kris stood there, like a huge black crow.

'He flew me with him to the States, where he was fronting his last tour with the Dominators and I was with him when he finished the whole thing in Philadelphia. When he told them all, before the last encore: 'This is the last show we'll ever do.'

Honestly, I'm like a Jonah. I'm the kiss of death to whichever band I'm with.

'I remember standing in the underpass at Philly airport at the end of the Eighties with Kris and we were both having a fag. Taxis were going up and down and pulling up and these fellas were dashing up to us, saying where did we want to go. It was so hot and bright in Philadelphia and the two of us looked like white-faced zombies by this time. Well, you know what Kris looks like. He was in his Bela Lugosi phase just then. We were both finishing our ciggies and these blokes were saying, Hey, guys, where do you want to go, guys?

'And Kris and I took one look at each other and one of us, I forget who, said: 'We just want to go home. It's time to go home."

'And you moved back to Blackpool?'

He nodded. 'Do you know what we should do now, Tim?'

I fingered the menu. 'Eat?'

'Find a hotel. For a couple of hours. Until we have to meet the others.'

My mouth went dry and I had to swallow down the rest of my pint suddenly.

So now it was me, following him, and doing what he was deciding and going to a hotel by the river that was an old coach house converted.

I hung back in the foyer while he did all the transactions and suddenly he looked less hapless than he had done of late; signing the receipt and telling the blousey woman that we wouldn't be needing breakfast.

The hotel was quite swanky and Tony was treating it blithely like a cheap motel.

She showed us to the room, up winding steps, ambling ahead of us terribly slowly. As she led the way Tony reached back and squeezed my hand.

We watched her unlock the door and I was hard already. The end of my dick was wet.

When the door came open he bundled me past the proprietress and once we were both inside (more chintz; green and pink and lacquered furniture) he slammed the door in her astonished face.

Tony was on his knees in front of me, grasping my arse in both hands and pressing his face into my jeans, finding the zip with his tongue, teasing it down with his teeth.

All of this, very deftly done.

He eased my cock out with his mouth and the warmth and wet of his mouth covered me. It was shocking almost, the completeness of it. But also because of how familiar it seemed, to have him take me like that. My cock was already well-covered in come, just from anticipation and he groaned at this, kneading my thighs and rolling me around in his mouth.

Different people's mouths feel quite different, of course. His teeth nicked at me as we both got used to this. He sucked me and I felt I was filling him up, right down his throat.

He pulled back, at length, and carefully kissed the tip of my cock, which was bursting and red. And then we started, hurriedly, to undress.

He smelled milky. He lay back on the duvet and we rumpled the thick covers and I took in the smell of him, pressing my face to his neck. There was a distinct smell of milk, an almost sour smell.

I lay on him and we pressed our weight together, grinding our cocks together and we paused, as if we didn't know how to go on. He kissed me hard, pushing his tongue into my mouth and it was rough. Rougher than I'd expected, the way he carried on; pushing his strength onto me and rolling me over onto my back. He wanted to be on me, pushing down on my chest and kissing, then sucking hard, at my nipples. As if he could get something out of me that way.

It had all happened so fast I hadn't seen him fully naked yet. I reached down for his cock, which I could feel, nudging its busy way against my thigh, and he was rock hard and smaller than I'd thought. He had a snug cock, hand-sized, with a tight foreskin that hurt him slightly when I pumped him, too hard, in my enthusiasm.

'I want to come on you,' he said, breathing hard into my face. His breath was all bitter shandy. 'From when I first saw you, I wanted to come all over you. All over your belly and chest. I want to come in your face and in your hair.'

'Do it,' I said. 'It's been a while since anyone has.'

I had a momentary stab of guilt about Debs then, who'd climaxed so nicely. Who'd been so friendly. This wasn't like that. Tony was kissing me fiercely and throttling my cock, bending it back as far as it would go, rubbing it hard on his tight, heavy balls.

We came quickly that first time and both of us, so pent up, came so hard it shot up past both our faces into my hair, the pillows, the padded headboard.

'We came together!' he crowed. 'That's never happened before!'

Simon would always jump up at this point, to rub us both clean and dry with towels. Like that advert for paper towels where they show you how much chip fat they can absorb. Nasty allusion. But Tony was content to lie with me, hugging me hard, in both our mess.

We kissed a bit more and recovered ourselves and then, without even thinking much about it, did it again.

Time was getting on and we had to meet the others and attend to business. But in a very leisurely and absorbed fashion, a formerly famous Eighties pop star manoeuvred us both into a position we'd be happiest with, and fucked me very deeply. But it was just Tony Tony who I'd known for a few days. And Tony who I'd assumed would be hopeless in bed.

He squeezed himself up inside me and grasped my chest like there was nowhere on earth he'd rather be.

Afterwards we showered together and my legs were shaking. W

dried, dressed and left the hotel and took a taxi to the marquee at the college, just outside of town, where the graduation concert was taking place.

It was eight o'clock and the sky was a lambent blue above black trees. To me, at least, the night smelled of lager, excitement and the milky scent of Tony's spunk.

We could hear the music, the shouting and dancing as we got out of the cab.

We heard it all before we even went round the trees and into the field and saw the vast white tent full of students and lookalikes.

Chapter Sixteen

'What am I going to do with you?' Franky asked, stroking her daughter's hair again.

It had been years since Debbie had let her do this. Now she was sitting at a glass-topped table in the centre of the empty restaurant and didn't appear to care how much her mother comforted her.

Usually Debs would flinch. She'd tell her mother she could deal with it herself. Even when she'd lost the baby, she hadn't wanted her mother's help. She didn't want to be held by her.

Franky had steeled herself and waited for Debbie to come back. One day, she knew she would. She would need her mother again.

'I've come back with nothing,' Debs said.

She looked up, at the bleak light coming through the venetian blinds into the restaurant. She hated how dark and sour the room was in the daytime. Lemongrass and ginger the morning after.

She hated having to be here.

'I've lost everything, Mum.'

Debs was talking to a woman who had lost everything a number of times.

'Clive will come back to you,' Franky told her. 'He loves you at heart. Why, didn't I see him on that video of yours? When you wore that beautiful coat? You threw him out and you were the one being brave and cruel, putting an end to it. He was heartbroken. You could see it in that man's eyes. He couldn't stand the thought of losing you.'

Debs snorted. 'That was all made up, Mum. It was just a video. It didn't happen like that at all...'

Franky took her hands off her daughter's shoulders and

pressed her palms firmly on the spotless glass of the table. She examined her fingers. 'Of course your mother knows that, Debbie. You think she is a fool? I know what is what, even in your pop music world and that these things aren't always true to life. But I tell you, I saw your Clive's eyes on that television when he sang about losing you and those eyes can't be made up. He looked utterly horrified at the idea of being without you. Those eyes went back to his very soul.'

'He hasn't got a soul,' Debs murmured. 'Brenda bloody Maloney sucked it out and swallowed it whole.'

Now here was a topic they could both agree on. 'That woman,' cursed Franky.

'At least they're not together now,' Debs said. 'If I can't have the bastard, neither can she. Not that she wanted him, really. She didn't want him longer than it would take to fuck up my marriage.'

'Hush now, Debbie Now,' cried Franky. 'Language at your mother!'

'She hated us. She hated the band. It wasn't enough to just leave us be. She had to destroy it all. Till it was all spoiled forever and people would forget where it was she started out from...'

'I hate her on the television, that girl,' said Franky. 'What a lot of nonsense she speaks. What right has a woman like that, with her legs, to talk to me about diets? I switch her off. It is immoral, anyhow, to watch TV in the mornings. She doesn't care.'

'No,' Debs agreed. 'She doesn't care.'

Daytime TV was huge, though.

It was, as Brenda had suspected, the thing of the future.

She married a man who read local news. It was passionless, convenient, and a step up for the pair of them. They looked good, sitting together by a wickerwork coffee table and addressing the nation.

They had a house that had reputedly cost two million pounds and magazines photographed them inside and outside their house. They became good friends of many of their celebrity guests. You couldn't be a celebrity without sitting at their wicker-work coffee table and drinking coffee with them on TV. You had to pretend you were just popping round for a chat and everyone loved the informality of it all.

Brenda made it seem that famous people did things just the same as everybody else. All they really wanted to do was talk about ordinary things; shopping and babies, health scares and holidays.

Brenda grew matronly. She brought on fresh young pop stars and quizzed them, knowingly, about the world they were entering. She dispensed good advice and viewers, enthralled, would recall that once, years ago, she too had been a singer.

One time, on the Christmas Day show, the family-like team behind her show gave Brenda a surprise and cajoled her into singing live. She protested and gave in with good-natured curses. She held the microphone awkwardly and fluffed her words, reliving her glory years in a studio full of well-wishers. They could see she had once been a wonderful performer, but now chat was her metier. It was a good life. Even the most stressful things involved in fronting a daily show she found easy to accomplish, smoothing the stresses with a casualness that came naturally to her. Luckily, she knew how to relax. She fucked the boy who did the weather reports and so did her husband, sometimes at the same time.

And it was with good grace that she interviewed Clive about his new exotica instrumental CD. They talked on her show as old and trusted friends. She eked out of him all the details of his forthcoming trip to South America and his campaign on deforestation.

In Blackpool Tony watched Clive talk with Brenda on his telly as he unpacked his few things in the house that Kris had bought them. Hardly any room in Kris's house for Tony's few belongings.

Sun-tanned now, Tony sat on the settee that was still sheeted with plastic, and watched his ex-colleagues flirt and chat about the beleaguered rain forests.

He waited for them to talk about the band. About the old days. He waited for them to mention Debs, or him.

But people who were moving on, into new directions, didn't like to rake over the past. Especially when they were on the telly like this. They had to be seen doing new things; more exciting things. They had to develop fantastic new projects and if people mentioned the great things they'd done in the past, they would just give a self-deprecating smile and they would shrug. They wouldn't elaborate. Successful people never did.

Some nights Tony left Kris at home and went out on the scene in Blackpool and Manchester. He stayed away and met fellas and they talked to him and he waited for the moment when they would suddenly click and say, 'Hey ... aren't you the fella out of that band?' He knew he looked a little different. New haircut, chunkier, less sharp all round. He kissed these men on dance floors and in private rooms and waited for that moment when it would dawn on them.

But the only way they ever recognised him was if, by chance, by rotation, he slept with them again and they remembered having had him before.

The music in Manchester was different now, anyway. Dancey stuff, ravey stuff, indie bands. What Tony thought of as student music. There was no place in it for him, but still he went to the dark clubs, and drank fizzy lager.

How fond they all were of each other. Tony was quite caught up in how they danced together, these boys, touching each other, sweat pouring off them. Then someone told him it was because they were on drugs. Tony had only just tried to give up sleeping pills for good, and he wasn't ready to get into anything else.

He watched them dance and sweat and touch each other. They clutched their bottles of water. He wondered about stepping into that crowd, disguising himself as someone younger. He wondered if he'd pass.

Then he stopped it all when, one time, he found himself saying:

'But don't you know? Do you have any idea who I am?' In a steam room somewhere, with someone down on him and others' hands crowding and stroking him. His voice bursting out in the sticky florid air. They shrunk back, appalled, not expecting chat nor people declaring who they were, and he had stormed out. He wasn't going near them anymore. He was staying at home where, at least, Kris knew who he was.

Kris with his fanclubs and network of correspondents and his outfits and his miming in the parlour to his own records. Kris who, now they were settled into their new home, swiftly turned the tables, so it wasn't Tony who needed looking after anymore. Kris was the one demanding unerring attention.

Kris was so pure, in many ways, with his love; training it unequivocally on Tony, so that he could shriek and rant and behave abominably. But it was all because his love was total and unconditional. Expecting Tony's to be the same.

'We have to be separate from them,' Kris told him tenderly. 'We're not part of the same world as them. They came into our world for a bit; dressing up for the part and living out a fantasy. But they soon settle down into ordinary life. Meanwhile, we're out here, just orbiting. Out here in Blackpool. And we should be happy to be here, and separate from the world...'

Gradually Tony let his own feelings subside.

He had to.

He got a letter from Debs, who had returned to London.

Tony, if there's anything I can ever do for you, financially or otherwise, you have to let me know. Your accident, well, it was all down to me, wasn't it? I sent you round there. To see Brenda Maloney, of all people! To protect that fat evil bitch who never gave a good shite about any of us! Who was only ever out to feather her own nest!

But if you want BUPA or whatever I can let you have a bit. There's still some money from the pay-off and my mum let me have a bit. And they reckon we'll still get residuals, though the song rights are mostly with Clive. I don't know why I gave in to that contract back then. No idea. I was so young and silly and trusted him and Roy and everyone.

The only ones you can trust though, I reckon, are the ones you've known the longest. Ones like you, Tony, who have been there for the whole long ride with me.

What am I going to do with you in the north and me down here? I'm used to seeing you more than that. I could get you work, you know. It might not look like much, what I'm doing. You might turn up your nose, but I don't think you will really. It's a good job for a professional like me, or you.

It's not like being famous, but it's close enough.

Would you want a job? I could have a word. There's always work. I'm quite optimistic about my new career, really. It's easy work. Just what we always did. Easier than before. I just turn up and sing someone else's words instead of mine.

Session singing. Easy. Do you fancy it?

Would Kris let you go?

I turn up in studios every day, all over London. I do jingles and chocolate adverts and car adverts and covers of songs currently in the charts. They're always delighted with my work. I tell them, I've had enough bloody practice, haven't I? I know how to carry a song and even put my own distinctive mark on it. Even when that's not what they want. Even when it's meant to sound like someone else.

I still manage to smuggle some of myself into it.

Maybe you've heard me already.

Pushing your trolley through the supermarket. The music they play in there, that's all session musicians and session singers. Music in shopping centres and on radio adverts. You'll never know their names but they're with you all the time.

Maybe you'll hear me somewhere today. When you're out and

about. I think you'll recognise me. You'll hear something in the voice and you'll know that it's me.

I want to think of you, doing your groceries and listening.

Sing along with me, Tony.

Loud as you like.

love,

Debs.

Chapter Seventeen

The copycats were excellent.

I don't know if the crowd around us were in any state to appreciate the fact. The marquee tent was swilling with boys in black tuxes and girls in those very unflattering chocolate box gowns. They were all pretending to be James Bond and Audrey Hepburn. They must have begun the evening feeling very elegant, as if, somehow, this was the first evening of a whole lifetime of smartness and they had to start to make an effort. By now, though, everyone looked to me a tad rumpled and sweaty. The party had begun early and was being conducted in a determined, businesslike fashion. By the time Tony and I got there they had already seen and applauded the lookalikes of Kim Wilde, Bananarama and the Human League.

We moved through the crowd towards the front. They were sweating and shouting and the air was ripe with their bloated vigour. I used to be a student. I could have gone on and done a PhD and, if I had, it was the likes of this lot I'd be dedicating myself to teaching. Fucking hell.

Tony grasped my hand, more for his sake than mine, and led me through them, through the lull in the performance. How could students afford the bottles of champagne they were brandishing? I'd lived on tuna chunks and Thunderbird back then.

But I wasn't here to see the students.

Tony's hand was hot against my skin and he was crushing my knuckles together.

Tony parked us under the sound system and we'd hardly exchanged a word before the final act was announced.

He turned to say something, his mouth opened, and he grinned at me instead. The music had started. His angel song.

In the way his face relaxed into that smile, and his hand fell away from mine, it was as if he suddenly felt more confident. He was out of his world, in a crowd of what were obviously kids with a bit of money and education behind them. But those opening bars of music, blaring keenly through the perfect sound system, belonged to him like nothing else did.

And on came the lookalikes. Two girls, two boys, as promised. They wore Venetian masks with hooked noses and dark eye slits. They wore cloaks of silver and gold and they struck dramatic poses as one of the boys stepped forward to croon the opening to Tony's song. Their presence filled up the entire marquee tent. I thought: the law of diminishing returns just isn't true.

Tony stood there enraptured.

As the tempo quickened the lookalikes threw off their cloaks, revealing tight-fitting outfits, more daring than their predecessors had ever worn.

They were beautiful. They were perfect and young.

For their second song they took off their masks and the audience of students roared with approval. A danced-up version of 'Let's Be Famous'.

'They're not just copy-cats,' Tony gabbled at me, between songs. 'They're like us, reborn!'

At the end of their twenty minutes, by which time the young band were sweating and fully worked out, Tony was louder than anyone, screaming his approval. The dancefloor beneath us was thunderous.

He watched them impassively take their applause and leave the stage. And then Debs had found us, her face shining, grabbing us both by the arms.

'Weren't they wonderful?' she cried as, all around us, the students started to dance to the music that had replaced the show. 'I had no idea,' she said. 'He's trained them well...'

Tony laughed. 'We could never have done dance routines like that...'

They had been like perfect automatons. I thought Tony and Debs were taking the proficiency of their replacements rather well.

'Clive's with them,' she said. 'Round the back. We're meeting them and having a drink in the beer tent next door. We can talk to them there...'

She took both our hands and led us into the dark between the tents.

We were in the special tent, like the place the Royals hang out at Ascot. That's what it felt like. It was cooller here and lighter than in the other place, where the students were still dancing. Debs ducked in and we followed.

At a table in the middle, all of the performers were sitting with champagne and they appeared to be hanging on every word from Clive, who was expounding, a bit pissed, like a silver-bearded Svengali.

Things Fall Apart Again were lathered in sweat, in PVC shorts and agog at every word of praise they received from him. The Bananarama girls were hanging on too, along with an intrigued Human League and a slightly disaffected Kim Wilde.

'Look at them,' Debs breathed. 'And look at Clive. He's got them in the palm of his hand. The new generation.'

They had those heat lamps, glowing orange and blue and smelling like vinegary crisps. The atmosphere of the place was like some military tent on the eve of battle.

Clive saw us and stood up.

'Here they are,' he told everyone present and all the lookalikes stared at us. 'Two of the original members of Things Fall Apart.'

The singers were on their feet and applauding us. Debs and Tony both gripped my arms - one each - and I could feel their fingernails digging in as they flushed with pleasure.

'You were all wonderful,' Debs said, as the clapping subsided. 'I don't know if you realise how wonderful you all are...'

Now the lookalikes looked embarrassed.

The fella out of the ersatz Human League was on his feet, running his fingers through his oily quiff. 'It's an honour to meet you, Ms Now. Really.' He kissed her on the cheek.

One of the Bananarama girls was saying, 'Clive's been telling us what you're planning...' She came over shy suddenly, standing there in her feathered bikini. 'And we're all behind you. We want to go with you and crash this thing.'

Debs looked up and down the cluttered table, at Clive and then back at us. 'All of you? You all want to come?'

The disgruntled Kim Wilde nodded and swilled back her drink. 'Absolutely. You've had such shitty treatment. And we all want to get ourselves on the telly. And you've got room in your tour bus, right?'

Debs nodded.

'Then we're all coming to the telethon with you.'

Clive laughed. 'So that's it, Debs. They're all behind us.'

The four young members of Things Fall Apart Again looked exultant.

Debs blinked back her tears. 'This means so much to me. This time last week, I thought it was just me against the world...' She turned quickly to me. 'And then there was Tim, of course. Tim who's been my staunchest supporter. Tim who's pushed me on, even when my nerve was failing, to get back on the road and face the public again.'

Then they were all staring at me and applauding again, ever so seriously, with gleaming faces, glitter gel in their hair and revenge in their hearts.

We drank champagne and laughed and made further plans for tomorrow. I tried to find out the real names of the members of Things Fall Apart Again, but they were too hard to keep track of, and Tony couldn't remember, either.

After a while Tony took hold of my elbow and led me out of the tent and into the woods beside the college.

We walked for a bit, crackling through the undergrowth.

We lay under the trees on damp earth and bracken. We fooled around a bit again, but mostly we listened to the various parties going on into the night, and thought about the day ahead.

I didn't really sleep. Suddenly it was dawn and we were creaking and damp and the branches above us were black against the brilliant blue.

I heard Tony saying, 'You know, they did the same as us. They went back to the bus. Clive and Debs - she told me - they slept together again. As soon as they had some time, yesterday, and shook us off, all they wanted to do was be alone and fuck again.'

I tried to regather my wits and sat up, to find myself lying naked on the forest floor, with Tony spread out across from me; all fond, moist eyes, tousled hair and puckish morning erection.

I was distracted by the rustling of the undergrowth and together we watched the fella and the two women from the fake Human League emerging from the woods, unsteady on their feet, and their make-up smudged.

'The woods are full of pop stars,' Tony grinned and waved across the copse at them.

I reached over to kiss him.

'I don't know what's happening, really, Tony,' I told him. 'But I'm glad we're together.'

He nodded.

'This is what I want to be doing.'

He shuffled over closer on the uncomfortable ground. 'Well, good,' he shrugged, taking my cock in his hand and tugging it.

'No,' I said. 'It's a big thing for me to say, that. I'm actually doing what I want to be doing. It's not often that comes off.'

I sucked his salty cock for a while, before we found our clothes and trudged back to the tour bus.

Which was quite full. The whole lookalike entourage was

aboard and Clive was at the wheel. We were ready to set off for Tyneside.

Debs hugged me.

'You and him,' I said, as music started up from the speaker system. 'You and Clive. You're together again.'

She looked confused. 'It just happened.' She laughed and corrected herself. 'No. We both wanted it to happen. I don't think it was just nostalgia. I hope not. We remembered how well we fit together.'

'Yeah,' I said.

'And you and Tony.' She looked mischevious. 'I reckon you've been finding out the same thing, haven't you?'

'I think so...'

She put a finger to my lips. 'Don't decide anything yet. You don't have to decide anything at all yet. Just you enjoy it.'

We rode up the motorway to Tyneside and we sang together, all the way there.

We joined the usual traffic, the commuters and weekend shoppers as we coasted into the Team valley and the excitement was building up in us. We had no real plan of attack and somehow that made it even more exciting. Clive switched on his tour guide's mike and tried to instruct us and form a rationale for when we got there, but we weren't really listening.

All the lookalikes were thinking about was getting on the telly and usurping the order, the routine of legitimate showbiz.

As we approached the long, low buildings of the Metro Centre, and gazed out at acres of filled, glittering car parks, they were all changing into their stage outfits. I had to laugh, turning to watch them struggle into sexy costmes, wriggling and tugging them on in the aisle.

Debs quietly opened a compartment above the seats and produced what were evidently original stage costumes, packed safely in polythene.

The lookalikes saw this and they were struck with awe.

She even found one for me and I felt honoured. I had to wear a chamois leather outfit of shorts and vest and boots. So I did.

I smuggled myself to the back of the bus and dressed myself in one of Tony's old outfits.

I was along for this ride as well.

Tony was grinning. 'I was just imagining ... what if this silver bus was a time machine? And we were all safely aboard, and Clive could take us back to any point in the past. Then we could, like, rescue people when things went bad for them. Pick them up and tell them to get on the bus...'

At first I didn't know what he was on about. He was gabbling away. Then I was thinking, who I would pick up on the bus?

I pictured us staying on the bus forever, flying low over the clouds and seas. All of life could be just like one of their videos, with every-one chorusing in and sweeping over the ordinary stuff, and never having to get involved.

Tony said, 'I used to dream about having a bus when I was a kid. I could stop at bus stops and give people a free ride. That's what I used to think.' He looked around and seemed to be counting the empty seats. 'If this was a time machine, you could change all the crappy bits in our lives. All the long, dull boring bits where it went wrong or nothing happened. If it was a time machine, you could make your whole life into your Greatest Hits. And that's all it would be. Just your chart-topping hits. Fuck the B-sides, fuck the album tracks and all the remixed filler material. Just the chart-toppers and highlights. *The Very Best of You.*'

'Yeah,' I said. 'That'd be great.'

When we parked the bus we realised we didn't look all that unusual here.

Other coaches were pulling up and disgorging their passengers and it was clear they were all here for the telethon.

As we clambered out, we were taking note of others' costumes: penguins, pirates, wombles, vicars, cowboys, prostitutes.

We were going to blend in all right.

The crowds were moving into the mall; a bright and variegated, excited mass; enjoying themselves; their deliberate eccentricity and the charitable effort they were making today.

'Stick together, everyone,' Clive warned us.

Debs' face was set in a rapt smile. She was wearing a tassled mini dress, studded with rhinestones. She winked at me broadly.

As we went through the automatic doors and I pushed past Steed, Emma Peel, Mrs Slocombe, Captain Kirk, Gandhi and Cher, I suddenly saw Shanna standing at the cashpoint. Her familiar face was painted black and white and she was grimacing out from her panda costume. Bad-tempered, she was drawing out her money, her furred behind all saggy in the panda costume.

I rushed over and touched her on the shoulder. She turned and screeched with laughter at my outfit.

'I can see your nipples and everything in that!' she laughed. 'Tim, you don't dress like that!'

I shrugged carelessly. 'I do now.'

'What are you doing here?'

I squeezed out of the way of Spiderman and the Bride of Frankenstein, both of whom were rather pushy.

'You'll see,' I said, and turned to see the others in my group moving on, through the press of the crowd, past McDonalds, the banks and Marks & Spencers. I would lose track of them if I didn't watch out.

A whole gang of fellas went running past us, laughing and shouting and dressed as sperm.

'I have to keep up with the others...'

'Wait,' she said. 'My lot are waiting by Marksies. You have to see them...'

'Is Simon there?'

She nodded and laughed. 'Dressed up as a seal. He has to see you ... like this...'

I followed her, feeling sexy as hell.

The staff of Natural World were sitting on benches, waiting for Shanna. All of them were in rented costumes; the middle-aged pouchy ladies were tigers, crocodiles and leopards. Pete was an American eagle, rapping out instructions from his clipboard and keeping tight hold of their oversized cheque. His legs looked very skinny in his yellow tights.

'Look who I've found,' Shanna said.

They all stared at me.

Pete's face went dark. 'Where the fuck have you been, Tim?'

I could see that his people-management training had all-but deserted him today.

He took a step closer. 'I had no choice but to sack you, and replace you.'

'I know,' I said, looking down at his feathers. 'Grrrreat.'

That was when Simon turned round in his grey seal oufit. All that was recognisably him was his rather flushed, hairless face, incredulous in all his plush.

'You've really fucked up,' were his first words to me.

'Have I?'

He nodded and his ears flapped. 'You really have. You can't hold onto anything, can you, Tim?'

I stared at him. It was a bit disconcerting to be confronted by him again. He seemed more familiar than I had expected him to, even dressed, as he was, as something endangered. Before I could start thinking of him as a real person again, as someone I'd been even slightly attached to, I took a deep breath.

'To be frank, Simon, everything I've had till recently ... it hasn't been worth holding onto.'

He went scarlet. At the next bench Noddy, Batman, the three little pigs and Robin Hood were all earwigging.

'You would say that,' he said.

'Yeah, I would. You were a frigging creep, Simon. Management material you may be, being the anally-fixated twat that you are. But boyfriend material, never. And you can't suck cock for frigging toffee. Did I ever tell you that?'

He looked alarmed, and the women dressed as endangered species were laughing. Shanna was laughing hardest of all.

'I reckon that's telling him, Tim,' she said.

I turned to look, and Shanna was standing with her two Elvis brothers. One was in a white sequinned suit and the other was in black leathers. Maybe I'd gone too far with Simon. But looking back at him, he didn't seem too cut up. Just cross.

'Actually,' I said, 'I've been thinkng about you all week. I even wanted to see you. I wanted to brag to you about what I've been up to. I was only doing it in the first place so I would have something to tell you...'

Simon was looking at me blankly.

'But really,' I said, 'I don't want to tell you about it at all.'

'Right,' he said.

'I've got to run,' I said shortly. 'And catch up with my friends.'

Shanna pecked me on the cheek. 'I understand. I'll see you later, I reckon.'

'You will.'

Then I turned and hared off through a gaggle of orcs and fairies, mermaids, knights, wizards and clowns.

'Tim!' Simon shouted. 'Hang on!'

But I ran, leaving the staff of Natural World far behind.

The stage area was in the central hub of the mall, under a crystal dome, with fake fountains, escalators and glass bullet-shaped lifts all descending into it.

Vans crammed with equipment for outside broadcast were ranged at intervals in the crowd, and people were dashing everywhere, dragging cables and chunky, complicated-looking devices. In amongst the professional chaos, the revellers were staring open-mouthed at the preparations and each others' home-made outfits.

A band was tuning up on the wide podium. Even from their diddling about, rehearsing on bass and synthesizers, we could tell it was going to be deafening.

At the head of our now rather large party, Debs was starting to have qualms.

'I can't go through with it,' she said. 'I've got us all here and now I'm scared. Look at all this paraphenalia! And all these people!'

The four young members of Things Fall Apart Again were limbering up and their eyes were bright with eagerness and hunger.

I grinned. 'We have to do it, Debs. We just have to.'

She looked pained.

'Just think,' I said, nodding to the stage. 'Pretty soon, Brenda Maloney's going to be up there, showing off and acting like she invented charity and showbusiness itself. You've got the chance to put the kybosh on that ... once and for all.'

Clive was listening. 'He's right, Debs. We can give her the shock of her life and, because it's live on camera, she'll be forced to be nice to us and welcome us back into the spotlight.'

"Us'?' she asked.

Clive nodded. 'We're not just sending the kids up there. I've decided. We're all getting up on that stage. Every one of us.'

There was a sudden hubbub amongst the rest of the audience. Evidently something was starting to happen. I saw an harrassed stage manager get up on the stage, fighting to be heard and, as the lights started to go down, causing the murmuring to increase in pitch, he explained breathlessly that there was only four minutes till we all went on air.

'Debbie!' came a raucous voice.

We all turned to see someone forcing their way towards us.

'Jesus,' said Debs.

Her mother was in her diaphanous yellow fan-dancing outfit and clutching her feathers to her bosom. She was accompanied by three of her young waitresses, all in similar, if less extravagant, numbers.

'You came!' Franky cried, folding Debs into her embrace. 'We are all here! And, you know what? They will not let my fan dance be on TV! They have told me I am too obscene!' She drew back then and suddenly gasped at the sight of Clive. 'Even this person is here!'

'Hullo, Franky,' Clive said.

She scowled at him.

'Now, Mum,' Debs said. 'We've got stuff to tell you...'

'That you are back with this man? The man who ruined your whole young life?' Before Debs could get a word in, Franky had turned to me. 'And this boy! Who you met only this last week? What has been going on here, Debbie? What have you been doing all week?'

She laughed. 'Now, there's a story.'

Franky had almost fallen over at the sight of Tony. 'You bring Tony back to me! What is going on, Debbie Now? How come you bring all these people to me? And who are all these others with you?'

'Can't explain now, Mum,' Debs said.

And it was true, the house lights were down and the stage was lit. The crystal dome of the mall cast an odd, pearlescent glow over the whole chamber.

The stage manager was forcing the audience to listen, to count down the last, tense minute till air time, and to be prepared to whoop when the whole mall went live.

'I'm feeling crushed,' Tony said. He looked a bit warm in his silver coveralls. 'We're too near the front.'

'We have to be,' muttered Clive.

Just then the entire audience erupted into wild cheers and shouts and the band started to play the telethon theme.

I looked up to see that the tiers and walkways above were thronged and packed with audience members too.

We were part of something big.

All eyes were on one of the glass lifts as it descended to the stage. To a synthesized fanfare, its door shot open and out stepped Brenda Maloney in a black strapless dress. She was encrusted in rhinestones, spelling 'Kiddies in Krisis' diagonally across her generous torso.

She was the fourth member. Now I had seen all four of them in the flesh.

Brenda grinned beatifically at her public and took stately little steps to the centre of the stage, holding out her palms to accept the welcome lavished upon her.

She beamed. 'Good evening, Gateshead! And good evening The World!'

She repeated this opening gambit in several European languages.

'This is bigger than I thought,' Tony whispered.

'She's looking good,' Debs said, tugging at her own well-preserved stage costume. 'I have to say that for her.'

Brenda was being chatty and adlibbing for the audience, who were lapping it all up. She brought on a few people from an electrical supply shop (Andy Pandy and Looby Lou) and a hair salon (the Spice Girls), all bearing their oversized cheques, which Brenda took off them and made us applaud.

'We're never going to do it,' Tony said. 'We're going to stand here the whole time, with the rest of the public, and never get up there. We'll never have the nerve.'

'No?' I said. Then my heart thudded and skipped a beat, because Brenda was announcing Peter the manager and his loyal staff from Natural World.

On came my workmates in their shabby endangered animal outfits. I watched Brenda get kissed by Peter and Simon and realised I was clenching my fists. Shanna was standing to one side of them, looking mortified, as Brenda took their cheque for a thousand pounds and waved them off without further ado. The endangered animals shuffled back into obscurity.

'What a bitch,' I heard Clive say. 'How sincere does she sound? A thousand quid wouldn't keep her in tights for a month. What does she care about kids in crisis?'

'Time,' boomed Brenda's voice, 'for our first, very special, musical guest.'

We all looked at each other as the audience's ears pricked up. There was a crackle in the air, I could feel it.

'My first guest will be extremely familiar to you all as the late, lamented Mandy Hopkirk from the smash hit TV series, *A Doll's House.*' Brenda paused and sighed. 'Remember how the whole nation watched, heartbroken, as Mandy died of a brain tumour last March? Well, thanks to the magic of television - she's back! Everybody - I'd like you to welcome to this year's Kiddies in Krisis telethon - Shelley Sommers!'

The whole mall went crazy as the arc lights fixed on a tiny figure in white at the top of the escalator.

With one hand bunching up her skirt, she descended slowly, in time to a version of her old TV show's theme, played by the band. She waved.

'Shelley Sommers!' Brenda bellowed again, just to work us up a bit more.

As the theme finished, Shelley stepped lightly off the escalators and onto the stage. Flowers were flung from somewhere in the crowd, to litter the floor she was crossing so carefully.

'It's a very special song you're going to be singing for us,' Brenda began.

Shelley lowered her head modestly. 'It's a song that has always meant a lot to me and it's the one I wanted to be my very first single. And it's quite relevant, in some ways, to the theme of tonight's telethon.'

Brenda smiled delightedly and put a motherly arm around Shelley's tiny shoulders. 'It's a song that means a lot to me, too.'

'Of course it does,' Shelley agreed.

'Ladies and gentlemen,' said Brenda, starting to emote. 'Over twenty years ago, four very young, talented people embarked on a life of fame and stardom and they did it with the song you are about to hear. Three of these young, talented people were very dear friends of mine. And the fourth? Well, ladies and gentlemen ... that girl was me. Back when I was even younger than Shelley here.'

The audience roared appreciatively and Shelley looked stung for only a second.

'When Shelley sings this song for us tonight, I'm sure I shall have to wipe away a tear of nostalgia. For my youth and all our youths...' Brenda lifted up her head bravely. 'But I'll be proud to hear Shelley sing this song that means so much - oh, so much - to me.'

Shelley toyed with her mike and you could see she was keen to get on with it and for Brenda to shut up.

'I only wish,' Brenda went on, 'I only wish I knew where those companions of my youth have gone to. I wish they could be here, with us, tonight.'

'Ha!' Debs hissed and suddenly she had found her nerve. 'Like she really means that!'

Then, before we knew what was happening, Debs had bolted. She pushed through the crowd, ducked the barrier and hopped lightly over the loops of cables. She was firmly gripping Tony's sleeve, and he grabbed my arm and so we all had to follow. Beside us, Clive wore a similar look of determination as he led his army of lookalikes out of the audience, through the barricades of camera and crew, towards the stage, onto which Debs was now hoisting herself.

The audience muttered and stared, aware that something was going on.

As yet, Brenda hadn't clocked a thing.

'Ladies and gentlemen! Tonight, for the first time ever in public, the delightful Shelley Sommers sings that all-time classic, 'Let's Be Famous'...!'

The band started up as Brenda backed respectfully out of Shelley's spotlight.

The familiar drum beat began, the throbbing bass, the synsthesizers slicing in...

Right on cue, Shelley Sommers opened her mouth to sing.

Debs was kicking the stage manager, who had grabbed hold of her foot. He cried out and was yanked out of the way by Tony and Clive.

Debs hurled herself onto the stage.

The audience gasped in horror as they saw someone lurch into Shelley's silver cone of light.

Shelley stopped singing, the words dying in her throat as she came face to face with the slightly deranged-looking Debs.

We were on the stage behind her. I don't even remember our getting there, but we were standing behind her. Once she was up there, it made it easy for us to follow.

We faced out the perplexing darkness of the crowd.

Tony was with me, and Clive, the four lookalikes, the Human League, Bananarama and Kim Wilde. We were all looking back at Shelley as the music crashed on, heedless, through the song. And Shelley could only stare at us with wide, breath-taking, baby doll eyes.

The spell was broken by Debs shouting: 'Give me that!'

There was a thunk, even over the noise of the band, of her grabbing the microphone.

She took it and Shelley offered no resistance. She stood there frozen, gaping.

'Everyone!' Debs bellowed and everyone in the place jumped. 'Everyone listen to me! We are back!'

Then, right as the band hit the chorus, Debbie Now started to sing. And we sang along with her.

I stopped only once, surprised, as there was further kerfuffle in front of us, and at first I thought security men were about to remove us. Instead, there was a fluttering of yellow feathers, as if a great bird was landing. But it was Franky and her waitresses.

They had found their own way up and were vigorously fan-dancing along with the song.

Three minutes long it lasted. The perfect length for a pop song. For us, with the younger lookalikes doing their strenuous routines and the original members pouring their hearts into the lyrics, it could have lasted forever.

But it didn't, of course. The band finished playing and the audience were silent for a moment.

Then: massive applause. They were on their feet. They were sending their love and approval in ragged torrents from the upper tiers and balconies of the crowded mall.

Debs cradled the mike and shook with tears. Clive put his arms around her.

As the applause subsided we waited to see what would happen next.

Like the consummate professional that she was, Brenda Maloney had managed to compose herself.

She stepped back onto the stage.

She drank in the applause, gathering attention to herself and, as she turned on us, her eyes were glittering and hard.

'What a *wonderful*, wonderful surprise,' she purred into her microphone. She stalked towards Debs, who flinched as she pecked her cheek.

'I had no idea,' boomed Brenda. To the audience she added, 'Honestly! No idea!' They chuckled. 'What a surprise! But what does it all mean? Tell me,' Brenda's voice hardened slightly. At last she was showing the strain. 'Tell me what it all means.'

There was a beat of silence.

Then a diminutive figure in a white sheath frock tottered back into the limelight, looking furious.

'I'll tell you what it means!' she screamed, snatching the mike back out of Debs' hands. 'I'll tell you!' Shelley Sommers spat, making the sound system whine in complaint. 'It means these fucking selfish has-been bastards have screwed up my career in pop before it's even fucking began!'

Gasps of horror from the crowd in the mall.

Brenda's eyes were out on stalks. With one hand she was making savage 'cut' gestures to the camera crew.

Shelley rounded on us all. 'You talentless fucking cunts! What right have you got to piss on my career? You had your chance - and you blew it! Now you do this, you evil fuckers!'

'Shelley,' Brenda warned. 'Remember, you're on television.'

'Oh, fuck television,' Shelley sobbed. 'The goddess promised me it would be brilliant. You told me it would be fucking brilliant, Brenda! You promised me!' She flung the mike to the floor.

'Quickly...' Brenda whirled to face the band. 'Music...'

The band members shrugged and started the same song again.

We were milling around in confusion.

Shelley tried to stomp off, twisted her ankle, and fell heavily on the stage.

We really had fucked the whole thing up.

Debs made a grab for the mike, intending to sing the song again, but Brenda darted forward and kicked it neatly away from her grasp. The audience howled and the lookalikes started to dance again.

Franky and her girls fan-danced obliviously.

Debs and Brenda rolled on the floor, tearing at each other's hair. Clive threw himself down on them and tried to drag them apart.

I was paralysed.

Suddenly, a different voice cut in over the sound system.

The voice of Zeus.

'Look at the state of you all,' it sighed. 'Look at the frigging state of you lot.'

A hoarse, guttural voice that had everyone on stage and in the audience craning their necks.

The rasping, booming voice started to sing along with the band.

> '*Let's be famous,*
> *Let's be famous,*
> *Let's be famous,*
> *It's what everyone wants to be,*
> *Let's be famous,*
> *Let's be famous,*
> *Let's be famous,*
> *Let's all be famous as me.*'

I saw Debs and Brenda freeze in their scrag fight at the sound of that voice. Clive started up on his knees. 'Who...?'

We all turned to the escalator. Someone was coming down on it, bellowing the song into a mike.

Tony seized my arm. He was rigid.

A gargantuan figure in a raven black wig was gliding down the stairs. It was backlit and made a formidable silhouette: the towering hair, bulbous earrings and monstrous breasts.

Terrifying, square shoulder pads.

As he sang he threw back his head and raised the mike to his succulent painted lips.

Tony's voice was right in my ear, shrill with terror.

'Roy,' he whispered. 'It's Roy!'

The stageful of performers shrank back as the new arrival slid effortlessly off the escalator and into our midst.

We were all transfixed as he sang his song till the bitter end. Even

Brenda Maloney, though she had wrested the mike from Debs, was silent, slumped on the floor.

Debs was on her knees, as if Our Lady herself had manifested herself in the mall.

Roy was in a black evening gown.

After everything they had said about him, he'd come back as a classy dame.

He stepped lightly to the front of the stage and finished the song. He took his applause with grace.

Automatically we looked to our hostess for guidance, but Brenda was lying on the floor, with tears rolling down her face.

Debs said, 'Roy...'

He turned slowly and flashed us a massive, voracious grin. He had tiny teeth and far too many of them.

'That,' he said, 'is how easy it is to upstage you all.'

This got him a laugh.

'What are you doing, Roy?' asked Tony, and he sounded frightened.

'Me?' Roy boomed. 'I'm being famous. I'm showing you all, as I always did, just how easy it is. I'm stepping into the limelight, at last, to demonstrate.' He froze us all with his smile. 'You've ruined my new protogée's career, I see.'

'Shelley?' said Debs. 'You're her manager? You were behind all this?'

'Oh, yes,' he sighed. 'I felt certain she was a sure frigging thing. But you've buggered all that up.'

Debs steeled herself and got to her feet. 'You left us, Roy,' she said. 'You left us to fend for ourselves.'

'You ought to be glad,' he grunted. 'You stopped being famous. Do you really want to go back to that, Debbie Now? To be famous again? I don't think you can. You were never really happy.'

'That's what she wants!' Brenda called from the gleaming, slippery floor. 'She wants fame more than anything! She always did, because then she could feel legitimately unhappy all the time. They all resent me because I kept up there in the public eye. I made a go of it and had a happy life, while they all faded away...'

There was a loud snort then and Franky stepped up to Brenda, thrusting a feather mockingly in her face. 'You should say less, you awful woman. You should not be on the TV at all, telling people what to do. You should be stopped.'

'Fuck you,' Brenda shouted, and remembered, too late, she was still being broadcast.

Debs took her mother's arm. 'It's all right, Mum.'

Roy was staring at us, shaking his head in wonder. 'Look at you all. And I'm responsible. Mr fucking Starmaker himself. But look around you. All of you.' He gestured outwards to the fancy-dressed audience. 'You've got all of them singing along. Look. Everyone's on camera. The stage is full. The audience is full. And everyone's in costume. Everyone looks frigging fantastic!'

Roy threw back his head and roared with laughter.

'Fame's not the same as it used to be. You should know that by now. You thought you ought to be famous because you thought you were someone special.'

He walked up to Debs and for a second she shrank from his massive embrace.

Roy told her: 'We all knew you were someone special anyway. But maybe it isn't like that any more. Face it, baby - *everybody's* famous now.'

MODERN LOVE
Paul Magrs

'This is the sort of smart, moving novel that good young British authors don't seem to be writing any more. If the Booker Prize meant anything, this one might win it.'

SCOTT BRADFIELD, *THE TIMES*

At nineteen, Christine is happy working in a bakery, hanging out with a succession of rough lads and battling with her indomitable mother, Margaret. When Margaret tries to set her daughter up with a nice young bank clerk, Christine is initially repelled by the idea. But when she falls pregnant after a visit to a safari park, she is forced into a shotgun marriage - to Michael, the clerk.

Chritine gives birth to twins, Jude and Jess, and life seems alright for a while. But the house is not a good place for children to grow up in; there are too many secrets, too much swearing and shouting. And the twins become increasingly strange: Jude is quiet, creepily passive, and Jess is a foul-mouthed trouble-maker. Immersed in their own private world, their violent games must end in tragedy ...

'A perfect entry point into the fictional world of this about-to-be-big young writer ... A tale of madness, mystics, miracles and murder, few young writers could match it for invention, comic timing, and compassion.'
HARPERS & QUEEN

'*Modern Love* is clearly the product of one of the smartest and darkest imaginations in contemporary fiction.'
LITERARY REVIEW

'*Modern Love* renders his excellent earlier work as dress rehearsals for this astounding performance ... a page-turning classic.'
TIME OUT

Available to buy from all good bookshops
Published by Allison & Busby - price £9.99
ISBN: 0 7490 0484 3